THE AVON ROMANCE

Four years old and better than ever!

We're celebrating our fourth anniversary...and thanks to you, our loyal readers, "The Avon Romance" is stronger and more exciting than ever! You've been telling us what you're looking for in top-quality historical romance—and we've been delivering it, month after wonderful month.

Since 1982, Avon has been launching new writers of exceptional promise—writers to follow in the matchless tradition of such Avon superstars as Kathleen E. Woodiwiss, Johanna Lindsey, Shirlee Busbee and Laurie McBain. Distinguished by a ribbon motif on the front cover, these books were quickly discovered by romance readers everywhere and dubbed "the ribbon books."

Every month "The Avon Romance" has continued to deliver the best in historical romance. Sensual, fast-paced stories by new writers (and some favorite repeats like Linda Ladd!) guarantee reading *without* the predictable characters and plots of formula romances.

"The Avon Romance"—our promise of superior, unforgettable historical romance. Thanks for making us such a dazzling success!

Other Books in
THE AVON ROMANCE Series

BRIAR ROSE *by Susan Wiggs*
HEART OF THE HUNTER *by Linda P. Sandifer*
HOSTAGE HEART *by Eileen Nauman*
LADYLIGHT *by Victoria Pade*
MIDSUMMER MOON *by Laura Kinsale*
PASSION'S GOLD *by Susan Sackett*
STARFIRE *by Judith E. French*

Coming Soon

MARISA *by Linda Lang Bartell*
RENEGADE LOVE *by Katherine Sutcliffe*

Avon Books are available at special quantity discounts for bulk purchases for sales promotions, premiums, fund raising or educational use. Special books, or book excerpts, can also be created to fit specific needs.

For details write or telephone the office of the Director of Special Markets, Avon Books, Dept. FP, 105 Madison Avenue, New York, New York 10016, 212-481-5653.

RECKLESS SPLENDOR

MARIA GREENE

AVON
PUBLISHERS OF BARD, CAMELOT, DISCUS AND FLARE BOOKS

RECKLESS SPLENDOR is an original publication of Avon Books. This work has never before appeared in book form. This work is a novel. Any similarity to actual persons or events is purely coincidental.

AVON BOOKS
A division of
The Hearst Corporation
105 Madison Avenue
New York, New York 10016

Copyright © 1987 by Maria Greene
Published by arrangement with the author
Library of Congress Catalog Card Number: 87-91589
ISBN: 0-380-75441-X

All rights reserved, which includes the right to reproduce this book or portions thereof in any form whatsoever except as provided by the U.S. Copyright Law. For information address Avon Books.

First Avon Printing: December 1987

AVON TRADEMARK REG. U.S. PAT. OFF. AND IN OTHER COUNTRIES, MARCA REGISTRADA, HECHO EN U.S.A.

Printed in the U.S.A.

K-R 10 9 8 7 6 5 4 3 2 1

For Ray,
whose faith never wavered . . .

. . . and for my three "crutches,"
Patti Barricklow, Carol Budd,
and Pam Renner

Prologue

Rouen, November 1660

The moment Monsieur Dubois arrived, Madeleine knew something was very wrong. Papa suddenly seemed on the verge of collapse. She swallowed hard to control her growing anguish. She would have to see to it that he got a much needed rest. They could go to Provence or Gascogne together—or even to Spain. His dear old face had looked a shade too gray earlier in the evening, and the purple smudges beneath his eyes had spread wider; it was pure agony to look at him.

Madeleine pulled on the high-necked flannel nightgown and plucked the pins out of her hair. The light curls spilled down her back, and she massaged her scalp to relieve the headache advancing up from her tense neck. Tears of pain burned in her eyes.

If it weren't for that bully, Dubois, whom the finance ministry had sent to examine Papa's work, Papa would be his old, happy self. Why was Dubois here at all? Papa was the most honest person she knew—and the King's most loyal tax collector; there certainly could be nothing wrong with the tax ledgers.

Madeleine brushed her hair and twisted it into a thick braid, then covered her head with a lace-trimmed cap. Her heart heavy with worry, she walked to the window and looked through the gap in the drab maroon drapes. Outside, the darkness was complete; there wasn't even a sliver of moon.

The wind moaned in the bare trees, the branches grinding against the panes. In the distance horse's hooves clattered on the cobblestones.

A resolution hardened in Madeleine's mind. Tomorrow she would confront Dubois and ask him to leave. Someone had to protect her gentle father, and there was no one but herself. She squared her shoulders, raised her chin, and climbed into the high four-poster bed. Having made that decision, she found that the immediate future looked brighter. She closed the bed curtains and curled up under the covers. It was fortunate that she had left the convent school at this time. Papa needed her support.

Drifting in and out of sleep, Madeleine heard a harsh scream from somewhere in the house. Instantly alert, she jerked upright in bed, her lacy nightcap tumbling down her back. Holding her breath, she clutched the edge of the blanket. Now she heard a groan and a hard thud. She slid from the bed, her legs trembling.

"Papa?" she breathed as she shoved her feet into a pair of slippers and pulled the blanket across her shoulders. Weak with foreboding, she hurried down the stairs. Yellow light poured from the crack under the study door, and sounds of struggle filled the air. Terror ran through her veins as she placed her hand on the cold door handle. Another scream sliced the air.

Faint with fear, she tore open the door and stared, unbelieving, at the scene before her. Her steps faltered on the threshold. Dubois, crazed, his face shining a furious red, was repeatedly plunging the glittering blade of a dagger into her father!

"Papa!" she sobbed, moving toward him. Her hands numb with horror, she hoisted the large iron doorstop with difficulty, the blanket slipping to the floor and the too-long nightgown hampering her movements.

Dubois had left her father inert on the floor and was slowly advancing toward her, the raised dagger dripping red. Her breath caught in her throat, strangling a whimper. As he suddenly leaped forward, she wielded the doorstop, a scream erupting from her lips. The iron connected with flesh; the dagger whirled through the air, whispered past her ear, and rattled to the floor.

With a cry of pain Dubois crumpled, clutching his head. A twitch went through him as he lost consciousness.

Madeleine moaned, biting her knuckles in a moment of indecision. Her eyes widening in agony, she stared at the blood covering her father's chest and his deathly pale face. Rushing across the floor, tears streaking her cheeks, she knelt next to him.

Urgent banging sounded on the front door, but Madeleine did not move. In despair she cradled her father's wigless head in her lap. "Oh, Papa, Papa, *mon pauvre!* Can you hear me?" An eternity seemed to pass before his mauve eyelids fluttered open. Oblivious of the blood soaking her nightgown, she held him closer. By sheer willpower she pulled him momentarily from the grip of death. Even as his eyes clouded over and his skin grew cold and ashen, he struggled to speak.

"Madeleine . . . *ma petite fille*, the diary . . . diary . . . in the secret place . . . take it to . . . the King . . . you . . . must . . . *must!* . . . Be . . . careful . . . trust . . . no one . . ."

"What diary?" she whispered.

Only a tiny flicker of light remained in his eyes. *"Ma petite . . ."*

"*Oui*, Papa, I promise! I'll do anything, only please, don't leave me!" she begged. But it was too late. Jean Poquelin slipped away, trying to form a last smile on his lips. Madeleine thought her heart would burst, and the moment was forever burned into her memory. Unable to release her last hold on him, she moaned softly, rocking back and forth.

She was dimly aware of the front door crashing open and heavy steps pounding on the floor. Suddenly she remembered Dubois. She looked up, expecting to see him on the floor where he had fainted. He was gone.

Part I

Chapter 1

Versailles, January 1661

Madeleine Poquelin studied the unfamiliar surroundings. Never had she seen such splendor as Versailles, the royal hunting lodge outside Paris. Gilded plaster moldings gleamed everywhere. Fresco paintings of angels and gods cavorting in idyllic landscapes adorned every ceiling, and crimson brocade panels graced the walls. The fishbone-patterned parquet floor shone from much polishing.

Madeleine thought she could never see enough of the royal salons—and the nobility! She had come a long way from that dark moment two months ago when her father had drawn his last breath and she had been forced to move to Paris and live with her uncle, the playwright Jean-Baptiste Molière.

The bitter grief in her heart was slowly lessening, but her desire for revenge still burned bright. Her father had deserved a better fate! But there was no use dwelling on the past if she was to execute his dying request. He had given her a mission to fulfill at this very court, and now she was here. At last.

The information that the diary contained weighed heavily on her shoulders. The King had to know, and tonight might be the perfect moment to approach him. What would he say when he found out the scandalous secret about his powerful minister of finance, Nicolas Fouquet?

There was a commotion at the enormous double doors. Noblemen swept plumed hats to the floor and bowed from their waists. The ladies sank into full curtsies, their embroidered skirts spreading around them like islands of silk. Madeleine's eyes grew round, and she shrank against a gilded wooden column. The King was coming! Then she remembered to curtsy in the manner that Uncle Jean-Baptiste had taught her. Still she managed to get a view of the King from under her humbly lowered eyelashes.

Louis XIV's majestic presence dwarfed every person in the room. He stood six feet tall, with the magnificent posture of an avid sportsman. A scarlet, gold-embroidered vest flattered his proud young shoulders. Thick, curly brown hair, parted in the middle, flowed down his back. White silk stockings picked out in gold showed off his splendid legs, and his rhinegraves were tied with a red ribbon just above the knees. The diamond buckles of his high-heeled shoes sparkled in the candlelight. He moved his hands with exquisite grace to accompany his speech. But it was his eyes that caught and held Madeleine's attention. His flashing black gaze seemed not to miss a single detail.

Madeleine wished she could hear what he was saying to the tall, blond courtier by his side. She noticed the blond nobleman because of the serious expression on his lean features—a forceful face wholly devoid of artifice. Then her breath caught in her throat. The very dark gentleman on the other side of the King was none other than Nicolas Fouquet, the very man who was responsible for her father's death! Madeleine shivered, but pinched her lips together in determination. She wouldn't turn into a coward now that she had come this far. She would denounce Fouquet right in front of the King.

Waiting until the courtiers began to mill about the salon, she walked toward the middle of the floor where the King was surrounded by a group of nobles. At the thought of the ordeal ahead, the color heightened on her pale cheeks, and the palms of her hands grew clammy.

An argument erupted unexpectedly right behind her. Two ladies were talking in angry voices, gesticulating and whipping their fans back and forth. As a gentleman sought to separate them, a minor fight broke out. Madeleine was shoved into the group of gentlemen surrounding the King. One more step and she would have his attention. Eagerly reaching out, she almost touched his satin vest. Licking her lips, which were dry with nervousness, she prepared to address him. Then someone gripped her arm and wrenched her away.

"Non!" she protested, watching helplessly as the King slowly retreated toward the other end of the salon without noticing her. Whirling around, her eyes flashing anger, she came eye to eye with Nicolas Fouquet. Her further protests dying on her lips, she stood as if rooted to the floor.

His dark eyes narrowed to cunning slits as he recognized her, and his thin-featured face hardened in anger. Calculation burned at the depths of his eyes, and Madeleine swallowed in fear.

"Voilà! Mademoiselle Poquelin, I presume," he drawled with a cold smile. "We have urgent matters to discuss. I have been searching for you everywhere."

Madeleine wasn't about to tell him that she had spent two months in a convent in Rouen recovering from her grief. Her mouth was parched with anguish; she couldn't speak. Loathing tasted bitter in her throat. She fully expected Fouquet to force her then and there to reveal the diary's hiding place, but he eased into the background. "I will know where to find you now," he said lightly. Giving her a final smirk, he disappeared in the crowd.

Madeleine breathed rapidly, her mind more than ever hardened on revenge. The man should pay for the evil he had brought to her father! Struggling to control her wrath, she discovered that she stood only inches away from the tall, blond courtier. She liked his assured face, and when his gaze met hers, the air seemed to spring alive and thicken. Madeleine's breath caught in her throat. Who was this gentleman whose eyes were like magnets? Then he looked away.

Germain de Belleforière, comte de Hautefort, was bored.

He did not care to return the seductive glances the ladies of the court kept sending him. He failed to appreciate their coy smiles as they fluttered past his eyes like nervous butterflies. Gowns, fashioned to seduce, shimmered in the light from thousands of candles in the chandeliers suspended from the ceiling.

His calm gaze followed the sovereign, who had eyes only for the golden-haired Louise de la Vallière.

In his thoughts, Germain was far away. He was conjuring up the picture of his peaceful estate, Les Étoiles, deep in the forests of Brittany. His heart ached with longing. What would he not give to spend some time there! He had not seen the ancient heap of stones for six months, and every day he grew more tired of the shallow games played at court, the endless rounds of balls, the card games, the late nights. The strict etiquette chafed him. He had to be in constant attendance to the King, the sun around which all the courtiers revolved like planets of more or less significance. He needed to get away, needed to taste the tangy air from the sea and the spicy fragrance of the forests.

As he toyed with a bunch of grapes in his hand, he felt a light tug on the cuff of his coat. Surprised, he looked down. Ah! The beautiful young woman who had stared at him so intently. She had the silkiest curls he had ever seen, and her eyes were large pools of deep blue, just the color of the forest ponds at Les Étoiles.

There was something faintly familiar about that innocent, heart-shaped face. Where had he seen it before? Or her silky hair, the color of pale morning sunlight?

"Monsieur, I'm sorry to interrupt your thoughts, but I desperately need your help."

She had a slightly husky voice that touched something deep inside him. His interest awakened, he studied the small, slim woman, then flourished a gracious bow.

"How can I serve you, mademoiselle . . . ?"

"*Oui*—I suppose I should introduce myself." A warm blush rose in Madeleine's cheeks. She hesitated for a moment, then gave him a shy look. "Excuse me for accosting you like this. I'm Madeleine Poquelin, the seamstress for Molière's ensemble," she explained in a rush, "but sometimes I play a part when one of the actresses is sick. This is the first time I've played in front of the King."

A slow smile tickled the corners of Germain's wide mouth. "Ah, yes, I remember now. Tonight you were the enchanting Célie. *Sganarelle* is the name of the play, isn't it?"

Madeleine nodded, and an urgency lit her delicate features. "I know it's very impertinent to approach you like this, monsieur, but I beg you to help me."

"I'm your slave, Mademoiselle Célie," Germain said with a seductive smile. He leisurely took hold of her hand, which rested tensely at her throat. Toying lightly with her slender fingers, he noticed under half-closed eyelids that her gaze was riveted to his hand.

Germain pressed a feather-light kiss on her fingertips. "Well?"

She started, torn from the spell his touch had woven. "I need an audience with the King."

Germain's eyebrows shot up. "An audience? Isn't it enough to attend his ball? You are lucky to have an invitation tonight."

"I know. The whole theater ensemble was invited."

He scanned her simple burgundy velvet manteau over the plain underskirt with its single lace flounce, and noticed her full breasts tightly laced by the burgundy bodice and a stiff busk. He felt a stirring of desire, and involuntarily his lips curved into a smile.

A sigh of exasperation passed her lips. "It seems impossible to approach the King without his explicit invitation. I have been in his antechamber every dawn for a week with my petitions—to no avail." She paused, a look of hesitation creeping into her eyes. "You are very close to him, *vraiment?*"

"*Bien*, you know me then?"

"*Mais non*, monsieur." Whispering, she beseeched, "But you must speak to the King for me."

His breath brushed her fingertips. "You *are* a daring young *fille*. What makes you think I would consider helping you with such an audacious request?" Soft menace touched his words. Outwardly his face was a polite mask while inwardly he chuckled at her daring.

"I thought you looked . . . different from the others." She blushed fiercely, her gaze lowered to the floor. What would he think of her now? She coughed discreetly into a handkerchief.

He got a closer look at the exquisite curls gathered into a chignon interwoven with a strand of pearls on the top of

RECKLESS SPLENDOR

her head. A corkscrew lovelock spilled over one dainty shoulder. What an enchanting creature, he thought. So frail—an ethereal sprite. "And what if I don't consent?"

He placed one long finger gracefully under her chin and lifted her face, perceiving the defiance in her clear eyes.

"You're not the only one who is close to the King."

"Now, now, you've made me curious. Tell me, what is so important that you have to bother His Majesty?"

"I can't tell you, but do believe me, it is important—very important."

Germain studied her in disbelief. He felt the undercurrent of her desperate sadness, and his heart reached out to her. This was a delicate situation. He had dallied much too long with her already. He felt the teasing glances from the courtiers as they gossiped around him. Tomorrow morning, the court would be abuzz with the latest *on-dit* that Hautefort had found a new mistress.

He let go of her hand with some reluctance.

Straightening the point de Venice lace flowing over his wrists, he said, "I can't do anything unless you confide in me."

Her expressive eyes filled with anger. He thought for a moment that she would turn her back on him, but after taking a deep breath, she composed herself.

Germain let his gaze linger on the velvety *mouche* in the shape of a heart at the corner of her lips, quivering with emotion.

"I thought you were a gentleman. A gentleman wouldn't pry into a lady's business," she whispered hoarsely.

He smiled wickedly. "I can't imagine what could be important enough to disturb the King at this time. A state matter can wait until tomorrow—unless it's a declaration of war with Spain." His low voice teased her. He paused. "Perhaps you're aspiring to catch his fancy. I know he favors blondes." He smoothed his thin mustache arrogantly, a diamond flashing on his little finger.

Madeleine turned her head haughtily, her eyes brimming with wrath. "I simply asked you to introduce me to the King, but I should have known better. You so-called *gentlemen* are all the same."

He stiffened. "I'm first and foremost a servant of the King; my duty is to protect him. I don't want to bother him with trifles. Things are just not as simple as you seem to believe."

He saw that she had an angry retort on her lips, but it was never uttered because just then a page, black as ebony, dashed to her side. The contrast between her fairness and his dark skin was striking. Urgently he whispered something in her ear, and she followed him, her skirts swishing on the floor.

Germain stood as if in a trance. He suspected his life was never going to be quite the same again. The flowery scent of her perfume lingered in the air, and he breathed deeply. Dread squeezed his heart. Why did he get the impression she was in some sort of danger?

As they left the warmly lit salon, Amul captured Madeleine's hand and pulled her along the corridor. *"Vite, vite!"* He resembled a brightly feathered parrot in his crimson and purple silk caftan and balloon pants.

"Stop! I can't see! I'm going to break my legs in these slippers." Madeleine panted and stopped, propping her hand on a pillar.

"No, you can't stop now! Fouquet recognized you, and who knows what he's planning at this very moment. When Molière realized you had stayed behind, he flew into a fit of rage. Nevertheless, he sent back the carriage for you. It's waiting outside. I'm here to escort you home."

Madeleine flung out her arms in exasperation. "I don't care about Fouquet now! I failed to contact the King. All because of that insufferable, odious—"

"Listen to me," Amul interrupted her, shaking her arm. "Fouquet has spies everywhere. He's too powerful to trifle with, Madeleine."

"Oh, *zut!*"

Silence fell as freezing as the air seeping through the cracks in the windows. Outside, the snow glittered ice-blue, frozen in a rigid drift on the terrace, and stars blinked.

"I'm cold; I have to have my cloak. Will you fetch it for me, *s'il vous plaît?* I have to get back to Paris tonight, or Uncle Jean-Baptiste will have my head for disobedience," Madeleine said with a sigh. As Amul prepared to obey, she placed a hand on his arm. *"Merci.* You are a good friend, Amul."

He let out a grunt and disappeared through a door concealed in the brocade panel on the wall.

Madeleine hid in the shadow of the pillar. Her gaze worriedly scanned the dark corridor, but she saw no one.

Her thoughts repeatedly turned to the words she had exchanged with the arrogant courtier. How strange, she thought. She had felt an immediate rapport with him, a subtle elation in his presence. He was the only person who had looked human in that gilded hall, his eyes lacking the calculating coldness of those of the other courtiers.

Towering over the crowd, he had been at least as tall as the King, the silver satin of his coat straining across powerful shoulders. And she had to admit it; except for the King, he was the most intriguing man she had ever laid eyes on. She recalled his strong, clean features, the deep cleft in the square, stubborn chin, and the glorious wheat-colored curls rippling over his shoulders. And his eyes—she had become overcome when glancing into his deep-set, smoky gray eyes, so wise and weary, framed by imperious eyebrows. *Dieu,* but he was a dangerous gentleman!

A sweet, breathless sensation flowed through her, and she forgot the icy touch of winter for a short moment. Then she recalled that her mission had failed. I'm the greatest fool there ever was! she thought. Believing I could grasp one of the nobility and make him do my bidding. I should have known better.

Amul appeared soundlessly at her side with her velvet cloak slung over his arm. Without a word he draped it over her shoulders, and she pulled it close, shivering as she realized how cold she was.

"I hope the carriage is still waiting," he whispered impatiently. "We have to slip away unnoticed. I don't trust Fouquet. He may have planned a trap for you."

Madeleine sighed and followed Amul without complaint. The arctic wind lashed them as they stepped outside. Deep drifts of snow impeded their progress. The weak light from the lanterns on the stable wall guided them. The enormous stable yard was empty, all the horses inside.

"Where is that carriage?" Madeleine stared at Amul, who shook his head in confusion.

"It was here ten minutes ago. I don't understand. Perhaps the coachman brought it around to the other side."

Madeleine's eyes widened in fear as she saw a dark shadow fall over the snowdrift by the timbered wall of the stables. She grasped Amul's arm, and he shot her a questioning glance.

"*Mon Dieu,* somebody is hiding in the shadows. I have a feeling he's waiting for *us!*" She could almost feel the wintry touch of eyes in the darkness. "We have to get away from here." Her voice was harsh with fear.

Amul did not need prompting. Noiselessly he slipped close to the stone wall surrounding the stables. Madeleine could barely move for fear and cold. Her thin satin slippers were wet through, and she trembled violently.

Unnerved, she huddled against the wall, scanning the inky shadows for movement. To her agitated mind the very air was filled with menace, hissing and breathing as if the yard were infested with ghosts.

A black, wraithlike form slid over the silver-blue snow and flitted behind a tree.

Amul pulled her urgently, and together they crept along the wall back toward the palace. Twigs broke somewhere behind them, and Madeleine tensed with panic. Imagining a freezing breath caressing her neck, she turned sharply, but the empty darkness ruled.

Stumbling and panting, they reached a door to the palace. To Madeleine's relief, they found it unlocked. After slipping inside, they closed the door carefully behind them, then pushed the bolt home.

"Do you see anything?" Madeleine's words were almost inaudible.

"Not a thing, but if we follow the wall we'll get to one of the salons. There might even be a secret door somewhere."

Madeleine sensed the page disappearing rapidly in front of her, and she followed the faint draft he stirred. In the distance, frail tunes of violins reached her ears. The festivities were still in full swing.

RECKLESS SPLENDOR

Slowly, she felt her way in the darkness. The only light to guide her was the weak glimmer of stars reflecting on the snow outside the narrow windows. Her hands numb with cold, she trailed the frosty marble wall.

The distant slam of a door alerted her, and raw fingers of air danced around her ankles.

"Amul?" she whispered into the darkness. An unspeakable terror gripped her when no answer came. "Amul?" Her voice echoed hollowly in the vaulted passage. She stood perfectly still, holding her breath. All she could hear was the faint whisper of cloth sliding over stone behind her—as if somebody was feeling his way along the wall. The sound rapidly came closer. She knew it could not be Amul.

Panicking, she hurled herself blindly into the darkness. She bruised her shin on an urn and stifled the urge to cry out with pain, biting her lip until she tasted blood.

Her flight ended abruptly as she stubbed her toe and fell down. The stairs! Not daring to stop to examine the extent of her injuries, she lifted her skirts and fled upward, ever upward, until she reached the top, almost falling headlong into the corridor on the first floor. For a moment she had to stop to painfully catch her breath, her heart beating so hard she thought it was going to burst.

A sconce holding a guttering tallow candle hung on the wall, and she detected a line of doors. There was no time to lose. She had to seek refuge behind one of them. She could already hear the approaching footsteps on the stairway.

She tried the first door. It was locked. The same was true of the second and third. The fourth door yielded to her touch, and she slid into the warm, dark chamber, a relief from the coldness of the passage. Quietly she closed the door and leaned against the door frame, breathing raggedly.

An orange fire caressed the tiny chamber with leaping lights, and she could make out the contours of a large curtained bed, a painted screen, and a stuffed armchair by the fire. The chair was occupied. She groaned in disappointment as she recognized the man in the chair; it was the man she had addressed earlier in the salon!

Only a few seconds passed as Madeleine digested the picture before her. The man uncoiled his lean body in one swift movement and came toward her, his white shirt a sharp contrast to the soft semidarkness.

Footsteps sounded outside, and Madeleine flung herself against the courtier, gripping his arms.

Taken by surprise, Germain held her in the warm circle of his embrace and was about to speak when she raised her fingers to his lips in warning.

The footsteps had stopped outside the door.

Burying her face in Germain's hard chest, Madeleine held her breath. His heart beat strongly under her cheek, reassuringly. Then the room filled with the creaking threat of the slowly turning doorknob.

Just as the door opened, Germain pushed her behind the screen in the corner.

"Who goes there?" he barked, his voice full of chilly authority. Two strides took him to the door, and he tore it wide open. Madeleine shivered behind the screen, hardly daring to breathe. Then she heard the voice, the voice of a nightmare.

"Monsieur le comte . . ." The whining voice grated along Madeleine's nerves.

"Dubois! *Diable!* What are you doing here? Did Lemont send you?"

"No, monsieur. I'm sorry; I opened the wrong door."

"Don't you know you're supposed to scratch before you enter?"

"No reason to be irritated, monsieur. I did apologize. I'm looking for the Marquis D'Ambrose," Dubois said nervously.

"D'Ambrose? He certainly isn't here. The marquis is away in disgrace." Germain's voice was fringed with suspicion. "You should know that, as close as D'Ambrose and your employer are."

Madeleine heard more footsteps approach.

The comte continued, "Lemont! You ought to keep an eye on your valet."

Madeleine stiffened, her mind numb with surprise. The chevalier de Lemont! Dubois was his valet. Was Lemont yet another of Fouquet's henchmen? Who could she trust at court? She couldn't hear Lemont's murmured response and could not breathe freely until the comte had closed the door behind the chevalier de Lemont and Dubois. At last silence reigned in the corridor.

She emerged, pale but composed, from behind the screen. The comte was waiting for her with his arms crossed over his chest, a black cheroot pinched between his lips.

"You look like you could use a glass of brandy," he commented dryly, motioning her toward the chair. "Please, have a seat."

Meekly she sank down on the chair. In the aftermath of terror, her legs shook like a blancmange.

Germain observed her closely as he poured a small amount of brandy into a tulip-shaped glass. She stared into the fire, her eyes glistening with unshed tears. Her shoulders sagged, but when she realized that he was looking at her, she straightened her back and raised her chin.

"I suppose a thank-you is in order here, monsieur le comte; you saved my life, and I'm eternally grateful."

Thoughtfully he swirled the brandy in the glass, regarding the amber liquid with studied indifference, holding the glass up against the light of the fire. Then, with a rapid movement, he handed her the glass.

"Vraiment, your life? That sounds overly dramatic. Most likely, Lemont had a desire to taste your tender lips this evening," he suggested, rubbing his chin. "But I must admit *that* is strange. His taste usually runs to the boys."

A shiver of unease rippled through Madeleine, and her cheeks grew red with indignation. "Monsieur le comte, I don't even know the chevalier."

A mirthless smile hovered on his lips. "That wouldn't stop him." He moved to stand next to the chair, pressing the side of his thigh against her upper arm. "The chevalier has crushed more hearts than I dare to count."

Madeleine pulled her arm away as if his touch burned her, and she folded her cloak more closely around her. "Not mine anyhow, and he never will."

The comte tapped the red heel of his high-heeled shoe on the floor, as if in thought. His next words were a soft, suggestive drawl. "I was preparing to spend a solitary night, but perhaps you can liven things up a bit now that you're here." To emphasize his words, he buried his long fingers deeply into her hair, scattering pins in every direction.

His touch was not unpleasant, but she resented his arrogant attitude. She tried to pull away.

"Monsieur le comte, I do not intend to enliven one of your lonely evenings; I need to get back to Paris tonight."

His roving fingers dislodged the strand of pearls and the last of the pins holding her chignon. Her hair tumbled down, the cascade of pale curls startling against the dark blue velvet of her cloak.

Winding a silky curl around his finger, he felt a hot wave of desire rise within, and he wanted nothing more than to bury his face in her fragrant tresses, to kiss her slender throat and the pink shell of her ear.

"Paris?" he muttered and placed a kiss on one of her curls. "It's much too dangerous to venture through the forests at night. Cutthroats, thieves . . . all kinds of rabble roam the roads."

"I'm aware of that, but it doesn't mean something would befall me."

He laughed hollowly, and Madeleine glared at him.

"Mademoiselle, didn't you just barge in here wild-eyed and frightened out of your wits, seeking my assistance? It's unthinkable that you should leave tonight. You're safe here. Nobody is going to disturb us, *ma chérie*. Make yourself comfortable and be grateful that you don't have to spend this freezing night outside in the snow. Here, let me help you."

Before she could protest, he bent down on one knee and deftly pulled off her wet slippers, revealing delicately arched feet. Propping her unwilling feet on a footstool in front of the fire, he began sliding his fingers up her ankles, but she immediately pulled her feet to the floor.

"Your stockings are wet. You should take them off," he said.

"It's not for you to take them off, monsieur le comte. I might be a simple seamstress, but that does not signify that you can take liberties with me."

He sat back on his haunches and observed her, a devil dancing at the depths of his eyes. "I thought you perhaps had singled me out for a night's pleasure. The lie about needing my help was a nice touch," he teased.

RECKLESS SPLENDOR

Madeleine shook her head in disbelief. "Of all the gall! You self-centered, oafish— You turn everything to your own advantage!" She gasped for air. "You know I was followed here. It was no coincidence that Dubois opened *your* door. He must have seen me enter." The brandy and the warmth of the fire made her unbearably sleepy, and a treacherous numbness filled her limbs.

"A cloud of mystery envelops you, enchanting Célie. Who are you, and why was the chevalier de Lemont so desperate for your company?"

"Who are *you?*" she muttered thickly, trying to cast aside his impudent fingers.

"The comte de Hautefort, but surely you know that already." His fingertips trailed the delicate line of her cheek.

"I do not! I need . . . to get . . . back to Paris." Why was it such an effort to pronounce the words? Then she remembered. Hautefort's name had been in Fouquet's diary! Fear drenched her, and she struggled to get up. His face wavered in front of her, and his smile looked diabolical. Her head was leaden, and the rest of her body seemed to have slipped into oblivion. Her mind refused to work. Had he poisoned her? Had she fallen into a trap? She had to give up her futile struggle, all her willpower drained at last. Finally she let herself sink into the frightening abyss of sleep.

Chapter 2

Where was she?

Madeleine struggled to get away from a suffocating warmth. With a jerk she forced herself upright, her eyes wide in confusion. A shaft of gray light filtered through the darkness.

Slowly she realized that she was in a soft bed, a thick cover wrapped around her. Yawning, she let her hand travel back and forth over the smooth satin. In awe, she touched the silky gold fringe bordering the brown velvet curtains around the bed. Her gaze wandered over the silver candelabras on the mantelpiece and the sumptuous coats and vests hanging in an open armoire behind the elegantly painted screen. An array of jewelry—emeralds, pearls, and sapphires—mingled with discarded lace jabots on a table and spilled carelessly out of a red leather-bound box.

She was alone, and her head ached.

Then she remembered—the comte. Where was he? She peeped around the half-closed curtain.

In the armchair, his face relaxed in sleep, rested the comte, his long legs sprawled out before him and the embroidered coat she had seen on the previous evening covering his lean body.

She looked down at herself, noticing that, though she was still fully dressed, her bodice had been unlaced.

Sighing with relief, she realized that he had not violated her in any way. He must be a real gentleman, after all—letting her sleep in his bed while he slept in a chair.

Trying not to disturb the sleeping man, Madeleine slipped out of bed and stretched her weary and bruised limbs. With the quickening circulation, the events of the previous evening swam through her memory, and her fears rushed back. *Dieu*, she had to escape before he awakened! The room was cold, and she shivered in her thin, rumpled dress. Close to the bed was a small window. Stars of ice crusted the panes like thousands of tiny diamonds, distorting the view. Cautiously she leaned forward and looked out to ascertain her exact whereabouts. Her warm breath thawed a small circle on the pane, and pressing one eye to it, she got a glimpse of the courtyard and the village of Versailles.

A misty orange-red glow in the east heralded the new day. Smoke from the chimneys flowed straight up in the cold, brittle air.

On tiptoe, she stepped over the comte's legs. Straighten my dress, don my cloak, and then away! she thought. Just one minute by the mirror.

Behind the screen she hurriedly laced up her bodice. Bending over a rose-patterned basin on a stand, she splashed some cold water on her face and dried herself on a perfumed cloth.

The mirror revealed dark rings under her eyes. Her cheeks were almost as pale as the curls she impatiently wound into a simple chignon in the back. She pinched her cheeks to force some color into them. Rapid steps sounded in the corridor, stopping abruptly outside the door.

Her heart jolted with fear, and she darted a glance at the comte. His hands tucked beneath his head, he was wide awake and smiling wickedly as if he had found her toilette vastly entertaining. *Mon Dieu*, she shouldn't have stayed to arrange her clothing! Now she was trapped.

A faint scratch on the door disrupted the charged silence.

"*Entrez*," the comte ordered, his voice lazy with sleep.

A slim young man in an oyster-colored velvet coat with a wide white collar stepped inside.

"*Bonjour*, monsieur le comte," he said briskly and bestirred himself to light the fire. Madeleine knew he had noticed her from the corner of his eye, but he did not acknowledge her presence in any way.

"*Mon vieux* Gaspard, you're awfully brisk this morning," the comte complained and yawned.

"You'll be late for the *levée* if you don't hurry, Monsieur Germain."

The comte grinned, and Madeleine could not believe the transformation the smile brought to his face, its charm making her weak inside. "Ah, *oui*, the *levée*," he said. "Gaspard is a stickler for etiquette, almost as bad as the King's brother," he explained to Madeleine. Sweeping his arm in a wide gesture, he introduced, "Gaspard Vincent, my *valet de chambre*." Raising his voice slightly, he added, "Gaspard, this is Mademoiselle Poquelin—none other than *petite* Célie in *Sganarelle*."

A flicker of interest darted into the young man's serious eyes, and he regarded her for a brief moment, nodding curtly.

"He's a surly Breton. Just ignore him," the comte explained with another smile.

Embarrassed, she snatched her cloak from a peg on the wall. She knew exactly what the valet was thinking of her. Before she could don her cloak, the comte seized it. Encircling her with his arms, he draped the garment over her shoulders.

Germain looked down at her alabaster face, noticing the rose-petal blush in her cheeks and the fire in her eyes. *I want her.* She was so charmingly fresh and frail—at least she looked frail. An unfamiliar sensation gripped him, a bittersweet longing in the area of his heart, and he wanted nothing more at that moment than to crush her to his chest, to trail her silky skin with his lips and fingertips, to feel the roundness of her breasts in his hands. A thudding, ensnaring desire held him in its relentless grip. None of the women of his numerous affairs had ever inspired such intense longing in him. In fact, lately he had been bored by his *affaires de coeur*, spurning all seduction attempts from the ever-scheming mesdames at court.

Nervously Madeleine tied the tasseled cords of her cloak at her throat. The comte's proximity flustered her. He radiated virile warmth and sleep, the blond stubble on his chin giving him a rakish air.

"I'd better leave now. Uncle Jean-Baptiste will be furious if I'm late."

"*Ma petite*, are you afraid of me?" His breath caressing her ear, he spoke in a whisper so as not to be heard by the valet.

"No . . . you behaved like a gentleman." *Dieu*, she hoped he really wasn't involved with Fouquet.

A short, intense pause ensued, and she eyed him warily. A teasing light danced in his eyes. "But perhaps I won't behave the next time," he breathed into her ear. "How would you like to become my mistress? I could set you up in style. You could have everything of your heart's desire."

A wave of crimson flooded her face. "You!" she exclaimed. "How dare you! And in front of your valet."

He chuckled. "He knows everything there is to know about me. We grew up together. He's discretion personified."

"You must be out of your mind! I take back my words—you are no gentleman!" She stuck her chin valiantly in the air. "The only thing I need from you is help to arrange an audience with the King. I would be eternally grateful to you."

Mischief flashed in his eyes. "What would it be worth to you?" His long fingers caressed her soft cheeks. He noticed her outrage, and added dryly, "Since you don't want to tell me your business, how can I help you?"

She kept her temper under control. She could see his point of view, but it didn't make her less disappointed. "It's really none of your business—for the King's ears alone. You will have to trust my word."

He did not answer, his gaze wandering slowly over every inch of her face. She wondered uncomfortably if she had a spot on her nose.

She sighed. "Well, there is nothing else to say then. Thank you for giving me shelter." She bent to slide under his arm, but, imprisoning her, he braced his hands against the wall on each side of her shoulders.

"Let me go!" Defiantly she looked into his eyes, seeing a mercurial fire burning in the gray depths.

"Not until I've had a chance to taste your lovely lips. Let's call it a just reward for . . . saving your life last night," he murmured.

He bent his face closer and closer until his lips assaulted hers. It was a surprisingly soft assault. Never had a man's lips tasted more heavenly or more dangerous, Madeleine thought, spellbound as his demanding mouth drained all willpower from her limbs, replacing it with honeyed sweetness. When his shameless tongue sought the moist recesses of her mouth, she was ready to dissolve in the escalating pleasure. Her arms automatically sought the strength of his neck.

A discreet cough brought them back to more mundane matters. Madeleine was breathing with shallow gasps. Germain reluctantly abandoned her lips.

Another wave of embarrassment swept over her when she discovered that she was still clinging to him.

"Monsieur—the *levée*." The valet's voice held a trace of disapproval.

Germain sighed gustily, and his eyes shone in admiration. "Mmm, *ma chérie,* how delicious are your lips!" he whispered, lowering his arms.

Madeleine took the opportunity to move away from his embrace. Her gaze riveted to his, she fumbled for the doorknob. Forcing her gaze away, she mumbled *"Adieu"* and fled into the corridor.

"Wait!" he cried, but she ran swiftly, aiming for the stairs at the end of the cold passage. Muted sounds came from behind the many doors. She pulled the hood up over her head and face. Sneaking down the stairs, she feared finding Dubois and Lemont lying in wait behind every corner. But there was no sign of them, and Hautefort did not pursue her.

In wonder, she pressed her fingers to her still-burning lips. Nobody had ever kissed her like that before.

The palace was awakening; doors slammed, and disembodied voices echoed in the vaulted marble passages. Madeleine decided she would try another round of petitions before returning to Paris. Perhaps the King would notice her today. Most of all, she wanted to see Amul. What had become of him?

Her breath was an icy cloud around her face. It must be bitterly cold outside to create such a chill inside.

The relentless winter mirrored the desolation in her heart since her father's murder. Every night she dreamed about him, helplessly watching the light of life draining from his eyes. Why should her father, a loyal and dedicated servant of the King, have to give his life for a silly little diary? Life was never fair.

Madeleine sighed and dashed away a tear. Her adversary, Fouquet, was formidable, the second most powerful man in the country. She was David against Goliath; in her hands she held the power to destroy him. And she would not stop until he had paid in full.

Her skin prickled as if someone was watching her. She hurried along the corridor and was relieved to step into the warmth of the King's antechamber.

Pinched and ragged petitioners from all walks of life crowded before the fire at one end of the room. Madeleine joined them. Noblemen of the First, Second, and Third Entrance waited outside the royal apartment for the *levée*, the King's dressing ceremony. They chatted in lisping voices, and Madeleine thought they looked strange, dressed at dawn in all their splendor. Were they never cold in their thin silks and satins? One nobleman hid a yawn behind the flashing jewels on his hand.

A numbing chill crept along Madeleine's spine as she recognized the chevalier de Lemont among the courtiers. He was talking idly with the King's younger brother Philippe, the duc d'Orléans—or "Monsieur" as he was generally called.

As if Lemont sensed her gaze, he turned his eyes to the group by the fire. Madeleine could not avert her gaze. In morbid fascination she kept staring at him. His yellow stare coldly measured her, his handsome face impassive, his stance slowly turning more frigid and threatening. She grew stiff with terror. Yet she could not lower her gaze.

"Still here, Madeleine?" Amul hissed testily from behind a screen where he could not be seen by the courtiers at the door. "You leave yourself open to all sorts of dangers. You ought to give up before you find yourself in the Seine with a slit throat."

His voice broke the evil spell. On trembling legs she retreated deeper into the rapidly increasing crowd, not daring to look back at the splendid group at the King's door.

As soon as the courtiers left the antechamber, Amul joined Madeleine by the fire. This morning he was somberly dressed in brown velvet.

"Thank God, you're alive!" she whispered to him.

"Here." Amul handed her a cup of chocolate. The liquid was tepid, but she drank with relish.

"I'll never forgive you for leaving me alone," she continued, and shifted her gaze furtively around the room. "I've never been more afraid in my life!"

"I thought you were right behind me. I escaped through a door under that moldy tapestry in the corridor, and when I realized you were not with me, it was already too late. You ran in the other direction." His large black eyes were anxious. "You got away this time, but don't expect to be as lucky the next." He scratched his head under the plumed cap. "By the way, did you find out who followed us?"

"*Oui,* I immediately recognized his whiny voice: Dubois. *Dieu,* I had no idea he was Lemont's valet."

"*Oui,* he's a shady one. He must be in Fouquet's pay. You ought to leave right this minute—before you get caught."

"I had to make sure you were unhurt, and I want to present another petition. It looks hopeless, but you know how important it is. I have to reach the King before Fouquet reaches me."

"Where did you sleep?"

Madeleine made a grimace. "The comte de Hautefort gave me shelter—and saved me from Dubois."

Amul laughed. "Did Hautefort try to make you his mistress? From what I've heard, he's very popular with the ladies, and an expert swordsman."

She drained the last dregs of the chocolate and looked at Amul in concern. "You're much too young to speak of such matters, Amul. It can't be easy to live in Monsieur's household. The court is corrupting you."

Amul shrugged. "I stay away from Monsieur." A smile spread across his face, exposing rows of perfectly white teeth. "He eats boys for breakfast, but such a small detail doesn't stop me from spying on him and his retinue. I did not sleep at all last night. Monsieur was up all night playing cards, and when he lost, he had a vicious fight with Madame. You know how biting his tongue can be."

Madeleine knew very well. Officially Monsieur was the patron of Molière's theater company, although he conveniently forgot to pay the yearly pensions that were his due. But Uncle Molière did not complain, so why should she? she thought. The theater was popular, and the actors earned enough to live comfortably. Yet, instinctively, Madeleine held the royal prince in aversion.

"Amul, it's dangerous! What if you are caught?"

He giggled. "I run faster than any of them. Anyway, Madame would never let any harm befall me."

All at once, as if by an unspoken order, every lady in the room sank into a deep curtsy, and the men bowed reverently. The King was coming out of his *appartement* to attend Mass. After Mass, he would collect petitions.

To watch the King at such close range was almost frightening. Every time she saw him, Madeleine could not help but stare. But however daunted by his presence she felt, she planned to speak with him at the first convenient moment.

Once His Majesty had passed with his retinue, the buzz of the petitioners' voices rose once more. It would continue until the sovereign returned. Among the burghers there were impoverished noblemen hoping to throw themselves at the mercy of the King, to beg for some small legacy to keep them alive. Madeleine knew that many courtiers became ruined overnight at the gaming tables, and how could a nobleman fend for himself when he had never done a day's work in his life? They were a pitiful sight.

The air was suffocating with the foul odors of unwashed bodies, and Madeleine sought refuge near one of the tall windows. She was still tired, and her legs ached from last night's exertions.

Amul leaned against the wall next to her and spoke under his breath. "You have to be extremely careful where you go from now on. You're next on Fouquet's list. You don't want to end up in the Salpetrière or the Châtelet. You'd never return from there."

Madeleine shivered in apprehension. Those were hospital prisons, so hideous that "guests" never survived for long within their walls. Amul continued his lecture. "And most of all, watch out for poisoned food!"

She turned to him in indignation. *"Bien!* Are you suggesting that I should go away and hide in a hole somewhere, like a coward?"

"That is an excellent idea."

She glared at him. *"Jamais!* You know I can't do that."

Amul shrugged apologetically. "I wish I could keep an eye on you."

"That is not necessary. You have your place, and besides, I need you to spy on Lemont and Dubois now. They are connected to Fouquet."

Amul paused, and she noticed that his lips were trembling. For all his grown-up ways and careful speech, he was very young and insecure. When Molière had returned to Paris from the provinces with his company of strolling actors, Amul had been one of the stagehands. He and Madeleine had soon become friends. He was devoted to her and spent every spare minute at the theater studying plays, dreaming of becoming a great playwright like Molière. It was a dream he never dared to voice to the great man himself. Madeleine loved Amul like the little brother she had never had; she had confided her secret to him since she needed his help and was sure that a small, young boy was not involved in Fouquet's evil schemes.

Ever since Monsieur's wife, Madame, Princesse Henriette of England, had taken a liking to Amul's chocolate face and round eyes, he had been in her service. He was her personal page, and since his arrival, Moorish pages had become all the rage at court.

"We should not be seen together here, Amul. Our enemies can easily add two and two, and I don't want you to suffer because of me."

"I know. I have to go back to the Saint-Cloud palace with Madame. Take care of yourself. I'll come to the theater soon—and you ought to confide in your uncle. He can help you."

"Mais non! Uncle Jean-Baptiste is not to be involved. Fouquet can ruin him with a wave of his little finger. Who

says the King would believe my uncle any more than he would me? I have a better chance, and I have nothing to lose."

"*Oui,* your life," Amul said darkly, his lips trembling. "Go home and stay there, please, Madeleine. Or go to work, and don't go out alone."

Madeleine smiled. "*Oui,* I have to go back to work. Uncle Jean-Baptiste has been quite the tyrant since the new theater in Palais-Royal opened. I'll be very busy making new costumes—that is, if I'm not dismissed for being late. But I'm not giving up my plans. It might take somewhat longer than I thought, that's all."

Two small pages from the Queen's household approached Amul and pulled him away. He sent Madeleine an apologetic glance, and she winked.

When total silence once more reigned in the antechamber, Madeleine knew that the King was returning. She jostled her way to the front of the line and sank down on her knees, holding out her petition in the path of the King and praying that he would notice it. If not, she would *make* him notice her.

She did not dare lift her eyes to his face, but she got a good view of his diamond-buckled shoes and strong calves.

He lingered here and there for short moments. She was about to throw herself in front of his feet, but the silk-clad legs of the nobles surrounding the King pushed her aside before she had a chance to move. The opportunity passed in a flash.

All of a sudden somebody snatched the petition from her hand and flung it on the floor, far from her grasp. Madeleine jerked her head up, and pain shot through her neck. Her eyes connected with the mocking, cold gaze of the chevalier de Lemont. He flicked an imaginary speck of dust from his lace cuff and proceeded to grind his red heel on the petition. Madeleine gasped with fury at his insolence and tried to throw herself after him, but the crush of people was too great. She was squeezed between two portly burghers who strained to gain the King's attention long after he had entered his study. Walking behind Monsieur and other noblemen, Lemont followed the King. With impotent wrath Madeleine could only curse him in silence.

Then, as if in a dream, she saw a strong hand poke a page gently in the back. A solitary emerald glittered on the index finger. Obeying the courtier's order, the page bent and picked up Madeleine's petition and handed it to the owner of the emerald. She had no difficulty recognizing the comte de Hautefort. Her breath caught in her throat.

He turned to look at her, his face a haughty, indifferent mask, but she observed the ghost of a smile in his eyes.

Amazed, she watched him place the petition on the table consigned to hold the petitions the King did not take personally.

Somebody would read it, one of the King's ministers perhaps. Now there was a faint glimmer of hope that someone would understand the urgency of her request.

Madeleine stared at the comte's broad back. He was attired in a pearl-gray silk coat with silver braids and ribbons, white rhinegraves, and gray silk stockings. His smile sent a beam of warmth into Madeleine's reluctant heart. What an enigmatic man he was!

Chapter 3

Amul's warnings lingered in Madeleine's mind. Every shadow seemed ominous; every unfamiliar face held a menace. And however much she denied it, she was afraid of poisoned food. Consequently she was not eating well. Yet she kept reminding herself that Fouquet surely wanted her alive if he was ever to retrieve his lost diary. But you never knew with him. He also wanted her dead to prevent his secret from reaching the King's ear.

Madeleine shuddered as she bent closer over the delicate embroidery in her hands. She was sitting in the enormous dressing room behind the stage at the Palais-Royal theater. Bursts of laughter echoed from the spectators, and Madeleine could hear Gros René's voice penetrating to every dark corner of the building. The candle at her elbow flickered wildly in the cold draft from the ill-fitting windows.

Heightening her tension was the fact that the King had made no effort to respond to her petitions. Had she been a fool to think that he would lend an ear to her humble person? If only he knew!

Day after day her dissatisfaction escalated, and she earned many reprimands for falling behind in her work. Costumes needing to be mended piled ever higher on the table in the tiny chamber at the theater that was her usual workroom. Escaping from that airless cubbyhole, she often sewed in the dressing room. Uncle Jean-Baptiste had threatened to dismiss her if her speed did not improve. She sighed and pinched her lips together.

He didn't know that in her mind she relived a nightmare over and over. Every time she closed her eyes, she saw her father's dying face. His last words reverberated constantly in her head: *Ma petite fille, the diary . . . take it to . . . the King . . .* She clapped her sore, needle-pricked fingers to her ears and fought back a wave of tears.

The performance was over. Footsteps shook the floorboards, and one by one the actresses danced into the dressing room, their voices and laughter loud and excited.

"Will you have dinner with us tonight?" Madame Du Parc asked Madeleine.

Monsieur Du Parc and his wife always invited her to share their dinner on Saturdays.

"*Non*, but thank you for the invitation." Madeleine held up the satin gown for La Du Parc's inspection. "I darned the tear and embroidered a flower on top. What do you think?"

Swinging her swan's-down stole, La Du Parc smiled and pecked Madeleine on the cheek. "*Petite*, your fingers are pure magic! I don't know how you see to make such fine stitches."

Madame Du Parc was one of the most beautiful women Madeleine had ever seen. She had a voluptuous figure, glorious red hair that curled and bounced like fire, and a passionate voice that could hold an audience captivated. She was a marvelous actress, a perfect foil for Molière.

His genius was steadily on the rise. Having secured the King's approval in 1658, the company had prospered rapidly. Molière's satirical plays were much liked by all the classes of Paris, and the actors rode on a wave of glory.

At Palais-Royal, performances were held four nights a week, Saturdays being the most profitable. Other days Madeleine spent frantically sewing and repairing the costumes, or in the noisy company of the actors. La Béjart, Molière's mistress, was like a mother to her and often helped her with the costumes. Molière harbored hopes that Madeleine would someday follow his tradition and become an actress. He had trained her voice, teaching her for long, frustrating hours. However, her obvious lack of interest had caused her uncle to tear at his long brown curls. He had failed to see that she was still numb with grief over her father's death.

It was so difficult to accept that her father was dead, and so shortly after her mother had died of smallpox. Madeleine felt as if her life was over; she had lost the two people who meant the most to her, and in such horrifying ways. Perhaps her nightmares would disappear if she could clear her father's name.

Nothing was left of her father's modest fortune, and Madeleine knew that her uncle's goodwill was the only thing keeping her from squalor. She owed everything to him. She knew that despite his terrible temper, Jean-Baptiste would always protect and support her.

She sighed listlessly and pulled out the pins from her untidy chignon. Bone tired, she brushed her hair. The curls spilled around her face. With an angry tug of her brush she gathered the errant waves and fastened them in the back with two tortoiseshell combs. Around her, the other ladies chatted and giggled. Their spirits were always high after a good performance. Although it was only five in the afternoon, darkness was falling, and they had to light tallow candles to see their images in the mirrors. Madeleine lit another candle from the sputtering stump and placed it beside La Du Parc. Meticulously the actress wiped off the excess rouge on her lips and cheeks.

With another sigh Madeleine braced her chin on the palm of her hand and stared at the beautiful woman.

"Why are you sighing?" Madame Du Parc asked as she pulled up her silk stockings and fastened them with gaudy satin garters.

"Oh, nothing."

"The crowd was rough today, but aren't they always on a Saturday? The loudest and the rudest are those strutting peacocks from court; enough to throw you into a fit."

"*Oui*, I looked at them from behind the curtain. All I saw was a sea of plumed hats. The theater was full."

"*Oui*, but such arrogance! They kept up an ongoing commentary on the play. Molière was furious and bid them to shut up."

Madeleine smiled tiredly. "Yes, Uncle Jean-Baptiste has a vile temper. But he's well pleased with you. The audience loves you and Gros René."

Madame Du Parc looked pleased. "I'm happy as long as it lasts. The taste of the audience is very fickle." Changing subjects, she said, "Are you sure you get enough sleep, *pe-*

tite Madeleine? You seem so . . . tense, as tightly strung as a violin wire. You need an assistant."

Before Madeleine could answer, running footsteps sounded on the wooden floor. One of the stagehands, a young boy, approached carrying a bouquet of pink roses. The ladies exchanged incredulous glances. Roses!

Madeleine believed without a doubt that the flowers were for La Du Parc, but to her surprise, the boy headed toward her.

Madeleine's lips parted in amazement, and she was about to protest, but the boy shoved the bouquet into her arms.

"*Dieu*, how lovely they are! Where do they find roses in the middle of the winter?" She buried her face in the balmy fragrance of the flowers. "*Who* sent me these?"

"Look for the card," La Du Parc advised and dabbed some perfume along the edge of the low décolletage of her gown.

Madeleine was truly bewildered. "I don't understand." She looked between the thick stems of the flowers, careful not to prick herself on the thorns. She soon found what she was looking for. As she pulled out the card, her heart hammered wildly.

It read:

> For the ethereal Célie, the sweet phantom of my thoughts. My offer still stands. Will you dine with me tonight? I'm waiting outside with my carriage. Hautefort.

Madeleine's hands grew clammy with excitement. "It's from a courtier, the comte de Hautefort. He has invited me to dinner."

A gasp escaped La Du Parc's lovely lips, and Madeleine glanced at her. "Something wrong?"

"You *do* understand what a courtier has in mind when he invites a seamstress-actress to dine."

Madeleine blushed and hid her face in the sweet fragrance of the roses. "*Naturellement*. I'm not an infant, and I know that a nobleman has no *serious* intentions—"

"*Bien*. Are you going to dine with Hautefort?" La Du Parc pursed her lips and patted a curl behind her ear. "Let's see . . . *Enfin* he's the master of the hounds. Very close to the King. I must say you do have a lofty admirer. He is very rich—and wildly attractive. Take care not to lose your heart to him," she added with a twinkle in her eye.

"You're right. It would be courting disaster to get involved with him." Once again Madeleine smelled the roses. "But he's so gallant—and persuasive."

"Where did you meet him, *petite* Madeleine?"

Madeleine's senses reeled, and she could almost feel the touch of his lips on hers. "At Versailles after the performance." Reluctantly she called the stage boy back. As he fidgeted beside her, Madeleine wrote a polite note on the back of the card, thanked the comte for the flowers, and declined the dinner invitation. "*Ecoutez*, Jacques, give this to the gentleman in the carriage."

La Du Parc's chuckle held a world of meaning. "Mayhap are you already the comte's paramour, *non*? You remained overnight at Versailles."

Madeleine gave her a playful shove. "*Dieu du ciel, non!*" she protested. But she felt a pinprick of regret at refusing the comte and sank down on the lumpy sofa in a corner, still smelling the roses. Her tremulous sigh wafted over the fresh rose petals, and as she closed her eyes, she could clearly see the comte's striking face before her . . .

When she looked up again, she was completely alone in the dressing room. Silence hung brooding in the air. The gaudy costumes were tossed about as if discarded in flight, creating an eerie effect. *Dieu!* I promised Amul never to be alone, she thought, panicking.

Why had she not heard La Du Parc or the others leave the room?

"Madame Du Parc?" Her voice echoed hollowly. Everyone was gone. The shadows expanded and shrunk, crowding in on her, and the only light came from the tiny flame of a faltering candle. Fear crawled along her spine.

With trembling fingers, Madeleine lit another candle and set it in the pewter holder overflowing with old tallow. Not knowing if she dared to move, she stared wide-eyed into the darkness, clutching the flowers close. Thorns pricked her through the wool of her bodice, but she did not notice the pain. She had to get out now. Feeling utterly alone, she took one faltering step.

Straining her ears, she thought she could hear a faint shuffle of feet in the area of the stage. She tried to extend her sight, but could see nothing. A draft of cold air made the flame of the candle shudder wildly, and a curl of black smoke meandered into the empty, dark space above her. Menace breathed around her.

Her heart thudded heavily. I'm only imagining this, she thought. Biting her lip, she took another step, her gaze darting from one side of the room to the other, seeing nothing but pitch darkness. She fumbled for her cloak and looped it over her arm.

Edging her way toward the exit, a narrow door next to the stage that the performers used, she stumbled and dropped the candle. Thus losing the guidance of that feeble light, she had to feel her way across the floor. Her stiff lips formed a silent prayer that she would find the door.

You're too fanciful, she told herself angrily, but the path to the door was the longest she had ever walked. All around her she sensed evil—eyes staring at her from the darkness. A loose floorboard groaned.

She touched the cold doorknob. Never had she been happier to reach a door. Tearing it open, she skipped down the shallow steps and flung herself into the snow outside. Terror gave her speed, and she hastily regained her upright position and rushed headlong down the dark and windy Rue de Richelieu. Anything to get away from the unseen horrors behind her.

Here and there the massive blackness was broken by the light of a lantern, and some windows were lit by candles.

Why did I stay behind everyone else? she chastised herself. In this dense darkness she was likely to be set upon by footpads or cutthroats.

Perhaps the person in the theater had wanted her to flee headlong into a more hideous trap. It was too awful to consider even for a moment, and she pushed away the thought.

She shrieked with fear as a shadow loomed in front of her. Thinking her last moment had come, she shied away, staggering. In the biting wind a cloak writhed like the flapping wings of a crow. Two strong, masculine arms encircled her, and her screams were muffled against a broad chest smelling of orris root. Delicate lace tickled her nose.

This is no ruffian! she thought.

"Célie? Are you hurt?"

She would have recognized that deep voice anywhere. It belonged to the comte de Hautefort.

Gulping for air, she could not answer, but she did not resist as he lifted her into a coach that she had not noticed before. The comte tapped the roof three times with his cane, and the coach began to move hesitantly. Madeleine heard the horses snorting and chomping at their bits. The air was so cold it seemed crystallized.

The moon emerged from behind a bank of clouds, its pale glitter providing the only light in the coach. It wove a haze of black and silver shadows on the seats and the ornate molding around the door.

Realizing she was safe for the moment, Madeleine sobbed. Without asking any questions, the comte cradled her against his chest, and his warm breath fanned her neck and hair as he leaned over her, whispering soothing nothings. His curls fell like a protective curtain around her face, and with admirable patience he dabbed gently at her eyes with a muslin handkerchief.

"*Dieu*, I—I'm so s-sorry." She gulped.

"Don't be. Are you hurt?"

"No, I don't think so—except that the thorns of the roses are pressing into my chest."

"Eh, *oui—pardon*, let me help you." The comte gathered the bouquet and placed it on the opposite seat.

"They must be sadly crushed. I meant to thank you. It was a lovely gift, and . . . sinfully frivolous!"

"I am in a frivolous mood."

Madeleine blushed in the seductive darkness. His warm voice caressed her raw nerve endings.

He continued, "I was disappointed when you refused my invitation. I waited and waited, and then I saw you careening out the door."

"I was frightened out of my wits. I think someone was lying in wait for me inside. Amul told me I should never be alone."

The comte groaned. "Not again! What is this new wild tale? Who are you involved with? And who is this Amul?"

"My friend. He's a page in Madame's service."

"Ah, the Moor." He paused. "I suppose these 'incidents' have something to do with your petitions to the King?"

Madeleine leaned eagerly forward. "*Oui.* Have you heard anything? Has the King mentioned my petition?"

The comte chuckled. "You're somewhat . . . naïve, *ma petite.*"

Her anger kindled at those words. "You have no right to—"

"Shhh." His voice held an edge of authority.

A current of excitement raced through her veins as he cupped her chin with his large hand, and her anger subsided. His tenderness taking her by surprise, she stared at his moonlight-washed features. In the sudden light of a lantern she noticed that his eyes shone like mercury, and their intensity made her breathless. He leaned closer.

The instinctive protest died before it reached her lips, and she yielded to his demanding kiss.

The strength of her reaction puzzled her. She went hot and cold all over as his lips roved warmly over hers. A thousand tiny fires sprang to life within her, all needing to be quenched, but his coaxing lips only increased the burning sensation. The kiss was slowly transformed into a deep, molten yearning in the core of her being. Her whole body cried out to him; the kiss felt wonderful, natural, and—new. Nobody had ever made her feel so excited or so aware of the secrets of her own body. For a short moment she forgot her fears.

As he reluctantly lifted his face inches above hers, his soft sigh brushed her lips. Neither of them spoke. The magic was all around them and in them—sheer as gossamer. The world had stopped.

Madeleine was the one to speak first, her voice a weak whisper. "Why did you come tonight?"

"I came to see the performance."

She laughed shakily and lowered her eyelashes. The intensity of his gaze daunted her. "I wager you were one of the loudly criticizing noblemen on the *parterre.* Uncle Jean-Baptiste almost had an apoplexy."

He laughed, throwing back his head. "In fact, I was on the first tier, to the right, and saw your sunshine hair when you peeped around the curtain."

"You're flattering me, monsieur le comte! I don't understand your interest in me." He did not answer immediately, and she sat up and moved to the opposite seat. The comte did not detain her.

He rubbed his chin. "I don't know. Perhaps I find you intriguing."

Those simple words made her heart throb wildly. No other man had ever touched her intimately with only a few words. He continued, his voice shrouded in amusement. "You also have a lovely voice. It stirs a man's, er, feelings."

"Comte, you're accomplished at showing those, er, *feelings* in a practical way. As for my voice, Uncle Molière deems it important to speak with clarity and beauty. But I'm somewhat of a disappointment to him; he despairs, he begs, but I will not follow his acting tradition."

"A pity. Your rendition of Célie at Versailles was charming."

"I have my uncle to thank for everything."

"You are a born actress."

Madeleine snorted in a way that the nuns at the Ursuline convent would have considered highly unladylike. "Hardly. I have no calling for the art. Fate changed the course of my life in mere seconds. I would never have thought of becoming an actress or costume maker if it weren't—"

A pregnant silence followed, and Germain waited for the continuation of her story, but Madeleine pressed her lips together and stared out the window. Suddenly she remembered that she had no idea where they were going.

She turned to him. "I forgot to inform you of my uncle's address." A shaft of moonlight caught the silver clasp of his cloak, and she sensed that he was smiling.

"Piliers des Halles, near Rue de la Réale," he recited. "Molière lives with your ancient grandfather, when he's not at La Béjart's house on Rue Saint Thomas du Louvre."

"How did you know?"

"I made it my business to know. Your grandfather is ailing with gout and taking the waters at Vichy. He has no idea that you are in Paris. He thinks you're as yet at the convent in Rouen. Also, he doesn't know the details of your father's death."

Madeleine was baffled. A stab of fear made her spine stiffen. "How . . . ?"

Something was wrong. How did he know about her father's death? And if he wanted a mistress, why did he pursue her when so many ladies at court, or at the theater for that matter, were more beautiful and more experienced? He was playing a cat and mouse game with her. Madeleine drew her cloak closer, completely on her guard.

As if he sensed what was going through her mind, he said, "I would like you to reconsider my dinner invitation. A special feast is being prepared at my *hôtel* on Rue Saint Antoine in the Marais. Please don't make me depressed by refusing."

Madeleine didn't answer. She stared at him intently and imagined that his tone was turning slightly sinister. Or was it? She swallowed, tasting the salt of tears. How confusing!

"Pauvre petite," the comte said with a soft laugh. "Are you frightened of me? I promise I will not take any liberties with you." He toyed with the knob of his cane.

"You nobles are not known for stability or reliability," Madeleine responded frankly. "I'd rather go home, if you please."

"The nobles? You can't judge me by those few dissipated characters whose reputations are first and foremost on the tongues of the gossips."

"And you're not one of them? You know as well as I do that said characters are in abundance at court. Do I have to say more? I'm not a woman of easy virtue to be toyed with and then discarded."

"I have understood. If I promise to behave myself, would you please reconsider? You would be brightening a rather dull evening with your lovely presence."

He was so gallant that Madeleine was charmed against her better judgment. Yes, she wanted to spend the evening in his company. Time fled by in his presence, and she was wildly attracted to him.

"You have won, monsieur le comte, but I will not let you take any more liberties with me. You have already stolen a kiss."

"I seem to recall that you gave it freely."

She could not see his face, however much her eyes fought to penetrate the darkness, but his voice held a smile as if he was taking pleasure in their banter.

"How do you know so much about me?" she asked.

The question hung between them, the wheels crunching over cobblestones the only sound.

"I make it my business to discover everything I can about my *petite amies*," he explained at last.

"I see. But I am not your *amie*." Madeleine's fear was gradually turning into annoyance. "Can you not be serious for one moment?"

He laughed, a low, rumbling sound.

A shiver of apprehension she could not hold back rippled through her. The comte was probably not one of her enemies, but she could not be entirely sure.

"Are you cold?" he asked.

"*Oui*—and *non*."

"We'll soon be there. I hope you're not regretting your decision." He placed a rug over her knees.

"Do I have a choice?" Her voice was very small.

"Perhaps, perhaps not; I'm a man who doesn't give up easily. Resistance is a delectable spice."

"Why do I get the feeling that I'm a lamb going to slaughter?"

The comte laughed and lightly tapped his cane three times on the roof. "You're too suspicious." The coach came to a sudden halt, and Madeleine was thrown forward, to her knees. The roses scattered on the floor. The next thing she knew, the door opened and a heavily caped figure jumped in. Madeleine's eyes widened, and her heart bolted.

The man sank onto the seat while she labored to untie the cords of her cloak, which were digging into her neck. The comte tapped his cane again, and as the carriage lurched forward, the scarf muffling the other man's face fell free.

"You!" Madeleine gasped. Her heart skipped a beat as she recognized Fouquet, her enemy.

Chapter 4

"*Oui*, I knew we would meet sooner or later," Fouquet said with a ghastly smile. "You are very careless to walk the streets alone at night."

Madeleine bit her lip to stifle a whimper of fear. Fouquet's white teeth gleamed in the darkness, and his black eyes glittered. She imagined hearing her father's voice, *Think, oh, think,* petite *Madeleine!*

"What do you want?" she breathed, her lips stiff. Momentarily she had forgotten Germain, her entire concentration focused on her adversary.

The minister of finance chuckled. "You know very well what I want, Mademoiselle Poquelin. Do not be foolish like your father. You saw what happened to him."

Madeleine shrank trembling into a corner of the coach. *Think!* "I have done nothing that would warrant that gruesome fate. You are a murderer, Monsieur Fouquet."

He gave a shrug. "When your father died, I was at a ball at the palace of Saint-Germain. There are hundreds of witnesses who will swear to that."

Madeleine clenched her hands until the nails bit into her palms. "*Peut-être*. But you know very well when my father died and who did the deed—on your orders."

Fouquet's voice was harsh and contemptuous. "Come now, mademoiselle. Do not throw empty accusations around. It only hurts your situation more. I am a very powerful man." He leaned toward her, and Madeleine recoiled in fear. "If you cooperate with me, mademoiselle, no harm will come to you."

RECKLESS SPLENDOR

Madeleine laughed, but the sound that came out was a frightened squeak. "I will never trust one of your words; you are a snake, Monsieur Fouquet!" Even though she thought she was going to disintegrate with terror—or at least faint—she held her chin high and turned her flashing eyes on Germain. "And you! You're no better than a worm, monsieur le comte. How could you do this—set up this trap!"

Germain held out his hands in an apologetic gesture. "Fouquet begged me to arrange a few minutes of conversation with you; I had no idea—"

Madeleine bristled. "Don't you dare lie to me! You knew about my father, about his . . . his death." Suddenly she felt drained of all strength, and in her chest where her heart had sung with joy a few minutes ago, there was now a black hole of despair. She made a rash movement toward the door, but Fouquet's bony fingers circled her wrist like a band of iron. She could smell the wine and tobacco on his breath as he leaned closer. Menace and formidable power poured forth with his every word.

"Tell me, Mademoiselle Poquelin, where is it?" His voice was infinitely soft. His fingers tightened until she gasped.

Lies and evasions flickered feverishly through her mind. "I have no—"

His nails bit into the soft skin of her wrist. "And don't try pulling the wool over my eyes. Tell me the truth! I know you have it." He leaned closer and closer, and Madeleine warded him off with her free hand.

"*S'il vous plaît*, release me. I will take you to it." She grit her teeth so as not to reveal her pain.

"*Alors*, I'm glad you're coming to your senses." He let her go abruptly, and she fell back into the corner, panting and rubbing her aching wrist. Her thoughts scurried from one plan to the other, and she swallowed hard. What would happen now? *Stall for time, stall him!*

"The diary is at my grandfather's house," she whispered. She thought Fouquet could hear her heartbeat in the heavy silence that ensued.

"*Where* in the house?" Fouquet sounded as if he was holding a tight rein on his temper.

"I will show you," Madeleine responded with as much calm as she could. "It is well hidden—in the cellar." That was as good an excuse as any. Let Fouquet stumble around the dank cobwebby cellars while she gave the comte de Hautefort a piece of her mind. Perhaps Uncle Jean-Baptiste was there. Oh, *Dieu,* let Uncle be there! He would know what to do. He would protect her from Fouquet, and in the worst case she would have to confide her secret to him. In a daze she heard the comte order the coachman to drive to the Rue de la Réale.

The harnesses jingled as the horses made a sharp turn, the carriage creaked, and the snow crunched under the wheels. Madeleine pulled her cloak closer, shivering with nerves and cold. She clamped her teeth together to stop them from chattering.

"For your own good, I hope you're not lying, mademoiselle," Fouquet threatened.

His icy voice made her blood run cold. All she could think of was how to get away from the two men. She was taking a risk by luring them to Rue de la Réale; now she could only pray that her wits wouldn't abandon her at the crucial moment. She knew every corner of her grandfather's house, and they didn't. With that small advantage, she would somehow escape from her assailants.

The closer they came to the Poquelin residence, the more afraid she grew; her heart beat erratically and her nerves were so tightly strung that she thought she would explode into a million fragments.

Fouquet was tapping his cane in a staccato rhythm on the floor. Madeleine sent a furtive glance at the comte, who was staring straight in front of him, but she could not see his features. A cold hand seemed to squeeze her heart. He was worse than Fouquet, who didn't pretend to be other than what he was—her foe. The comte's kisses and smooth words had been very convincing, and she would never forgive him for toying with her. Never!

The coach came to an abrupt halt in front of the dark portico of the tall, narrow house belonging to Grandfather Poquelin. Madeleine threw herself against the carriage door, but was gripped from behind by Fouquet. He forced her down on the seat and pushed past her. The wind tore at the door as he opened it and stepped down. He extended a hand toward her, but she refused it and climbed down, stumbling on the cobblestones. Instantly Fouquet's hard fingers came around her arm. As he pushed her toward the front door, she was dimly aware of the comte descending and following.

A weak light glowed in the hallway, but the rest of the house lay in silent darkness. There was a slightly musty smell of age and mildewy brocade wall panels. Her grandfather had maintained a prosperous upholstery business for many years; the house had once displayed elegance. But as her grandfather's health had slowly deteriorated with time, the house had crumbled with him.

"*Bon*, where did you hide it?" Fouquet's voice was impatient.

Madeleine pointed a shaking finger toward the corridor leading to the kitchen. "In the cellars. Through there; the cellar door is in the kitchen. The diary is behind the cognac barrel in the corner." *Dieu*, if I could only reach the pistol that Grandfather's manservant always keeps loaded and hidden under the stairs.

That hope was instantly crushed as Fouquet shoved her in the back. "You'll fetch it for me," he ordered coldly. "I'll be right behind you, so don't try any tricks."

Embers glowed in the kitchen hearth, and Madeleine's gaze darted around the room, searching for a weapon. Two sets of footsteps echoed behind her. The comte was still there. Was he coming to gloat? Madeleine wanted to take a swing at his head with the heavy iron poker by the fireplace. As if Fouquet could read her thoughts, he prodded her in the back, urging her on. Total silence reigned, even after she deliberately overturned a chair. No one was in the house. Just her luck that no one was there to help her!

She turned the heavy iron key. The odor of damp earth and sour ale rose from below as she swung the door wide. The comte lit three candles on the embers and offered her one. She accepted it with a defiant thrust of her chin and refused to meet his gaze.

Fouquet pinched her, and she protested loudly, taking the first step down.

"I think Mademoiselle Poquelin will do as you bid without your abuse, Fouquet," came the comte's icy voice.

"I do not trust her," Fouquet retorted, and followed Madeleine onto the stairs. "Don't concern yourself, Hautefort. You always had a weak spot for the ladies, you fool. Be quiet—you owe me that. You owe me much more, so don't tell me what to do."

Madeleine prayed that their quarrel would develop into a fight, but the comte remained silent. What did he owe Fouquet?

They reached the uneven earth floor. The candles created eerie circles of light, making the darkness seem more dense around them. Madeleine's breathing was uneven. What would she do now? There was no diary behind the barrel, and she wanted to be far away from Fouquet when he found out. "There." She pointed at the dusty, dripping barrel.

Against her heel she felt the hard side of a brick. As soon as Fouquet was moving, she would bend and hoist her impromptu weapon. But Fouquet didn't move; he jerked his head toward the barrel and demanded, "Show me—now! I don't have all night."

Madeleine's hope seeped out, but in a last desperate effort, she threw her candle at him and gripped the brick. Fouquet sprang at her, was on top of her before she had time to use her weapon.

"Let her go, Fouquet, and put your hands in the air," came a youthful voice from the top of the stairs. "And you too, comte. I have two pistols, and they are loaded." The voice faltered as Fouquet turned and stared motionlessly at the small figure.

After a short, tense pause, Fouquet labored to his feet and dusted off his knees with studied indifference.

"Amul!" Madeleine breathed. She ran up the narrow steps. He handed her one of the pistols, and she noticed that his hand trembled violently. His eyes were wide with fear, and a thin layer of perspiration covered his face. *"Merci,"* she whispered. "Thank you so much. Give me the other pistol."

RECKLESS SPLENDOR 47

"Stay where you are!" she ordered shrilly as Fouquet took a step toward the stairs. "One movement, and I will shoot."

She backed into the kitchen. Amul grasped the door, and as Madeleine slowly retreated, both pistols aimed at Fouquet and the comte, he closed the door with a slam. Madeleine hurriedly placed the pistols on a bench, and helped Amul turn the rusty key. Then they pushed a table up against the door and wedged it under the key.

Madeleine leaned against the table and pressed a hand to her heart.

"I'm exhausted."

"Come, let us leave," Amul whispered, rolling his eyes in fear. "They will break down the door."

Madeleine laughed, a high-pitched sound of relief. "*Non*, the door is solid oak and at least two inches thick."

Amul made a grimace. "Don't underestimate Fouquet—or the comte."

"Bah! That traitor. I hope they both rot in hell!"

Amul gave her a sharp glance as he hefted one of the pistols. "Where shall we go?" he asked and scratched his head. He was dressed in a scarlet velvet cape with matching velvet beret and blue silk rhinegraves that billowed around his knees. He looked incongruous in the dark, dingy kitchen.

"I don't know—to La Béjart's house, *peut-être*, or to Saint-Germain. La Béjart's house will be full of actors as usual, and we'll be safe." As they hurried out of the room Madeleine asked, "Do you have any money?"

"*Non*. Molière sent me here for a script. He is going to Saint-Germain to see the King about the new play. The King wants to have a part in it—add some sort of ballet."

"Oh. We cannot leave without funds. I will take a gown or two to sell at Pont-Neuf tomorrow. We have to eat, and I don't know when I can return here."

"We don't have time to go upstairs," Amul said, his voice worried. "The longer we delay, the more the risk that Fouquet—"

"Don't worry about that. We are safe for now," Madeleine consoled him with more assurance than she actually felt. "This will take but a minute. We cannot go anywhere without funds."

Opening the door to her room, she was surprised to find it icy cold. The door to the small terrace outside flapped in the wind, making a hollow sound as it hit the wall. She took one step and stumbled over something on the floor. "What is this?" The candle in her hand blew out.

Close to the door she kept a small candlestick on a dresser. Fumbling with a tinderbox, she managed to light the candle. The weak flame leaped and fluttered in the draft, making huge, wavering shadows on the walls.

Amul's breath rasped in shock.

Madeleine looked around the chamber. All her things were strewn over the floor, dresses, petticoats, shifts, hats, books—everything. Her hand to her throat, she gave a strangled cry and knelt in the middle of the room. Tears flowed freely down her cheeks as she pressed her favorite dress to her chest. The icy wind pinched her, but she didn't care.

Amul closed the flapping door, shutting out the furious wind. Furtively he glanced around the room, as if expecting the shadows to leap at them from every corner.

Madeleine began sorting through her ruined belongings. "This is Fouquet's doing, I just know it. When he didn't find the diary here, he came after me."

Many of her books had been torn to pieces, and every single one had a broken binding. Her leather-bound and wooden boxes had been turned over, spilling the trinkets that she treasured—a dried four-leaf clover, a seed pearl brooch, a string of pearls with matching earrings, her parents' wedding rings, a brittle pink rose from her mother's bridal bouquet, an ornate silver crucifix, and a miniature painting of the Holy Mother.

Madeleine crossed herself and stared listlessly at her bed. The sheets and blankets lay in a heap on the floor, and her feather mattress had been slit up the middle, its contents poured all over. At least they had not found the diary, she thought with grim satisfaction—because it was not in the room.

With a tremulous sigh and mumbling a prayer, she straightened her things. She placed her torn garments back into the drawers and stacked her ruined books onto the bookshelf. Amul swept up the torn book pages and the glass shards and deposited them in the fireplace.

Madeleine shivered with cold. If they could do this to her things, what were they capable of doing to *her?* She was lucky to have escaped Fouquet this evening. And the comte. She could trust no one, just as her father had warned. No one.

"Look," Amul said, and pulled a gown from the back of the deep armoire. "They didn't notice this. It is intact."

Madeleine's features lit up. "I hate that gown, but it is by far the most valuable of the lot. Papa, poor soul, had it made for me last year. He thought the King would come to Rouen, and that I would be presented. How naïve Papa was, such a dreamer, so romantic!" She reverently fingered the heavy cream satin. "His taste was not the best, but the trim is real Venetian lace." She sighed. "It is the only link I have with him, yet we need the money it can bring. He would have wanted me to sell it. Trust him to care for me—even now." Her voice broke, and she turned away from Amul.

Silence ruled for a long moment until Amul said, "Let us not spend another minute here. It is not safe, and it is so—sad." Furtively he wiped his eyes on his sleeve.

Madeleine nodded and bundled the overdress into a pillowcase, the flounced petticoats into another. After slinging a warm wool shawl that had a single tear down the middle around her shoulders, she followed Amul down the dark stairs. There were no sounds from the cellars.

The wind battered them outside, whined around the corners, rattled down chimneys, and fought with loose shutters. Hautefort's carriage still waited, the coachman having difficulty controlling the four restive horses.

"We're in luck," Madeleine whispered to Amul, sliding into the shadow of the carriage. "A free ride somewhere. Why not to Saint-Germain and the King?"

The coachman in silver and blue livery, hanging on to the leader's bridle for dear life, didn't notice as Madeleine crept up behind him and stuck the pistol into his back.

"Do as we say, or my pistol will go off."

The coachman's eyes bulged in surprise, and he panted with the exertion of calming the horse, whose eyes rolled in terror. A branch crashed to the ground behind the carriage, and the horses shied and whinnied, creating more confusion as they trampled each other.

"Diable!" he swore. "What do you want?" His coarse horsehair wig was awry, his feathered hat tilted over one eye.

"Drive us to the palace of Saint-Germain, and *vite!*" Madeleine ordered. She pulled Amul toward the carriage door. "I will have the pistol trained on you from the window," she warned.

The wind carried the words *sacre bleu* to her ears, and she smiled grimly. To use the comte's carriage was but a small revenge. Let that traitor starve in the cellars and ponder his sins!

Amul opened the door and pulled down the steps. The wind grabbed his velvet beret and tossed it high in the air. He wanted to rush after it, but Madeleine tugged at his sleeve. "I will give you another one. We have no time to lose."

"That is—was—my favorite hat," Amul protested.

She jumped into the coach, closely followed by a muttering Amul. He bumped right into her as she stood frozen in the middle of the floor.

There was a moment of tense silence.

"So we meet again," Fouquet said silkily as he ripped the pistol from Madeleine's nerveless fingers. She found herself staring dumbly down the black barrel of her own weapon.

Chapter 5

Hautefort pulled Madeleine down next to him on the seat and shoved the pillowcases underneath. "I advise you not to try anything foolhardy," he murmured. "Fouquet means business with that pistol. He is very angry with you."

"Bah!" Madeleine wrested her arm from his restraining grip and moved as far away from him as possible. Amul huddled into a corner, fear making the whites of his eyes seem doubly bright as he stared unblinking at Fouquet.

The carriage moved with a jolt, and Fouquet put the pistol down next to him on the seat. The horses tore down the street at breakneck speed, the carriage skidding over the cobblestones. Madeleine held on to her seat, struggling to recover from the shock of this latest turn of events.

"How did you get out of the cellar?" she asked, her voice pinched with chagrin.

Fouquet chuckled. "If you could see our ruined garments, mademoiselle, you'd know that we crawled out of the window."

"The window?" Madeleine breathed.

"*Oui*. I see that you have forgotten that there are two windows in the cellars. They are quite narrow, but then the comte and I are hardly what you call plump."

Madeleine pictured the cellars in her mind, but could not recall any windows. Nevertheless, they had not come through the door—she was sure of that.

"And you lied; I did not find what I sought behind the barrel. I cannot abide people who lie." Fouquet's voice rasped across her raw nerves, and Madeleine could not find a hasty excuse.

51

Suddenly the comte addressed Fouquet. "This diary—what is it? Perhaps I can assist you, Nicolas."

Madeleine stared incredulously at the comte. The nerve of him, playing the innocent! She was too angry to speak, but her mouth fell open as Fouquet's unnaturally soft voice wound in and out of her mind.

"Ah, Hautefort, I know that you're an expert in matters of the heart, but this time I'm afraid you cannot help me. In one of my weaker moments, I fell for Mademoiselle Poquelin's innocent charms. On one of my travels to the provinces. Unfortunately, I recorded the details of my infatuation in a certain diary, a small, nondescript book that mademoiselle now uses to extract, er, large sums from me. In other words, it is a matter of extortion. *Oui,* an ugly word to connect with such an enchanting face."

Madeleine made a strangled noise, but he raised his hands in a rebuffing gesture. "She will deny it, *naturellement*. I dare not take the chance that the contents of the diary will reach the ears of my current mistress, the comtesse de Durenne. Hautefort, as a man of the world, *you* must understand the delicacy of the situation."

"He is lying!" Madeleine was so choked with anger that she could barely speak. "Every word is a lie."

Fouquet chuckled softly, ignoring her. "As I said—she will deny it."

Madeleine could feel the comte's eyes on her, and she swallowed hard.

"I don't know what to believe," the comte murmured.

Madeleine recognized the hesitation in his voice. She took a deep breath. An urge to defend herself washed over her, but no words came from her lips. Fouquet had cleverly planted doubt in the comte's mind, where it would grow like a weed. Besides, why did she feel a need to defend herself to the comte? He was nothing if not Fouquet's accomplice. Tears burned under her eyelids, and she gulped for air. Like the devious snake that he was, Fouquet had twisted the truth into a snarl of lies that she could not begin to untangle.

Amul had not moved since the carriage lurched forward, and Madeleine wondered what was going through his mind. Poor child, having to witness the ugliness of Fouquet's lies. Amul had always witnessed the dark side of life, had never known the love of parents or siblings, had never known his real name, had never really belonged anywhere. Still, he had the kindest, most generous heart and a sweet, innocent smile. She felt a powerful urge to protect him. Reaching out, she patted his knobby knee under the cover of her cloak. He jerked as if startled and gave a long, shuddering sigh.

The carriage came to a halt; voices floated on the wind outside, cursing and bellowing. Fouquet pressed down the window and leaned out. "*Diable*, what is going on?"

"A tree is down, monsieur. Across the road," the coachman shouted over the din.

Madeleine caught a glimpse of shadows moving back and forth, of men struggling to clear the road. The wind had risen in force and moaned through the branches and along the side of the carriage.

Taking the pistol, Fouquet muttered, "Keep an eye on her, Hautefort," and stepped down, sweeping his cloak around him and covering his face with a scarf. As he moved away from the door, Amul slid to the ground and disappeared. It all happened so fast that Madeleine barely noticed. She glanced at the comte, who had not moved to stop the boy.

She flung one of her legs outside and was about to follow Amul when the comte grasped her. His arm snaked around her waist, and she made futile efforts to free herself.

"You let him go! Now let me go," she sobbed, pummeling his arm. "Fouquet is a liar and a cheat. Don't ever believe him."

"Should I believe you then?" came Germain's voice close to her ear. His warm breath fanned her cheek, and he pulled her closer.

Anger and despair exploded inside her, and she twisted around and sank her teeth into his arm. All she tasted was satin and hard muscle.

"Wildcat! What Fouquet says is probably the truth. Your innocence fooled me." Twining his fingers into her curls and yanking her head back, he pulled his arm free from the vise of her teeth. He laughed wearily. "Luckily I wore a heavy coat tonight, or my arm would carry teeth marks for life."

Madeleine's fists drummed on his chest; she gritted her teeth in frustration. "Beast! *Imbécile!* I hate you." She labored to free herself from his warm, roving hands that touched now her face, now her hair, now her neck.

"You allowed Nicolas to touch you. Relax. I promise you, my touch will be just as pleasant. I can bring you delights that you have never tasted before," he suggested softly.

"Of all the inflated, pompous— You are a *bouffon!*" With a mighty heave, Madeleine pushed him away, gathered her cloak tightly around her, and retreated into a corner. Her voice trembled with loathing as she said, "Don't you dare touch me again, or I will kill you. I swear I will."

Germain chuckled. "Chew off my jugular while I'm asleep, *oui?*"

Madeleine gasped for breath and didn't trust herself to answer him. Wrath glared red behind her eyes.

His voice slithered along her nerves. "You may have bitten off more than you can chew now, *ma belle.*" She snorted, but he continued relentlessly. "Fouquet is a very dangerous man, and he would rather, er, dispose of you than give in to your demands." He lifted his shoulders in a Gallic shrug. "I understand that a seamstress's wages must be pitiful, but to try extortion on a powerful state official, one of the King's ministers—well, that is pure folly." He tapped his head. "Think, *ma petite.* Use your brain."

Madeleine wanted to scream, but instead she fumed in silence, tapping her toe on the floor.

Fouquet returned and slammed the door behind him, and the carriage moved once more. For a moment he didn't notice that Amul was missing. Then he inquired sharply, "What happened here?"

"The boy sneaked out, Nicolas. What do you want with a mere boy? You haven't turned to abusing innocent children, *non?*" Germain's voice held a frosty edge.

Fouquet shrugged. "One less problem, I suppose," he said, but his voice was ripe with discontent. "I told you to guard both of them. We don't know how much he knows, and I don't want any rumors at court. The page belongs to Madame at the palace of Saint-Cloud, and you know what a hotbed of gossip that is."

Donc, he knows where Amul lives, Madeleine thought, and shivered. It would be her fault if anything happened to Amul. She had dragged him into her problems.

The carriage rattled across a bridge and pulled into a courtyard. Silence enveloped them suddenly since the wind could not disturb the sanctuary of the closed-in yard. Madeleine could not stop herself from peeping out the window, but the night shrouded the building from her sight.

A servant emerged from the house with a torch to show them the way. Prodded by Fouquet, Madeleine cautiously stepped through the snow and climbed the long, shallow steps, a stray gust of wind whirling around her ankles.

The interior of the old mansion took her breath away. The salon into which the steward showed her was the epitome of luxury. Even the steward, wearing blue and silver livery, looked like a person of wealth. As her feet sank into the thick jewel-toned Persian carpet, Madeleine felt insignificant and poor.

Awe rounded her eyes at the sight of the gleaming mahogany furniture with gilt and mother-of-pearl inlays. The draft from the open doors made the crystal teardrops of the chandeliers tinkle like bells.

She barely noticed when the comte took her fingertips and led her to a brocade-covered sofa in front of the roaring fire. "Welcome to *hôtel* Belleforière," he said with a smile. "You heeded my invitation at last."

"Enough of that nonsense, Hautefort. What I want is a nice hot dinner—now," Fouquet demanded. He rubbed his hands and glared at Madeleine, who got a good look at him for the first time that night.

He wore a black satin coat embroidered with black flowers, silver-gray rhinegraves, and white stockings that were torn and muddy. His gaunt face was dusty, and the lace jabot at his throat hung awry, dotted with spots of grease. Her gaze shifted to the comte, who looked equally disheveled, his gold brocade vest sporting a long rent down the back and his unruly curls covered with cobwebs.

Madeleine stifled a sudden laugh and turned her eyes toward the fire so as not to meet Fouquet's narrow black gaze.

"You must be very hungry, mademoiselle," he said in a deceptively soft voice.

His words made her aware of her growling stomach. She had eaten nothing since breakfast. Swallowing convulsively, she tilted her chin upward. "*Mais non*, Monsieur Fouquet. I'd prefer to leave now."

He cackled evilly. "I'm sure you would, but how can you be so rude as to shun Hautefort's hospitality?"

She glanced suspiciously from one to the other. "*Oui*, I can be that rude."

"A pity. However, I desire your company at the supper table this evening; you must obey, this once. And if you tell me the diary's true hiding place, I will release you tonight."

Madeleine's doubtful gaze was riveted on Fouquet as he moved to an ebony cabinet to fill glasses with apricot brandy.

"We need to chase the chill from our limbs, don't you think?" With a wide flourish, he handed the comte one of the glasses, then crossed the carpet to give her a glass but changed his mind, covering the glass with his pale hand. "*Non*, mademoiselle shall tell the truth first."

"I will tell you nothing," Madeleine said with a toss of her curls.

Fouquet shrugged and sipped the brandy. "You will—very soon." The comte sighed and sat down. There came the sound of running paws on the polished floor. Into the salon bounded two giant Irish wolfhounds. They leaped straight at their master and wagged their tails and whined in a greeting. The great hounds tried to climb onto the comte's lap without concern for the silk of his rhinegraves.

"Down, now! Down, I said!" Reluctantly they sat at the comte's feet, and he gently stroked their long, narrow heads. Their coats were shaggy, gray like a wolf's, and their bright peppercorn eyes stared at Madeleine and Fouquet with wary curiosity.

"Let me introduce Ariel and Claudine." The comte fondly rubbed the hounds behind their ears.

"They are awfully large," Fouquet commented, evidently disliking the animals.

"*Oui*, but gentle as lambs unless I order them to guard." The dogs lay down at his feet. "The King loves his dogs.

RECKLESS SPLENDOR

He has hundreds of them and feeds them himself every day so that they'll know and obey him."

"Like good courtiers then?" Madeleine could not hide the irony in her voice.

He was not annoyed. "It is a very good observation," he said with a sigh and smoothed his mustache.

"Are you hinting that you . . . dislike life at court?"

The comte smiled enigmatically and slanted an amused glance at her. "Louis is a great king," he responded noncommittally.

She challenged Fouquet. "Why are you not at court? The King will miss you both."

Fouquet gave a smile that was stiff around the edges. "Don't deviate from the main issue! I ask the questions here. I admire your spirit, but it is foolish to make an enemy of me. Also, you didn't answer my question. Where is the diary?" His eyes gleamed hard and snakelike, under the shadow of his heavy eyelids.

The look made her feel like a fly under a magnifying glass. Wanting to scream with vexation, she sent him a scornful glance. "A band of wild horses could not pry it out of me—only the King, Monsieur Fouquet."

He chuckled softly. It sounded infinitely menacing. "I'll find out."

More heated words might have passed between them if the steward had not entered, soft-footed, to announce that dinner was served in the dining room.

Madeleine instinctively did not like the steward. Perhaps his narrow weasel face was the most repugnant feature to her, or his cold eyes, but she rose and meekly followed him. The others trailed behind.

A small damask-covered table stood by the fireplace. Burning candles provided the only light in the room, forming a circle of glowing warmth around the table.

Madeleine looked in wonder at the silver plates and exquisite crystal glasses with slender stems.

Pulling out a chair, the steward motioned her to sit down. With measured movements, the comte sat across from her, arranging the lace of his shirt cuffs to prevent them from dipping into the food. "I pray you're hungry because the cook has prepared some special delicacies for us."

Madeleine was completely taken by surprise when Fouquet, standing behind her, gripped her arms and twisted them in back of her. She protested, but he deftly bound her hands to the back of the chair.

"What are you doing?" she cried, pulling against the tight leather thongs.

"No supper for you until you confess," Fouquet said and sat down, tucking a napkin inside his collar.

She fumed, utterly humiliated. Her gaze challenged the comte to help her, but his eyes remained dark, inscrutable.

"Your hospitality leaves a lot to be desired," she spat at him. She thought she saw a flash of pain in his eyes, but she wasn't sure. He addressed the steward. "Maurice, please serve us the wine and bring in the food. After that, you may retire."

Maurice bowed stiffly and filled their glasses with ruby wine. The comte inhaled the bouquet and nodded slightly. Maurice withdrew soundlessly.

Madeleine tapped her foot on the carpet to soothe her boiling temper.

Coolly, the comte took a sip of wine. "Ah . . . excellent!" Quirking an eyebrow at Fouquet, he pushed a glass toward Madeleine. "One glass, *non?*"

Fouquet scowled but nodded reluctantly. "It might loosen her tongue."

A ghastly thought flitted through her head. What if it was poisoned? The comte seemed to sense her fear.

"If you're superstitious, I can offer you a toadstone in your glass—not that it will protect you from poison."

"Poison? I don't know what you're talking about." He held the glass to her lips, and she swiftly took a deep draught, noticing his soundless laughter from the corner of her eye. Like a wave of warmth, the wine flowed to her stomach, and her heart pounded with anxiety. But there followed no sudden pain or nausea. A silly toadstone—formed in the belly of a toad and used as a charm against every evil—wasn't needed here, she thought, secretly relieved.

Maurice returned with covered silver dishes from which wafted enticing smells of hot food. A serving wench carrying a tray followed him. Maurice lifted the domed covers and presented the food, releasing aromatic steam. Madeleine had never seen a more elegant repast. Her mouth watered.

First came a plate with roast suckling pig garnished with baked red apples. Hot and cold vegetables added color to the pale, succulent meat. Cuts of doe served on artichoke hearts were thronged with pâtés and thick, spicy sauces in silver tureens. Ravenous, Madeleine took note of the other courses, including fragrant pigeon pies, chestnut-stuffed pheasants, and—most treasured—a dish of green peas, a delicacy that was all the rage in Paris and very hard to come by.

"All this for supper?" she croaked.

With a twist of his hand, the comte dabbed at his lips with a damask napkin, hiding a smile. *"Naturellement."* He winked and saluted her with his wineglass.

"Bouffon," Madeleine scoffed. She wanted to cry, unable to satisfy her hunger.

"It could all be yours if you'd tell me the truth," Fouquet purred close to her ear. "Look at these delicacies, mademoiselle." He speared some peas on his knife. Madeleine noticed that they were not using the newly introduced forks from Italy.

"I hate peas," she lied, but could not stop the tip of her tongue from darting across her lips.

Fouquet muttered angrily, attacked a slice of doe, poured a thick layer of sauce on top, and devoured it in silence. Madeleine kept her eyes trained to the floor and forced her thoughts to concentrate on Amul. She wished she knew what had happened to him. At least he was free.

She would not tell Fouquet the truth. Ever.

She wavered between anger and fear. Fouquet would never give up—he'd kill her first. He would not let her out of his sight until she had confessed. She prepared herself for a long battle and suddenly doubted that she would emerge the victor.

Suppressing a bout of fear, she forgot to keep her gaze on the floor. She watched the comte eat his meat with his fingers and a knife. The jewels on his long fingers, emeralds and diamonds, glittered seductively in the soft orange light from the fire, and he moved with easy elegance, an elegance that seemed to spring from a well inside. He was dangerously attractive. She sighed. A first-class villain!

She watched as he rinsed his fingers in a silver bowl filled with lavender water and dried them on his napkin before he unhurriedly helped himself to another dish.

"Do you always eat this many culinary masterpieces?" she could not help asking.

"It depends on my mood and . . . company," he replied. "Your presence makes my appetite improve greatly." He gave her a smile that lit his face and made his eyes sparkle.

Madeleine glared at him. "I don't care much for this kind of company—liars and murderers."

"I choose my company with care." Somehow his glance excluded Fouquet, and she could not stop a flow of desire from coursing through her veins. Her cheeks grew hot, and she hated herself for it.

Her heart pounded as if she had sprinted up a flight of stairs. She had no idea how to deal with this man. He was nothing like her actor friends, who treated her like a younger sister who had to be accepted because she was the niece of the great Molière himself, or the young stagehands who sometimes stole a kiss or two.

"I hate you," she breathed.

Fouquet chuckled. "She probably does, Hautefort—but only to cover up a quite different feeling."

The comte stiffened, his lean cheeks suffusing with color. He tossed down his napkin and spoke, his voice filled with ice. "I have had enough of your abuse, Fouquet. Get this charade over with and get out of my house!"

"Oh-la-la, temper, temper," Fouquet chided and dragged his sleeve across his lips. "I leave when I wish, and you, of all people, should know that, Hautefort."

Madeleine stared wide-eyed from one to the other as they challenged each other across the table. Then Fouquet smiled thinly and said, "*Bien*, if that is your wish. Trust me, I will have the truth in half an hour."

Madeleine shivered and cringed as Fouquet's cold gaze seared her. "Hautefort, I need one of your bedchambers."

Chapter 6

Fouquet pushed Madeleine into the bedchamber.

The comte stood in the doorway, his arms crossed over his chest. "What are you going to do with her?" he demanded, his voice steely.

"Wait and see, *mon ami*. She will spill the truth as sure as rain falls in the spring."

Madeleine cringed as Fouquet jerked her toward the bed and tossed her down. Then he snapped his fingers, and two burly men in rough peasant clothes and greasy stocking caps stepped past the comte into the room.

"*Diable*, where do they come from?" the comte barked.

"Wait and see the spectacle, if you want. I will step downstairs and finish my supper," Fouquet said in bored tones. "The truth will be mine soon—very soon."

Madeleine whimpered as the two louts leered at her, displaying rotting teeth and tobacco-stained lips. They advanced on her, fingering the frayed cords holding up their dirty culottes.

Her hands still bound at her back, Madeleine crawled awkwardly across the bed, trying to reach the other side, but heavy hands caught her legs and pushed her down, pinning her to the mattress. She screamed as one meaty hand touched her breast. Marshaling all her strength, she kicked out, her toes connecting with one bearded jaw.

Suddenly a roar of fury reached her ears. One of the louts was jerked off the bed by the scruff of his neck. His face was a study in surprise, and his eyes bulged as the comte's fist smashed into his face—once, twice. The ruffian crashed to the floor, moaning and holding his head. The other hairy

61

fellow jumped into the fray, and Madeleine's eyes widened in fright as he slammed his head into the comte's back. The comte went down, groaning, but in an instant he was back on his feet, whipping forth his sword and lunging.

Madeleine gasped as she saw the steel tip penetrate the back of her attacker's arm, sending a rivulet of crimson blood coursing down onto the carpet. The man yelped and clutched at his wound. Germain's face was contorted in fury; his fist shot out with concentrated force, an uppercut colliding with the ruffian's jaw. The man toppled over without a sound, and Germain rubbed his fist and grimaced.

But the other lout was back on his feet. He grasped a handful of Germain's hair and jerked the nobleman off his feet. Then he leveled a kick to the comte's groin and a fist to his eye. Gasping, the comte crumpled like a rag doll, holding his groin and rolling in excruciating pain on the floor.

The ruffian stepped forward to aim a last kick at the comte's head, but stumbled over one small foot that was thrust in his way. Staggering, he lost his balance and fell, pulling a tablecloth and an antique vase down with him. Porcelain shards rained in all directions.

Sitting on the floor and panting hard, Madeleine pulled her foot back under her skirt and propped her back against the side of the bed. Abruptly she was deafened by the blast of a pistol. The room filled with the acrid scent of gunpowder, and plaster cascaded from the ceiling. She stared unbelieving at the black hole in the painted sky on the ceiling.

Through the veils of smoke she recognized the Breton Gaspard's serious face. "What is going on here?" he shouted. "Things have come to a pretty pass when a nobleman is attacked in his own home."

Germain sat up with a groan, shaking his head. He looked ghastly, his cheek swelling, glaring red, and his eye beginning to blacken. "*Sacré bleu,* get rid of the scoundrels in some way. Throw them into the Seine!" he ordered between panting breaths.

Gaspard called for assistance, and two lackeys arrived armed with blunderbusses. They coaxed the ruffians onto their feet and forced them out the door, digging the wide barrels of the weapons into their ribs.

RECKLESS SPLENDOR 63

Fouquet strolled into the room, his hands folded behind him, and viewed the ruins of the chamber. He raised an eyebrow; otherwise his pale, narrow face was expressionless.

Madeleine glowered at him and clenched her hands until her knuckles whitened. Then she looked at the comte, and her expression softened. He had saved her. Even though he was involved in Fouquet's shady dealings, he had saved her.

"I am ready, Monsieur Fouquet; I will tell you the truth," she whispered, her voice hoarse.

Fouquet's lips parted in a satisfied smile. *"Bien!* I knew you would come to your senses, mademoiselle. Where is it?"

Madeleine felt as if she was shrinking, and she avoided his probing gaze. Tracing the red and green rose pattern on the carpet, she explained, "It is hidden in the garden wall at my father's house in Rouen. You know very well where the house is located. You'll find the diary under the second stone to the left of the back gate."

"Clever of you, mademoiselle, to hide it so carefully," he said, and Madeleine could feel his eyes probing her. Taking a deep breath, she raised her eyes and squarely met his gaze. She flinched at the malicious glitter there. He continued. "To make sure that you are telling the truth, I will keep you a prisoner here until my men return with the diary." He rolled on the balls of his feet and pointed at Germain. "And to make sure that you won't escape, Hautefort here will guard you—with his life."

Madeleine pretended that this new obstacle didn't concern her in the slightest. "As you wish," she responded meekly. "I wish you all speed so that I can leave this place."

Germain shot her a suspicious glance. Limping, he followed Fouquet into the corridor. He closed the door carefully behind him and locked it, then caught up with Fouquet at the top of the stairs. His hand shot out, twisted around the other man's jabot, and squeezed, almost lifting Fouquet from the floor. The finance minister sputtered; his face turned red, and his eyes started out.

Germain's eyes were thin slits of fire, and he pushed until Fouquet was barely balancing on his toes, flailing his arms as he hung suspended over the stairs. He was dangerously close to toppling over.

"You have gone too far, Fouquet," Germain snarled. "That you would stoop to persecution to lay your hands on some romantic folderol doesn't surprise me. But that you resort to rape and violence is unacceptable. *Diable*, you cannot expect me to stand by and watch and *support* such actions! I still consider myself a gentleman, despite my connection to you. You have your information. Mademoiselle Poquelin goes free tonight." He jerked Fouquet back from the stairs and let go of his stranglehold.

The slighter man fell to his knees, coughing and gasping for air. *"Imbécile!"* Fouquet croaked, clutching his throat. "You have no choice but to obey my orders." He cleared his throat and straightened the mangled jabot. "Mademoiselle Poquelin stays. Always remember that I know about your little *affaire de coeur* with Brigitte Delchamps. One word to Monsieur Delchamps and he'll kill his wife—after he kills you; he's a jealous lunatic. Think about that, Germain. I'm sure you want to protect *belle* Brigitte's reputation. You wouldn't like her shame on your conscience, *mon ami*."

Germain snorted. "Life doesn't mean much to you, does it? At least not other people's lives. You'd do anything to reach your own goals."

Fouquet managed a derisive smile as he hoisted himself to his feet. "We are forever linked together in our little secret. Don't do anything foolish." He patted Germain on the shoulder. "Take good care of Mademoiselle Poquelin—I give you a free hand with her. She may have a hot temper, but she's quite good in bed." Laughing contemptuously, Fouquet descended the stairs. "Love makes you weak. Methinks you have lost your heart to Mademoiselle Poquelin, while she calls you miserable worm. Ha-ha-ha-ha."

Germain stared grimly at Fouquet's back, clenching and unclenching his hands. A muscle worked in his jaw, and his eyebrows pulled into a thick bar above his eyes. "Love!" he spat and stalked down the corridor. "Common decency has nothing to do with love. I cannot abide rape, no matter how heartless the woman," he added to no one in particular as he ran up another flight of stairs. I made one mistake and now I have to pay for it for the rest of my life. Oh, poor Brigitte, old friend, what won't I do to protect you from shame.

He slammed the door to his bedchamber. The gilt mirrors and old oil paintings trembled on the walls.

Gaspard looked up and frowned in the act of pouring water from a copper pitcher into a hip bath. "You smell . . . of mold, Monsieur Germain," he stated with a fastidious wrinkling of his nose.

Germain scowled. "*Oui*, it is all Mademoiselle Poquelin's doing. Because of her, I crawled through a mouse-infested coal cellar, and then through a window white with dove droppings. I was attacked by two ruffians; I—"

"*Pauvre petit*," Gaspard chided gently.

Germain smiled. "Whining, am I?"

The valet nodded sagely, then chuckled. "Your temper is frayed, like the plaster in the green bedchamber."

"*Oui*." Germain sighed and peeled off his ruined coat, shirt, and jabot, then sat on the edge of the bed and held up a booted foot. Gaspard pulled off the tight, dusty boot with some difficulty.

Germain growled in contentment, flexed his toes, and stretched his legs. Then he looked in the mirror, and the satisfaction died on his face. His jaw and eye throbbed relentlessly. Gingerly he fingered the contusions and shook his head.

"Take a bath, and I will return with a slice of veal," Gaspard said. "That might stop the swelling, but it is too late to prevent a black eye now."

Germain shrugged and sighed. "*Bon*. And, Gaspard, make sure that Mademoiselle Poquelin is served a hot meal and some mulled wine. She has been through enough abuse for one day." He tossed the key to Madeleine's prison to the valet.

Gaspard nodded and left the room. Tearing off his remaining garments, Germain slid into the bath. He scooped hot water over his muscular shoulders, and the knotted tension in him melted under the water's soothing caress. A purple bruise was forming on his forearm. He inspected it closely and chuckled ruefully. The bite of a wildcat.

Pouring water over his head, he thought about Madeleine. Even now he could feel an invisible pull toward her chamber. He wanted to jump out of the water and rush naked down the corridor, perhaps scaring the wits out of Madame Barbette, the cook, if she was close by. He laughed out loud at the thought. The fat Barbette would toss her apron over her head and scream abuses at him.

Oui, he wanted to lift Madeleine into his arms and deposit her on the bed and make love to her all night. Kiss every curve and shadow of her alluring body, trace his tongue along her shoulder, and tickle her neck. That was just what he needed, a long night of lovemaking.

Groaning in frustration as his loins hardened and ached, he soaped his hair with more vigor than it warranted. Wildcat. Was Fouquet right? Had he fallen in love with a little seamstress with hair the color of morning sunlight? He flinched from the thought. Ridiculous! He never fell in love with his mistresses.

He would make her his mistress. If what Fouquet said was true, she wasn't the innocent she pretended to be. If she had been Fouquet's mistress, she had probably tasted every vice in creation. Grinding his teeth in a sudden flash of jealousy, Germain shook his head until water drops flew in all directions. Then he lit a black cheroot on a nearby candle, leaned back in the bath, propped his elbows on the edges, and planned his strategy.

Madeleine devoured a small dish of buttered peas. They slid like nectar down her throat, and she closed her eyes in sheer pleasure. Then she attacked the crusty rolls and the slices of veal with truffle sauce. Methodically she worked her way through a pheasant leg, a small meat pie, sugared plums, two iced apricot tarts, and a plate of chocolate-covered marzipan birds. "Ah, *délicieux*," she said blissfully and wiped her hands and mouth on a napkin. "This is quite the best meal I have ever tasted." It was the least the comte could do—feed her royally after the misery he had let her go through.

She rose from the table and studied her luxurious prison. The room was decorated predominantly in green and gold. A huge four-poster bed was topped by a pleated green silk canopy and surrounded by matching curtains tied at the corners with tasseled gold cords. Stately gold brocade draperies framed the tall windows, and in a corner stood a walnut escritoire inlaid with tortoiseshell and ivory.

Madeleine tried the chair in front of it and flourished her arm as if writing. She pretended that she was a lady—*oui*— a comtesse, the comtesse de Hautefort, writing a letter. *Imbécile!* she chided herself. A comtesse was the last person she wanted to be. The real comtesse de Hautefort most likely lived her dull life in some smelly old castle in the provinces, while her husband, the comte, lived a life of vice in the capital.

She made a grimace and said, "Bah! I hate him."

"Who?" asked a deep voice from the doorway.

Madeleine started and whirled around. The comte was outlined in the door opening. Except for the disfiguration of his face, he looked the epitome of elegance in a royal-blue silk coat with gold braid and pristine lace at the neck and wrists. As he walked toward her with an enigmatic smile on his lips, she could smell the spicy aroma of orris root. His heavy curls were parted in the middle and brushed back over his shoulders. They gleamed like gold silk. He emanated vital strength and purpose, and Madeleine's breath caught in her throat. Warning signals went off in her head. He was her enemy—and he was pure temptation. Her heart pounded wildly.

"*Moi?* You hate me?" he prodded.

Madeleine colored and lowered her gaze. "I do have a reason," she muttered.

The comte sighed. "*Oui*, but I cannot undo the pain. I can only offer my apology." His gray eyes were dark with emotion and followed her every movement.

Anger flashed in her eyes. "It is too late! You could have stopped Fouquet at any time if you cared. But no, you played along with him at every turn."

Germain spread out his hands. "I had no idea that he would stoop to such crude methods as threatening you with rape. Why didn't you simply hand over the diary? Fouquet never gives up when he gets an idea into his head." Germain shook his head and crossed his arms over his chest.

He continued. "He is like a spider in a web. The webs he weaves are glutinous, and once he has wrapped his threads around you, you'll never be free of him." He paused, his gaze probing her. "I hope you didn't lie to him. Save yourself, Mademoiselle Célie, before it is too late."

Madeleine stared up at him, her eyes narrow with suspicion. "What hold does he have on you, or are you just his mindless puppet, ready to execute any dirty deed?" she challenged.

"What do you think?" he threw back at her and sauntered to the table holding the leftovers from her meal. He sank his strong teeth into an apple.

Madeleine tapped her foot on the floor in frustration. "That is the kind of evasive answer *he* would give. You're just like him, as slippery as an eel." When Germain didn't respond, she glared at him. "You owe him a large amount of money," she suggested, craving to know his real reason for being hand in glove with Fouquet. She wished she was right. She could forgive him if he was under a monetary obligation to Fouquet. All of a sudden it seemed so innocent when compared to other, darker possibilities. She *wanted* to forgive him.

She shivered, angry with herself because she cared.

Nervously she straightened her plain blue wool gown and hoped that the lace fichu crossed over her bodice wasn't too grimy. She tugged at the modest lace trim edging her white elbow-length blouse sleeves and adjusted the tightly laced bodice. Her clumsy clogs peeped under the hem of her gown, and she straightened her back so as to hide them.

"I would not have assisted Fouquet had I known his crude methods." Germain's face was serious; his bruises looked painful. "I do not expect you to forgive me for leading you into a trap—and all for some stupid diary."

Madeleine's bottom lip trembled. "*Mon Dieu,* why did you do it?"

"I cannot tell you that. All I can say—do not play a cat and mouse game with Fouquet."

Madeleine closed her eyes and rubbed her neck. A headache was coming on. She wanted to be angry with the comte, but she was too weary. She felt deflated.

"Thank you for saving me from the . . . louts," she said reluctantly.

He took another bite of the apple, intently studying her. "That was the least I could do, *ma petite*. I was very angry."

She smiled tremulously. "Do your wounds hurt much?"

He nodded and gave her a crooked smile. His bottom lip was cracked. Their eyes locked, and they stared at each other for a long time. Madeleine sensed his desire, like a tangible thing reaching out to her. She felt herself respond. Her skin tingled; her breathing became labored. Her lips remembered his touch; her skin yearned for the caress of his fingertips.

"My offer still stands," he murmured. "Do you want to become my mistress?"

His voice made her heart go berserk, but she refused to show him the emotion boiling within her. She pretended to study an ormulu clock on the marble mantelpiece.

She was very tempted. It would be so easy to succumb.

"*Non*, monsieur le comte, I repeat what I said before—I don't want to be a man's plaything, only to be discarded on a whim."

"You were free with your favors to Fouquet." Germain could have bitten his tongue as the words spilled out. How clumsy!

Madeleine pinned him with a look of utter loathing. "And you believed his lies?" She flung out her arms in exasperation. "*Dieu*, I do not believe it! You are all the same; the only thing on your minds is how to get under petticoats any petticoats." She turned her back on him and folded her arms across her chest.

He took a step toward her. "I'm sorry. I formulated my words badly."

"Oh, *zut!* Your words mean nothing to me. Go away, or let me go!" she demanded. "I do not want to split words with you any longer." Tears burned in her eyes. She was exhausted, and she couldn't bear to look at him. Disappointment tasted bitter in her throat. "Please let me go home," she begged, her voice breaking.

"I cannot do that. If you lied about the hiding place, Fouquet will be back. He sent the chevalier de Lemont and

Marquis D'Ambrose after it. I know now why the chevalier came to see me that night at Versailles. You were right; they were trying to capture you." He sounded weary. "And here you are, caught up in a web of intrigue. God only knows who possesses the entire truth."

A shiver of fear rippled through her. She could almost feel Fouquet's dark tentacles reaching out for her, winding around her throat and squeezing the breath out of her. "I can take care of myself," she said, but her voice lacked conviction.

His steps echoed on the floor, and he touched her back, his finger tracing her spine. "I would like to take care of you," he murmured. "I'll protect you from Fouquet. He will never touch you again."

His breath fanned her neck, and Madeleine stiffened. The molten yearning she had once experienced in his arms returned. It would be so easy to surrender, to let him deal with her foe.

Her father's dying face flashed before her eyes, and she strangled a whimper. She felt the comte's lips on her neck, so exhilarating, so warm. Then she pictured the diary—the proof that would bring Fouquet's downfall if she could put it into the King's hands. She was the only one who could accomplish that.

She slid away from Germain—one of the hardest things she had ever done. "*Non*, you are very arrogant to believe that I would submit to your dulcet words after what you have done. I can never trust you again. I don't like you," she lied.

She faced him. He stood very still, his face white and tense. "You are candid, *petite* Célie." He bowed stiffly and walked toward the door. Holding the doorknob, he turned to her. "I will not give up."

Then he closed the door and locked it.

Madeleine threw herself on the bed and buried her face in the soft pillows. "*Alors*, we will see who is the more stubborn," she said between gritted teeth. Curling up under the down cover, she fell into an exhausted sleep.

Chapter 7

Madeleine awakened as someone shook her shoulder vigorously.

"Madeleine," that someone hissed in her ear.

She struggled to open her eyes and stared into Amul's round face. She jerked upright. "Amul!" she whispered. "How did you get in?"

"It is a great household. I slipped up the back stairs. No one saw me. The key was in the door, and I saw a tray with food outside. That must be Madeleine's prison, I thought, and *voilà,* here I am."

Madeleine's mouth widened into a grin. "Thank God!" Impulsively she hugged her small friend. "Let us escape before they find you." She scrambled out of bed and straightened her wrinkled garments. "What time is it?"

"Close to seven in the morning." He held up two bulging pillowcases. "I fetched these from the carriage in the carriage house. That's how I knew you were here."

Madeleine clapped her hands together and knotted the cords of her cloak. *"Bien!* The pillowcases with my satin dress and petticoats. You think of everything. Let us go to Pont-Neuf and sell them."

They slid into the silent corridor and managed to slink unobserved down the back stairs and out onto the street. Rue Saint Antoine, Madeleine read at the corner of the building. She pulled the hood deeply over her head and clutched one pillowcase.

"I am so happy that you escaped, Amul. Where did you go?"

71

"To La Béjart's house. Molière was there. He asked for you, and I told him that you had gone to Rouen after receiving a note that the mother superior at your old convent school was seriously ill." He rubbed his head and looked anxious. "I knew you didn't want me to tell him the truth."

"*Oui*, that is the best. I'm sorry you had to lie, but I don't want to place him and the whole theater ensemble in danger—as I have done to you." She placed an arm around his bony shoulders. "What did he say?"

"He was angry that you hadn't asked his permission."

Madeleine sighed. "He will understand when I explain everything later. *Maintenant*, I have to concentrate on delivering the diary to the King. Without you I would still be in Fouquet's clutches."

Amul climbed over a mound of snow. "Where is he now?"

Madeleine giggled. "Waiting for the men who he sent to Rouen on a wild-goose chase."

"*Non!*" Amul's eyes were round with surprise. "You told him the truth?"

"*Mais non!* I said the diary was hidden in my old home. Most likely they'll end up tearing down the entire wall around the house—and find nothing."

Amul gulped audibly. "You will be in grave danger now. If Fouquet ever finds you . . ."

Madeleine pressed her lips together. "He will not find me again." An icy wind whipped them as if in protest, and Madeleine shuddered.

Amul's silence was ominous, and she clasped his shoulders. "We have to use our wits. You know, if you hadn't rescued me, I would have been hard pressed to find an excuse for Fouquet. I can easily picture him breathing fire and threatening me." She glanced at Amul's trembling lips and downbent head.

Taking a deep breath, she added, "I think you should return to Saint-Cloud and stay away from Fouquet and his henchmen. Fouquet won't hurt you if you're not with me. I could never forgive myself if something happened to you. You're my only friend." Anguish squeezed her heart as he blew his nose and refused to look at her. Then she felt his little hand touch hers shyly.

RECKLESS SPLENDOR 73

"You are my only sister, my only family, Madeleine," he muttered in a tear-choked voice. "I'd rather be with you than at Saint-Cloud worrying about you. Anyway, I'm in disgrace with Madame because I broke an expensive vase."

"I see," Madeleine said, her lips twitching. "*Bien*, we'll stay together until she calms down."

"What will we do now?" he asked, clearly relieved.

"Sell the gown and visit Monsieur Colbert, Fouquet's assistant. I hear he is high in the King's favor."

With the pillowcases tucked safely under their arms, they aimed their steps toward Pont-Neuf. Today I am going to solve the problem of the diary, Madeleine thought. Luck had been with her so far, and strength expanded in her chest. Life looked brighter.

It was a lovely morning despite the biting cold. Her fur-lined cloak protected her nicely. Although the ground was covered with crusted snow and icicles hung like daggers along the edges of the roofs, the bustle on the streets continued as if it were a summer day. The chime of the bells at Notre Dame floated over Place de Grève as they passed the construction site of the elegant Hôtel de Ville. On Place de Grève the gibbet was erected, awaiting some condemned criminal. She shivered. That square had seen more suffering and death than any other spot in France. Witches were burned at the stake, thieves drawn and quartered, and traitors beheaded with a single stroke of the ax. Fouquet deserved to meet his maker on Place de Grève, she thought grimly. She would like to be there and pelt him with rotten tomatoes!

On Pont-Neuf clusters of stalls huddled around the statue of King Henry IV. Burly fishwives and peasants dressed in voluminous coats and scarves, their hands covered with half mittens, warmed their frozen fingers and posteriors over glowing braziers. They offered their wares in loud, coarse voices. Sparrows, like fuzzy balls, jumped around the feet of the people, looking for bread crumbs.

Bony hands clutched at Madeleine from all sides. She looked down at a motley crowd of beggars crouching on the ground. Bloodstained bandages covered heads and arms. Old hags carried infants whose faces were covered with sores and blisters.

Blue, frozen, shaking hands stretched toward her. Her heart contracted at the pitiful sight. They crowded in on her, dirty fingers reaching toward her face.

Somebody tried to snatch her bundle, but she yanked it back. "Get away from me!" she cried and pushed at their evil-smelling bodies. She hurried after Amul, who was watching a barber-surgeon blowing a horn to attract customers—or victims. He cried a slogan: "Painless tooth extractions. Big Hercule has the softest hands in Paris!"

An elegant carriage bowled across the bridge at a dangerous speed. Madeleine recognized the Hautefort crest and retreated into the crowd.

As the carriage squeezed through the throng, the rabble scattered so as not to be run over. Madeleine could not believe her eyes when she saw one of them, a lame man running at full speed toward the Quai du Louvre, his crutches tucked under his arm.

"Did you recognize the carriage?" Amul whispered in her ear.

"*Oui*. The comte must have found out I escaped. Let us take care of business and proceed to Colbert's house."

They went to a stall where everything from wigs to coughing medicine for horses was sold, and opened the bundles.

"What have we here?" asked a ruddy individual, peering at her from behind a tin canister of gingerbread.

Madeleine pulled out the satin gown. "I want to sell this to you. The lace is pure, exquisite Venetian."

The man fingered the satin with dirty fingers. "Hmmm. Stolen goods, eh? You stole it from your employer, didn't you?"

She stared at him in outrage. "Are you mad? Of course I didn't steal it! It's mine!"

The man cackled evilly. "And I am King Louis XIV."

"The gall! This is my dress!"

"You aren't exactly dressed like a duchesse, now are you, *petite*?" His rheumy eyes traveled the length of her body to rest on her clumsy clogs.

She had to admit she did not look like somebody who could own such a sumptuous dress.

"Nevertheless, it *is* my dress!"

He narrowed his calculating eyes. Then he shrugged and said, "I'll give you two livres for it." He leaned negligently on the edge of the stall.

"Two livres! You must be mad! It is worth at least twenty livres. Look, Venetian lace and three petticoats!"

The man laughed. "Twenty livres, ridiculous! Two at the most. Take it or leave it, mademoiselle."

She glared at him. He was stealing from her, but she knew it was no use arguing. With a contemptuous toss of her head, she held out her hand. She desperately needed the money, and she snatched the meager payment from his hand.

Without a word, she reached into her pocket to place the coins in her empty purse. Gone! She had kept it in one of the voluminous pockets of the cloak, but even as she turned the garment inside out, there was no sign of the purse. She wanted to cry when she realized that the beggars must have stolen it. Beggars? Thieves was the right name for the villains.

"Lost something, mademoiselle?"

"*Oui*, my purse has been stolen," she shouted.

"That cutpurse the Mouse—Le Souris—stole it."

"The Mouse?"

"*Oui*, the Mouse; you don't notice him because he's small and gray like a mouse. You could stand right next to him without really seeing him, but he's the most clever cutpurse in all of Paris, fast and nimble like a squirrel."

"What gall! Why didn't you stop him if you saw him?" Madeleine cried angrily. "I thought they were all pitiful cripples."

The shopkeeper shrugged and chuckled maliciously. "Cripples? Ha-ha. They have not done one hour's worth of honest work in their lives. They are no more crippled than you or me!"

"Oh." Madeleine had to digest that. Were there no honest people? Like a sleepwalker, she pocketed the two livres, which was all she owned in the whole world.

Amul tugged at her sleeve. "You're not used to Paris yet."

Madeleine grimaced in exasperation. "A city of fake beggars and robbers." She rattled her thin savings for emphasis and held the coins tightly in her hand all the way to Colbert's house.

The interior of Colbert's townhouse was as simple and precise as the man himself. In the long, narrow waiting room a mixed crowd was assembled. Aristocracy mingled with peasants and burghers. Madeleine sat down on the edge of a long bench next to a stocky man reeking of garlic.

So many people! Could it be that Colbert was more powerful than she had ever dreamed? One thing was certain; nobleman and peasant alike were here to beg for a favor.

An icy draft curled along the floor, and Madeleine shivered. A smell of cabbage soup seeped through the crack of a door behind which muffled voices and movements spoke of other activities than business of the state. How did Madame Colbert feel about having her home invaded by strangers from morning until evening?

Another door opened, and all faces turned expectantly. Colbert stepped out holding a stack of papers under his arm. His brown gaze flickered around the room.

He was dressed in a drab coat and vest. Coarse brown wool stockings came to the tip of his knees, and the buckles of his shoes were plain silver.

Was this the man with whom the King spoke every day? It was truly hard to believe, Madeleine mused.

She tried to catch his glance, but it had already turned to the topmost paper of his stack when he spoke. "Since I cannot deal with everything, all petitions not involving monetary matters will be handled by my assistant, Monsieur Simeon."

He bowed stiffly to a nobleman, who followed Colbert into his study. The door closed behind them. How would she ever be able to pass through that door since she had no "monetary matters" to discuss with him?

She fidgeted and rolled her eyes at Amul. "Where is this man Simeon?" she whispered. Amul shook his head so she turned to Monsieur Garlic Breath beside her. As if he knew what she was about to ask him, he pointed at another door. The silence in the room became threatening as she rose.

"Mademoiselle! You have to wait your turn," a shrill voice chimed.

"*Oui*, go to the end of the line," another voice echoed.

RECKLESS SPLENDOR

Crestfallen, Madeleine stared around the room. Fingers pointed to the very end of the opposite bench. It was packed with people. Her spirits plummeted. Sighing in defeat, she sat down at the very end to wait her turn. Amul smiled behind his hand.

Noon found her still at the end of the line. Nobody had seen the elusive Monsieur Simeon. Did he really exist?

Madeleine was becoming more and more dispirited and angry by the minute. Her stomach growled with neglect. The all-pervading scent of cabbage whetted her appetite.

Petitioners of "monetary matters" came and went from Colbert's office in an even stream. He was not wasting his time.

At the end of her tether, Madeleine suddenly had a brilliant idea. She would just change her plea to a "monetary matter" and be able to see the great man himself!

She moved to the other bench, feeling the withering glances of the other petitioners, but she kept her gaze lowered to the floor.

Within half an hour she stood in Colbert's study. She licked her dry lips. It was important that she get the words right.

Forming a steeple with his fingers, Colbert studied her intently. "Mademoiselle?"

"Monsieur Colbert, I'm Madeleine Poquelin, the actress." She thought actress sounded better than seamstress.

"Ah, *oui*. I saw you once at Palais-Royal. Are you ill?"

Madeleine was taken by surprise by his abrupt question. "No, I'm fine. Why?"

Colbert lifted one brown eyebrow over one brown eye. Everything about him was brown!

"You're coming here to beg for a small pension, eh? Too lazy to work, eh?" He threw his hands up in a gesture of anger. "What is it with the youth today—don't want to do any work!"

"Monsieur Colbert." She steadied her voice. "I'm here to . . . through you . . . warn the King."

Colbert's bottom lip dropped in surprise. She had his ear now. She braced herself, her nerves vibrating now that the opportunity had come to voice her secret, the whole secret.

"Monsieur Colbert, I hope you will understand the importance of what I have to say. It will sound farfetched, but please hear me out." She took a deep breath. "Monsieur Fouquet is an embezzler and a murderer. I have proof." She bit her lip. It sounded preposterous. She had become nervous before his fusillade of accusations and blurted out the words too fast. This was bound to set up his hackles.

She was right. Colbert's gaze scorched her. He looked her up and down disdainfully. "Who are you to burst in here, throwing accusations at Monsieur Fouquet? Don't you think I have more important matters on my mind than listening to raving lunatics?"

His words set Madeleine's anger churning. "Monsieur Colbert, if you would give me a few moments, I will explain it all to you," she said icily.

"Of course." He mimicked her tone. "And I can spend those moments doing honest work. I have no idea why you left your position at the theater company to come here. Mark my words, I will not help you in your schemes to gain some favor from the King. Thank God, he doesn't have to be bothered by the likes of you!"

At that moment Madeleine felt intense dislike for the brown man. "It is unbelievable how a narrow-minded and—and—yes, stupid man like you could have reached your position. I feel sorry for the King to be surrounded by the likes of you every day!"

Monsieur Colbert turned white with fury. "Guard!" he barked, and before she knew it, Madeleine was seized and dragged out of the room. Sniggers greeted her, and fragments of malicious sentences floated in the air. "A just payment . . . brazen hussy."

She was set down on the steps outside. Add another enemy to your list, she chided herself. "Let go of me!" she ordered the guards still holding her arms, as if they suspected that she would dash back into the building and attack the brown man.

Finally heeding her, they released her with a shove in the back, and she fell down the steps. Tears of rage streamed down her face.

Amul bolted down the stairs and knelt beside her. "Are you hurt?"

RECKLESS SPLENDOR 79

She shook her head, and ignoring her bruised limbs, stood up and walked toward the Seine, boiling with anger and disappointment. Amul placed a thin arm around her shoulders. His compassion comforted her.

The sunlight glittered in the snow, and her angry tears turned icy on her cheeks. The long wait in Colbert's corridor had made her ravenous. She bought a meat pie from a vendor on the street corner. Breaking the steaming pie in two, she handed one half to Amul. In companionable silence they downed the pie. It appeased Madeleine's hunger but did nothing for her plunging spirits.

Hailing the brandy vendor, she drank deeply from the pewter mug he filled to the rim with the fiery liquid. It coursed down her throat like a burning ribbon.

"Come, let us leave this area. Fouquet might visit Colbert," she said.

As they got closer to Pont Saint Michel, the groans of huge ice blocks grinding against themselves and against the heavy timbered foundation of the bridge reached their ears. The current was desperately trying to deliver the river from the thick, silvery mantle that the freezing temperatures had created. Madeleine's tears flowed in icy rivulets down her cheeks, and she dashed them away as she turned her eyes to the serene sky. "Argh! I am so angry!"

Then her shoulders moved in a deep sigh. "What are we going to do now?" The cold numbed her toes and fingers. She had no refuge and very little money, but she had scores of enemies.

Amul screwed up his face in concentration. "There must be some other possibility." As he thought, he pushed handfuls of snow off the railing and onto the ice.

Madeleine blew her nose. "I have no idea."

Suddenly Amul danced a little jig in the snow. "I know! Why didn't I think of that before? I will speak with Madame on your behalf and beg her to arrange an audience with the King."

Madeleine's face lit up. "That really is a good idea. But that means you have to return to Saint-Cloud and grovel at Madame's feet—beg her forgiveness."

"*Oui*, I don't like that part, but the diary is more important than Madame's displeasure."

Madeleine playfully tweaked his snub nose. With a nervous giggle, he dashed her hand away.

"You are very brave," she said. "How long will it take? We will have to decide on a meeting place."

"I don't know. It depends on Madame's temper, which is short at best." He rubbed his head. "I will try to be at the statue on Pont-Neuf at noon tomorrow."

"I'll meet you there." Madeleine clapped her hands together. "I'm so excited. I can already *smell* our success."

"Where will you spend the night?" Amul asked with a worried frown.

"I'll stay with La Du Parc and swear her to secrecy. I can always tell her some romantic tale. She already thinks that Hautefort is my lover." She hugged Amul tenderly. "Be careful. Hautefort is bound to look for you at court since he won't find me. Good luck."

Amul smiled. "I'm not afraid. I will hurry now."

Madeleine's gaze followed him as he bounded across the bridge, her heart contracted with fear.

Chapter 8

La Du Parc was not at home. The concierge told Madeleine that the actress was at the palace of Saint-Germain and would stay there for the next two days.

Madeleine pinched her lips together and tried to think of a solution to her problem. She counted the coins in her pocket. If she spent the night at an *auberge*, there would be nothing left for food tomorrow. She thought of asking one of the other actresses for lodging, but could she trust them? La Du Parc was her friend, but were the others?

Lingering in the portico of the building where the Du Parcs lived in Faubourg Saint-Germain, Madeleine toyed with every possibility. Darkness was falling rapidly, and she didn't want to spend the night in the streets. She would have to try one of the other actresses since she had no desire to return to Rue de la Réale and possibly run into Uncle Molière.

Afraid of the moving shadows in the dark portals and the scurrying rats in the frozen sewers, Madeleine decided to take a chance and stay with La Rodin on Rue Saint Honoré.

She stifled a scream when she felt tiny paws running across her clogs. Determined to reach her destination without mishap, she clutched her cloak closer and turned her steps toward Pont Royal. She pulled her hood deeply over her face and made herself small, sneaking along the walls.

It was cold and windy, getting colder every minute as the pale sun descended below the horizon. Needlelike snowflakes whirled through the air in wild abandon, stinging her face. The ghostly hoot of an owl nearby made her jump with fright.

The wind carried whispers and cackling laughs, proving she was far from alone. But she saw no one. Here and there a lantern swung in the wind, and the signs over the shops creaked forlornly. A carriage drawn by six horses passed at high speed, and Madeleine pressed herself against the wall so as not to be trampled.

The sound of raucous laughter and hoarse cursing voices erupted from a bawdy tavern as she turned onto Rue Saint Honoré. Roughly dressed men with painted women on their arms came and went from the taproom. The sign read The Greedy Cat, and she knew it would be dangerous to go too close to the door alone.

She could not stop now, and there was no other route without making a long detour. Knowing she had to pass the tavern, she kept well away from the square of light spilling from the door of the ramshackle building. The cobblestones were icy, and she was afraid of bringing attention to herself by slipping in her clumsy clogs.

Hiding in the shadows, she edged closer. Two men with tattered clothes and bushy beards passed nearby without seeing her.

After flitting past the open door of the wine shop, and just when she thought she was safe, Madeleine felt a bony pair of hands shoot from the shadows to grasp her arm.

"Oh-la-la, what have we here? A plump little pigeon," a high voice piped in the darkness.

Frightened, Madeleine lost her footing and tumbled against a tall, thin form. Breath reeking of sour wine and garlic washed over her face, and she recoiled in revulsion.

The reedy man was amazingly strong as he pulled her toward the rectangle of light cast by a window. He peered closely at her face. She yanked hard to get away from his steely grip.

On both sides of his long, thin face hung greasy strands of rat-colored hair topped with a tattered woolen hat. He wore a threadbare coat hanging limply from his shoulders. Spindly legs were encased in coarse stockings. His evil eyes studied her.

"Hmmm . . . I think the chief will be pleased with you. My catch could not have been better. You even look innocent, but we know better, don't we? Ha-ha-ha." He spoke French with an accent.

One bony finger lifted her chin, and she shuddered. Her voice seemed to have left her, but not her indignation. Angrily she kicked his shin until he howled and swore, but he did not loosen his hold on her.

A large shadow filled the opening of the tavern.

"What is going on here, Spider?" a voice boomed.

The man called Spider groaned, rubbing his shin. "I have a real wildcat for you this evening." He shoved her toward the tall man by the door. Stumbling on the cobblestones, she fell against him. An acrid scent of gunpowder mixed with tobacco and stale sweat assaulted her nostrils. A wide-brimmed felt hat with several limp plumes shadowed his face. A wide, drab cloak hung from his shoulders to his knees. He caught her arm.

From the ashes to the fire, Madeleine thought desperately.

"*Sacre bleu*, come inside, *petite*. It is foolish to be out on a raw night like this when you can sit in front of the fire with a mug of mulled wine."

Before she could protest, he had propelled her into the dark, smoky tavern. Fifty pale faces turned to her, and whistles and cheers rose to the dirty ceiling. The floor was sticky with spilled ale. Rough-looking customers snored with their faces lying in large puddles of ale on the tabletops.

Madeleine wanted to bolt out of the room. Distressed, she jammed an elbow into the ribs of her escort and at the same time stepped on his foot with all her weight.

He laughed, a deep rumbling sound, and failed to budge. "Spitting fire, eh? Don't you like the company?" He dragged her roughly to the fire and pulled her hood away from her face.

She glared at him, ready to spit out a string of suitable epithets.

"*Diable*, if it isn't a little beauty! And such spirit! It must be my lucky day." The man laughed, and Madeleine got a good view of his toothless gap. He was menacing and awfully dirty, his beard in a matted tangle. He swept off his hat in mock gallantry, and she noticed the wrinkles on his face and his gray-streaked hair. His small eyes leered at her. Her fear grew. His was the most repulsive face she had ever seen, eclipsing even those of her attackers at *hôtel* Belleforière.

He reached out to undo the knot of her cloak. "Let's find out if you have more to offer than a lovely face."

She slapped his hand hard, but it did not deter him. He only guffawed, again baring the empty cavern of his mouth.

As if they were thin as gossamer, the tasseled cords of her cloak snapped under his fingers, and her cloak slipped to the floor.

A deafening roar rose from the eager audience, and Madeleine blushed furiously.

"Spider, look at these curls! Don't you think the wigmaker would be happy to get his hands on these tresses?" A dirty finger held up one of her curls for inspection. Angrily she jerked her head away.

She realized that the man called Spider stood right behind her, and the rest of the audience were mostly men. A sprinkle of noblemen, elegantly dressed and wearing half masks, stood drinking wine out of large goblets. Their handsome swords, attached to gilt-edged leather baldrics, glinted in the light. Perhaps she could ask one of them to rescue her, or get her hands on one of the swords.

Spider cackled. "As you say, Capitaine Roland. Let's lop off her curls."

A shiver rushed along Madeleine's spine. She felt Spider's bony fingers around her arms. "Capitaine, this lace collar is surely worth a few pistoles." His black-rimmed fingers flicked her fichu.

"Take your grubby hands off me!" Madeleine squirmed to get away from his grip.

"*Par bleu*, easy now, little filly! We're only evaluating your assets." Without ado, Spider lifted her up on a table and made her turn around slowly. When she tried to kick him in the face, he took hold of her ankle and made her topple over, revealing her legs.

Tears of desperation flooded her eyes. "Let me go! I have done nothing."

RECKLESS SPLENDOR

"Ha-ha-ha . . . but you soon will." Capitaine Roland bellowed with laughter. "You will bring me a pretty penny."

Spider stared at her intently. "She might not be as innocent as she looks."

"*Sacre bleu!* Spider, you have sharp eyes." Roland paused. "If her maidenhead has been plucked, she is worthless to us. We'd better make sure."

Madeleine could not believe her eyes when the capitaine grabbed her skirts and was about to lift them to reveal her bare bottom for all to see. Her head reeled, and she fought to keep her skirts down.

"Stop it, you clods!"

Abruptly the roaring cheers ended, a threatening silence suffocating the drunk patrons.

Dazed, Madeleine raised her eyes. Against the jutting beard of the capitaine, a steel blade glinted icily. The villain looked as if he had turned into one of the gargoyles of Notre Dame. Only his mean eyes glittered, steadily trained on the owner of the sword.

Madeleine whipped her gaze to the nobleman whose sword threatened to slit the capitaine's throat.

"Get down!" he barked at Madeleine, who obeyed instantly. Where had she heard that voice before? The gentleman's elaborate velvet costume looked out of place in the run-down wine shop.

That blond hair!

How had she failed to recognize that rippling mane? What was the comte doing here?

She clutched his arm to get a look at his face. Although his eyes were covered by a black velvet mask, she instantly knew that angry glare. "You!"

Without taking his attention from the capitaine, Germain shoved her behind his back. "Keep out of this!" he ordered.

Seconds trickled by. Nobody moved.

Madeleine decided to make a dash for the door, but before she reached it, arms from all sides halted her.

It was a nightmare to hear the comte's voice, taut with anger, saying, "Defend yourself, Roland!"

Instantly the grim room filled with a din of cheers and the jarring clash of steel.

Somebody pushed Madeleine into a chair, and she pressed her hands to her ears to shut out the noise. Her eyes were riveted to the comte, who parried back and forth, his footwork pantherlike. He had taken off his coat, and his white, full shirt billowed around him.

The clashing swords shot blue flashes as the two men's fury increased. Although he was larger and clumsier than Germain, Capitaine Roland was not a bad fighter. He wielded his sword with skill, feinting and thrusting like a fiend.

Madeleine could barely breathe. What if the comte were killed? It would be all her fault!

As Germain danced over the rough floor, the spurs of his high boots jingled ominously.

She screamed when the capitaine's sword made a slash in the comte's shirt and blood soaked the white linen. But Germain did not fall or cease to fight. Instead the wound appeared to increase his fury, because his thrusts came faster and more viciously. Madeleine saw perspiration pearl on the face of the capitaine. He breathed heavily, and his sword arm no longer had the same force.

Germain rained a crescendo of thrusts at his foe, the finale coming rapidly. Receiving a deep gash in his arm, the capitaine howled in pain, and his sword clattered to the floor.

As dark blood welled out of the wound, Madeleine wanted to retch. He roared like a wounded bull and clasped his hand to the wound. Ashen-faced, he sank onto a proffered chair.

"She's yours," he grunted.

Germain sent Madeleine a burning glance. Without a word he wiped his sword on a spotted tablecloth and sheathed it. His shirt was stained with blood, and he walked with difficulty.

Donc, he had been in the tavern all along! Madeleine thought. What was he doing here?

Shrugging off an offer of assistance, he pulled on his coat. His face turned pale; momentarily he had to steady himself against the table.

What was going to happen now?

A carriage stopped noisily outside the tavern, and Germain walked slowly toward it.

Is he going to leave me here? Madeleine wondered in dismay. She almost wished he would, but he speared her cloak with his cane and tossed it to her without giving her as much as a glance.

As soon as they stepped outside, she was tempted to run, but then she noticed all the leering faces in the doorway and rapidly changed her mind.

She followed Germain into the carriage. With a curse, he leaned stiffly against the squabs.

"You are hurt." Madeleine was all concern and sat next to him. "Let me help you."

"Take your hands off me—firebrand!" he roared. "Not only did I have to humiliate myself by borrowing this carriage, but I have to listen to your drivel."

As it crossed Rue Saint Denis the carriage lurched and tossed Madeleine against him.

"I told you to leave me alone!" he warned.

"What's eating you? I didn't ask to accompany you!" She was seething with anger by now. The nerve of the man!

She sensed him turning to her in the pitch-black interior of the coach. "We can stop right now and set you down," he threatened. "Or do you demand to be set down at some other point? At Versailles perhaps, or Saint-Cloud where your devious friends reside?" He pressed hot fingers around her throat. "You are nothing but trouble, mademoiselle. This world would be a better place if I just squeezed a little harder."

Madeleine could not believe her ears. She fought off his hands; he let them drop with a weary sigh.

"*Dieu!* You . . . *bouffon!*" She rubbed her sore throat, then slapped him, but still he did not move. "Let me off right here!" she demanded.

"*Non.* You're not going anywhere until you have given me some answers, Mademoiselle Poquelin. Have you already forgotten that you escaped from my custody this morning?"

Madeleine laughed, a high brittle sound. "Ah! That's what's eating you. You're afraid to look like a fool because I managed to escape."

His laughter was dry and humorless. "You always land on your feet, don't you?"

"It is none of your business, Monsieur High and Mighty."

An uneasy silence descended. Madeleine stared stonily out the window. Not that she could see anything; she was aware only of her anger boiling all the way to her fingertips. She itched to slap him again, but what would it help? She was at the mercy of the arrogant comte.

The carriage rattled into the courtyard of *hôtel* Belleforière. Lackeys descended with torches to light their progress up the stairs. At the top stood Maurice, the steward.

Germain stepped down and with a motion of his hand indicated to a lackey to assist Madeleine as well.

Due to the evening's nightmarish events, she was overcome with exhaustion. Her legs felt wooden, and it was with difficulty she walked up the stairs. Puppetlike, she followed Germain to his study, a room she had not seen before. Her eyes ran across the filled bookcases, the wide leather-topped desk, the paintings, a collection of yellowed maps, and the beautiful Oriental carpets.

Germain sank down in an armchair by the fire. He looked ghastly. Maurice stood motionless next to the chair.

"Bring me a decanter of brandy, Maurice," Germain said tiredly.

"Your master is wounded. Please fetch some lint and boiling water," Madeleine ordered, seeing that Germain was not about to help himself.

If the steward was startled, he kept the emotion admirably to himself. His face a cold mask, he left the room. What a sour man! Madeleine thought.

Without delay, she hurried to Germain's side. "Take off your coat immediately!" she commanded sternly, not about to let him bully her again.

A mirthless smile spread across his lips. "Are you so eager to see me undressed?"

Delicate color suffused her cheeks. "Not at all! But whether you like it or not, I'm going to help you since you won't do anything to help yourself."

To show him that she was serious, she began tugging at his velvet coat. She expected a fight, but he sat motionless

RECKLESS SPLENDOR 89

when she pulled the coat away from his shoulders. She gasped when her gaze fell on the blood-soaked shirt.

Looking at her green face, Germain smiled weakly, the smile reaching his eyes this time. "It is only a scratch."

Taking a deep breath, she ripped the shirt down the middle and exposed the wound.

To her surprise, Germain was chuckling. "You have a forceful way of undressing a man. It is very exciting."

"Oh, *zut!*" Madeleine scoffed. "Have you nothing else on your mind while your lifeblood is seeping out?" But the sight of his broad chest covered with curly blond hair made her heart beat faster.

When he noticed her gaze lingering on his chest, he took her hand and placed it on his warm skin, right over the heart. His eyes had narrowed, and a dangerous rapier-sharp gleam burned in their depths. His heart thudded rapidly under her hand.

"You should not overexert yourself," she said nervously.

Maurice entered carrying a tray containing a wad of lint, a bowl of steaming water, a poultice, and a bottle of Queen of Hungary elixir. He lighted a candelabra on the small table next to the chair where Germain sat sprawled. Germain's hair glinted golden in the soft light, and his face was covered with a fine sheen of perspiration.

Maurice placed the tray on the table. "Monsieur le comte, can I help or call your physician?"

Germain hesitated for a second. "*Non*, Maurice, Mademoiselle Poquelin will assist me. You may retire."

"*Merci*, monsieur." With a bow the steward left the room.

Madeleine bit her bottom lip. She wondered what excuse she could use to touch Germain's bare chest again.

He stared at her, his wide lips stretched in a mocking smile. "*Bien?* Are you going to let me bleed to death?"

Compressing her lips, she knelt at his side. She mixed some elixir with the hot water and then soaked the lint in the solution. She dabbed at the gash, her fingers trembling. As Germain had maintained, the wound was not deep, yet a trickle of blood oozed steadily from it.

When he did not complain, she grew braver and washed the wound once more, this time pressing harder.

"*Zut!* . . . the devil!" he groaned.

"There, almost done." She arranged the dough of powdered oyster shells on the wound. To keep it in place she needed to wind strips of gauze around his chest. To reach around him, she had to embrace him. It took all her determination to do so. His chest was broad enough to be difficult to wrap, and she was not going to press her face to his chest!

The musky scent of him, mingling with that of tobacco and orris root, enticed her nostrils until she wanted to cover his warm skin with kisses.

"What are you doing?" he mumbled in her hair.

Madeleine realized her hands lay motionless on his back, her head against his chest. She was mesmerized by the feel of his fingers twining into her hair. She could have stayed like that forever, but his voice brought her back to the task at hand.

"Oh, I'm sorry." She secured the gauze. "There! You will probably survive." Her voice was breathless, and she did not dare meet his gaze.

She did not resist when, with two fingers under her chin, he lifted her face to his, but her gaze was still lowered.

It came as no surprise when his lips forcefully swooped down on hers. Like a flower opening up to the sun, her lips parted, and she tasted his impatient tongue against her own. A sweet pounding began in her loins, magnifying, echoing to all the nerve endings of her body as his lips slowly seduced her.

Her arms went around his neck, and she felt safe in the warm haven of his embrace. Kneeling, she failed to notice the pain in her knees as she sought to quench the wild yearning that he had lit in the core of her being.

A deep sigh flowed over her lips when he began to rain tight kisses along the arched column of her neck, on her shoulders, and in the hollow of her throat.

She leaned weakly against him, her lips throbbing and half open, awakened, waiting. His hands eased the fichu from her shoulders and unlaced the bodice, revealing her full, round breasts. Rosebud crests rose and fell with her shallow breathing.

Madeleine felt a tremor run through him and the gust of his breath on her bared nipples before his lips greedily fondled one of the pink buds.

A wave of desire engulfed her, making it increasingly hard to breathe. She whimpered with pleasure, curling her fingers into his hair to drag him closer.

A storm of desire raged in Germain's loins. He was shaking all over, and cold sweat trickled along his spine. The softness of her skin, the pliant curves of her yielding lips, the seductive sweet scent of her arousal, her beautiful breasts, made him desperately want to thrust himself deeply into her. He would drive her mad with slow pleasure until she cried out and entreated him for release.

He was ready to lower her right then and there to the rug in front of the fire, but he glimpsed her widely staring eyes. The daze of arousal mixed with fear made her excruciatingly vulnerable, and Germain had to curb the rage in his loins. Taking several deep breaths, he slowly released his convulsive grip on her shoulders.

With a sigh of defeat, he leaned back in his chair. He struggled to make his voice normal. "*Bon*, I feel better already," he lied. "If only you would serve me a snifter of brandy, things would be perfect."

After fulfilling his wish, Madeleine shakily sat down in the armchair on the opposite side of the fireplace. What was going to happen now? She laced up her bodice, fumbling.

On edge and more than a little confused, she knew that Germain was studying her, but she stubbornly kept her gaze lowered to the carpet. She could still feel the tingling sensation left by his lips on her breasts and on her lips. Yearning still pounded dully through her body.

"The *capitaine* was right. You are a very beautiful woman, Madeleine," he drawled after a few moments of silence.

Her haze of delight evaporated. She whipped her gaze to his face. "What of it? Since you're not above taking advantage of me, you're no better than the ruffians in the tavern."

He shook his head in exasperation. "Hedgehog, pull in your spines. What are we going to do with you? You cannot accept a simple compliment. I'll have to give you a lesson in the game of flirtation."

"I will leave now."

He laughed without joy. "Have you already forgotten that you are my prisoner? Now that I have found you, I will not let you slip away again." He rubbed his mustache. "Tell me, how did you escape? I was disappointed to see you gone."

"Were you?" A wicked gleam lit her eyes. "Afraid of Fouquet's wrath?"

"You would like to think that. Well, explain yourself!" he countered.

Madeleine sighed and explained how Amul had helped her, making much of how easy it had been to slip unseen out of the house.

Germain could not help but smile. "So? I hope you had a delightful day because it won't be repeated tomorrow."

Madeleine pursed her lips. "Why? Fouquet will have the diary in his hands and won't need me any longer."

Germain crossed one long leg over the other and twirled his cane. "*If* you told him the truth, that is, and even then he may want to, er, silence your lips. The word whispered at court today is that you're a disgrace to Molière. You know who planted that slander, don't you?"

Madeleine laughed. "That is the most idiotic thing I've ever heard. Fouquet never rests, does he? It is astonishing that *you* believe him rather than me. I thought you more perceptive than that." She laughed, a bitter sound.

Germain did not see the humor. Irritably he tapped his boot with the cane. "Enough! I have been warned to stay away from you. The contents of your petitions must have been explosive, to say the least, to put such fear into an exalted individual like Fouquet. You had better tell me the whole truth."

"Why? You will never believe me. It is obvious that my petitions ended up in Fouquet's hands. The King doesn't even know I exist! I know it sounds odd to you, but His Majesty would be very pleased to read Fouquet's diary."

She watched Germain's brow darken.

"But don't worry, I won't burden you by asking for that particular favor again—an audience, I mean. I'm on my own."

"Favor? Where do you think you would have been tonight if it weren't for favors? Let me tell you." He leaned forward, his eyes twin silver daggers boring into her. "Capitaine Roland is a white slave merchant. He lures lovely ladies like you with promises of great riches and a pleasurable life in harems on the Barbary Coast. Whether they come willingly or not, he makes sure they are on his ship when he's ready to sail. None of those girls ever see France again."

Madeleine stiffened as if in pain. She owed this man so much already, even though he was allied to her enemy. Did she dare confide in him? There was a small chance he would let her go. And when Fouquet found out that she had lied about the diary—well, then the comte would have to explain why she was gone. If only the comte understood the urgency of her mission, he would let her go.

She did not want to die or disappear at Fouquet's hand before she had fulfilled her mission. It was the only way she could avenge her father's death. The minister of finance was a very devious man. It was almost too much to bear that he was trying to undermine her credibility with the King, and she hadn't even met Louis. A disgrace to Molière, indeed! What more lies was Fouquet spreading?

She compressed her lips. "I suppose I should thank you for what you did for me at the tavern. What were *you* doing there?"

"Why should I tell you?"

Madeleine's eyes narrowed. "An eye for an eye?" Then she said, "You seemed to know everyone. At least you know Capitaine Roland, or know *of* him."

Germain chuckled. "Everybody who frequents lowly taverns in Paris knows him. He's a prominent character in the underworld. A dangerous character; he doesn't think twice before killing a man."

He winced as his wound throbbed. For a moment he stared intently at her. "You're not going to give me any more information about this . . . diary, are you?" He sounded tired, disappointed.

"I would like to, but only when I'm sure that you'll believe me."

"*C'est bien*, time to rest now." He stood with difficulty and stretched. "Thanks to you, I'm covered with bruises and cuts."

Seeing the veil of guilt covering her pale features, he laughed. "Don't worry; you make me feel alive, *ma belle*." He waited for her, and she walked listlessly before him up the stairs.

"I will order a maid to assist you and to give you some clean clothes. This time you'll stay in the blue guest room—and don't try to jump out the window; it's on the third floor. Jerome, the lackey, will be guarding the door."

Madeleine felt sick with hopelessness.

Chapter 9

The next morning Madeleine stretched in the comfortable bed, her eyes painful and gritty, and her nose stuffed. She grimaced and blinked. Apparently a cold was coming on, and at such an inconvenient time. Yet she was warm and cozy under the down coverlet behind drawn bed curtains. To avoid placing her warm feet on the cold floor, she dreamed of staying in bed all day. Then she remembered that she was supposed to meet Amul at noon. She would have to find a way to escape.

Carefully she opened the bed curtains a crack. A merry fire blazed in the hearth. "What luxury!" she said out loud. Flinging the curtains wide, she lay back on the pillows, her hands tucked beneath her head.

The guest room was beautifully appointed. The ceiling was painted light blue, adorned with fluffy clouds and smiling angels. An ornate molding covered with gold leaf marched along the top of walls that were upholstered with deep blue silk. Exquisitely crafted furnishings made of ebony and gold leaf graced the room.

Madeleine curled into a ball and stared at the fire. Was Germain still in the house? She could not forget the conversation they had exchanged in the study. The memory of his lips on her breasts and throat made her heart thud faster, and she blushed a deep pink.

A soft knock sounded on the door. Madeleine was startled out of her reverie and rapidly pulled the eiderdown coverlet to her chin.

"Entrez."

She watched a young girl, younger than her own eighteen years, enter. A huge white mobcap covered her head, and she had a freckled face with a pert nose and round eyes that ogled her curiously. She wore a gray fringed shawl and a dark corduroy dress.

"I am here to assist you, Mademoiselle Poquelin."

Madeleine sat up, her hair streaming wildly around her face.

"Would it be possible to have a bath?" she asked eagerly.

The maid gaped. "A bath? You cannot mean it. Water is dangerous!"

"Nonsense! At Vichy, patients are submerged several times a day in the sulphuric waters. Have you not heard of it? By the way, what is your name?"

The maid stared dumbly at her for a few moments, then answered hesitantly. "Nicole. I will see if a bath can be prepared." As if she had just spoken to a raving lunatic, Nicole ran out and slammed the door behind her.

Madeleine smiled and slipped out of bed. Her toes immediately sank into the luxurious carpet patterned with pink roses. She walked to the window, enjoying the feel of the soft carpet with every step.

Flinging aside the curtains, she opened the shutters, and sunlight streamed into the room. Pressing her nose to the windowpanes, she got a glimpse of the street below.

Carts and carriages rumbled by, toward the busy intersection of Rue Saint Denis. The brandy vendor and a baker with his covered basket offered their wares in high, shrill voices. A barber with his tools in a cloth bag hurried by. Horses snorted big clouds of frozen air. It was still bitingly cold, but Madeleine was snug in a room with a fire roaring in the hearth behind her. She tried to push away the thought of being a prisoner. Absently she massaged her aching neck.

The winter had been bitterly cold so far. This morning the sun shone from a brilliant blue sky. In the glittering air she glimpsed the square towers of Notre Dame on Ile de la Cité. Between the houses across the street a narrow ice-blue ribbon of Seine water glowed like diamonds in the sun. Horns and trumpets blared in the distance, aids of the hawkers on Pont-Neuf.

Another timid knock heralded Nicole's return. "Mademoiselle, monsieur le comte's hip bath will be moved downstairs to the kitchen. You see, if you were to take a bath in monsieur le comte's dressing room, he might—"

"The kitchen will be fine." Madeleine looked the girl over. "Nicole, we're much of the same height. Could I purchase a set of garments from you? This is all I have," she said, pointing at the crumpled and stained wool dress hanging over the back of a chair.

Nicole gawked with her mouth open. "My clothes, mademoiselle? Le comte would be angry. You'll find everything you need in the armoire. Monsieur le comte keeps extra clothes for his guests. Look!"

Nicole tripped over to the armoire and opened wide the double doors. Madeleine stared at a row of sumptuous velvet dresses and a row of men's vests and coats. Nicole pulled out drawers filled with shirts, shifts, and stockings. A waft of sweet-smelling lavender reached Madeleine's nose.

Nicole presented a deep blue dress adorned with gold embroidery and bows. "This would suit you, mademoiselle."

Madeleine turned her back on the dress. "I'm not interested. If I cannot buy your clothes, please go out and buy some for me." She sent the maid a beseeching glance.

Nicole shrugged her shoulders. "Of course." But it was said without conviction. Obviously the maid thought Madeleine was mad not to accept one of the elegant dresses in the armoire.

Madeleine picked up her little leather pouch containing the rest of her money.

Tonelessly Nicole recited the price of the different garments she wore, and Madeleine realized she could only afford a new skirt and bodice of the coarsest material.

Curtsying, Nicole prepared to leave the room. "While I go shopping for clothes, you can take your bath. At this time, Madame Barbette is the only person in the kitchen."

Madeleine threw her cloak around her shoulders to cover her near nakedness and followed the maid through the corridors of the elegant mansion. Going down the back stairs, they reached the warm kitchen.

In the enormous hearth hung a huge black iron kettle filled with steaming water. Two lackeys were filling the tub with alternately hot and cold water until it was full.

The rotund Madame Barbette hovered over them with her fat arms akimbo. Nicole slipped outside, and the movement made the *cuisinière* shift her ferocious eyes to the newcomer.

With a look that said, *You must be the madwoman who wants a bath in* my *kitchen,* she waved her hand, indicating a chair at the table. She set a cup and saucer and a plate of steaming white rolls and assorted cakes in front of her guest.

Pouring cocoa into the cup, she said, "It isn't right that you should have to take your bath in the kitchen, Mademoiselle Poquelin."

Madeleine smiled. "You don't share Nicole's opinion that water is dangerous?"

"Pshaw! We eat it and drink it every day and nobody has died from it yet, as far as I know. You should have had your bath in your room."

Madeleine shrugged. "I'm a prisoner here—not a guest. You must know that. By the way, this kitchen is so cheerful," she added, studying the spotless room with new interest. The wolfhounds, Ariel and Claudine, slept in a square of sunlight on the floor. Copper utensils gleamed on the walls, and the aroma of cinnamon and freshly baked bread permeated the air.

The *cuisinière* beamed at her. "You're a sweet little thing. Not at all high and mighty like the ones he usually brings around from time to time. Eat your rolls, *petite.*"

She must mean his mistresses, Madeleine thought. *Naturellement,* he would not live a life of celibacy; she knew that. Blushing, she took a sip of cocoa. He could make a woman tremble in his arms.

The cocoa scalded her tongue, and she spluttered and coughed. Madame Barbette slapped her in the back.

"Th-thank you—madame, er?" Madeleine wheezed when her breath returned.

"Madame Barbette." The older woman pounded her ample bosom. "I'm proud of my kitchen, and it is a pleasure to work for the comte. He's a kind man—even if he has his wild ways." She rolled her eyes. "I heard that shot yesterday, and I'm not ashamed to confess that I hid in the pantry." Every layer of flesh shivered. "I don't know what the comte is thinking of, letting his valet shoot a hole in the ceiling like that. I cannot abide that Monsieur Fouquet, who orders the household around as if he were King Louis himself and brings big, hairy ruffians into the house." She took a deep breath, her three chins trembling.

"*Enfin*, I've been with the family for a long time, ever since Master Germain was a tiny tot with hair as pale as yours. He wasn't as wild then." She leaned over in confidence. "He's the spitting image of the old comte." She looked at a small watch pinned to her gray serge dress. "*Donc*, 'tis time for his breakfast. And you, *petite fille*, should take your bath before it grows cold."

Armed with an iron skillet, Madame Barbette made sure no lackeys were peeping in the passage as Madeleine slipped out of her shift and settled in the tub.

Wonderful. The steam smelled sweetly of jasmine. Around the rim the tub was decorated with painted pink roses. Madeleine giggled. "Does the comte like this feminine touch?" She traced the roses on the porcelain rim.

"Oh, it belonged to la comtesse, his mother. He keeps it as memory of her, I should say. Our comte is mighty finicky about his toilette. He cannot stand the foul smells of Paris. I don't mind."

He did not wrinkle his nose at the tavern last night, Madeleine thought.

Picking up a sponge and a bar of soap smelling of roses, Madeleine spoke. "Tell me more about the comte's family. Is he married?" She could barely keep the eagerness out of her voice.

As Madame Barbette worked by the hearth, the air became redolent with the scent of fried eggs and ham. Judging by the look on her face, she could not be more delighted to have an opportunity to let her tongue wag.

"*Non*, so far he has been too wild to settle down. A pity." She sighed. "I came into service twenty-eight years ago at Les Étoiles."

He wasn't married. "Les Étoiles?" Madeleine said innocently.

"*Oui.* Hautefort's country estate in Brittany. Of course, Master Germain has other estates throughout Poitou and Normandy. Les Étoiles is by far the loveliest of them all. Made out of gray stone, it has two turreted towers and an adjoining circular chapel." Madame Barbette's eyes grew dreamy as she described the castle. "There are many dark, narrow passages and odd-shaped rooms, dark paneling and mullioned windows. You should see how worn the stone steps are after hundreds of years of use. Master Germain is fond of the old heap."

Madame Barbette pushed an errant strand of hair under her cap, then continued. "There is a ghost in the west tower. I've seen it myself, one of Master Germain's ancestors. He wears one of those awful armors, clanking as he walks through the corridors at night. *Oui,* Nicole does not dare to sleep alone at Les Étoiles. She always sleeps in my room." Madame Barbette snorted in contempt.

"The old comte was a wild one. He and the father of our King were close friends, if you could ever call that sourpuss Louis XIII a friend. Now, our Louis, he's different. Full of charm, he is. He will crush many hearts."

Madame Barbette rubbed her bulbous nose. "I guess I'm rambling a bit." She heaved a rumbling sigh and speedily invented an excuse to continue her story. "See, I don't often talk to strangers—strangers who are interested in the family. Master Germain's mother, La Comtesse Eveline, she was a beauty. Unfortunately, the beauty stopped with her face. When she opened her mouth, the sharpest tongue in Brittany came to use, spewing out sharp criticisms about everything and everybody. I'm afraid she wasn't much loved."

Madame Barbette slapped a thick slice of ham on a plate. "I do remember one time when Master Germain and Gaspard dipped all the horses' tails in a bucket of glue. The tails had to be cut off, and Master Germain and Gaspard were thoroughly spanked and had to eat a diet of bread and water for two days. Unbeknownst to the comtesse, I slipped them a few delicacies." She laughed, her stomach wobbling. "Master Germain could not sit without a pillow under his sore parts for at least a week."

Entranced by the story, Madeleine had quite forgotten her bath.

"*Donc*, Master Germain and the bailiff's son—Gaspard—were always thick as thieves. I suppose it came out of Master Germain's loneliness. There were brothers and sisters, but they all died in infancy. Perhaps it is no wonder that the comtesse was so sharp-tongued. She couldn't bear the loss, and I don't blame her."

Placing the plate on a tray, she proceeded to pour out a tankard of ale from a keg on a wooden stand.

"Then Master Germain went abroad. He sailed with his Uncle Armand, the old comte's youngest brother, who was a seafaring man. I cannot even begin to pronounce the names of the places they went, but Master Germain came home a grown man and took over the management of the estates. The old comte was failing then." She paused and wrinkled her nose. "It was in those foreign parts Master Germain picked up that nasty habit of smoking those black cheroots."

She took a step closer to Madeleine and spoke in a lower voice. "Let me tell you in confidence; Master Germain is not a happy man. I'm sure he loves the King well enough, but he doesn't like the . . . harness. He's a freedom-loving man, likes to roam around. King Louis is one for rites and rituals from morning to night."

"What is going on here? What garbage are you saying about me, Barbette?" snapped Germain from the door. "I've waited this age in the dining room for my breakfast."

Then he noticed Madeleine. A flicker of surprise in his eyes, he stepped into the kitchen. "Well, well, if this isn't a quaint sight! The maiden in the bath."

The dogs whimpered with delight and threw themselves at him.

Madame Barbette waved her arms. "Get out of here, Master Germain! It's not fitting for you to come into the kitchen. An aristocrat *never* enters the kitchen, as if I have to remind you, and the poor girl's taking a bath!"

Like a mother hen flapping her wings, she tried to chase him out of the room with the aid of the iron skillet. He laughed and fought her off. "It looks interesting; I think I'll have my breakfast in here. It is my house, and if I please to have breakfast in the kitchen, so it shall be." Resolutely, Germain folded his tall frame onto a plain wooden chair in front of the bare pine table. He faced Madeleine, whose red face showed over the rim of the tub.

"A shame on you, Master Germain!" Madame Barbette cried, outraged.

He chuckled and took a deep draught of ale. "No harm done! All I can see is her beet-colored face and a mop of limp curls."

"Oh! *Zut!*" Madeleine wanted to throw the soap bar in his face, but instead she pulled her head under water. As she emerged, water streamed down her face and she began soaping her head and rinsing it until the water grew milky, concealing her nudity.

"It looks very comfortable in there. Perhaps I should join you? My wound is rather stiff today—could use a soaking," Germain suggested with a wry smile.

"Don't even think it!" she exclaimed. "Thank God there is no room for you."

Unconcerned, he ate his breakfast. Flustered, Madame Barbette hovered at his side, arms akimbo, uneasy with his unconventional behavior.

She threw Madeleine a series of reproving glances as if she blamed her for his invasion of the domestic regions.

"I should punish you, Barbette, for filling Mademoiselle Poquelin's ears with much exaggerated tales of my life," Germain said. "She will have an advantage over me, because I know nothing about her."

Madame Barbette snorted in disgust. "She's a sensible girl. Never trust a man, I say. Especially when he wears a smirk like that on his face!" To emphasize her words, she stood over him and swung her skillet, looking like an angry Leghorn hen with her three chins trembling.

Germain gave Madeleine a mischievous glance, his eyes caressing her. His gaze kindled a spurt of excitement in her veins, and her heartbeat accelerated alarmingly. What was happening to her? She didn't dare to examine her feelings too closely.

The comte finished his breakfast, but made no move to leave the room. Contented, he stretched out his booted legs toward the fire. The dogs lined up along his legs, the *thump-thump* of their tails declaring their appreciation.

A few minutes later, Nicole stepped into that domestic picture, her arms laden with packages. Taken by surprise, she stopped, undecided, right inside the door. Her mouth fell open, and she blushed furiously.

"*Entrez*, Nicole, you ninny," Madame Barbette ordered irritably. "Just step over his legs. He won't bite you. He ought to take his legs elsewhere so that I can do my work." She wagged her fat finger at Germain. "You are an ogre, Monsieur Germain. And the poor Mademoiselle Poquelin; her water must be quite cold by now."

Nicole sent a frightened look in Madeleine's direction.

"It is, but I'm not getting out of the tub until *he* leaves." Madeleine glowered at him, but the only response she received was a lazy chuckle.

"I promise I won't look," he said.

"Ha! I wouldn't believe a word, mademoiselle. He's got the devil in him today," Madame Barbette said with a sniff.

Madeleine was beginning to feel cold in the tepid water. She shivered. With a note of desperation in her voice, she pleaded, "Monsieur le comte, if you leave us alone, I promise to clean your wound and bandage it."

Germain looked at her through half-closed eyelids. "Will the treatment include the . . . other things, too?" His voice was ever so soft.

"How dare you! *Non*, they won't be included. You ought to know better! Now, *leave!*"

Madeleine knew he was not going to stir a finger, but she rapidly devised a plan on how to get rid of him.

"Gaspard already dressed my wound," he drawled.

Madeleine said matter-of-factly, "*Bon*, then he's going to have to do it again."

Before he knew what hit him, Germain was dripping wet. With an angry curse bursting from his lips, he stood, overturning his chair, his curls plastered to his face.

Madeleine could not help laughing, and before long, the mirth of Madame Barbette and Nicole mingled with her own.

The dogs, their fur wet, crawled under the table. Tails limp, they stared at Madeleine with mournful eyes. She held onto the wooden dipper, once again filled to the brim with liquid ammunition.

"My poor floor!" Madame Barbette wailed to hide the fact that she was enjoying herself hugely.

Germain rapidly collected his wits. "You want war? You shall have war." His arm lashing out like a whip, he grabbed a bucket and poured the icy contents over Madeleine's head. She squealed, sputtered, and tried to knock the bucket from his grip. In return, he pushed and held her head under water until, between bouts of coughing, she begged to be released.

Spitting anger and soapy water, she glared at his laughing eyes—loving eyes. Her breath caught, and she squeezed her eyes shut and rubbed them as the soap stung. But in her mind she clearly saw the tenderness in his gaze.

When she looked up again, his eyes were not on her face but on the swell of her breasts discernible through the milky layer of soap. Her nipples stood erect and hard, and his eyes widened with interest. She closed up like a clam, pulling her knees to her chin.

Taking a good grip on his limp jabot, Madeleine dragged his face down until his glowing eyes were only inches from hers. "Get out!" she ordered.

He laughed all the way to his study at the other end of the house.

Chapter 10

"I knew nothing but trouble would come of this bath," Madame Barbette grumbled as she poured herself a glass of ale and fanned her perspiring brow. "A bath in the kitchen—bah!"

Madeleine dried herself and dressed in a clean shift, petticoats, and a dark blue corduroy skirt and bodice. A white shawl warmed her shoulders, and sturdy wool stockings kept her legs protected from the fangs of winter drafts. What a blessing to be warm, she thought. Yet her headache had worsened. She dried her hair in front of the fire while the lackeys emptied the tub and removed it from the kitchen.

One of them, Jerome, a huge man with awkward movements, returned to mop the wet floor.

Madame Barbette clucked as she helped braid Madeleine's hair and fastened it into a neat chignon on the back of her head, allowing soft curls to frame her face.

Madeleine pressed her fingertips to her temples. Her eyes were gritty, and her head was throbbing. In fact, she was miserable and longed to crawl back under the eiderdown and sleep. Even her hands had begun to shake.

"You look very pale, mademoiselle," Madame Barbette commented as she fastened the second comb. "Are you feeling ill?"

"*Oui*, I have a headache."

A look of compassion crept into Madame Barbette's eyes. "*Pauvre petite*, I know how it feels. But I have a remedy. I will brew a cup of herb tea. That should relax you."

As she filled a cup with boiling water, she muttered, "The thought of that dreadful Fouquet always gives me a headache. I don't understand how you can stand being, er, intimate with him."

Restless, Madeleine rose from her perch at the edge of the hearth. "I don't know what rumors you've heard, but they are false. Everything he says is a lie." A vertical line formed between her eyes as she said, "I loathe Monsieur Fouquet as much as you do."

Madame Barbette gave her a searching glance as she handed her the tea.

Madeleine's eyes lingered on the kitchen entrance. If only she could escape! Jerome's shadow was visible in the window. Too late!

"I need to speak to the comte," she said tiredly.

Madame Barbette's ferocious gaze softened. "I think he ought to thank you, Mademoiselle Poquelin."

"Why?"

"You put the smile back into his eyes. He has been very troubled lately." Madame Barbette patted Madeleine's shoulder. "You're always welcome in the kitchen, mademoiselle."

"Call me Madeleine."

"The master is in his study, but you'd better hurry because he'll be leaving for court any minute now."

Madeleine met Maurice in the front hall. He stared at her, his pale face set in lines of displeasure. He was guarding the front door—of course—so that she couldn't escape. Ignoring him, Madeleine knocked on the door to the study.

"Entrez!"

The sound of Germain's voice made her feel weak and vulnerable. Like a drug, the memory of his touch lingered in her blood.

He sat behind his desk in his shirt sleeves. The desk was littered with sheaves of paper and open ledgers.

"The sprite has turned into a serving maid," he commented dryly as she advanced toward the desk.

Madeleine looked slightly embarrassed. "Nobody will be searching for a kitchen maid."

"It would have pleased me to see you wear something frivolous from the armoire upstairs."

Madeleine shrugged. "I didn't come to discuss my wardrobe. I'm indebted to you; your timely intervention at the tavern saved my life. I cannot thank you enough. However . . ."

He leaned back in the high armchair and laughed softly. "I can think of a way to show your gratitude. But we have plenty of time; you are my prisoner until I get the word from Fouquet."

"*Oui*, Fouquet—always Fouquet. You are a puppet, monsieur le comte," Madeleine spat. "A coward." She drank more of Madame Barbette's headache cure, but it didn't seem to help. The pounding was intensifying, the pain pulsating from the base of her neck.

He studied her for a long moment, a silver gleam in the depths of his eyes. Madeleine's heart hammered, but she didn't avert her gaze.

"What were you planning to do today—if you were free to go?" he asked, sharpening a goose quill.

"I told you I need to see Amul. He may have the solution to my problem. I have to see the King, have to speak with him." Madeleine could have bitten off her tongue. Why was she going on about it when he didn't believe her? Her head was swimming, and the headache was growing unbearable. Her mind was a quagmire; she couldn't think clearly.

"Madeleine, how can you conceivably believe that you are strong enough to do battle with the pinnacles of the state? Forget the King, little fool. He will never listen to you." He rose, quickly advancing on her. Placing a finger under her chin, he tilted up her face. "You look sick, mademoiselle."

She jerked away from his grip. "I don't need your concern."

He pulled her up, and she didn't have the strength to fight him. Her eyes were level with his neck. His pulse beat rapidly in his throat, and a few tufts of golden hair peeped from the opening of his shirt, loosely held together with a ribbon at the neck. Her eyes wandered upward to fasten on his firm lips. An ironic twist marred the perfection of the wide curves.

An errant hair protruded from his mustache and Madeleine could not prevent herself from reaching up to smooth it down.

The next second found her in his arms. Her shawl fell to the floor as his hands wandered over her back and his tongue wildly sought the inviting, moist recesses of her mouth. Her lips throbbed sweetly under his onslaught, and his strong fingers squeezed her arms and shoulders with an intensity that almost frightened her.

"Desist . . . now." Her voice was a hoarse whisper as she reluctantly pulled away. Dizzy, she leaned against the desk and pressed the back of one hand to her forehead.

"You invited me," he drawled softly.

"I did not!"

"Whatever it was you were doing, I distinctly got the impression that you wanted a kiss—and a hug. Don't deny it." He pulled her into his arms once more, and as she was about to protest, he held two fingers to her trembling lips.

"Why don't you take me up on my offer, *ma belle?* As my mistress you may have anything." He towered over her. With one long finger he tilted her face and looked into her stormy eyes. His gaze glinted silver in the sharp morning light.

Mesmerized, Madeleine stared, drowning rapidly.

"I . . . cannot. Whatever you think, I'm not that kind of woman," she said in a dreamlike voice.

"Liar."

Her eyes followed his lips as he bent his face over hers. When his lips were upon hers, she felt as if all her nerve endings went out to meet him, springing vibrantly alive, afire. She melted into his arms, moaning against his lips. "I . . . cannot."

His hands cupped her buttocks and pressed her greedily against his hard manhood. "Madeleine, this is what you want." He undulated his hips, grinding himself boldly against her. "Let us go upstairs," he urged as he lifted his lips inches from hers.

"Never!" Her sanity returning, she pulled away. "How dare you!" She wanted to weep in frustration and anger. "You take advantage of me; I'm so confused," she whispered and staggered forward. The room tilted crazily, colors swirling behind her eyelids, and her ears roared.

"Amul," she whimpered as she crumpled in Germain's arms.

RECKLESS SPLENDOR 109

* * *

She was swimming through a hot red sea. Blue, green, yellow tentacles, long glutinous arms, reached out to catch her; they wrapped around her legs and pulled her deeper down, where the water was purple, thick, and ice cold. She fought for her life against the dark abyss below—gigantic black eyes, a cauldron of evil that waited to gobble her up. One of her feet disappeared in the blackness, then the leg. She was powerless. She screamed, and the darkness ate more of her. Long, bony fingers, every one belonging to Fouquet, dragged her ceaselessly, effortlessly down. And she could not stop him.

As the blackness poured into her mouth, she screamed again. Something warm tickled her throat, and she swallowed, finding that she wasn't choking to death. Now she seemed to be under clear water—pure, sweet water. Sunlight. Faces wavered above the water, but she couldn't speak. They didn't know she was there. Germain, trailing yellow weeds in the water. The fat man in the moon, folds upon folds of flesh wavering above her.

Germain tenderly cradled the feverish Madeleine in his arms as Madame Barbette spooned more lemon and barley water between her cracked lips. "There, I think she is on the mend. She had a terrible ague—must have become very chilled yesterday."

Germain relaxed, giving a long sigh of relief. Tenderly arranging the pillows behind Madeleine's head, he said, "I feared she would die."

Madame Barbette glanced toward him. "You would have been sad, very sad, if that had happened," she stated sagely and gathered her medicine bottles on a tray.

Germain averted his gaze and walked to the window. Arms crossed on his chest, he looked at the high, clear sky dotted with pink-edged clouds. *"Oui,"* he confessed, "I would have been sad. I have never known anyone like Mademoiselle Poquelin. She is all fire and determination."

Madame Barbette smiled knowingly at the broad back and sailed out of the room with her tray.

Germain returned to the bed where he had kept vigil for twenty-four hours. With a frown of worry, he smoothed back an unruly curl from Madeleine's sweaty brow. Her skin was hot, too hot, but not as burning as before. She looked peaceful, and so young. He wiped her face gingerly with a handkerchief, tracing every delicate feature, the shell-like ears, the small straight nose, the impetuous eyebrows, and the delicate, blue-veined eyelids. They flapped like tiny bird wings and revealed her deep eyes, unfocused as yet.

He held his breath and stepped back, watching as consciousness slowly crept back into her gaze. Her little face was vulnerable, innocent as a child's.

"Comte? Where am I?" she rasped and swallowed convulsively. "I ache everywhere."

"*Oui*, you have been ill, but are getting better by the hour," he explained kindly. Then he smiled. "You fainted in my arms as we argued; you wanted to leave."

"Amul?" she whispered.

"He has not been here." Germain sat down on the edge of the bed and took hold of her hot hand. "But Fouquet was here. You lied to him, didn't you? He was furious—wants your head now."

"You . . . you didn't betray my whereabouts?" she whispered, squeezing his hand in anxiety.

He shook his head. "I'm not a complete villain. I told him you had escaped." He gave her a lopsided smile. "Fouquet wanted *my* head then, but I managed to persuade him that it would be very foolish to soil his hands with my blood. I told him that we would visit Hades together if he tried."

"*Merci*," Madeleine whispered. "I'm more indebted to you. I wish you would tell me the . . . truth about you and Fouquet."

Germain averted his gaze and patted her hand. "I'm not sure I'd like to see your eyes turn away from me in loathing."

Madeleine gazed at him, her eyes wide and vulnerable. "Do you care about my opinions? That is a change." She smiled as she noticed the flush creeping above his collar.

"I do care," he said in a brisk voice to cover up his embarrassment. Rising, he started to pace back and forth, his thumbs hooked into the armholes of his vest. Then he stopped abruptly in the middle of the floor. "Ah, *diable*, I cannot tell you anything yet. Besides, you have Fouquet on

RECKLESS SPLENDOR 111

your brain—always talking about him as if you want him dead."

"Perhaps I do," Madeleine said coldly and turned on her side, presenting her back to him.

"Why? Because he dropped you for another woman?"

"Of course not!" she exclaimed. "The diary that Fouquet is so desperate to confiscate contains no romantic drivel, as he maintains. It contains something that could send him to the gibbet. Does that convince you that I have to speak with the King?" She peered at him over the edge of the eiderdown. "If you care, you should believe me—not him." She was so tired, and he kept pestering her like a gnat.

"I don't think it is that simple. I haven't seen the diary. It is your word against Fouquet's, and he is the minister of finance, the superintendent of France. You are a seamstress, so what is the connection between you, if it isn't amorous?"

Madeleine sighed. She would have to tell him everything. "My father was a state official, just like Fouquet—if not that exalted. He was a tax collector all his life in Rouen. Each official has to send in a report every month from the different provinces. And who is the manager of all the taxes of France? Fouquet." She smiled weakly. "So you see, the connection is far from romantic."

Germain's brow was furrowed in concentration. She quieted for a moment to regain her strength and her rapidly crumbling composure.

"I loved Father so." She fumbled for a handkerchief, and Germain gave her his. She blew her nose noisily. "He knew how to love people, always lending an ear to their grievances. Most of the peasants are extremely poor. It wasn't Father's fault that they were so heavily taxed."

She took a deep breath and twisted her handkerchief into a tiny ball. "We had little if no contact with the nobility of Normandy, but when things started to go wrong with the house of the Beaumonts, my father was alerted."

Catching her breath, she continued. "It all began when they did not pay their taxes. It had never happened before. Naturally Father had to report it to Fouquet. We never believed other than that the Beaumonts were fabulously wealthy. Then one day Fouquet arrived. I never spoke with him, but he was closeted with Father for several hours, and after that, my father was never the same. I don't know what transpired exactly, but I know that Fouquet forgot a diary on my father's desk. It contained records of several monetary transactions from the treasury to the Beaumonts—a loan with an interest charge of seventy percent. I know after reading the diary that Fouquet pocketed the interest money himself. My father carefully listed every sou the Beaumonts paid. The treasury did not see half of that money.

"Father wrote down in the same diary every sliver of evidence that Fouquet was embezzling funds. Keeping his ears open, Father came across some other transactions with a few families of minor nobility in our province. The diary lists many powerful names in the country, and Fouquet has painstakingly written down how much he lent them, and how much interest they paid to him. He is nothing but a lowly moneylender, using state funds for his own underhanded transactions."

Madeleine's voice was fading with the effort of talking about the painful subject. She had kept the sorrow inside her for such a long time.

Germain flung himself into an armchair, lit a cheroot, and watched the smoke curling toward the ceiling.

Madeleine continued. "I'm sure Fouquet demanded his diary back, but Father denied having seen it. I know because I saw a couple of letters concerning this business."

Madeleine propped herself on one elbow and stared at Germain, her eyes burning with fever and distress. "I was very worried. I had no idea that the diary was that important. Father changed so much after that meeting with Fouquet. It was as if everything he had believed in all his life was crumbling around him."

She collapsed against the pillows, and Germain threw the cheroot into the fireplace and joined her on the bed. As he caressed her hair, she was grateful for his presence. In sharing the secret, she felt that a great burden had fallen from her shoulders. He did not comment, only waited until she was strong enough to continue.

"I knew things were becoming really bad when Dubois moved in. Father was lying when he told me that Dubois might be a prospective bridegroom for me. He only said that to conceal Dubois's real business. I loathed the man! He is a murderer." She swallowed to control a wave of tears.

"The tension at home was insufferable. Father was turning into a shadow of himself; he stopped smiling entirely. Then it happened. I heard a terrible row in Father's study. I watched Dubois stab my father to death. There was nothing I could do; Father died in my arms." Madeleine clenched her hands and bit her trembling bottom lip. Germain took hold of her hands.

"The diary?" he asked softly.

"Father asked me to deliver the diary to the King, and I will do it, if it is the last thing I ever do!"

"Where did you hide it?"

Madeleine's eyes narrowed, and silence hung between them for a long, tense moment. "I won't tell you that. I won't take the risk of your going straight to Fouquet with that information."

Germain rubbed his mustache. "It is the most preposterous story I've ever heard—but I believe you. I am going to help you."

Madeleine leaned forward, brightening. "Really?"

"Oui. The King will be pleased to be forewarned. I think he has suspected that not all is well with Fouquet, that the minister is too greedy for power. But it is hard to believe that he is such a villain. Fouquet is a truly brilliant man."

"Peut-être he would like to shine brighter than the King." She gave a watery smile.

Germain chuckled. "There is never a dull moment with you, Madeleine. I will have a word with the King."

"Merci. I only wish you would confide in me as I have confided in you. You used my weakness to force my confession." Her face clouded over. "I hope I haven't made the mistake of my life—since your name is in the diary as well."

Germain stood, his lips a determined line. Then he stalked to the door.

"Where are you going?" Madeleine asked, alarmed.

"To Fouquet."

Chapter 11

Madeleine tossed and turned. How could she have been so stupid as to confide the whole to Germain! He was going to Fouquet. Then Fouquet would come and force her to reveal the hiding place and after that . . . kill her?

A gray mist began to swirl at the perimeters of her vision, and she felt so ill. Her head pounded. She wanted to cry, but it was too painful.

Amul. Where was he?

She must have fallen into a fitful sleep, because when she awakened, Madame Barbette was leaning over the bed, placing something cool on her brow.

"There, *petite fille*. Feeling better?"

Madeleine jerked upright. "The comte. Where is the comte?"

Madame Barbette patted her hand. "Don't worry, he'll be back. He left the house yesterday in a hurry. Went to court, I'm sure." She placed a napkin around Madeleine's neck and fluffed up the pillows. "Now you should eat some breakfast so you get your strength back."

Madeleine swallowed and viewed the food with dislike. "I am not hungry, but I feel a lot better. My headache is gone, and I don't ache all over."

"Bien!" You'll be on your feet in no time. You have slept for fifteen hours straight. You have to eat, mademoiselle."

Madeleine shrugged and sipped the hot cocoa. It tasted good, inspiring her to nibble at the fragrant, steaming ham omelet. "You are an excellent cook, Madame Barbette."

"And you are a good patient." She winked. "If a little impatient. Already longing for Master Germain, eh?" She clapped a plump hand to her bosom. "Ah, to be young again, and in love!"

Madeleine's mouth dropped open. "In love? Who is in love?"

Madame Barbette snorted. "You are, and Master Germain, *naturellement*."

"Nonsense!" But Madeleine's cheeks turned pink, and she couldn't meet Madame Barbette's knowing gaze.

The rest of the day she pondered that idea, and knew in her heart that the fat cook was right. She also mulled over the rest of her breakfast conversation with Madame Barbette.

She had asked the cook about Germain and if she knew why he had befriended Fouquet.

"*Enfin!* Master Germain knows everyone at court," she had responded, and at Madeleine's question if Germain owed Fouquet money, she had flung up her arms and scoffed. "*Non!* I don't believe that."

"But Fouquet has some hold on the comte. He forces him to do—well, evil things."

The cook had laughed. "Evil things? Bah! Besides, *mon petit* Germain is the kindest, the most loyal, the most thoughtful man I know. He doesn't do 'evil' things, mademoiselle."

Those words were etched in Madeleine's memory, and she found herself fervently hoping that Madame Barbette was right. She had to speak with the comte—force him to tell her the truth. Tonight she would ask him. She also dared to acknowledge that she longed for his arms, his warm lips. She would taste them again, and more—tonight. Then she would escape. Tomorrow she would find Amul.

As the day turned into night, she heard laughter and voices floating up the stairs from the vestibule far below.

Madame Barbette stuck her face around the door and said, "Monsieur Germain has company tonight, but I will have Jerome bring your dinner on a tray."

Madeleine glimpsed the stalwart fellow guarding her door, and her face fell. How would she get beyond that door now?

Though still feeling weak, she dressed and paced the floor. She was admiring a chubby cherub covered in gold leaf on the marble mantelpiece when Germain stepped into the room. Trembling, she turned to face him. Her heart seemed to have become lodged in her throat. Her rapid pulse and Germain's presence were the only things on her mind.

He looked so handsome in an ice-blue satin jacket edged with silver braid and lace at the neck and wrists. His face bore a distant cool expression.

For once, her fighting spirit was gone. She only wanted some human warmth, some comfort.

"*Mon Dieu*, you are out of bed! Feeling better?" he asked, and sat down on the edge of a desk, his satin-encased leg dangling carelessly. "Would you like some mulled wine? I'll send Jerome for a tankard."

"I don't care. Tell me, did you go to Fouquet and tell him all my confidences? Is he perhaps downstairs this very moment waiting to abuse me?"

He chuckled, a low seductive sound that sent rills of breathless delight along her spine. He sauntered toward the spot where she stood, his face alive in the orange light of the fire. His eyes shone dark and mercurial. "Suspicious to the last. I told him I had seen neither hide nor hair of you."

She had a wild urge to throw herself headlong into his arms, to cover his face with tiny kisses, to let her fingers play along the silky curls rippling over his shoulders.

There were two steps separating them, then one step, and then she was crushed to his chest. Instinctively, she lifted her face to his in eager longing, and her lips were captured by his warm ones, tasting of wine and spice. Her thoughts fled.

She forgot their differences, forgot the huge gap between their stations, forgot Fouquet and Amul, and drank deeply from his passion. Her shawl fell from her shoulders, and he loosened her bodice to let his palms roam over her back. Her thin shift slid erotically under his fingers, and she clung to him for more warmth, more contact. Inside was a large, empty hole that desperately needed to be filled with light and love.

"You're freezing," he murmured. "I will instruct Madame Barbette to place a hot brick in your bed." If he had planned to say more, he was effectively stopped by her lips pressing on his, her tongue boldly seeking his.

RECKLESS SPLENDOR 117

Germain was dizzy with the impact of her fiery kisses. His loins burned with desperate longing. No woman before her had ever ignited his passion to such a fever pitch. Madeleine's presence in his house, the memory of her kisses, had increased the pressure for release. And now, with her in his arms, it was clear that he wanted nothing more. Madeleine, the clinging, sweet, elusive, temperamental, but oh so erotic sprite in his arms. Her breasts pressed blatantly to his chest, separated by more layers of corduroy and silk. He wanted to take her right there, to raise her skirts and . . . and . . .

His sexual daze was pierced by her husky voice.

"Do you remember the first time we met, at Versailles?"

He nodded.

"You asked if I wanted to become your . . . mistress."

The last word hung breathlessly in the air. He stood rooted to the floor, not daring to move lest she disappear. He cupped her neck, her silky hair tickling the back of his hand, and looked deeply into the bottomless pools of her eyes, reading her sincerity as she said, "I was afraid of you—afraid of the feelings you ignited inside me. I still am, but . . ."

"We have all the time in the world," he assured her, when all he wanted was to lay her on the bed.

"*Oui.*" She was pale, but two bright scarlet spots flamed on her cheekbones.

"Madeleine, I want you more than I have ever wanted another woman," he responded frankly. "Here. Feel this." To see if she dared to touch him, he took her hand and placed it on the bulging ridge of his manhood.

To his amusement, a wave of color suffused her face, but she staunchly let her hand rest cautiously on him. He sensed a tender sweetness in his heart, spreading warmth throughout his body.

If he did not stop now, he knew he would take her right then and there. Easy, easy, he chastised himself. *Sacre bleu!* He didn't want to frighten her away, now that he was so close. He traced his fingertips along her nose. "I have to return to my dinner guests."

Madeleine turned away from him. Her back looked so fragile, so insecure. He decided it was best to leave her to sort out her feelings. Planting a light kiss on the top of her head, he walked swiftly to the door.

"Wait!" she cried. As he raised an eyebrow, she continued, "Am I free to leave the house now?"

"You are free to go whenever you want." He didn't show her the deep sense of defeat welling up inside him. *She will leave now. I have lost her.*

She smiled gratefully, and he stepped outside. Stopping for a few moments in the hallway, he steadied his boiling emotions, but gained little ease.

Germain and his guests were playing vingt-et-un, and he was a steady winner. The streak of bad luck that had followed him for some time appeared to have disappeared at last. But his mind was not on the play. He did not care whether he won or lost. Madeleine hovered constantly in his thoughts. Finally, he hid a yawn behind the lace cuff of his shirt.

"It is clear that our host is bored with his company!" the prince de Condé bellowed. Fastening his hawklike gaze on Germain, he said, "Have you perhaps some other, more tempting pastime in mind?"

Germain was stung by the truth of those words. *"Mais, non!* I'm excessively rude. Nothing pleases me more than your brilliant company," he lied glibly.

"Your turn," the comtesse de Durenne said brightly. To emphasize her words, she placed her hand over his and squeezed his fingers. She had let him know all during the evening that she would gladly welcome his advances. She leaned forward to give him an opportunity to look down her cleavage. But after his encounter with Madeleine, La Durenne's charms held no interest, even though she was a lovely, sensuous woman.

Dawn was not far away when the assembly finally broke up. La Durenne hung back when the others left. Germain offered her a glass of brandy and then hinted her away.

"Au revoir, mon cher, there will be another time," she said and batted her eyelids. He accompanied her into the hallway, and she placed her crimson lips over his and sucked greedily. "Mmm, my rivals at court say you're the best—the very best lover. How will I sleep tonight?"

RECKLESS SPLENDOR 119

Highborn whore, Germain thought, glad that he had been saved from an exhausting night with her.

Her carriage already waited in front of the door. As she turned to walk through the door, she halted, remaining perfectly still. Germain followed her gaze to see what had caught her interest. Madeleine stood on the stairs, dressed in a loose velvet *coutouche* from the wardrobe in the guest room.

Diable! he thought. Very soon, *everybody* would know that she was here. Fouquet would find out.

La Durenne turned malicious, triumphant eyes on Germain. "Shocking!" she breathed.

Madeleine remained motionless. *Mon Dieu!* She had thought that everyone was gone. For some time the house had been quiet, and she had taken for granted that the party was over. Unable to sleep, she had stepped downstairs for a glass of water.

She felt the impact of the other woman's flashing gaze, burning with envy. When she had seen the woman press her lips to Germain's, Madeleine had tasted the bitter bile of jealousy for the first time.

Germain kissed La Durenne's hand and saw her out to the carriage.

A wave of wrath preceded him as he stalked up to Madeleine, two steps at a time. "How foolish of you to venture downstairs," he snapped. "What are you doing? Leaving?"

"I was thirsty."

"You could have summoned a maid." When he noticed tears beginning to fill her eyes, he relented. "I should not scold you, but it's better for your own sake if nobody knows your whereabouts."

"You're right. I behaved thoughtlessly." She turned and ran up the stairs.

Germain sighed and went into his study. Things were getting too emotional for his taste. Sloshing some brandy into a snifter, he stared broodingly into the fire. Life had become too damned complicated since Madeleine had entered his life! Remembering her soft lips, her delicious hair, made him want to rush up the stairs and storm into her room, throw her down on the bed, and make wild love to her, to spend all his pent-up longing inside her. His heart beat rapidly at the thought. But no, he would be a fool to give in to the urge. He didn't want to be in love. He smiled grimly. As it was, he was already up to his neck in trouble. With her beguiling smile, Madeleine had wormed her way under his skin.

Slapping the snifter roughly on a table, almost breaking its base, he stormed out of the room.

Pale moonlight washed the walls of his bedchamber, penetrating the secret shadows of his canopied bed. He needed no light to undress. Sliding naked between cool lavender-scented silk sheets, he grasped one of the long, fluffy down pillows and held it along his chest, pretending it was Madeleine's soft body. He wanted desperately to run the length of the corridor to her room, yet a thin thread of sanity still clung to him. If he took her to his bed, he would be a lost man, a prisoner of love.

He tossed and turned, cursing out loud. Sleep refused to touch him with its magic peace, and his frustration chased it still further away.

Folding his hands under his head, he stared at the dark circle of the canopy over his head. Silver light made patterns on the dark surface as the wind outside tossed the spidery tree branches back and forth.

Dissatisfaction drove him wild. With a growl, he propped himself on one elbow to light the candle in its holder by the bedside. The pale golden circle cast shadows around the bed. He would read the letter from his bailiff at Les Étoiles.

Tossing off the down cover, he jumped out of bed and helped himself to more brandy from a crystal decanter. He downed a good measure, and while appreciating the warm flow seeping through him, he heard a soft *click* behind him. Someone was at the door. Turning, he saw the dark gap fill with a slender form in a white shift. Madeleine glided toward him like a soft apparition.

Moonbeams caught the blond hair cascading to her waist. She stopped a few steps from him, her eyes huge pools in her thin face.

He remembered that he was naked, and that he stood in full relief in the moonlight, yet he made no move to shield himself from her eyes.

He sensed her womanly need; it echoed inside him, and his heart began to pound heavily. An intense, sweet pull in his loins made his manhood harden. He noticed her gaze fall to that impudent member of his body. Germain chuckled in delight. He could clearly picture her blushing cheeks, but moonlight washed away all the color.

"Have I guessed the reason why you're here?" he asked softly.

She nodded wordlessly, and a wild joy flooded him, making him curiously weak. He opened his arms, and she walked into his embrace. Her silk shift whispered against him like thistledown, and she felt wonderfully warm and tantalizing in his arms.

"Are you sure?" His words were a mere breath in her hair.

"*Oui* . . . I'm sure. Show me how." Her breath wafted over his skin. "Show me how a man loves . . . a woman."

Germain thought he was dreaming. "Am I really your first lover?"

She nodded. He did not know how much courage it had cost her to step into his arms. Yes, she wanted him. Her body screamed for his caresses, and between her thighs a throbbing ache begged to be relieved. She knew that Germain could give her that relief. To touch his naked skin was a sweet shock to her senses, a breath-stopping delight. She let her fingertips glide over the rippling expanse of his muscled back.

Instinctively she tilted her face toward his. When his brandy-flavored lips caught hers in a ravenous kiss, she wanted it to go on forever.

Never had she experienced anything so exquisite. His tongue played over the soft flesh inside her lips, and she gripped the springy waves of his hair, loving every sensation. Pleasure made her bold. She had never been close to a naked man before, but nakedness was not a mystery. She was the mystery. The touch of his hard manhood against her silk-clad belly evoked feelings that were entirely new to her. His wiry hair rasped against the silk, tickling her tender flesh. Desire spiraled through her and formed a swollen knot between her legs, an uncharted area, a place for new discoveries, a thrilling promise. She became eager to taste the full delight promised in that desire.

"Germain, show me," she whispered urgently, clinging to his broad shoulders.

"Do you really want—"

She put two fingers to his lips to silence him.

Through her thin silk shift, her hard nipples pressed into his chest, driving him savage with ardor. He knew he had to go carefully with her—if he could hold back. At the moment he felt ready to explode.

Slowly he pulled up the shift and eased it over her head. It fell in a whisper to the floor.

He thought he was going to ravish her right then, her beautiful body fully revealed to his hungry eyes. He steadied himself by taking several deep breaths.

Closing his eyes, he encircled her waist and pressed her to him. His other hand slid over her stomach, palm down, reaching silky curls. His fingers found warm, wet flesh, and he heard her gasp in surprise. One finger slid back and forth with ease, and with each stroke she quivered in his arms. Her pleasure flowed like honey into him, arousing him further, making his loins grow more taut and more urgent. She was hot and responsive to his every movement. Her flesh swelled and throbbed under his fingertips. He tingled all over as if magic dust had fallen on every pore of his skin. His nostrils were filled with the heady scent of her arousal.

She moaned when he slipped one of his fingers deep into her. He held his breath at the luscious, soft feel of her.

He lifted her into his arms as easily as if she were a feather and carried her to his bed. Placing her gingerly on the ivory silk, he sank down onto the mattress next to her, holding her against the length of his body.

Her breath came in fiery gasps on his throat, and his hair fell thickly over her as he bent his head to catch her kiss-swollen lips between his own. She began to move against him, instinctively thrusting her hips toward him.

Denying his own frenzied craving, he made a trail of tight kisses between her breasts to her belly. Although hankering to taste her arousal, he let his lips travel back up along one side of her body. He sucked greedily at one enlarged nipple, and she writhed under him as he covered her with his body.

"*Mon cher* . . ." she whispered against his lips.

The undoing of his control came when she shyly encircled his hard shaft. He had to take her. In wonder, he noticed that she was trembling and ready, her legs spread wide in welcome.

Their hair tangled together, shadowing her face from his eyes as he moved over her, between her legs. Her breath coming in hot gasps against his throat, she urged him on.

Grasping her round buttocks in a hard grip, he placed himself against her wetness. Flesh touching flesh. A slow, sweet penetration. He heard her gasp and held off, even though stars had begun to swirl in his head. He waited until she urged him on with a whimper. He was so big, and afraid that he might hurt her, but she forced him deliciously all the way to the very center of her being, while a moan flowed from her lips. He saw her surprised, darkened eyes stare up at him.

"The first pain will pass, I promise," he muttered. "Let me . . . pleasure you, let me show you . . . heaven," he muttered in her ear, caressing her face until she relaxed completely. Her silky wetness enfolded him like ambrosia, and he could barely breathe. A groan surged over his lips. He lay still, bending his head to her breasts, laving, teasing, nibbling, biting until she sobbed with pleasure under him.

Perspiration trickled from his brow into her hair. Moonlight bathed her pale limbs with silver. He savored the moment infinitely, tremors of wild rapture coursing through him, amplifying with every breath.

To watch her face grow more sensuous after each deep, heavy thrust was a revelation. Somewhere in his brain he registered that there was no calculation, no greed on her face, only innocence and mounting ecstasy.

She convulsed around him; she cried out. The heat and fire of his own longing exploded in her, the glory of his ecstasy brighter than the sun.

Still filling her, he felt another frenzied peak course through her as he watched every nuance of rapture cross her face.

As she lay limp and sated in his arms, he covered her face and neck with tender kisses. Curling her arms around his neck, she pressed closer. "Ohhh, *mon cher,* you didn't lie. It was sheer heaven."

Chapter 12

Madeleine opened her eyes, not knowing where she was though she felt warm and suffused with well-being.

Not able to recall one other time in her life when she had been so happy, she turned her head, afraid to move lest the contentment should evaporate.

A thick curtain of wheat-blond curls covered her bosom, and she instantly remembered the previous night. Next to her head on the pillow, Germain's face rested peacefully. He was sleeping heavily, one arm thrown across her middle and the other tucked under his head.

He did not move as she leaned over him and placed a light kiss on his lips. She flinched. The soreness between her legs was ample proof of the ardor they had shared.

She had shamelessly given herself to this man. Never again would she be an innocent girl; she had passed over the threshold to womanhood. She had become the mistress of a nobleman. She had never dreamed of doing anything so wanton. Her dream of marriage and children would never come true with Germain. He was a comte, and she was a nobody. She had accepted that. Yet she had followed her heart; yes, she loved Germain and feared she would always love him. This kind of situation could not last. Mistresses were temporary; wives were for life.

Amazed that she did not feel any shame, only blissful satisfaction, she burrowed closer to Germain. Reveling in his nearness, she wanted to stay there forever.

Then reality burst upon them with a crash of the door. With a start, she sat up, pulling the covers over her nakedness.

Over the edge of the mattress peeped two pairs of peppercorn eyes. Two plumes of gray tails wagged in unison.

Germain lifted a sleepy head from the pillow. "*Zut*, Ariel! Claudine! . . . Close the door!"

To Madeleine's surprise the dogs trotted to the door and pushed it closed with their noses.

"They do this every morning," Germain explained, a glint of laughter in his eyes as he studied her sleepily. "Madeleine, come here." He held out his arms, and she nestled close to him, her chest pressed to his. The blond stubble on his cheeks grazed her tender skin.

"Full of regrets today, eh?" he murmured.

She hesitated for a moment. "*Non*, I don't regret anything."

"You're wrinkling your brow, *ma belle*. Problems?"

"Oh . . . nothing. Just a bit sore."

Twin sighs surged from the invisible dogs beneath the bed.

"My kisses will make you forget," he muttered and pulled her face down to his. "Don't doubt your feelings." The sweet, demanding touch of his lips sent spurts of pleasure through her veins, and she responded by sagging against him. Was this the foreplay to another swooning experience of ecstasy like the one she had tasted on the previous night? She now knew the secret her body held. Never in her life had she believed it possible to feel such rapture. And she didn't need a wedding ring to savor it.

The delight began to repeat itself as his hands moved down her spine to her round buttocks.

"Still having problems?" he drawled, letting his hand slide over the silken mound between her thighs until she gasped.

"Oh . . . *cher* Germain," was all she could whisper. She wanted him madly.

His hands slid over her until they came to rest on both sides of her head, pinning her face until she had to look into his eyes. A haze of desire lay in their smoky-gray depths, and Madeleine wanted to melt, to drown into him.

His voice came with great effort. "Now that you are my mistress, what is the payment going to be? Is this enough for this time?" Leaning over her, he pulled out a drawer in the bedstand and produced a black velvet case. When he opened it, pale yellow satin gleamed, and nestled in the folds were double strands of magnificent pearls. He placed them between her breasts, where they shone with divine luster against her pale skin.

With a thud, she plummeted from her euphoria. She had not expected this development. Anger welled through her, and she flung the pearls across the room. "How dare you insult me!"

Looking shocked, he stiffened. Wanting to strangle him, Madeleine sat up in bed, crawled away from him, and crossed her arms over her breasts.

Germain rose without a sound. Sauntering over, he bent and picked up the necklace. He did not bother to cover himself, and Madeleine could not help but stare at the beautifully proportioned man who looked so daunting and arrogant in the sober morning light, the honed muscles, the tapering waist, the hard, round buttocks, the—

Madeleine blushed, drawing her breath in sharply. Noticing her embarrassment, Germain laughed and sat down on the edge of the bed.

"I only wanted to give you a taste of what is going to come. You satisfied me deeply." He held the necklace toward her. "Look, aren't they lovely?"

"I'd like to kill you!" She crouched like a small fury in bed. "Is that all I am to you, a piece of merchandise to be paid for with expensive trinkets?"

"I thought you wanted to know the size of your reward," he answered dryly. "There was a frown on your forehead, you know. I'm only eager to show my appreciation."

What was wrong with her? he thought. He had only wanted to assure her that, as his mistress, she would not lack any of the luxuries of life. Had he been too blunt?

Disappointment drowned her and killed any hope that he felt true love for her. How could she have been so blind! So foolish, so ignorant! Love only existed in girls' dreams! Reality was always something else. Angry with herself, she wanted to lash out at him.

"All I want is an audience with the King." The words cut the stillness like shards of glass. "That is my price."

As if sensing the icy tension in the room, the dogs whimpered under the bed.

Madeleine shivered. Germain's voice turned frosty. "That I cannot promise you. Yet." With an impatient glance, he strode into his dressing room, calling to Gaspard, who slept in a small adjoining room. *"Enfin! Les femmes!"* he muttered angrily.

Madeleine wanted to lie down and die, such was her humiliation. She had only herself to blame. Her weakened state was at fault. She had fallen around Germain's neck like a lovesick monkey.

Pulling on her shift and winding a sheet around her, she fled to her room to indulge in a bout of crying, ignoring the fact that self-pity would not help. She wanted only to hide away from the world.

Night fell over Paris. The bells tolled for vespers. The stars emerged one after the other like diamonds on a black velvet cloth. Moonbeams silvered the roofs and the trees. Night turned the ugliness of the city into a fairyland.

Madeleine stood by the window looking toward Notre Dame. All day she had stayed in her room, brooding. She was empty, with no more tears to shed.

Every time the door slammed downstairs, her heart began to beat faster, but Germain had not returned to her. She went to sit on the floor in front of the fireplace, her wide petticoats spread out around her on the bearskin.

All day she had tried to convince herself to leave, but she had nowhere to go. She felt like a trapped animal, afraid of seeing Germain again. Was he going to order her out of his house, or was he going to take her into his arms? She couldn't leave until she had spoken with him. She wanted to be in his arms. He had awakened something in her, a deep powerful well in the core of her being, and he was the only one who could tap it. That realization nagged at her like a bittersweet pain. But she was proud as well, and hated herself for succumbing to his charms. To him she was just a mistress whom he could drop at will. She doubted he was even capable of loving deeply. A groan of helplessness rose in her throat.

RECKLESS SPLENDOR 129

The next moment the door flew open and there he stood, splendid in a golden coat over a white batiste shirt. Danger gleamed in his eyes, and they stared at each other for a long moment. Her heart did somersaults in her chest, and her breath grew ragged.

Three long steps bore him to her side, and taking her shoulders in a firm grip, he lifted her to her feet while she held her breath in nervous anticipation.

A charged current of emotion quivered between them.

"You're back," she whispered.

"Did you miss me?"

She wanted to scream *oui*, but she shook her head in sullen resistance.

"What did you expect? That I would not return to my own house . . . and you?" Deliberately he mocked her while his hot gaze challenged her. "I was afraid you had gone."

Madeleine pulled her hands through his long curls while he traced the delicate contours of her face.

"Are we friends?" he asked softly.

She nodded, too overcome with emotion to say anything. They stood entwined until the fire needed replenishing. Cold drafts curled along the floor. Germain added more wood to the embers, and soon the fire crackled merrily. Madeleine sat in an armchair, her feet tucked under her.

From a pitcher, Germain poured two tankards of spiced wine. He handed her one and wondered how long the peace would last when he confronted her, which he had to do. He had to make her talk about her father and the diary.

"Madeleine, I spoke with the King today. I told him about you and your . . . mission. He was intrigued, but before he sees you, he wants to read your petitions. Then he will give you an audience."

"I only hope he will believe me. You do, don't you?"

Suddenly she needed his reaffirmation.

He chuckled. "I believe you. The stained sheets proved that you've never been Fouquet's mistress—other than in his dreams." He sighed. "I would like to get my hands on that diary."

Her stomach turned into a knot. "I will give it to the King—only to the King."

"Naturellement. He will reward you handsomely."

"Thank you for talking to the King." Her forehead furrowed. "I admire your strength. Fouquet could destroy you for helping me."

"I have to humor my, er, mistress," he returned lightly, a smile lurking in his eyes. "Come sit on my knees." He beckoned her with outstretched arms, and she leaned gratefully against his chest, his strong arms cradling her in a cocoon of warmth.

"You never told me why your father's murder was covered up," Germain said.

"I thought you knew all about his death."

"I never realized that Dubois killed him. Fouquet told me about you and said that your father had been murdered. I cannot believe it! Lemont's valet! Lemont must be involved with Fouquet if his valet is. There is a mystery here."

Madeleine sighed. "When the neighbors, attracted by the sound of the fight, stormed into the house, Dubois was already gone. Nobody believed that the high official from Paris—presumably from the treasury—could have done such a dastardly deed. They maintained that I was overwrought, that some thief from the street had killed my father."

She clenched her hands. Germain hugged her tenderly.

"Your family here wasn't notified?"

"Oui. Fouquet took care of that. He made sure they heard the thief version of my father's death. If I had insisted on the truth, who would have believed me? Who would have believed a grieving, half-crazed daughter claiming that the minister of finance was behind her father's death? Tell me!"

He shook his head, and she continued. "I could never bring up the true cause of Father's death to Grandfather. He would have died with grief."

Germain tapped the armrest with his fingertips. "You are carrying a heavy secret." He thought for a moment. "Why did your father not approach the King himself?"

"I think he wanted to have enough evidence to present, so that there could be no doubt of Fouquet's guilt."

"You have a point there."

"Fouquet must have thought that I didn't know about the diary, because he never contacted me. Fouquet was only alerted when I began petitioning the King."

"You did well to be suspicious. You don't know who your enemies are in a case like this."

She caressed Germain's ear and whispered, "I would never have succeeded in contacting the King on my own. I know that now, but I *knew* you would help me—sooner or later. With you by my side, Fouquet doesn't stand a chance, *n'est-ce pas?*"

He smiled crookedly. "Ever the optimist! I wish Fouquet could have been stopped before he destroyed your father and your life in the process. Now, let's compose another petition for Louis. I'll hand him this one myself."

Madeleine sighed. "The King is nothing if not thorough, and so slow! Petitions, bah!" But she obediently collected paper and sharpened a quill.

At an elegant *hôtel* in the heart of Paris, the comtesse de Durenne addressed the man whose black hair was the only thing visible over the high back of the armchair.

"Nicolas, I know where the woman you're looking for is hiding. She's at *hôtel* Belleforière." The last words were spoken in anger.

Fouquet rose and turned to La Durenne. He seemed gaunter, dressed in a black silk coat and culottes. Against the paleness of his face his eyes burned black with an inner intensity. His full-bottomed wig curled to his shoulders. He was holding a black cat in his arms, its yellow eyes slits of contentment.

"Belleforière? *Vraiment?* Germain lied to me then, and my contact in that household did not speak up."

"Perhaps he didn't know."

"I have a very reliable contact in that house."

"As in so many others," La Durenne echoed maliciously.

He strolled across the precious carpet and, looking deeply into her eyes, bent down and pressed a kiss on her crimson lips. "I'm pleased with you, even though your tongue is as acid as ever," he murmured. "Will a diamond bracelet suffice?"

She nodded.

"Do I detect a disturbance in your eyes? A streak of anger, perhaps? Could it be that you wish you were in Mademoiselle Poquelin's position? I know you have been burning for the comte de Hautefort's attention. Is he cold toward you?" His tone mocked her, but a shadow of envy crossed his face. La Durenne noticed it, and she taunted him, even though he had been her lover and still was upon occasion.

She pouted and searched for the right words. "Hautefort has a certain . . . finesse which you don't have. He's handsome, has a very virile body, and a well-filled purse." She clapped her hands to her heart in a theatrical gesture, emphasizing her words.

Fouquet laughed evilly. "Do you know why all of you hens flock to him? Because none of you has been able to snare him."

La Durenne glared at him. He was right, of course, but that did not give him the right to point it out.

"Comte de Hautefort is much more of a man than you'll ever be!"

With satisfaction she witnessed something very nasty creep into his expression. She was going to have her revenge on Hautefort for scorning her yet. He didn't know what he had missed when he turned her down.

Chapter 13

Wrapped in a thick, fur-lined cloak, Germain rode across Paris toward the palace of Saint-Germain where the court was assembled this bright morning.

Sunlight flashed over the snow, making him squint. For the first time in weeks, a waft of sweetness flowed in the air, a faint promise of spring. The sun did not look like a pale lemon any longer; it more closely resembled a large orange. Germain breathed deeply of the fresh air as he rode away from the heart of the city.

He could not deny that nerves fluttered in his stomach. Madeleine was an experience of wonder, like a new awakening of life, something he had not felt since he was a boy on the verge of manhood. It was hard to admit that he had never felt such intense pleasure when bedding other women. After all, he was a ripe thirty years of age. It was unbelievable that a mere slip of a girl, an innocent virgin, could have given him such scorching pleasure.

She acted as if she truly loved him. His brain barely dared to brush by the word. It was one he did not like to include in his vocabulary. She was making him weak, vulnerable. She flowed like poison in his blood. And now he was involved up to his neck in her problems. Who would ever believe that a young girl from the provinces was fighting to bring justice to the minister of finance? Germain laughed out loud, a gritty sound.

Grimly he pressed his lips together into a thin line. His horse Apollo snorted in protest when he pulled the reins too hard. Sharing Madeleine's secret made him responsible for seeing the mission through to a satisfactory end. Fouquet would turn against him and set his threat in motion; the minister would approach Brigitte Delchamps's jealous husband and tell him the truth. *Diable!* Could he afford to make Fouquet a deadly enemy? He wanted to protect Brigitte at all cost, but he also wanted to help Madeleine. If the diary could spell Fouquet's downfall, then the King should have it at the first available moment. By helping Madeleine, he was doing France a favor, and by God, he had to put France's safety before Brigitte's humiliation. There wasn't a perfect solution. He clenched his jaws in frustration.

"Apollo, *mon vieux*, what do you say if we just ride on home to Brittany and leave all this behind?"

It was one thing he could not do, although he was very tempted.

The Belleforières could trace their ancestors back to the Crusades. Being of such old and proud lineage, Germain was an obvious member of the inner circles at court. It was unthinkable that he would not serve the young King, as his father had served the old King, and with most illustrious glory.

All his life, Germain had known King Louis. He had been at his side fighting the civil war of the Fronde; he had been at the magnificent coronation and at the wedding between Louis and the Spanish infanta, Marie-Thérèse.

He had been there to notice the growing love between the King and Louise de la Vallière. Their love shone so embarrassingly bright that nothing else was talked about at court. The Queen was devastated with jealousy since she was madly in love with her handsome husband. The court was steeped in an explosive atmosphere, which was not unusual—it was always a place of seething passions, intrigue, and debauchery.

Germain had had his share of passion and intrigue. Having been offered only the best of everything all his life, he found his tastes were jaded. He had never had to search for a new mistress or company since he was one of the richest men at court. Women were always eager to share his wealth.

Arriving at Saint-Germain, he melted into the crowd watching the King at his dinner. He impatiently tapped his cane against the side of his boot, wanting to remind the

RECKLESS SPLENDOR 135

King about Madeleine. Time was of the essence. Fouquet would be after him like a bloodhound.

The royal dinner was a ceremony of many dishes that the King methodically sampled with dignified slowness. He had a passion for boiled eggs and green peas, and every meal was accompanied by a dish of each. Germain saw him eat three eggs in a row, and then roast turkey stuffed with chestnuts, braised lamb tripe, eel stew, and hot and cold vegetables. The enticing aromas in the air caused Germain's stomach to rumble with hunger, but he could sample none of the tasty dishes. The King ate alone. For dessert he would choose from an assortment of almond pastes, tarts, and dainty cakes.

Luxurious gold plates and crystal glasses shimmered in the sunlight bathing the room. Pink and green jellies quivered in transparent bowls. When the King wanted to drink, he had to wait several minutes while the procedure of tasting the wine, pouring it, handing it to a page who handed it to the King, was painstakingly followed.

Germain smoothed his mustache in irritation as time appeared to stand still.

The King never showed any impatience with the rigorous protocol. With charm and elegance he bore everything. Mostly he kept his eyes on his plate, but now and then his inscrutable black gaze would sweep over the assembled nobility and take note of who was absent. Germain knew very well that the King had noticed the exact moment he had entered.

An arm slid seductively under his. It belonged to La Durenne, and Germain quirked a disdainful eyebrow at her. She tapped his arm with her fan, a malicious gleam marring her lovely eyes. "Germain, *mon cher*, you're late. The King will be displeased."

None of your business! he thought angrily. He did not answer. If she hoped to make him nervous, she was working on the wrong man.

"*Enfin*, we both know *why* you're late. New mistresses can be very demanding."

Germain did not bother to answer her. He knew that she had not wasted any time airing the new gossip.

"I say she isn't of your usual class, Germain. Your taste must be slipping, or perhaps the novelty is amusing." She fluttered her fan in front of her face.

"I rather think my taste has improved." With haughty insolence he let his eyes wander over her grass-green satin gown covered with purple rosettes. He made sure she noticed the disgusted wrinkling of his nose. How annoying it was to have his private life scrutinized by all and sundry! *"Pardon,"* he murmured, pulling away from her.

La Durenne gave him a murderous glance.

The King had decided to take a walk in the park. A mad run for cloaks and hats followed as the courtiers were expected to join him. When he did not hunt in the afternoon, the King liked to walk in the park, especially in the summer when the walks were bordered with a riotous mass of flowers drenching the air with sweet scents.

The lackeys had swept the snow off the walks and the King sallied forth, dressed in an ermine-lined brown velvet cloak and a wide felt hat dripping with plumes. The gold knob of his cane shone in the sharp sunlight as he swung it back and forth.

He had not shown any inclination to speak to Germain. Disappointed and frustrated, Germain fell back in the brilliant crowd. It did not surprise him when he was flanked by the chevalier de Lemont and the shifty-eyed Marquis D'Ambrose on one side and Monsieur, the royal prince, on the other.

"Messieurs, I'm sure there is plenty of room for all of us. We don't have to walk so closely together," Germain drawled with a studied sneer of his lips.

"You know why we're here. Certain information has come to our ears." Monsieur paused to let the words sink in. "You know, last night Molière's ensemble gave a wonderful performance in front of the King. A certain amateurish actress was gone, and in her place was a star, a shining talent, a rose of such beauty it cannot be described—Madame Du Parc. What contrast!" His tone was aimed to gall Germain, who remained unperturbed.

"Donc?" With an extravagant gesture, Germain smoothed his mustache with the side of his forefinger. "Tell me about this new . . . incomparable in the ensemble."

RECKLESS SPLENDOR 137

Hostile silence seethed among the three men. A cloying scent of too much jasmine water emanated from Monsieur, and Germain's nostrils quivered in dislike.

"Don't be a fool, Hautefort. We know Mademoiselle Poquelin is under your protection," D'Ambrose snarled. "Not that I don't understand her attraction. You obviously like the elfin type."

"I have yet to figure out what type *you* like," Germain taunted, arrogantly eyeing the small, effeminate man down the length of his nose. There was something secretive about D'Ambrose, as if you never knew when he might stab you in the back. He would be a bad enemy to have. Germain shivered involuntarily.

His words were enough to provoke a duel, but Germain knew that neither Lemont nor Monsieur would risk the King's displeasure. Duels were illegal. D'Ambrose was another matter, but he kept silent and clung to Lemont's arm, his amber eyes full of malice.

Germain could see the plumes of the sovereign's hat bobbing up and down ahead of the crowd and wished he were there.

"Do not speak with the King. If you do not heed our warning, Hautefort, you will soon find out what a mistake it was, not listening to your superiors."

"I had no idea that you gentlemen—superior as you are—could be afraid of a slip of a girl who has nothing to recommend her except her beauty. Tell me, what does Nicolas have on you that you so desperately want to keep secret?"

That sealed their lips for a moment, and Germain slanted a glance at Monsieur's painted and powdered face. His mouth, of proud Bourbon lineage, was pursed to resemble a red cherry.

Germain continued relentlessly. "What does he know that turns your knees to jelly? It must be something very important." He waited with secret amusement for their answer. Funds naturally. Always under the hatchet, they had borrowed heavily from Fouquet. Germain knew he was treading on dangerous ground. How far could he taunt them?

And if Fouquet demanded their services, how far would they go to silence Madeleine? *Mon Dieu,* he thought, she was utterly vulnerable. Their malevolence knew no bounds. He had to get back to Paris to protect her. He recognized the importance of speaking to the King so that he could return to Paris with all speed.

Monsieur said cleverly, "Mademoiselle Poquelin must have a strong hold on you since you're prepared to stand up for her. But why? Is her . . . body so alluring that you've lost all your senses? And how indiscreet—keeping her at your *hôtel*. Like a lovesick moonling!" He spat out the last word.

The truth hit Germain hard. He drew his breath in sharply, trying to ease the gnawing pain in his middle. He struggled to salvage what was left in the verbal battle.

"You ought to know me better than that, Your Royal Highness." He swept his arm in a wide gesture. "Take the ladies assembled here today. They all have as much allure as Molière's little niece."

Germain was lying, but he prayed the others would not pick up the infinitesimal edge of insincerity. Just mentioning Madeleine's name made his heart beat faster. He had to think. No woman could be so important that he could not leave and forget her within the week. He was only helping Madeleine because he believed her story.

"You say that, Hautefort," Lemont lisped, "but if the ladies at court hold such allure, how come you haven't had a mistress for so long?"

Silently Germain raved, *Because they're whores and mean in the bargain!* Aloud he said, "A man has to rest sometimes."

It was a truth that could not be denied, but the royal prince and his consorts were not easily misled.

"We've heard you possess exceptional stamina . . ."

Germain thought his blood was going to curdle with disgust. When he felt D'Ambrose's roving hand on his buttock, he jammed his elbow into the other man's stomach, sending him sprawling in the snow.

The entire party had stopped. Germain stood without moving a finger, tense, ready to spring.

One of the King's personal Swiss Guards stepped up to them, his spurs jangling. "What is amiss here?" He reached out and helped D'Ambrose to his feet.

"The marquis slipped and fell," Germain said in a loud voice. His eyes challenging D'Ambrose, he dared him to tell the truth.

"*Oui . . . oui*, that's right. Slippery spot back there," the marquis said peevishly, and brushed the snow from his satin cloak. Germain turned to Monsieur and bowed stiffly. "Your Royal Highness." Then he walked briskly toward the King, who was waving angrily.

"Remember what we talked about," Monsieur threw after him, and the crowd was now agape with curiosity. Like a wave, whispered speculations rippled through the throng.

Germain bowed low in front of the King, clasping his hat under the arm. Nobody was allowed to wear a hat in the presence of the sovereign.

"Ah, Hautefort."

"Sire, forgive the disturbance. It was not important." It secretly gladdened him to know that the scuffle had given him an opportunity to speak with the King.

The King smiled blandly, but his eyes remained cool. "Walk with me awhile." The King sent La Vallière away with a glance.

"You were late this morning, Hautefort, and you have caused quite a stir at court lately. When you attend, some tempers fly high, scuffles occur in public. The traces of your black eye is ample proof of that. Tell me, why is this phenomenon happening?" The King's voice was light and friendly, but Germain did not miss the icy edge of displeasure.

"Sire, I have under my protection—"

"Molière's niece. I knew she would find a powerful, rich friend sooner or later. Such delicate beauty, such an exquisite flower! Not that I thought it would be you. Not quite your type, eh?"

"Eh, well, she is delightful. Sire, do you remember my request? An audience?"

"Ah! *Oui*." No emotion sneaked across the royal face at Germain's insistent plea for his mistress. "Colbert told me she had pestered him with the same nonsense. Tell me, Hautefort, did she tell you *why* I am in danger?"

"*Oui*, it is all in this petition." He delved into his cloak pocket and pulled out a piece of parchment whose message he had helped Madeleine compose the previous night. It was sealed with red wax. "The diary is real. I could swear to it, even though I haven't seen it. It should contain some astounding proof of Fouquet's villainy. Fouquet is undermining your power, sire."

The King stopped for a short moment, glancing with hard scrutiny at Germain. "It is the most preposterous thing I've ever heard! Do *you* believe this nonsense?"

Germain flinched. "*Oui*, I do."

To Germain's surprise, the King chuckled. "I thought the girl was trying to catch my personal attention, eh?" He slanted a sly look at Germain, who felt his face turn red in mortification. "She wouldn't be the first."

"I thought so at first, but—I don't want to disappoint you, sire, but I don't think that is her goal at all," he said boldly. "She desperately wants to see you concerning the diary."

"Who says I would be interested?" The King paused. "*Bon*, I'll give her a few minutes." Then there was laughter in the King's voice. "*Alors*, Germain, so you don't think I'm a desirable goal for a beautiful, scheming female, eh?"

"I don't know," Germain answered truthfully, realizing the answer was dangerously close to insolence. "I believe you would be," he added to cover up his *faux pas*.

The sovereign's voice turned brisk. "Very well. I've had enough of this tiresome business for one day. You may make an appointment through Colbert. And whatever your differences are with Monsieur, my brother, solve them!"

The King walked away without another glance at Germain.

Chapter 14

Madeleine knew that Germain would remain at court for two days, but by the end of the second day she cried with boredom at being stuck in the house without his company to amuse her. She needed him to reassure her that the King would allow her an audience. In the late afternoon she fell asleep and did not wake up until darkness had long since fallen.

Her limbs were cramped and aching. The fire had died down, and the hands of the clock on the mantelpiece showed eleven. Germain had not returned, but she was confident he would. He was probably attending a ball until the small hours of the morning. How she wished she was there with him, if only to be close! And he had promised to bring news of Amul. She worried about the boy every minute.

While waiting for Germain to return, she would dress and make herself beautiful

Looking out the window, she noticed that the moon and stars were covered with a heavy blanket of clouds. Snowflakes whirled outside, and the wind slapped against the windows, creating an incessant rattle.

The icy draft made her shudder. The house was so quiet, so empty!

Reclining on the bed, she covered her legs with the down coverlet, feeling heavy with sleep. Winding one of her curls around her finger, she brought it to her nose. It held a faint memory of Germain's scent, a mixture of orris root, tobacco, and the indefinable virile scent that was his alone. Madeleine wanted to cry. Why was he taking so long? Desperation clawed at her. What if he had not managed to get an audience, and what if the news of Amul was bad?

She refused to dwell on it. Restless, she stood. She wound her tresses into a chignon, letting a few curls spill over her shoulders, then, shivering, forced herself to build up the fire. Listlessly she fingered the dresses in the huge armoire.

Where was Nicole? she wondered fleetingly, and then remembered that all the servants had their day off.

Finding a lovely velvet mantle dress with a short train, she put it on the bed and went to search for the matching underskirt. It was of white silk, embroidered with rosebuds and layered with lace. The pink of the rosebuds exactly matched the color of the velvet. The bodice was cut low and tight.

Slender at the waist, she could get into it without stays, but after lacing the bodice, she could barely breathe.

Why was Germain taking so long? She wished she could go outside, but he had impressed on her the importance of staying out of sight, safe in the house until he returned.

She stood in front of a mirror and impatiently brushed the curls falling softly around her face. She applied a *mouche, à la passionée,* near the eye, and placed the strands of pearls Germain had given her around her neck. Their milky luster made her skin look translucent. She hated what they represented and tore them off. Turning her head this way and that way, she was at last satisfied with her toilette. Sitting on the edge of the bed, she pulled on a pair of silk stockings and fastened them above the knee with lacy garters.

The ticking ormulu clock kept drawing her gaze. The hands moved at snail's pace. Midnight. She pictured Germain leaving the ball and riding hell for leather to be with her.

Imbécile! she chided herself. On the King's whim, Germain could be at the palace for days yet. *Mon Dieu,* please let him come tonight, she begged silently, pacing the floor like a caged tiger. I should prepare some cocoa. It will keep me from brooding.

Standing on the landing above the stairs, she looked down into the dark hallway. Not a sound. Eerie shadows wavered on the walls from a lonely taper burning in a sconce on the wall. In a few moments it would go out and throw the house into total darkness. One of the lackeys must have lit it before he left the house.

The stillness held a strange waiting quality, and shivers ran up her spine. The same threatening feeling she had experienced at the theater closed in. Why were *all* the servants gone? Obviously they took liberties when Germain was at court.

Her throat parched with fear and thirst, she decided to squelch her misgivings and go to the kitchen. I'm too fanciful, she told herself.

Downstairs, stillness reigned. The only light guiding her in the corridor to the kitchen was the orange glow of the dying fire in the huge hearth. Even the hounds were gone from their customary spot under the table.

Her eyes darted around the kitchen as she lowered the dipper into the water bucket, filled a glass, and drank greedily. She had forgotten the cocoa.

She heard a chinking sound from the front hall. Had Germain returned at last? Sudden joy leaped in her heart as she sneaked along the passage. She would surprise him. But when no more sounds followed, she stiffened with foreboding. Absolute stillness hung around her. Her heart hammering in her throat, she edged toward the study. The hallway lay in total blackness, the taper gone. The door was closed, and ever so carefully she opened it without making a sound. The room was empty. Only the faint scent of Germain's orris root remained in the room.

Madeleine's sharp ears detected a muffled noise coming from the upper floor. Pressing next to the stairs, she waited. It could be one of the servants, but the little warning signal in her mind kept ticking: danger, danger.

Clearly she ought to leave the house before the person, or persons, on the second floor detected her. She crept to the front door, but as she was unfamiliar with the lock, she needed a light to find out if there was more than one bolt. But a light would attract whomever she was trying to avoid.

She could clearly discern the sound of steps now. Two pairs of steps, heavy steps made by men. Her hair stood on end at the base of her neck, and a dart of fear flashed along her spine. A door closed, and something crashed to the floor. A curse reached her ears. Muffled voices argued now, but she could not detect the words. Were they looking for her? Lame with fear, she forced herself to touch the oak front door. She touched the cold key. Above it, a bolt was wedged into the other door. She tried the key, and it did not turn. It was not locked. They had entered through the front door.

A faint cough echoed from the outside, and Madeleine's blood froze in terror. Someone was out there! She bit her lip out of pure nervousness. What was she going to do? The kitchen door!

The footsteps upstairs neared the landing. In a moment, the light from their candles would show the pale oval of her face against the darkness of the walls. She had only one thought in her head—to hide.

The kitchen door was too far away. The study! After sneaking into the book-lined room on jellylike legs, she closed the door soundlessly.

Moonlight spilled into the room, and her gaze darted around the perimeter. Where could she hide? The voices were coming closer. Would the intruders look in the study for her? She did not wait to find out. As her eyes adjusted to the darkness, she sprinted across the room and crouched behind the high back of the armchair by the desk. Her heart raced, and she wanted to scream when the door opened. She could almost sense the sweeping glance of the intruders.

"There is no one in here," a peeved voice grated.

Madeleine would have recognized that voice among a thousand others. Dubois. It made her body stiffen in horror.

"We should have another look." That was Maurice's voice. "I know she was in the house twenty minutes ago. It is the oddest thing! How could she have slipped through our fingers?"

Dubois sounded impatient. "We don't have much time. Someone could return to the house any minute, although you paid them all to stay away for the evening. I don't like it. That *cuisinière* Barbette is a snooping sort."

"Don't worry, Hautefort won't be back until tomorrow."

Tomorrow! The word penetrated Madeleine's mind.

"The servants?"

RECKLESS SPLENDOR 145

"I assure you, all the lackeys are dead drunk at the alehouse. They are a dumb lot, anyway."

Madeleine hated him. She had been right all along to suspect Maurice. He was one of *them*. Did Fouquet have spies *everywhere?* It was frightening to see the magnitude of his power unfold right in front of her. Hysteria bubbled up, but she bit her knuckles hard, holding back the building agitation.

She heard the clinking of glasses. "Excellent brandy, this," Dubois mused aloud.

"*Oui*, the best—only the best for Hautefort."

Madeleine could imagine the sneer on Maurice's face. He hates Germain, she realized.

"What if he comes back?" Dubois sounded nervous. He had no wish to be caught red-handed.

"Relax, he won't. Besides, if he did, I wouldn't be surprised if he'd *help* us to find the girl. He changes women as often as he changes shirts. I'm sure he will thank us for getting rid of this one for him. She is a high-spirited little thing, thinks she has a chance against Monsieur Fouquet."

Madeleine was crushed. Did Germain really change mistresses that often? She did not even want to consider the possibility.

He was not coming back until tomorrow.

All she wanted was to get out of the house before they detected her, away from the heaven and the hell within its walls.

The light moved, expanding as it came closer.

"*Enfin*, let's take a fast look. Perhaps she's hiding behind the drapes."

Madeleine shivered uncontrollably with horror. They would find her now!

The light danced and flickered around the room. As soon as they stepped up to the window they would see her.

The desk was next to the window.

Pure instinct made her move. Immersed in shadows, she could still clearly see Maurice's pale face in the circle of candlelight. Blinded by the light, he could not see her.

On her knees, inching away, she pressed herself against the side of the large desk, making herself small and praying that they would not see her.

Her heart thudded so hard she was sure they could hear it. Her ears roared. If they found her, there would be no chance of escaping. Dubois was no fool.

"What was that?" Dubois shuffled toward Madeleine's hiding place. He stopped.

If she were to reach out, she could touch him; that was how close he stood. She held her breath and stared at his black shoes. If he turns around now, he'll see me, she thought, her mouth parched with panic.

"I hear something," Dubois whined tensely.

Madeleine heard it also. It was the patter of eight paws on the wooden floor. Ariel and Claudine.

"The hounds! Didn't you lock them up in Hautefort's bedroom, Maurice?"

"Oui—"

The rest of his words died on his lips. The two huge hounds surged into the room, their fangs bared and menacing growls erupting from their throats. Madeleine hoped they would not reveal her hiding place.

"Get out!" Maurice ordered, but that seemed only to infuriate them more. I'm not the only one who dislikes Maurice, Madeleine thought.

Dubois stood closest to the door, and since the dogs did not recognize him, they attacked him. Ariel sank his teeth into the man's leg.

"Argh, oooh," Dubois wailed and shoved his fist into the hound's head, but it only increased Ariel's fury.

Bravo! Madeleine thought. She knew Ariel by his deep growls. Peeking around the corner, she saw Claudine standing stiffly in front of Maurice, her fur on end.

Dubois began pulling himself toward the door, Ariel's teeth firmly lodged in his shin. The dog's savage growls urged the man on.

Maurice still held a candle and the light wavered, making the whole scene seem unreal.

Ariel finally let go of his victim, and Dubois stumbled noisily into the hallway. Pulling his bleeding leg awkwardly behind him, he reached the front door, loud curses streaming from his lips.

Closely guarded by Claudine, Maurice hurried after him.

Madeleine could not believe her good luck. She had escaped, thanks to the faithful dogs. Their claws pattered on the floor. Rising on shaky legs, she caressed their heads as they flanked her. Licking her hands, they showed their devotion.

"*Merci,*" she whispered. "It was very close this time. Strange that Maurice did not know you can open doors. It must have slipped his mind."

But she might not be so lucky next time. She had to get away from there.

Chapter 15

Madeleine stretched out her stiff and aching body. All night she had crouched close to the kitchen hearth in the darkness, close to the door and ready to escape if there was another attempt to capture her. The dogs had kept watch from under the table, once in a while dozing off, snoring loudly.

She had not slept a wink. She could not go on like this. Deciding to go to the palace of Saint-Germain and locate Germain, she rose. She needed to hear him say he loved her. What if what Maurice had said was true, that Germain changed mistresses as often as he changed his shirt? Perhaps Germain would laugh at her and turn his back on her now that she had given herself to him.

Things were different now. No longer was she the innocent girl she had once been. She swore that even if Germain had another woman in his arms when she found him, she would not break down! She would make him plead with the King and make it very uncomfortable for him if he did not help her.

Tension gathered into a knot in her middle. How could she even consider that Germain would treat her so shabbily after the tenderness he had shown her? Where was her faith? Maurice's predictions had to be wrong. But the only way to learn for sure was to find Germain.

Dawn colored the ice on the windows pink. She hung a pot of water on the hob and built a fire. The warmth made the room more cheerful, and the light chased away the ghosts.

RECKLESS SPLENDOR   149

Still wearing the elegant clothes of the previous evening, she sat at the table eating bread and cheese, a steaming cup of cocoa in front of her.

Her mind kept conjuring up Germain's face, and she wanted to weep. Longing sat like a dull ache in her chest.

Having finished her breakfast, she walked down the passage to the front hallway. Listening, she could hear no sounds of life in the house. Feeling an odd revulsion, she hurried back to the kitchen and donned her cloak.

The dogs whimpered under the table, and she bent to caress them.

"*Peut-être* we will not see each other again," she told them sadly. "Guard the house." She looked hesitantly up the back stairs. What if the servants were bound in their beds? It was strange that nobody had returned to the house in the night.

Tense with fear, she ran up the stairs and peeped into Madame Barbette's room in the attic. It was empty, as was Nicole's.

Relieved, she returned downstairs and slipped out the back door.

As she turned the corner of Rue Saint Antoine, the wind shook her, and she narrowly escaped being drenched by the contents of a chamber pot being emptied from a window in the house next door.

The vendors were already hawking their wares, and their breath billowed in white clouds around their faces in the freezing air.

With the hood pulled over her face, she walked briskly west. She hoped to reach Rue Saint Thomas du Louvre before La Béjart left for the theater. She would borrow the actress's carriage.

Crossing Rue Saint Denis, she heard a coach rumbling behind her. The horses' heads stayed abreast with her, clearly without intention of passing. Madeleine glanced behind her. The coach was elegant, red with ornate gold trim. The two lackeys in the back and the coachman wore a blue uniform with red facings and gilded gorgets. She immediately recognized their distinctive uniforms: the King's

French Guards. What were they doing with a luxurious coach in the middle of Paris?

She stopped to watch them, but to her surprise, the coachman halted the horses and the guards jumped down and saluted her.

"Mademoiselle Poquelin?"

"*Oui?*"

"I have an order from His Majesty the King to escort you to the palace of Saint-Germain. It concerns your petition."

Madeleine was too shocked to respond. Finally she said, "How—how did you know where to find me?"

"We were informed we could find you at *hôtel* Belleforière. And, if I may be so bold, mademoiselle, I saw you at the theater once, and as you stepped out, I recognized you."

Madeleine stared at him, still not recovered from her shock.

"If mademoiselle would be so kind as to step into the coach?"

The other guard held the door open for her.

She hesitated, eyeing them warily. "How do I know you're speaking the truth?"

The guard fished a folded paper from his pocket. It looked stiff and official; he handed it to Madeleine.

She read silently. "In response to your petition, you are herewith expected . . ." Her eyes traveled rapidly down the document. It was signed Jean-Baptiste Colbert. She smiled excitedly. How simple! After all this struggle to get an audience! It was unbelievable.

Slowly her spirits began to rise. At last she would be able to let the burden of her secret fall on him whom it concerned—the King.

Her steps were light as she climbed into the coach. She sank down onto the soft seat covered with pale blue velvet and let her hand slide along the material, awed at the sight of the gilded and painted ceiling. Was this one of the royal coaches?

With a jerk the vehicle began to move.

Madeleine wanted to sing and yell her triumph. The nightmare was turning out to have a happy ending.

The sovereign would instantly recognize the importance of her discovery, that much was sure.

When the coach turned right on Rue Saint Denis, she was puzzled. Surely the King was at Saint-Germain or Versailles? They should have turned left!

The coach picked up speed, skidding over the icy cobblestones and lurching through big holes. Madeleine was jarred by the sudden knowledge that something was very wrong.

The King would be nowhere near the Porte de Saint Denis looming up ahead of the coach. This area was a haunt of all sorts of unsavory characters; no respectable individuals would venture into this realm. Madeleine leaned out the window to tell the coachman to turn around, but the raging wind pushed her back into the coach.

Speeding through the gate, the coach entered Villeneuve-sur-Gravois, an area with old villas, most of them in bad repair.

Despair coiled through her, and she shivered. She had fallen into a trap!

Disoriented thoughts swirled through her head, and she leaned out the window once again. The wind whipped loose the pins holding her chignon, and her hair fell in a wild mane over her shoulders. To jump was unthinkable; the coach was moving too fast. If she tried, she was bound to break her neck. The icy road caused the coach to slide sideways, throwing her across the seat. She hit her head on the wall, and the blow dazed her temporarily. Tears of fear and pain rose to her eyes, and she beat and clawed helplessly at the squabs.

Mon Dieu, what was going to happen to her now? Pulling herself upright, she hit the ceiling repeatedly to make the coachman listen to her, but no one paid any attention.

"Stop! Halt the horses!" she yelled, but she knew her cries were useless.

As a last resort, she hung out the window, heedless of the cold stinging her face. They met a few carriages, and she waved and yelled to them in despair, but nobody stopped. Leather curtains were let down in the windows of the coaches, and the coachmen did not even bother to look at her.

Soon there were very few carriages on the road. Paris lay far behind. Madeleine sat listlessly on the seat, her face burning with cold and her fingers frozen blue. But she did not care—not now. Fouquet would have her killed now.

Never in her life had she felt more miserable, not even when her father died. All the tension that had accumulated since she had begun her mission was coming to a peak in a powerless, hateful sense of defeat. *Mon Dieu*, why was this happening now? The summons had looked quite genuine, but she should have known! Fouquet could easily have falsified the document.

The coach lurched and swayed, but all of a sudden it slowed and turned down a narrow lane flanked by rows of leafless trees. Madeleine leaned out and stared ahead.

A few minutes later a pink brick house came into view. It had once been elegant, but now it had a seedy, unused look.

The carriage jolted to an abrupt halt in front of the door, and Madeleine was thrown to the opposite seat. Before she could recover her balance, the carriage door was torn open and she saw staring at her a face, round and pale like the moon, the long nose protruding parsniplike, the small whitish eyes like those of a dead fish. It was the same face that had bent over her dying father.

Dubois.

What an awful way to die! Madeleine thought, and shrank away from the revolting visage. Was she going to follow her father's fate? Unable to move or speak, she stared wide-eyed at the living monster bending toward her.

Clawlike fingers gripped hold of her cloak, and although she braced her legs against the seat, she was pulled roughly out of the carriage.

"Well done, *garçons!* There will be ample reward for you inside," Dubois whined. His sour breath washed over her face.

"Our little pigeon is finally going to get her wings clipped. Too much time has already been wasted chasing her all over Paris!" He chuckled evilly, and with a bone-crushing grip on her arm, dragged her up the shallow stairs. He walked with difficulty. Ariel had obviously done his job well, Madeleine thought with grim satisfaction. The thought

RECKLESS SPLENDOR 153

of Ariel made her pull out of her chilling trance, and she tried to wrench out of Dubois's grip, but he was stronger than she expected.

Anger surged through her; she aimed and kicked him on the shin where Ariel had bitten him.

"Hellcat!" he shrieked and lost his grip on her.

She smiled grimly when she saw how white and tortured he looked. Then she flew down the stairs.

But her triumph was short-lived when the two bogus French Guards caught her and carried her back up, ignoring her kicks and screams. She was delivered back into Dubois's custody, and this time there was murder in his eyes. His cold fingers closed around her slender throat, and she truly believed her last moment had come.

Never had she looked into such cruel, cold eyes. A lust to kill glared at their depths. These are the eyes of the devil, Madeleine thought before pinwheels of pain and red mists began dancing in front of her eyes. She hurriedly crossed herself. Numb with pain, she prepared to die. Then the merciless grip on her throat loosened and she fell back, hitting her head on the stone steps. The pain exploded, and she slipped into darkness.

When she opened her eyes, she was blinded by bright sunlight that jarred her raw nerves.

It was still and cold, but her head lay against something soft and warm. A damp cloth was pressed to her forehead. Painfully she shifted her gaze and looked straight into a huge pair of dark, liquid eyes.

"Amul? What are you doing here?" she croaked.

"Don't speak! That monster almost killed you. You have to rest until you get your voice back."

"I thought he *had* killed me." It took enormous effort to speak.

"Shhh. *Non,* he was interrupted by the other men. Fouquet wants you alive. Only you know where the diary is hidden. Dubois was wild, screaming. He wanted to kill you. He is a dangerous madman!"

Madeleine shuddered and felt sick. Her head throbbed as if it was clamped between the jaws of huge tongs. She did not dare to move for fear of aggravating the pain.

She glanced at Amul. At least she was not alone, but the fact that Amul was present boded ill.

Brave, loyal Amul, she thought, and closed her eyes. How long would he stand this pressure? *Dieu*, what had she dragged him into?

She tried the door, already knowing it would be locked.

She heard a cough outside. Guards. They did not take any chances.

Silence prevailed again, a tense silence vibrating with invisible threats.

Madeleine slumped down on the mattress, curling her feet under her and staring at the pinkish patch of sunset framed by the windows. The colors changed by the minute, the pink changing to pale green, light blue, and purple. Perhaps it would be the last sunset she would ever see. With growing grief tightening her chest, she greedily drank in the sight and swallowed the painful lump in her throat.

A sparrow chirped on the windowsill. If only I were a bird! Never would I have to be locked up.

Amul awakened, stretching and rubbing his eyes. A gray tinge of misery clung to his ebony skin. He looked awful.

"How long have you been here?" she whispered.

He made a brave show of a smile, but it did not fool her. She shook her head, and he became serious.

"Three days."

She nodded. "Did they hurt you?"

He shrugged, but agony was inscribed on his patient face.

Madeleine raged, her wrath a white-hot ball in her chest. She pulled him close and leaned her head against his. "Fouquet thought you knew where the diary was?"

"*Oui.*"

"How did you get caught?" she asked softly, holding his thin shoulders in a firm grip.

"Dubois must have kept an eye on me. I was careful, but that night at Saint-Cloud, when I planned to talk to Madame, I was caught. You know the secret stairway I told you about at Saint-Cloud? It runs all through the palace, and there are little slits in the walls for spying. Anyway, Lemont was present, and D'Ambrose. They played vingt-et-un for high stakes. To hear what they were talking about, I slid through a secret door. I don't know how Dubois came to be in the room, but he must have seen a movement by the tapestry. I was exposed right then and there."

He chuckled. "You should have heard the outcry! Dubois looked so pleased with himself. He already knew about our connection, *naturellement*."

Chapter 16

The sunlight had diminished to a mauve glow, a sprinkling of orange streaks across the shabby furniture in the cold room that was their prison. Madeleine sat up, her eyes adjusting to the gathering dusk. Her headache had dulled, but her throat still felt unbearably sore.

Rolled into a ball, Amul slept next to her on the lumpy mattress on the floor. A cheerless fire burned in the crumbling fireplace, sending out a minimum of warmth. The huge window had no curtains, and Madeleine tiptoed over to look outside.

They were on the third floor. To jump out would mean risking broken bones, even death. As long as they were alive, hope remained.

A carafe of water stood on a rickety table. Madeleine needed a drink badly. The water held a thin layer of ice on top, and she had to break it before the water could be poured into the one and only glass. Would it be poisoned? At the moment she didn't care. Most likely death awaited her at the end of her imprisonment anyway.

Gingerly she sipped the water, which soothed the burning sensation in her throat.

Her feet were numb with cold, and she stood in front of the bleak fire, coaxing some warmth into her toes. How long had she been sleeping? Darkness had almost fallen outside. Was it one day or two days?

Judging by the soreness of the large lump at the back of her head, she thought it was only one day.

Was there any possibility of escaping this latest disaster? And Amul—how was she going to get him out?

Madeleine nodded thoughtfully. "Dubois is a more devious man than we thought."

"Madame was screeching with anger when they took me away."

Madeleine could not help but smile wryly. "She would do that, of course. Madame goes nowhere without her black page in tow."

"I wish we could get out of here. They'll stop at nothing to get the truth about the diary."

"We'll find a way to escape," she stated grimly. She wanted to keep up his spirits at all costs.

Amul studied her, his face tense and drawn. "Perhaps."

They could talk no longer because the key turned in the lock and two guards, the same who had escorted Madeleine in the coach, entered. In place of their royal guards' uniforms they now wore ragged peasant garb.

"You come with me!" one of them barked gruffly. None too gently, he poked Amul in the ribs with his halberd.

"Don't do that, you brute!" Madeleine demanded and pushed the guard. She was taken aback when he slapped her hard across the face. Reeling against the wall, she stared in disbelief at the stone-faced ruffian. She did not resist when he pushed her out the door, her ear still ringing. The cold of the passage swirled around her, and she shook with fear.

On the first floor they were ushered into a room that had once been a handsome library. Now the paint was peeling and mildew bloomed on the walls. Large damp stains were proof of even deeper decay.

Behind a worn desk sat Dubois in a large, frayed armchair. His face was wreathed in a sinister smile, as cold as the air in the room. He rose awkwardly.

"We can get this business over with in a minute if you cooperate. If you don't—you've had a taste of our little methods of persuasion." His eyes lingered with satisfaction on Madeleine's bruised throat. She shrank back. He limped across the floor and loomed over her, his foul breath washing over her face. She recoiled.

"We know that you have the diary. It's no use pretending that you don't. Let's get on with it. Where is it?"

Amul and Madeleine exchanged glances. How long would she be able to keep the truth from Dubois? Fortunately she was the only one who really knew where the diary was hidden. Amul would never be able to tell them.

She spoke with difficulty. "I will tell you if you let Amul go. He has nothing to do with this!"

"The little rat was spying on Monsieur. That's enough to have him hanging from the gibbet on Place de Grève."

Her voice threatening to fail, Madeleine said, "If you want to know where the diary is, you'll have to treat me in a proper courteous manner!" It sounded so brave. Inside she was a mass of quivering nerves.

Dubois's moon face turned an angry red. His eyes bulged with the force of his fury.

"The gall! If I used proper methods, you'd be spilling the information right now. But Fouquet has forbidden me to harm you. He wants to have a go at you himself."

He leaned over her once more, his words softly menacing. "I know ways to persuade a reluctant prisoner, ways that show no outside marks but cause the most unendurable pain. Would you like to try that approach?"

Madeleine's heart almost stopped with fear, but she stubbornly stared into his cold fish eyes. His very threat made her want to fight. A fierce anger flared in her. What right did he have to stand over her with his filthy breath and threaten her? He had killed Father! She was the one who had been wronged!

"I will never, I repeat never, tell you where the diary is. And if you kill me, there are other persons who have instructions to fulfill my mission," she lied. Her legs shook so much she could barely stand. In fact, her whole body trembled like jelly.

He backed away two steps, and she drew a long breath to regain her equilibrium. His eyes narrowed to slits. He assessed her for a long moment, aiming to ferret out if she really meant what she was saying. Madeleine met his glare stonily, and he was the first to avert his gaze.

Madeleine dared to let out her breath, but she did not relax her stiff stance, afraid that she would dissolve into a puddle on the floor.

"When we're through with you, your song will be different, Mademoiselle Poquelin," he whined. "Tell me why

RECKLESS SPLENDOR 159

you lied to Monsieur Fouquet. After all, the diary is not your property."

"But it is! It was my father's diary," she fibbed.

He leered at her. "No, it wasn't. He stole it from Monsieur Fouquet."

"The diary is ample proof that Fouquet is a crook and that he wants to be the most powerful man in France. You know it. I don't know how much Fouquet pays you to do his dirty work, but is it really worth it? Do you hope to gain a prominent place in a government controlled by Fouquet? Chancellor, perhaps?"

She was startled as Dubois lunged forward to bend over her, his eyes flashing fire. "If you want to keep your life, you'll have to return the diary."

She did not answer.

"Bon. Let me tell you what Fouquet does when spurned. You know about his inflammable temper." He made a slashing movement with his forefinger across her throat. "He hires cutthroats."

"Like you?" It must be the unbearable tension, the odd situation, that made her want to laugh hysterically. Compressing her lips hard, she tried to resist, but the urge was too strong. She threw back her head and laughed.

A deafening crack across her face silenced her abruptly. Pain shot through her brain, and a wave of dizziness engulfed her. Tears sprang to her eyes, and something warm and wet flowed from her nose. She touched her face and realized in a blur that her fingers were stained with blood.

Madeleine noticed from the corner of her eye that Amul was fighting to get away from the guard's clutches, but to no avail. He was no match for the heavy villain.

"Are you going to tell me?" Dubois's voice cut the air like a whiplash.

Madeleine shook her head in defiance.

That was the last she remembered before a searing ball of pain invaded her head. She slid down a black tunnel, ever down into a numb void.

Chapter 17

Germain flung the kitchen door open. Madame Barbette was sitting by the hearth. Startled, she stared at him in disbelief.

"Where is she?" he demanded stormily.

Madame Barbette dropped the pewter mug with brandy that she had been nursing fondly between her hands.

"Who?"

Germain glared at her. "Mademoiselle Madeleine, of course."

"I have no idea, Master Germain."

He could see that she was telling the truth, her eyes round as saucers.

"Her cloak and shoes are gone."

The fleshy cook stood up, her arms akimbo. "I can't say I blame her, you always going back and forth to court, leaving her alone to brood. Madeleine has some brains, not like your, er, other women." She slanted him a cautious glance. Had she gone too far? He growled something unintelligible and stalked out of the room, slamming the door.

She waddled after him and prodded him in the back with one fat finger. "And don't you dare slam my kitchen door!"

"Maurice, where is he?"

"I've always said he was a shady one. He quit, master. Just like that." She snapped her fingers in disdain.

"Left?"

Her chins wobbled. "*Oui*, monsieur, the same evening you went off to court. We all had the evening off, except Maurice, and when I came back the next morning, all the fires were out, the house ice cold, and not a soul anywhere.

It gave me the shivers, it did. Even the dogs were different. If you'd asked me, I could have told you that Maurice would take off any day, his bundle filled with silver and gold, I don't doubt.''

"Apparently nothing is missing, and there's no sign of any struggle."

Madame Barbette coughed. "I'm sure Mademoiselle Madeleine had enough of your gall; bored with being cooped up here, she went out to amuse herself." Barbette knew she had overstepped her boundaries because he glared at her, his face dark with anger.

She shrugged, rolled her eyes, and trudged back to her kitchen. She sniffed and closed the door. Did she not have a right to vent her opinions at times? Especially since she was right! It miffed her that Madeleine had left without saying as much as a good-bye. And she worried. A suspicion that things were not right with Madeleine kept nagging at her. She did not dare to speak her suspicion to Germain. He would blow his top sky-high, and if she mentioned the spots of blood she had cleaned off the library floor, who knew what he would do?

She shook her head and went back to the familiar task of cooking a culinary masterpiece, as she had done so many times before.

Something was different. A sense of unrest filled the air. Perhaps Master Germain had really fallen in love at last. He acted wild enough, Madame Barbette thought, and pursed her lips in satisfaction—and worry.

Germain was more upset than he would have thought possible. She had left. Why? She knew he had gone to court to arrange an audience with the King. That he had to stay two extra days at the palace at the King's request was something he could not change. Had she so little faith in him that she could not await his return?

He sat behind his desk, drinking deeply from a glass of burgundy. The warmth began spreading slowly through his frozen limbs. He had returned to Paris in all haste, and for what? An empty house? Why had she not waited for him? Confusion mixed with anger churned in his mind.

Ariel and Claudine lay in front of the fire, staring mournfully at him. He bent over the papers spread out on the shiny surface of the desk. The finances of Les Étoiles. The figures blurred in front of his eyes. He would have to find a new steward. *Diable,* what a nuisance! As if he did not have other things of graver concern!

Across the papers floated the image of Madeleine's face, and he groaned out loud. With a savage sweep of his arm, he hurled the papers to the floor, hoping to wipe her haunting face from his mind.

It was fruitless.

All he knew was a powerful longing to hold her once more in his arms; a growing anxiety poisoned his blood. He would not be able to relax until he had found out what had befallen her.

He walked up the stairs and entered the room that Madeleine had occupied during her short stay in his house. Although the room was shrouded in darkness, he found a candlestick and lit the wick. Misshapen shadows leaped instantly around the walls.

He missed her. It hurt having to admit how much she meant to him. He longed to see her standing by the bed, her golden hair streaming over her shoulders and curling beside her breasts, her lips half parted in desire.

He felt a familiar tightening in his loins and a surge of warmth in his heart. What wouldn't he do to have her in his arms at this moment!

He had had so little time to get to know her, but he sensed there was so much more to her. She was not just a beautiful body. He had never before met a woman whose whole existence was not consumed with costumes, jewelry, and plans to snare a wealthy husband to sustain her expensive demands.

He was fortunate to have seen through the shallow games of the ladies at court, but here was one who wholly intrigued him. She was not of his class, of course, but she was a lady with more honesty and courage than any he knew.

He pressed his face to the pillow upon which Madeleine had rested her head. The faint scent of rosewater lingered in the silk.

A brilliant idea hit him. The dogs! Of course!

He rushed downstairs and called to Ariel and Claudine. Catching his excitement, the hounds bounced around him like huge puppies.

Placing the pillow to their noses, he instructed them to search. With eager whimpers, the scent of Madeleine in their nostrils, they rushed in unison toward the kitchen.

"Halt! Wait for me!" Germain shouted while snatching his cloak from the cloakroom. When he reached the kitchen, the hounds were whining by the door.

Madame Barbette stared in disbelief at the spectacle before her eyes, but before she could open her mouth to speak, the hounds followed by Germain had rushed out the door. Icy air flowed into the room.

Germain had difficulty keeping pace with the dogs. Repeatedly he ordered them to slow down. By the time he reached the corner of Rue Saint Denis, perspiration trickled along his spine. The dogs stood with hanging head and limp tails as he joined them. Ariel scraped the icy ground and wailed. Claudine had a confused look on her narrow face.

The scent ended here. Madeleine had disappeared at the corner of Rue Saint Denis. Thoughtfully he looked up and down the road. Somebody had taken her up in a coach, but who? That he might never know now.

Defeated, Germain retraced his steps. The dogs trailed after him, disappointed that the chase was over so soon.

He paced the floor in his study, deep in thought. What had happened to her? Was she in danger, or had she really left out of boredom?

With a frustrated snarl, he shouted to one of the lackeys to have Apollo brought around.

He had to go out into the icy streets to search for her. Where should he start? Had she gone back to Molière?

Reaching Rue de la Réale, he slowed his horse.

He glanced at the second-floor windows where the Poquelin bedchambers must be located, but he could see no signs of life. He hid in the shadows of a portal across the street. For a long time he remained staring at the building, hoping for a sign of Madeleine, but the upstairs apartment remained dark and empty.

As cold seeped into his bones he had to move. Disappointment coursed through him. Where was she? Worry ate at him like a canker.

In the vicinity of Pont-Neuf, he decided to stop at The Greedy Cat for a tankard of mulled wine.

The usual din enfolded him as he stepped inside. The smell of smoke and rancid grease mingled with the odor of unwashed bodies, and he wrinkled his nose as he swept off his heavy snow-encrusted cloak.

The host himself served Germain at a rough table in a dark corner lit by a tallow candle. Germain gripped him by the filthy apron and stared coldly into his small, piglike eyes. "Send Weasel here," Germain growled. "Now!"

Something like a whimper came from the man's lips. "Right away, monsieur le comte. He is in a nasty mood . . . has drunk a lot. Has been playing dice and lost a bundle. I warn you, he will try to relieve you of your purse . . ." The host's voice died as he staggered back behind the counter.

A few minutes passed before a ragged man came reeling among the tables and joined Germain. "What do you want?" His voice was so wheezy that he spoke with utmost difficulty.

Germain glanced coldly at the drunken individual on the opposite side of the table. The name Weasel fit him to perfection. He possessed a thin, incredibly agile body and a long, narrow face that tapered into a long nose topped with a huge black wart. His nose resembled a weasel's snout. Weasel was a master thief, the best bloodhound in Paris, and he could always be bought for a price.

"I have a job for you, Weasel. You will be fully paid when it is completed."

Small jet-black eyes bored into Germain. "Spill the beans."

"I want you to stake out a house for me tonight. Find out if a certain Mademoiselle Poquelin has been seen at this address lately. But, I warn you, don't let Monsieur Fouquet find out that you're looking for her. Is that understood?"

"*Oui*, a bagatelle." Weasel's lips curled in contempt.

Germain's eyes shot daggers. "Impudent scoundrel! It's important that you follow through." He pushed a pouch of gold louis across the table. "Here's part of the payment, but don't drink yourself into a stupor. You should start the vigil now."

Downing his wine in one gulp, Germain rose and left the stinking tavern, heading for home.

Germain spent the afternoon and half the night pacing the floor, too worried to eat or sleep. At three in the morning he heard a scratching sound on the library window. He stiffened. Peering out from behind the draperies, he recognized Weasel's nose. He opened the window, and lithe as a cat, the thief heaved himself over the ledge.

"Unorthodox entrance. You could have come through the door," Germain commented with a faint smile.

"And be kicked out? No, *merci!* Your lackey's shoes are too hard. I treasure my behind."

Germain laughed. "Never get caught in a compromising position, do you?"

"Not if I can help it. The mam'selle is not on Rue de la Réale. In fact, no one has seen her in the vicinity."

"How do you know?"

"I have my ways. The neighbors are nosy, know everything that goes on across the street." He grinned maliciously. "We kept an eye on the Poquelin Upholstery Shop, too, but there was neither hide nor hair of her."

"You have done well." Germain pulled out a bulging purse from a drawer in the desk.

Weasel whistled. "Not bad!"

"Let's say I might need you again soon."

"Just leave word at The Greedy Cat." He stared closely at Germain. "*Enfin*, this . . . mam'selle . . . is she perchance the filly Capitaine Roland had his clutches on a while ago?"

Germain nodded curtly. *"Oui."*

Weasel chuckled. "Must be a nice piece of flesh since she's causing such a stir and—"

He had no time to wheeze out the last words, as the air to his lungs was rapidly cut off by Germain's forceful grip on his grimy cravat.

"Don't you ever call her a piece of flesh again!"

Weasel made a movement of appeal with his hands, and Germain reluctantly set him free.

"She belongs solely to you then?" Weasel rasped.

"*Oui*, damn it!" Germain barked. The thought of anybody else laying his hands on her made him sick.

"Keep your eyes open. I need to find her. If you come up with a clue tonight, I'll double the size of that purse."

Weasel whistled. "Oh my, you have it bad for her, comte." Before he received the blow he knew was coming, Weasel slid out of the window as quietly as a shadow and disappeared. But a last whisper drifted through the air. "I will let everybody know that she's yours. Not one of her hairs will be touched."

Madeleine struggled as if she were drowning in a deep river, swimming desperately to reach the surface before she suffocated. A bleak light stabbed her eyes as she blinked once, twice, and then labored to sit up.

Her face and head ached. Gingerly touching her nose, she noticed that it was swollen and numb. She turned her head, only to regret the action as flashes of pain shot through her. "I'm thirsty," she rasped, and looked into a pair of black eyes.

She stared aghast. "You!"

Fouquet's expression was evil, his lips set in a sneer. "So we meet again," he said with a mocking bow, laughing. "*Oui*, clever mademoiselle, but I am cleverer."

Speechless, she struggled to sit up. She remembered her father's dying face and squared her shoulders. Somehow she had to beat this man to avenge her father's death. Coldly she returned his icy stare. As if he could read her thoughts, she was aware of a subtle change in him. Gone was any trace of patience, replaced by a look of hard determination. A flurry of disquiet raced along her spine. She was not sure how much more abuse she could take, yet she had to think of Amul. The invisible trap squeezed tighter, closing around her.

Fouquet snapped his fingers, and the guard jerked Amul high in the air by the scruff of his neck. He whimpered.

Madeleine flinched, and cold sweat drenched her. "Monsieur Fouquet, Amul does not know where the diary is. Why don't you let him go?"

He snorted. "Let him go? So he can run like a hare for help? Hardly."

Madeleine saw how weak Amul was. He had not eaten for days, and his spirit was broken. Understanding Fouquet's brilliant strategy in capturing Amul, her zest, her will to fight back, lessened. They knew of her affection for the boy.

"Tell me where the diary is and the page will live."

Madeleine sucked in her breath. She heard Amul scream, and she thought she was going to faint again. The room tilted crazily. Warning signals pounded in her head.

"If you don't deliver the diary to me, Amul will die now." Fouquet spoke so calmly, so menacingly, that Madeleine knew he meant every word.

He had known how to get to her. Perhaps with her stubbornness she could have withstood a lot of pain, but when the threat was directed at someone she cared for, she lost.

It was the lowest point of her life when she had to face his triumphant gaze.

"The diary is in the Ursuline convent in Rouen," she said, swallowing hard. Excitement leaped into his eyes, but he made no move.

Having one last reckless ace up her sleeve, she blurted out, "I'll have to accompany you because I hid it in the stone wall of the convent, and I don't remember which stone it's behind. I'll recognize it when I see it."

His eyes narrowed.

"It's true; I swear it! As a precaution I didn't count the stones. You will not be able to find it without me," she said firmly, glaring at him. "I suspected something like this might happen."

He studied her suspiciously, and as Madeleine did not avert her gaze, he finally accepted her statement. "We will go to Rouen together, tomorrow."

"Bien," she agreed, knowing that Amul was safe for the moment. Fouquet needed her, and with all her might, she held on to the hope that she would win in the end.

Chapter 18

Madeleine sat on a lumpy mattress, leaning her back against the wall. Feeling stronger after the meager meal of bread and water she had wolfed down, she looked at Amul, who was sitting next to her, quiet but alert.

"I know how we can escape; well, at least there is a slight chance." She could not see Amul's face, but she could feel his eyes on her. She continued. "*Oui*, there is a way, but no guarantee we will succeed."

"What do you have in mind? We're too high up to escape through the window."

"*Oui*. The only hope we have is if the guard outside falls asleep. Only one is posted at night. "We will stay awake all night if necessary."

Amul's intent but doubting gaze bored into her. "What wild idea have you concocted now?"

"Didn't you notice the key to this door?"

"*Oui*, it's a regular key and a common keyhole."

"I thought the key looked remarkably small."

"If it did, I didn't see."

"I also perceived that the gap between the door and the floor is wide enough for a key to pass. Tonight, we are going to lay our hands on that key, and then—freedom!"

"I wish it was possible, but we have so many obstacles to pass before we're free."

"You mark my words, you doubtful imp! We will be free tonight!"

Amul grew quiet. He did not want to destroy Madeleine's last hope. "How are we going to do it?"

She whispered in his ear, and then they sat close together to keep out the cold, listening to the sounds of the house. A carriage left, its wheels crunching through the snowdrifts. Doors slammed, and male voices floated up the stairs.

The guards outside were mumbling, and Madeleine crept along the floor to put her ear to the door. Straining to hear what they were talking about, she could only recognize a few words, most of them juicy curses.

"It'll never work, Madeleine," Amul said, knowing how high the odds were stacked against them.

She answered by holding a finger to her lips, cautioning him to keep quiet. The house didn't grow quiet until dawn was almost upon them. Madeleine stared tensely into the blackness of the night, waiting. Ghostly pale moonlight filtered into the room.

The faded wallpaper had been peeling for years. Great flaps hung like bird wings from the walls, and Madeleine carefully pulled down the largest piece. The crumbling paper made a ripping sound, and she listened for movement in the corridor, holding her breath.

There came the abrupt sound of a single snore. What she had fervently wished for had happened; the guard had fallen asleep, secure in his belief that the prisoners were too weak to do anything but sleep. He did not know that said weaklings were kneeling only three feet away from him, their ears pressed to the door.

"We need patience now," Madeleine whispered. "We have to make sure that he's deeply asleep before attempting this."

Crouching by the door, they grew stiff and numb, but at last they were rewarded by a steady stream of snores.

"That's it. Now, pray for our success," Madeleine said between her teeth. Gently she began easing the flap of wallpaper under the door until only a narrow edge remained on their side.

She straightened a hairpin, one of the two still left in her hair. Angling her eyes to the dark keyhole, she tried to figure out which way to turn the key.

Gingerly she applied the end of the hairpin to the key, which moved, slowly, slowly, making a creaking sound.

Despite the noise, there was no interruption in the stream of snores outside.

A thin rivulet of perspiration coursed along her spine even though she was chilled to the bone. She manipulated the key until it teetered on the very edge of the keyhole, and taking a deep breath, she gave it a last gentle push and it tipped over the edge.

With a loud clang it fell onto the paper.

The snores were cut off in midstream, and the guard sputtered and snarled. Madeleine could almost feel his head swivel and his gaze dart back and forth along the passage.

She shut her eyes tightly, praying he would not see the key on the wallpaper.

Sleepily, he rumbled something, and his chair groaned as he shifted his weight.

Madeleine and Amul sat as still as statues. An intolerable eternity passed before the blessed sound of his snores resumed. Madeleine saw Amul's teeth flash whitely as his face split into a grin. He had finally caught the spirit of adventure since luck appeared to be in their favor—so far.

Slowly she pulled the paper back under the door. Black against the lighter pattern lay the key. They had done it!

For a long moment they held hands, expressing their silent exuberance.

After several nerve-chilling moments, Madeleine managed to unlock the door. It slid open without much noise, just as she knew it would. Fingers entwined, they tiptoed out of the room, their shoes in their hands.

Madeleine shot a curious glance at the guard whose head was propped against the wall. His mouth was open, letting out gust after gust of snores. On a stand next to him flickered a candle.

The darkness in the passage soon swallowed them as they edged along the wall, feeling blindly for obstacles. Madeleine's muscles tightened, and she felt a powerful urge to flee headlong down the corridor.

When steps sounded on the stairs ahead of them, Madeleine almost jumped out of her stockings with fear. Someone was coming up!

RECKLESS SPLENDOR 171

* * *

Germain leaned his elbows on his desk, propping his throbbing head in his palms. He stared blindly at the gilt-edged leather inlay on the desk top. He hated to sit helplessly waiting, unable to act.

For the rest of the night he waited for Weasel to come back with the information on Madeleine's whereabouts, but he had no guarantee that Weasel would appear. Germain was at the end of his tether.

Slamming his fist into the mahogany surface, he rose impatiently. As he crossed the room, Ariel and Claudine sleepily lifted their heads and eyed him affectionately.

He poured a measure of brandy into a snifter. After one sip his headache instantly intensified. Gloomily he stared out the window into the desolate courtyard. Snowdrifts piled against the walls. It must have been wishful thinking, but he thought he saw a black shadow sliding along the wall. Weasel would come that way, like a thin, black shadow.

Then the pale face with the telltale wart peeped straight at him over the windowsill.

Relief flooded through him in hot waves. Weasel had returned! He had said he would return only if he had some vital information.

Germain flung open the window, and Weasel crawled inside.

"I have what you want, monsieur le comte, but first give me the promised payment and then some brandy. It is a murderous night out there," he said, wheezing.

Weasel rubbed his slim hands in front of the fire while Germain poured a liberal amount of brandy into a tumbler.

Smacking his lips in appreciation, Weasel told the story of how he had gained the information about Madeleine. "I was at The Greedy Cat as usual when a cutthroat called Paul Dijon entered. He's one of those rats you can hire for a few sous to kill your enemies. He'll do any dirty work at all. Cold as death, he is." Weasel rubbed his wet nose vigorously on his sleeve.

"Anyhow, he owed me a favor. I had let word out that I'd pay well for any information on this Mam'selle Poquelin. He struts right up to me and tells me of the hiding place. But not until he has seen the gleam of gold, *naturellement.*"

"Get to the point!" Germain barked, his patience worn thin.

"She's at an old house in Villeneuve-sur-Gravois. Fouquet has her. Dijon was one of the men who brought her there. He said that Fouquet and that slime Dubois are interrogating her. Dijon took pride in telling me that he himself slapped her a few times."

Germain let out a roar of fury. "There is no time to lose!" He flung another purse at Weasel and rushed out of the room.

Weasel scratched his greasy head and pulled his battered hat over his ears. How strange that the comte dared to leave a master thief alone in a house full of precious baubles. He shrugged his thin shoulders. Somehow he was not in a mood to nip anything. Some other time, perhaps.

The circle of light grew wider and sharper, and Madeleine's heart hammered wildly with fear. She sensed Amul shrinking against the wall next to her, and they exchanged frantic glances: Where to?

Sinking to the floor, they pressed into the shadows. The light did not touch them directly, and since they were dressed in dark cloaks, the guard did not see them. He stared stonily ahead as he passed them only a few feet away.

Realizing that the hue and cry would rise sooner than they had thought, Madeleine and Amul hurried down the stairs as fast and as silently as they could. Their stocking feet made no sound, but some of the wooden steps creaked under their weight.

No use stopping and worrying about it now, Madeleine thought doggedly. Like two wraiths, they slipped into the darkness on the second floor, aiming for the back stairs—wherever they would be.

Standing somewhere in the middle of the house, they heard a hoarse cry ringing out above. Their escape had been detected.

"*Mon Dieu*, we should have locked the door behind us," Madeleine exclaimed.

"Too risky. What if the guard had awakened? We had to get away from there fast."

"What if there are no back stairs?" she dared to whisper.

"There must be. This was a grand house at one time. There is bound to be more than one set of stairs."

Running steps sounded along the passage above. Amul pulled her faster toward the end of the corridor. Their hands touched draperies frail with age, sending out clouds of dust that tickled their noses.

As Amul had predicted, a door was hidden behind the draperies. Madeleine tried the handle. Locked. She searched for a key, but found none in the keyhole.

"Come, we have to go back and use the other stairs," she whispered.

"Guards will be posted downstairs, and by now they're alerted of our flight."

"*Enfin*, I don't think we're strong enough to kick in this door. What other choice do we have?"

Forced to agree, Amul groaned in disappointment. Their odds of escaping were diminishing with every second.

"Come! We'll outwit them somehow. We can't lose now that we've come this far."

Amul led her along the corridor, back toward the sounds of the guards above.

"They're going to come down here any second now," she whispered.

Reaching the stairs, Amul felt along the surface of the wall under the staircase. The next moment he had miraculously opened a door concealed in the wallpaper.

I would never have found that door, Madeleine thought as he pushed her into the gaping hole.

A rank odor invaded her nose, and she grimaced. The space was so small they had to kneel on the floor among foul-smelling debris. Madeleine fervently hoped she had not disturbed some mouse nest. It was pitch black, without the tiniest glimmer of light.

Outside, she heard loud voices and several pairs of boots pounding past their hiding place. In the meanwhile Amul's fingers wandered restlessly in search of yet another opening.

"There might be a secret passage from here," he whispered.

Doors slammed, and Madeleine worried. The metallic taste of fear filled her mouth, and her heart beat wildly.

Steps echoed and stopped outside, stealthy steps, then something hard butted into the wall. A methodical *thud-thud* sounded on the door. Madeleine grew paralyzed with apprehension.

An endless moment of silence stretched in the darkness. Madeleine and Amul sat poised for flight, not daring to breathe.

Another thud reverberated. It echoed in Madeleine's head like a gong, then receded, leaving only ominous silence.

The steps disappeared, and the corridor was empty once more. Cautiously Amul opened the door, letting in a sliver of moonlight. "I could find no other door," he whispered.

In the next breath they were hurrying down the last flight of stairs, their ears and eyes open, alert to further danger.

The hallway was empty and brightly lit. At any moment the front door could burst open and the house swarm with guards.

They must leave immediately.

Thrusting her ears to the door, Madeleine tried to discern movements from outside, but stillness prevailed.

Sounds exploded in the stairway above, and without prompting, Amul turned the key. It would not budge! Madeleine put her hands over his, and together they applied all their strength, but the stubborn iron would not turn.

They fled into the adjoining study, which fortunately was empty, shrouded in shadows.

Amul pulled Madeleine toward the tall, moonlit windows. Panting, they went to work on the rusty window latches. Reluctantly the window yielded a crack, groaning loudly.

With frantic effort, they managed to push the window open. Grinding and resisting, it finally flew open and banged into the wall.

Without waiting to see if the guards had noticed, they plunged through the aperture and landed in a deep snowdrift outside.

The air was crystal clear and cold, as smooth as nectar to Madeleine's lungs after the damp, malodorous air in the house. Following Amul, she waded through the deep, soft drifts, her icy petticoats plastered to her legs.

As soon as they reached the drive, the going became easier, and Madeleine wrapped her thick cloak closely around her, running behind Amul.

Entering a curve lined with dark trees with spidery branches, she halted. The sound of slamming doors reached her ears. Across a landscape bathed in milky moonlight, she spied the silhouettes of the guards rushing up the drive.

Swords gleamed like blue ice against the somber sky, and Madeleine counted at least five guards. The orange flames of two torches leaped into the air.

"I can't run any faster," she blurted out, winded, clutching Amul's cloak.

"You have to! They'll catch up with us if you don't."

"They'll do that anyway."

Looking left and right, she searched for cover. In the distance she saw a large boulder covered with snow and surrounded by a clump of trees.

"In there!" she breathed and pushed Amul into the high banks of snow bordering the drive. She ran back toward the house for a few yards and peeled off her cloak. With it, she began sweeping the ground, obliterating their tracks.

She had just jumped behind the snowbank when the men turned the bend in the lane.

Having no time to join Amul behind the boulder, she burrowed into the snow like a rabbit, quietly accepting the frigid embrace. She was already stunned with fear.

Hearing the men halting farther down the lane, she knew they were confused by the disappearance of the tracks. The sound of raucous voices reached her ears, and she curled deeper into the snow. "They can't have disappeared into thin air!"

Silence.

"Perhaps she's a witch, a she-devil. You never know with those—they can fly," voiced another man.

Madeleine willed them to return to the house, but yet another voice spoke. "It's only a trick to get us off their tracks. See here—brush marks. They're hiding somewhere close by. We'll have to look behind all the trees and rocks."

A murmured curse slipped through Madeleine's stiff lips. Had they come this far only to be caught again?

One of the men slashed the snowbanks with his sword only a few steps from Madeleine. She could hear his virulent curses. The men were obviously as cold as she was, and angry to boot.

Her relief was monumental when she heard the call, "Come here, I think I've found a clue." The voice came from farther down the lane. All the guards hurried to comply, and Madeleine could not believe her luck. Sitting up, she furtively looked for Amul, who was already crawling toward her.

"Let's leave before they realize they're on the wrong track. Look!" She pointed to the high shoulder of snow, its symmetry brutally hacked to pieces a mere two feet from where she had been hiding.

With no time left to linger and express their luck, they flitted like two small spirits up the lane, away from the guards.

Nearby hooted a melancholy owl. As birds flapped their wings in the trees, snow rustled from the branches and fell with a faint *plop* to the ground, dusting Madeleine's and Amul's heads with white.

They did not dream of complaining of cold, numb feet, wet clothes, or snow falling on their heads. Their only goal was to reach the road and find someone to escort them to Paris.

It would not be easy, but they had managed to get this far and could bear the rest.

Out of breath, they reached the road and began walking rapidly in a westerly direction, toward Paris.

Sending repeated glances over her shoulder, Madeleine saw that they were not being followed—yet. How she prayed that their pursuers would not find their footprints too soon!

A few minutes later, the distant sound of horses' hooves reached her ears. Not stopping to listen, she strained to hear what direction the sound was coming from.

RECKLESS SPLENDOR 177

The *clip-clop* swelled in the hushed night. More than one horse, Madeleine thought. And they're heading toward Paris!

Holding Amul's arm, she halted by the roadside, nervously waiting for the equipage to appear. When it did, she stepped boldly into the middle of the road.

The coach loomed out of the darkness, and the horses shied in fear. The animals and the coach were as black as the night.

"Please, help us, monsieur!" Madeleine pleaded to the coachman, letting her hood fall back to reveal her long blond hair.

"A woman!" a voice barked. "What do you want?"

Madeleine was temporarily taken aback by his rudeness. Then she stared in surprise at Amul who stepped out in front of her.

"That is no way to address a lady in distress, monsieur," he said coldly.

A smile tugged at Madeleine's lips. He looked like an angry chicken that a whiff of wind could topple over.

The man stirred uneasily in his seat, peering closely at Amul in the eerie light of the moon.

It struck Madeleine that he could not see Amul's black face.

"I assure you, monsieur, that we're not evil spirits, but people of flesh and blood, freezing to death. Please, have mercy on us," she pleaded.

He grumbled for a moment while the horses stomped the hard ground. Madeleine did not even stop to wonder what kind of man he was; she only wanted to put as much space as possible between herself and the evil guards.

"I have business at the graveyard of Saint-Innocents, but if you dare, you may sit back there. Just open the door and step inside." He pointed toward the coach with the whip.

"*Merci.* May God bless you for your compassion," she added to imprint on him that she was a respectable woman.

Hurriedly they ran to the side of the coach, but could not find the door. As they saw the door in the back, they recognized the undertaker's wagon. The coffin inside looked ominous.

"*Enfin*, what are you waiting for?" the coachman cried as he heard their involuntary gasps.

Madeleine and Amul crossed themselves and exchanged frightened glances before squeezing in next to the coffin. As they closed the door, they heard a horse galloping in the opposite direction at breakneck speed, but they could not see the rider—did not see the mane of blond hair whipping out behind him.

Chapter 19

Madeleine thought she would never get warm again. The undertaker let them off just inside the Porte de Saint Denis, and they were fortunate to find a warm stable nearby.

The interior smelled pungently of horses and leather. An animal snorted. In a corner a huge mound of hay beckoned, and Madeleine sank into its dusty crispness.

Amul surprised her with his inventiveness. Finding a horse blanket, he spread it over her and finally joined her beneath it for warmth. Back to back, they discussed the evening's events.

"I wish we could see Germain tonight, but it's dangerous to walk through the streets at night, unarmed," Madeleine said sleepily. "And I'm exhausted."

"*Oui*, me too. We'll go first thing in the morning. He will help us."

She laughed with relief, anticipating the feeling of Germain's arms around her. "We fooled them! But, oh, how close it was. And Fouquet doesn't really know where the diary is." She thought for a moment. "When they realize that they cannot catch us, they will go to Rouen and torment the nuns. I don't like that part one bit."

"Hmmm, I don't think so. Not even Fouquet would have the gall to do that. He'll try to catch you first."

"Will I ever see the King?" Madeleine exclaimed in exasperation.

"Tomorrow," Amul muttered sleepily. Within a minute, he was asleep.

Madeleine did not fall asleep as fast. She pictured Germain's face, his demanding lips, his proud nose, and his beloved eyes that could read her very soul. I miss him so, was her last conscious thought.

The next morning they were abruptly awakened when a muscular stablehand entered to do the morning chores. Madeleine rubbed her eyes and blinked sleepily.

"Beggars! Scum!" the stablehand shouted and hoisted a pitchfork. "Begone from here!"

Madeleine and Amul stumbled to their feet, barely having time to don their cloaks. They sprinted outside. The door slammed viciously against the wall in the fierce wind. Running swiftly along the lane, Madeleine looked once over her shoulder. The man had not bothered to pursue them. She slowed down, catching her breath.

"Phew. I thought for a moment that Fouquet had found us," she said, panting.

The bright morning light blinded them. Shading her eyes from the intense glare, Madeleine took a good look at herself. Her elegant velvet dress was stained and terribly wrinkled—like a rag. After a night in the hay, it was covered with a fine layer of dust. Her hair was like a bird's nest, and when she tried to smooth it down, her fingers encountered innumerable straws. In dismay, she stared at Amul, seeing that he looked just as bad, his velvet outfit a bundle of torn rags.

"We do look like two beggars now."

Amul glanced at her in distaste. "I agree. That gown looks awful."

"And you, Master Amul, certainly don't look the royal page."

Their eyes meeting, they burst out laughing. Madeleine brushed the dust from his back, and Amul picked the straw from her hair and helped her comb out the tangled tresses.

"There, that looks better. Just straighten your jacket and collar now," Madeleine said.

"Bien! I am sick and tired of the ridiculous costumes Madame forces me to wear every day," Amul complained, tugging at the grimy collar. He stared in growing fear at Madeleine. "I don't have to go back there now, do I?"

She smiled slyly. "Well . . . I don't know," she joked. His lips drooped, and she pounded him in the back. "You ninny! I don't want to be separated from you again." His face lit up. Taking her hand, he held it adoringly to his cheek. "I'll protect you with my life."

Madeleine dashed away a tear. Like two happy children, they walked hand in hand along Rue de Saint Denis, past the graveyard of Saint-Innocents, toward the hub of the universe, Pont-Neuf.

"Let us go to the *hôtel* Belleforière now," Madeleine suggested.

Due to the lengthy cold spell, the air had been purged of the prevailing foul odors that usually pestered the city. The air was exhilarating, and the wind held a whiff of warmth, a definite promise of spring. Madeleine skipped a dance step. They were free, free, free!

As they neared *hôtel* Belleforière, Madeleine placed a hand on Amul's arm. "We'd better be careful. Let's wait and see if the coast is clear before we barge in." They waited for at least half an hour behind a carriage parked on the stable side of the house. Built around a courtyard, the impressive town house was attached to the stables on one side, with the guest wing and servants' quarters on the other sides.

"Oh, no! Look," Madeleine whispered, tugging Amul's sleeve. "There, behind the curtain in the window. I could swear it is Dubois." She held her breath. "*Oui*, it is! Hurry, let's run!"

They ran all the way to Pont-Neuf and mingled with the peasants pushing wheelbarrows filled with cabbages and onions up and down the bridge. "Phew, that was a close call!" Madeleine held her side as she caught her breath.

"What are we going to do?" Amul asked, his eyes huge.

"We'd better wait until tonight and try to leave a message with one of the stableboys. Oh, *zut!* We were so close."

The day dragged on forever. Madeleine could not wait to see Germain again. She was counting the minutes as she and Amul strolled along the Seine.

Amul pointed out strange, crumbling places, explaining that they were old Roman remnants, now used as gang holds. Madeleine was beginning to see the extent of power the people of the underworld had and how their lawless pursuits terrorized the law-abiding citizens. Finally she managed to worm out of Amul how he knew so much.

"I never told you, but I was born in a hovel outside Porte de Saint Michel," he explained. "My parents were less than beggars. They stole a piece of jewelry to buy food because they were starving." He sighed. "They were unsuccessful thieves. My mother was hanged on Place de Grève, and my father was sent to the galleys; he was a huge, muscular man. I took to the roads, and that's where I joined up with Molière." Amul rubbed his head. "I love him," he said simply. "A very kind man."

Madeleine's lips widened in a fond grin. "So are you."

Amul blushed and kicked a snowball. "Girl talk!"

As dusk threw its blue veil over Paris, they walked into a maze of backstreets and alleys that eventually brought them to Rue Saint Antoine and Germain's *hôtel*.

After climbing through a window of the stables, they stopped and listened. Silence reigned. Eight horses turned their velvet eyes toward the intruders.

"We'd better wait upstairs in the loft until someone comes to groom the horses in the morning. I don't want to risk running into Dubois or Fouquet," Madeleine whispered. She was standing on the wooden ladder, poking her head through the dark opening. "It smells fresh, and it is warm."

Amul climbed after her, two horse blankets under his arm. Burrowing into the hay, he said, "Might as well be comfortable while we wait."

"Shhh, there might be lodgings on the other side of the wall. The coachman usually lives over the stables."

Their tempers were beginning to fray, and both realized it was better to keep quiet or they would end up quarreling. Tension was mounting, and expectations.

I'm so close to him now, but so far away. Madeleine conjured up Germain's image, and her heart beat faster. But she was so tired!

Weasel had been awake when the odd couple climbed into the loft. He had immediately recognized Madeleine's light gold hair. Staring into the inky shadows, Weasel had listened to their mutterings. What a piece of luck that he had chosen the comte's stables, this night of all nights! He could already hear the chink of gold when he told the comte this little morsel of news.

Weasel had learned to live like a shadow. It was second nature to him to always move without making a sound, to melt into the wall if necessary.

This night was no exception. Waiting and brooding, he did not move at all for an hour. When his sharp ears detected the steady rise and fall of the sleeping couple, he rose lithely, barely leaving a dent in the hay. Then he slid across the round timbers that constituted the floor of the loft, gliding so close to Madeleine that he could have touched her foot with his.

The horses were not fooled. Moving restlessly, they snorted in their boxes, and eight pairs of eyes stared at him in the darkness. Good at almost everything he did, Weasel whispered a few words, instantly quieting the animals.

He did suffer from one flaw: a difficulty in making friends. He was the loneliest person in the world—just like the comte de Hautefort. The man had everything a man could wish for—enormous riches, and the most beautiful women of the kingdom as his mistresses. Weasel could not help but like the man, although there was an enormous gulf in their stations. The strange thing was that the comte treated him as an equal, one lonely soul to another. He scuttled past a deep snowdrift. Without stealing, he was going to earn a well-filled purse this evening. He rubbed his hands together. A good day was going to have a better ending.

He knocked on the library window and peeped into the brightly lit room, but could see no sign of Hautefort. Wrinkling his brow, he evaluated the situation. Was the comte out? *Non*, he had seen him earlier. Weasel slid around to the opposite side of the house where candles burned in every window. Standing on his toes, he glanced into the salon.

The comte was sitting at the table in the dining room, and he was not alone. Elegantly dressed gentlemen were sharing a sumptuous repast. Weasel's mouth watered, and he licked his lips.

What pickings! I'll just wait in the shadows by the front door and when they walk by—*snip-snip*—I'll relieve them of their purses. *Oui*, indeed, Weasel mused, but he was soon brought back to reality as he felt his feet stiffening with cold.

A hoot of laughter erupted inside, irritating Weasel. It wasn't fair that he should stand out in the cold while the gentlemen were having such a good time. *Non*, he would sneak into the library and warm his feet. As good a place as any to sleep; he would take a catnap in front of the fire.

No house existed that could keep Weasel out if he wanted to get in.

Germain found a strange bundle of rags in front of his fireplace, a snifter of his best brandy to one side. Weasel was sleeping heavily, sitting up, his neck tilted forward at a ninety-degree angle.

"It must hurt," Germain barked as he shut the door with a slam.

Weasel jumped, bouncing immediately to his feet. He eyed Germain cautiously, ready to flee out the window if necessary.

"I see you found some brandy." Germain smiled sardonically. "Nothing like brandy to chase the chill out of your limbs, eh?"

Weasel nodded, still wary of the nobleman. He knew Germain could be dangerous if provoked.

Germain sat down behind his desk and put up his feet. From a silver tray on the desk he helped himself to his own snifter of brandy. "What urgent business brings you here in the middle of the night?" he asked idly, studying the amber fluid.

"Mademoiselle Poquelin." He watched Germain. The man's reaction was startling. Down came the feet from the desk, and before he had time to react, the comte was towering over him.

"If that is a bad joke, retract it this instant!" the comte ordered.

"*Non*, it is true. I know where Mademoiselle Poquelin is."

He noticed the aristocrat's face paling even more and the tense jumping of a muscle in his jaw. "*Oui*, monsieur le comte, she is in your stables, sound asleep." Weasel thought the man's eyes were going to pop with surprise. "Her and a little blackamoor."

"Amul." Germain paused. "Then they did get away."

Weasel stared at him in confusion. "What are you talking about?"

"Last time you were here with information, I rushed off to Villeneuve-sur-Gravois to rescue her. A gang of ruffians in the lane leading to the house were searching the grounds. I bound the horse to a tree and stole up close to hear what they were talking about. I heard enough to know that Madeleine and Amul had escaped. I prayed they would not be found." He laughed out loud. "You are a scoundrel, Weasel. Let's go and fetch her."

"*Non*, you go alone, comte."

It never occurred to Weasel to leave. Without asking permission, he curled up again on the rug in front of the fire.

Madeleine was dreaming about Germain. They were lying in the middle of a meadow of fragrant red poppies, daisies, and cornflowers. The scents were earthy, intoxicating, and warm. The male scent of Germain enticed her, taunted her. As his hand cupped one of her breasts, he rubbed his palm over her growing nipple until swirls of desire danced through her body. She wanted him, needed him.

Awakening, she breathed raggedly for a long time. Darkness still ruled. The only sound was the tranquil munching of the horses in the stables below.

Extending an arm, she felt for Amul. He was gone.

"Amul—*pssst*, where are you?"

No answer. The little rat, she thought, frightening her like this! A stab of anxiety pierced her. Where was he? What time was it, anyway?

The train of her thoughts was broken by a soft sound, like a muffled step. She sat up, fully awake now, listening. There it was again, a step. She could feel the shaking of the timbers in the loft. Someone was climbing up the ladder. Her fear mounting, she pressed into the hay, pulling the blanket over her head. She trembled, her heart lodged in her throat.

The steps came closer, and she had to look. Against the faint grayish light of the tiny window, she recognized the silhouette of a man. Madeleine gasped.

"Who are you?" she croaked.

"Madeleine?"

The next second found her in Germain's arms; he hugged her and rocked back and forth while sobbing and laughing into her hair. "I thought I had lost you forever," he murmured.

Tears streaked her face, and she covered his neck with kisses. The air between them vibrated with urgency.

Germain threw himself on his back into the hay, pulling her with him. She landed on top of him, her heart racing with anticipation. This was no dream; he was really here.

"It has been so long, *ma belle*, oh, so long." His words slowly faded as he pulled her face close, cupping a warm hand around her neck. Their lips barely touching, they savored the charged eagerness that radiated between them. Madeleine traced the tip of her tongue along the perimeter of his lips, and he groaned.

"I have missed you, too," she whispered.

He groaned and fused his lips to hers. A tidal wave of euphoria surged through her, a frenzy urging her to surrender to the demands of her body, to touch him, to melt with him. He tasted of brandy and desire.

The pads of his thumbs caressed the smooth peach softness of her cheeks. She heard him sigh, a deep sound of contentment. "I've dreamed about you, worried about you; in fact, life has been pure hell without you," he said.

Putting all the tenderness she felt for him into a kiss, she reverently touched his lips with her own in an eternally sweet moment. She wanted so much to tell him that she loved him, but she got caught up in the moment of swelling passion. He had already unlaced her bodice and bared her breasts, stroking them eagerly until she quivered with pleasure.

"Ahhh," she moaned when he took one hard peak between his lips and sucked hard. Liquid fire spread in her veins, and she dragged open his shirt and covered his warm chest with kisses. Her hands found their way under the waistband of his rhinegraves. She luxuriated in the feel of his smooth skin and honed muscles.

Spreading her legs across him, she touched his hard manhood, and her skirts became an irritating obstacle. She breathed with relief when he found the tiny hooks and deftly slid the skirt and petticoat over her hips. Sensing his mounting desire, she guided his hand under her shift and gasped as he caressed the soft folds of her femininity. She was already throbbing, and his intimate strokes created dulcet agony. "Oh, Germain, I . . ."

He wriggled out of his rhinegraves and coat. "I need you," he muttered hoarsely and rolled over so that she ended on her back on top of his cloak. "More than I can say." Relentlessly he teased and nibbled at her throat, her ears, between her breasts, down her flat abdomen. His skillful tongue made every hair on her body stand erect, and she could barely breathe for the exquisite torture.

"Please, take me," she begged, but he only chuckled, letting his fingers play in and out of her, slowly at first, then more rapidly, until she arched and felt a cry of pleasure building inside. The only thing she knew was blossoming rapture, and then she went over the edge . . .

He placed himself between her thighs and deeply filled her, holding her close, savoring her for a long moment. "Please," she moaned.

Undulating his hips, he massaged her profoundly inside until she gasped and quivered like a bowstring in his arms. He laughed triumphantly when a few hard thrusts sent her into blissful oblivion, and she shuddered in his arms.

Engulfed in his own pleasure, he was completely enslaved as he spilled his seed into her from the crest of an ecstatic wave.

Chapter 20

Dust was dancing in a beam of sunlight pouring through the tiny window of the hayloft. It was the first morning ray, still rosy and timid. Madeleine stared at the swirling particles. Her head rested on Germain's shoulder, and he was still asleep.

No sound except Germain's steady breathing disturbed the silence, but she knew that the grooms would be entering the stables at any minute.

Stroking Germain's cheek covered with blond stubble, she whispered, "Time to wake up. We don't want to be found up here." The urgency in her voice made him sit up with a jerk.

"What's going on?" he muttered thickly, sleep still clouding his eyes. Madeleine watched him gradually grow wide awake. A grin spread across his face, and he ruffled her hair, which was already an unruly tangle of curls. "Enchanting sprite," he whispered and kissed her swollen lips tenderly. Then he nuzzled her nipples until they ached with renewed desire.

"*Non*, Germain, I will not be a victim of the stableboys' leers and catcalls. And we will be, if we remain here," she said with a sunny smile, springing from the hay in one graceful movement. Languorous as a cat, she stretched her slender limbs.

"Beautiful, exquisite," she heard him murmur. "Delicious curves."

She shivered with pleasure and took delight in flaunting her nudity before him. Her arms extending above her head, she smiled down at him. "Time to rise, *mon cher*."

He growled and lunged for her, but she was faster. She slid her shift over her head. "Brrr, it is so cold. Look at the ice on the window." She slanted him a glance. "That ought to cool you off."

He flexed his body with a groan.

"Ah! The soft man is broken after one wild night in the hay," she taunted with a coquettish wink.

"*Diable*, Madeleine—you witch! If you don't take care, you might earn a sore rump before long." He captured her in his arms and hugged her hard. His naked skin was a heady sensation, and she could barely let him go when he released her after smacking her loudly on the derrière. Then he bent to retrieve his crumpled clothes.

"Where is Amul?" she asked.

"I carried him to one of the guest rooms. He was exhausted, the little mite. Didn't stir. Look—madness must have gripped us last night. Look at this vest."

Madeleine suppressed her mirth when he held up his buttonless vest. "We won't be able to find them in the hay," she stated.

Germain sighed. "Some unlucky horse will break a tooth on those buttons. Made of pure silver, too."

Though they dressed as best they could, they still looked as if they had just finished a wrestling match in the hay. Laughing, they picked straw from each other's hair. Madeleine loved to pull her fingers through his curls.

"Silver and gold," she whispered. Standing on her toes, she kissed the tip of his nose.

"What?"

"Silver eyes, golden hair."

He ceased to move, staring deeply into her eyes. Tenderness softened the clear silver to a smoky gray, and Madeleine felt her heart leap in response, flooding her eyes with love. She could not hide her emotions.

"I like that," he whispered, and held her fiercely. "Those blue pools should always be filled with . . . love."

Too fragile, too new, was their mounting love, and they separated, each bending, partly to pick up their cloaks but mainly to hide the strong emotion throbbing in their hearts. Madeleine thought, I will not be the woman he discards as easily as a shirt!

* * *

Madame Barbette hovered by the sideboard in the dining room. Although it wasn't her custom to preside over the serving procedure, wild horses could not have dragged her out of the room. The skulking Maurice wasn't there, and the lackey serving the breakfast did not care. Madame Barbette had her ears cocked. Madeleine was back, and she wasn't going to miss one single word of her story.

Only the best food was served on this memorable morning: for the master ham and eggs, a leg of mutton, and a wedge of pigeon pie, while Madeleine nibbled on a roll spread thickly with golden honey. Madame Barbette's mouth fell open as Madeleine told how Fouquet had starved Amul and threatened to kill him if Madeleine did not divulge the diary's whereabouts.

"Did you tell him the truth this time?" Germain prodded.

Madeleine made a moué. "Well, sort of, but he cannot find the diary without my help."

"*Bien*. The King will see you—us—very soon. I'm still waiting for the summons."

Madeleine muttered gloomily, "There is no time to waste."

Amul entered noisily. He looked refreshed, the strain around the eyes and the gray tint to his skin now gone.

"I could eat a pig!" he exclaimed and immediately proceeded to fill a plate at the sideboard.

"Good morning to you, too," Madeleine greeted him. "You left me without a word this morning."

Amul shrugged. "I knew you were in good hands." He did not confess that he had no idea how he had ended up in the comte's guest room.

Germain bellowed with laughter, and Madeleine could not maintain her stern expression.

"The cheek!" she teased.

"Things always turn out right in the end," Amul said with youthful glibness and shoveled large chunks of ham into his mouth.

That night Madeleine stepped into the corridor, dressed only in a loose silk robe. Aiming her steps toward Germain's bedroom, she knocked softly on his door. He opened it silently, and she slipped into his outstretched arms.

"At last," he whispered. "I don't like the way we hold up a façade of respectability in front of the servants. They all know that you, er—"

"They are people, too, with their own moral codes," she chastened him.

"*Oui*—and very loose ones at that," he said with a laugh. "You never cease to surprise me, *ma belle*."

"By the way," she said, "how did you find me in the stables?"

He grunted evasively. "Oh, I have my ways—informants, you know." Leading her to a chair by the fire, he inquired if she wanted something to drink.

"*Non*, I only want to spend a delicious night with you."

He chuckled. "Whatever happened to the chaste maiden I once knew?"

Madeleine pursed her lips in mock concentration. "You transformed her yourself, remember? Like this." Recklessly she pushed him down onto the wide canopied bed. "You taught her to do certain things that she'll never forget."

He lay still, his eyes twin silver flames of desire burning into her. Straddling his muscular thighs, she said with an exaggerated pout, "You are my prisoner now."

Throwing his arms above his head, he whispered, "I surrender. Do with me as you please."

Slowly she unbuttoned the diamond-studded buttons of his long waistcoat, then unlaced the white batiste shirt at the neck. Burying her fingers under the lace jabot, she caressed his throat, dipping her fingers into the tight curls on his chest.

Bending forward, she nuzzled her lips along his lean cheeks, smelling the spicy orris root.

"Kitten," he whispered. "I wish I could always cradle you in my arms like this." Stroking her back, he swiftly undid the laces of her dressing gown.

"I do, too, but according to Maurice, you change mistresses as often as you change shirts," she said matter-of-factly.

He pinched her nose and laughed. "That is very flattering gossip, but you should not believe everything you hear.

You have no reason to be jealous." His eyes gleamed wickedly, and Madeleine felt foolish.

Hiding her blushing face in his hair, she murmured, "Tonight we are together, and I want to savor it to the fullest. As long as Fouquet hunts me, there is no future for me—for us. Only *now* exists. You make me very happy."

He stiffened, and she lifted her head to gaze fully into his beloved eyes, those rich, penetrating gray eyes that were like no others.

"*Chérie*, you are already tearing us apart by saying that we don't have a future—as if we are about to be separated any minute, never to meet again," he complained. "I have just found you again. I will never let you go now."

She eyed him candidly. "Sooner or later you will. You know that we are worlds apart; but I'm sorry I brought that up now. I didn't mean to. I want to be with you now, to savor this moment always."

"Oh-la-la, how tearful we grow!"

Somehow the magic had gone, some obscure future separation looming like a ghost between them. Germain lifted her to the side and jumped out of bed. Trained to hide his feelings, he helped himself to some brandy.

The gulf yawned between them.

In a fraction of a second Madeleine realized that she wanted more than to be his mistress. She wanted to marry him, to spend the rest of her life with him. But it could never be. She would never preside at his table, never converse with the aristocracy. She would never be accepted. If Germain married her, he would be pulled down in disgrace.

But he never would marry her. A comte did not marry a seamstress, even though she was the niece of a famous playwright.

Why develop a relationship that was doomed from the start? Madeleine was overwhelmed by a sense of futility. The urgency of the moment, her fear of Fouquet, had pushed her into Germain's arms. Now she was falling deeper and deeper in love with him. She couldn't stop it. It was an avalanche. If she had only one night left with Germain for the rest of her life, she would, by *Dieu*, enjoy it to its fullest!

"Germain, please come. Let me sweep away those dark clouds on your brow," she cajoled. Seeing the tension ease from his back, she knew she had won a small victory. She would never mention the word *separation* again.

He came to lie beside her, propping himself on his elbow so that he had a good view of her face. "My life was empty before you came, *petite*. It changed the moment you stepped into my life at Versailles." He traced his index finger along her white throat, his expression grave.

"*Oui*. Whisper sweet words in my ears," she replied lightly, digging her fingers deeply into his curls. "Tell me about the seamstress maiden who was swept away on a white steed by the handsome prince with golden hair." She couldn't hide the slight trembling of her voice.

He threw back his head and laughed, dispelling the brittle atmosphere between them. "My stallion, Apollo, is black," he explained. "Don't be sad. I will make you forget all sadness. Kiss me here, here, and here." Alternately he pointed to his mouth, eyes, and throat.

With a seductive laugh, Madeleine hurried to comply.

The audience with the King was set for twenty-five minutes past ten on the following day, a Friday, a sunny morning late in March. No difficulties had arisen, and the King was eager to meet with Madeleine.

"It's more than I can fathom—that the man has been embezzling me right under my nose," the sovereign had said to Germain when the date was set. "It's clear that he is aiming for Mazarin's post." He paused, frowning. "I will not have it! I will rule without a prime minister. Fouquet must be crushed."

"*Oui*, sire," Germain responded, following the pacing King with his gaze.

"But we will not be able to walk into his house and arrest him," the King said, thinking aloud. "He is too powerful. We have to create a trap, a way that he might hang himself."

Germain related every detail of this meeting to Madeleine later that evening after they had made leisurely love. Her eyes were shining with relief. "At last! The wheels are turning. I will yet have my revenge."

"A passionate, young mistress should not be thinking of bloodthirsty revenge, but about pleasing the man who is bending backward to help her," he teased and buried his face in her hair.

"I'm spoiling you, comte." She sat up in bed, crossing her legs and propping her chin in the palm of her hand. "You know, you never told me what hold Fouquet has on you. It is not fair! I've shared my deepest, saddest secrets, and you have told me nothing."

Germain played with one of her curls. *"C'est vrai.* It is more than fair that you should know." He took a deep breath. "When I was a young man of twenty, I fell in love with a young girl, Brigitte Delchamps, of the estate neighboring Les Étoiles. She never loved me, and my heart was crushed. You must know that it was a bout of calf love, because when she married a few months later, my eyes were already on—well, that is not important here. Brigitte and I have remained good friends. She lives here in Paris and is married to a member of the Paris parlement. She is very happy. Six months ago, Jules, her husband, traveled to the provinces on business for the King. During that time Brigitte's brother died, and she was extremely distraught. Jules wasn't here to console her, so she turned to me. I truly don't know what happened, but one thing led to another, and I, er, bedded her. I was either drunk or momentarily insane. It should never have happened. And who do you think entered my study two hours later and found us?"

Madeleine nodded grimly. "I have my suspicions."

"Oui. Fouquet sauntered in as if he owned the house. I can tell you he was surprised to see Brigitte there, and she was frantic. Jules is notorious for his jealousy, but Brigitte loves him dearly and had not planned the tryst with me. It just happened." He sighed, his lips a thin line. "She ran out, crying. I made Fouquet vow to keep the secret, which he did with aplomb—in exchange for certain favors. Ever since then, he has used me to execute some underhanded deeds—like kidnapping little blond sprites with secret diaries," he added lightly, though his face was drawn. "I'd do anything to protect Brigitte. It was all my fault that she ended up in my bed."

RECKLESS SPLENDOR 195

Madeleine's lips quirked. "I'm not sure she was completely unwilling." She caressed his cheek. "But it's noble of you to put her happiness first. I respect you for it."

"That's what makes you so endearing, *chérie*. You don't create scenes, and you always struggle to understand."

"Fouquet could use you forever," she mused.

Germain shrugged. "If the diary is what you say, he is already digging his own grave. That will be the end to his power. Louis will be pleased. When Louis came into power, he knew he had many enemies—high-ranking enemies. He still has. Mayhap you are too young to remember the struggle of the Fronde, but many nobles didn't want Louis on the throne. The King is still suffering from those hard times, from constant opposition, from lack of funds. He has such great plans; he wants to create a strong France, wants to establish French tapestry and lace mills, French silks, and more. He has long suspected high state officials of dealing with his enemies behind his back." He paused and placed a kiss on her knee. "Fouquet is but one of those state officials. The way it looks, he may be the most villainous of the lot. The diary will prove that, I hope."

"It will," Madeleine promised grimly.

Madeleine had butterflies in her stomach. She was dressed in a deep blue satin gown shot with silver threads. The blue was the exact color of her eyes. Lavishly trimmed with Venetian lace, it was the most elegant gown she had ever worn. The satin parted over a quilted white petticoat embroidered with silver thread and pearls. Wearing a velvet cloak lined with soft fur, she looked exquisite.

Nicole had helped her to put up her hair in a myriad of ringlets clustered at the back of her head. A *mouche, à la Coquette,* adorned the corner of her mouth, contrasting with the alabaster smoothness of her skin.

Germain was to escort her to the most important meeting of her life.

Joining him in the hallway, she could not but draw in her breath with pleasure. He was dressed in an ice-blue satin coat and a shirt of silver cloth. At his throat gleamed a jabot of spiderweb-thin lace. White boots of soft leather reached above his knees. A baldric of the same leather crossed his broad chest, and a dress sword shone at his side.

When he placed the wide plumed felt hat on his head and took her outstretched hand, he whispered, "Is this the ragamuffin I found sleeping in my hay?"

Madeleine smiled prettily. "*Oui*, but underneath all that grime, a princess was hiding."

"So I notice," he complimented her and assisted her into the coach. Holding her hand tenderly, he leaned over and placed a light kiss on her warm lips. "My princess with lips like fresh rose petals and skin of such softness, of such translucent beauty, it goes forever unchallenged. Not to mention those dangerous eyes in which I've drowned many times." He kissed each of her fingertips.

"*Alors*, you've turned into a poet. Well, continue! Let me hear some more lies! I will be so inflated by the time we reach St. Germain that I will be incapable of climbing out of the coach."

He rubbed his mustache thoughtfully. "*Non*, you have to earn the compliments first. These are the ones I owe you for last night's ecstasy," he responded silkily. Madeleine hit him playfully over the head with her painted ivory fan.

She wished she could always remember this perfect early spring morning when the clouds looked benign and the sun was caressing the earth with warm and golden light.

"I'm going to see the King. I don't believe it! I know I won't be able to say a word, my tongue will tie itself into a knot."

"Nonsense. The King will be utterly charmed with you. I have a mind to hide you away from his eyes. I don't want him to get ideas."

Germain looked quite serious, and Madeleine had to laugh. "You're jealous."

"I'm not!" He glowered at her. "Who knows, you may take a fancy to him, and then where would I be? Would you leave me helpless by the roadside since you've stolen my willpower?"

Madeleine tapped the toe of her slipper on the floor, a teasing smile playing over her lips. "I just might, *mon cher*, I might. But let's see the King first."

Chapter 21

"We will arrive in time to attend Mass with the King," Germain said, looking at his gold pocket watch.

The coach halted abruptly, and Madeleine stared at the chaos in the stable yard. She had never seen so many grooms and ostlers in one place, as well as pages of all ages and sizes dressed in the King's livery.

A lackey let down the carriage steps, and Germain handed Madeleine down. They had to walk to the inner courtyard since Germain was not of high enough rank to bring his carriage into that sanctum. Only royalty, dukes, and duchesses were allowed that privilege.

The wet mud ruined Madeleine's shoes, and water seeped through the satin, making her toes uncomfortably cold. Bewildered by the crush of elegant courtiers, Madeleine clung to Germain's arm. He patted her hand.

The chapel was hot and airless, the odors of cloying perfume and unwashed bodies mingling with the scents of burning wax and incense. Germain handed her a handkerchief drenched in lavender water. Laughter danced in his eyes, and he winked at her. She felt shy and awkward. This was his natural environment, so far removed from her own. She doubted the abyss could ever be bridged.

"You're the loveliest woman here," he murmured behind his hand.

"Don't be ridiculous!" she scoffed to hide her insecurity. Shyly she met the courtiers' curious stares. It did not occur to her that the picture she and her noble escort made was stunning indeed. Many jealous glares were sent in her direction.

Madeleine focused her gaze at the dark brown curly head of the sovereign at the front of the chapel. Was he disturbed by the unrest and talk at the back? Sending Germain a worried glance, she was reassured by his calm expression. Evidently the restless chatter in the chapel was a common occurrence. Whispers and muffled giggles flew through the air. Was the King the only one who cared about Mass? Where he led, the others had to follow whether they liked it or not. King Louis wanted all his courtiers around him. Madeleine wasn't sure she envied them.

After Mass, Madeleine watched the King lead the procession out of the chapel. She swallowed convulsively. It was almost time.

She was startled when a soft voice reached her ear from behind. She turned. The chevalier de Lemont was standing at her side, lazily chewing a sugar-coated pastry.

"I see the fugitive has reappeared, and in style. Very clever, Mademoiselle Poquelin. Fouquet has been searching everywhere, but he has been powerless to find you." He indicated Germain, who was talking to a painted and powdered lady in a lilac gown. "I know who shielded you. But sometimes even high-ranking friends are useless. Your protector will soon be stripped of his power, you just wait and see. Fouquet does not have a forgiving nature."

He smiled maliciously, and Madeleine shivered. "The comte de Hautefort is the only one who has shown any decency. Your threats cannot touch him."

Lemont curled his lips into a sneer. "Just because you managed to wangle an audience with the King doesn't mean you have won. Fouquet will be waiting when you least expect it." His voice was silky with menace, and she smelled the faint aromas of brandy and sugar on his breath as he leaned closer. "Remember that!" he spat.

Anger caught like wildfire in her blood. "Let him tell me. Is he too cowardly to come himself? Sending fops—lackeys—like you to scare me is the height of cowardice!"

A muscle twitched in Lemont's jaw. He was white with fury.

Immediately she regretted her rashness. To have an enemy like Lemont could only spell ruin. Fop or not, he was an important man at court. Madeleine knew he could be as charming as he was vile, and he was known to amuse the King with his wit. As long as Fouquet was after her, she could not afford to antagonize Lemont further.

Trying to soothe his anger, she said, "Chevalier, I don't know what you want with me. We have never been introduced, and since you loathe my lowly class, I see no reason why you should speak with me at all."

"You have dipped your nose in affairs that do not concern you," he answered icily, "and I'm only protecting what is important to me—and the state."

"Fouquet is a burgher like me," she continued. "I know he must have some sort of hold over you or you would never deign to speak to him. You must be heavily indebted to Fouquet to be running his errands. Don't you see? You need to get free of Fouquet and his threats. Even if he divulges your secret to the King, it will still be your word against his. Whose word will the King believe, yours or Fouquet's? *Yours*, of course! You can throw off Fouquet."

She was trembling with the effort of making him see reason. For a moment it seemed to work. The wrath slowly subsided from his eyes, and he rubbed his chin.

"What are you doing here, Lemont?" Germain barked as he handed Madeleine a cup of cocoa.

Lemont did not answer at first, and the cold steel crept back into his eyes. Then he said, "Hautefort, I warned you before. Fouquet is a powerful enemy, and I would watch my every step if I were you." Without another word, he turned on his heel and marched off.

"I tried to talk some sense into him. He told me that Fouquet has not given up," Madeleine explained. A line of worry deepened between her brows. "Do you think Lemont was referring to Madame Delchamps? Perhaps Fouquet is going . . . or has already gone . . . to her husband with your secret."

Germain stared grimly after Lemont. "I don't think so, or I would have heard from Jules Delchamps." His voice softened. "But I have realized that you come before everything else now, *ma belle*. I'd do anything to help you and the King. Brigitte would understand that."

Madeleine's throat tightened, and she squeezed his hand. *"Merci."*

Germain rubbed his mustache. "I'm going to ask the King for armed guards for you," he said with a frown. "The faster this business is settled, the better. Whatever Fouquet is planning, it's not good."

"I don't know why Lemont is involved with Fouquet in the first place."

"He must be in a hole financially. It's likely he has large outstanding debts to Fouquet, who is putting pressure on him, just as he does on me. Lemont is a coward, has always been. He goes nowhere without Dubois, and we know what he is like. Lemont leans on him." Germain discreetly indicated another nobleman dressed in a pink pearl-encrusted jacket. "I don't trust D'Ambrose either; he has his finger in every pie at court, always mixed up in some intrigue. Most of all, he's malicious."

"How I wish the diary were in the hands of the King!" Madeleine exclaimed.

Her stomach made a somersault; she felt as if she were going to the ax block on Place de Grève. Her legs shook as Germain led her past the staring crowd in the King's antechamber. The crush was greater here than in the chapel.

As she faced the gilt-inlaid double doors to the King's study, she wanted to turn around and run, but Germain's firm grip on her fingers did not loosen. The Swiss Guards hastened to open the doors, their stiff-pleated ruffs looking very uncomfortable.

Dressed in a gold-embroidered vest and a white shirt, the King stood bent over a huge ledger spread out on the enormous desk. Books and papers were stacked on the gleaming surface. On one of the walls hung a map of France, and in a corner stood a globe.

As the doors closed behind them, Madeleine sank into a curtsy, her skirts ballooning around her. She dared not lift her eyes to the royal face.

Silence stretched, a comfortable, industrious kind of silence. Then the sound of a book sliding across leather and the scraping of a chair announced that the King's attention was directed at her. Madeleine kept her eyes to the floor.

"*Enfin,* Hautefort, *mon ami.*"

"Good morning, Your Majesty. This is Mademoiselle Poquelin."

Footsteps echoed on the parquet floor, and Madeleine found herself staring at a pair of silver buckles in the shape of bows.

"I am your humble servant, Your Majesty," she mumbled, her mouth dry with fear.

"Shy, *non*, Germain?"

"Awed, I believe, sire."

How dared Germain speak to the King so calmly? Her own tongue had grown to triple size.

The King chuckled, a low, soft rumble. She was paralyzed with shock as he reached out and lifted her chin. Her eyes wide, she met the dancing, black royal gaze. He was frightening, awesome, but he instantly put her at ease with a boyish smile. Only a few years older than herself, he was so sure of himself, already so much a king.

A faint scent of jasmine wafted around him as he moved.

Knowing his place, Germain retreated a few steps to remain unobtrusive during the interview, but the King addressed him all the same. "An unusual beauty, isn't she? I can see how she managed to melt your icy heart when no one else was successful." The sovereign flashed Madeleine a mischievous smile.

"*Oui*," Germain said, clenching his teeth. What woman could resist Louis's smile?

"She blushes prettily. Modest, too?" After leading her to a chair, the King sauntered off to stare out the window. Madeleine was shocked at the honor he showered upon her; the highest favor was to sit in his presence.

"*Donc*, tell me all about your extraordinary accusation against my minister of finance."

Collecting her wits, Madeleine slowly and clearly told all the details of her adventures. When she had finished, the King was quiet for a long moment. She feared she had angered him, but when he turned to her, his eyes were merely pensive.

He sat down behind his desk and tapped the mahogany surface with his fingertips.

"Sire," Germain dared to interject, "Mademoiselle Poquelin is in great danger."

"I'm aware of that," the King admitted. "I will allot six French Guards for your protection. They will accompany you to Rouen. I want that diary with utmost speed. Germain, you will escort Mademoiselle Poquelin as well. I have complete faith in you; she must travel to Rouen safely."

"Sire, I'm honored to escort her." Germain bowed at the waist, indicating with a glance that Madeleine should rise and curtsy.

The King nodded gracefully. "I wish you luck." Smiling at Madeleine, he added, "I'm indebted to you. You're a loyal subject. I wish I had more subjects like you." He sighed. "You will be richly rewarded." With a wave of his hand, he showed that the audience was over. Germain and Madeleine backed out of the room.

As the doors were about to close, the King added, "It will please me to see your lovely face at court often hereafter, mademoiselle."

Madeleine was too overcome to do anything but nod, her cheeks pink.

Wending their way through the crowd, Germain said from the corner of his mouth, "When he says he *wishes* something, it's an order."

"*Vraiment?*" Madeleine stared at him wide-eyed.

"*Oui.* It appears that you'll be another, er, prisoner at court." He didn't sound happy at the prospect.

"What do you mean? Don't you like life at court?"

"Louis wants control more than anything; that's why he keeps us here all the time. He's afraid of brewing conspiracies. My estates are falling into disrepair since I cannot go and inspect them."

"I'm sorry." Placing a comforting hand on his arm, she continued, "I thought you were happy here." She hesitated. "If we can be together—"

"*Oui*, times are looking brighter." A smile wiped away the stiffness around his mouth. "First we're going to Rouen, together. Ah, it will be good to smell fresh country air again!"

Chapter 22

Six royal guards escorted the large crested carriage out of Paris on its journey northwest to Rouen.

The roads were bad, but on the first leg of the trip Madeleine and Amul stoically accepted the coach's jarring contact with bumps and holes. Amul had nagged her until Madeleine had allowed him to accompany her.

"I wish I could ride like monsieur le comte. This carriage is for women and children!" Amul complained with a sigh and looked longingly out the window.

Madeleine's lips curved, and her eyes flashed. "Women and *children*," she replied sweetly.

"Bah!" He eyed her darkly. "I wish you would throw out that scented handkerchief. I vow I will throw up if you keep waving it back and forth under my nose."

"Do you prefer the stench of rotting refuse?"

They were traveling through a poor suburb of Paris, and the sudden warmth in the air had released all the pungent odors from the filthy streets. In the heart of Paris, the streets were kept clear to a moderate extent, but in the outskirts no efforts were made. In places the smell was so bad that Madeleine thought she was going to faint.

"I can't say I like it," Amul admitted grudgingly.

They were jostled together as the wheels hit an unusually deep hole.

"*Diable!*" Amul kneaded his head where it had made contact with the door. His elbow had hit Madeleine in the ribs, and they exchanged grieved glances.

"The comte is teaching you bad language, Amul! I will not have it!"

As if he sensed that tempers were rapidly disintegrating in the carriage, Germain rode up and ducked his head through the window. "We will soon be out of this pit. The roads will be better and the air pure."

He was right. By the time the sun was setting, the flaming orange ball streaking the sky with red and peach, they had left Paris behind. The road was smooth, and the air was scented with the sweet promise of spring.

Amul sat brooding in his corner. The next time Germain stuck his head into the coach, Madeleine put her hand over his on the windowframe.

"Amul is longing to ride. Why don't you travel with me in the carriage?" Her eyes bore a suggestion of pleasantries to come.

A tingle of desire kindled in his blood. Not to appear too eager, he shrugged. "That will be fine. Amul, do you want to try Apollo?" he asked the boy kindly.

As when the sun breaks through the clouds, Amul's expression changed drastically, and he clapped his hands in excitement.

"Really?"

"*Oui*, but he's a bit temperamental; you have to be on your guard." He eyed Amul. "By the way, where did you learn to ride?"

"At Saint-Cloud. One of the ostlers taught me. Madame likes to ride, and where she went, I went—"

"Fine," Germain interrupted him. He called a halt, and the carriage stopped with a jolt.

Madeleine took the opportunity to stretch her legs. In a ditch, she found the tiny yellow heads of coltsfoot peeping out of the moss, and she picked one and stuck it into the bodice of her gown.

Germain came up behind her and snaked his arms around her waist, pressing against her. His mustache tickled her neck as he bent to kiss the hollow behind her ear.

"Lovely," he whispered.

Desire flowed through her like a languorous wave.

"I want to make love to you," he breathed, and Madeleine felt the hard thuds of his heart against her back. Leaning her head against his upper arm, she glanced into his eyes, drinking in the ardor from the gray pools. She went weak with love.

Bouffon! You will lose him when he finds a wife of his own class, said a voice in her head, but she resolutely closed the door on the voice. Life was too short to waste.

"Hark!" one of the guards shouted. "Let's leave this copse. Highwaymen lurk in the forest."

Reluctantly Germain loosened his hold on her waist. "*Oui*, we'd better go on, alas. It's almost dark now, and we want to reach The Golden Stag by seven. I'm hungry—for more . . ."

"I'm starved," Madeleine admitted and planted a kiss in the hollow at the base of his throat. Germain assisted her into the carriage.

Sitting atop the huge stallion, Amul was a king for a day. He aped the guards who were sitting ramrod straight on their mounts.

The light had turned into a mellow mauve glow, shrouding everything in a mist of softness.

Germain smiled at Madeleine, and her heart raced. Leaning across her legs, he pulled the leather flaps over the windows, and a soft darkness enfolded them.

"Come here, you temptress. Tell me what you had in mind when you asked if I wanted to change places with Amul." His voice held a world of suggestion.

"This." Curling her fingers into his hair, she pulled his face down to her avid lips and let her tongue assault the soft velvet of his mouth before he could protest.

He gasped. "What . . . a . . . pleasant surprise," he managed to say before her bewitching lips claimed his once more.

The wheel floundered through a hole, and they fell helplessly to the floor in a tangle of limbs.

Germain shielded her head with his arm to prevent it from hitting the door.

"*Petite*, are you hurt?" he murmured, his breath fanning her neck.

"*Non* . . . I feel wonderful."

He paused, stroking her cheek with one finger. "Madeleine, I love you. No woman has ever touched my heart like you do." Germain could not fathom the strength of his emotions, his need to take care of her, his longing for her when they were not together. It was true. He really loved her. It was an emotion that threatened to break open his chest.

"I love you, too," she whispered, starlight in her eyes. He loved her! "I thought I'd never be happy again. The sorrow is still here"—she pointed at her chest—"but your love is healing me."

His fingers trembled along her neck. "That was the finest compliment a woman has ever given me." His warm breath rushed over her face as he tried to see her eyes in the darkness.

"Oh . . . Germain, I've loved you since the first moment I saw you at Versailles." Her voice quivered with suppressed tears. "I know I have."

With a groan he buried his face between her breasts.

"You have shown me wonderful things," she continued.

"And you have shown me that I have a heart. If this is the beginning, there is no end to our love." Gladness colored his voice. "I want to, I *need* to, know everything about you, to touch every inch of your body, to find every hidden mole or mark—and I will kiss them all!"

Madeleine giggled in breathless expectation.

Germain continued, his eyes serious. "And I've been thinking; I would like to make you—"

The coach halted with a thud, sending him crashing against the seat. *"Diable!* What was that!" he exclaimed and scrambled up.

Madeleine sat up and rearranged her hair.

Smoothing his mustache, Germain opened the door and jumped down. "What is going on here?" he barked.

Madeleine stuck her head out the window. The tableau in front of her eyes did not appear real.

The six French Guards were still on their mounts. Torches held high in their hands combatted the falling darkness, grotesque shadows dancing over the still figures of yet another group of guards standing on the ground.

Madeleine recognized them as part of the Life Guard by their blue uniforms with silver braiding and the wide baldrics from which swords hung. She counted ten guards, three of them old and distinguished.

"Comte de Hautefort?" the grizzled leader asked, stepping forward, a parchment roll clutched in one hand. "You're to return to Paris immediately." He waved the parchment. "I have an order here."

Confused silence fell. "Why?" Germain asked, genuinely puzzled. "His Majesty ordered me to escort Mademoiselle Poquelin to Rouen."

"The plans have changed. The guards will escort Mademoiselle Poquelin. You're to go back without delay."

Germain stared hard at the quiet circle of men. He didn't know what to believe. "This is ridiculous! I'm not going back," he said. "Let me see that scroll." He unrolled the parchment and scanned the words.

Amul edged up to the carriage, afraid of the building tension among the men.

Madeleine jumped down and flew to Germain's side. "He's coming with me!" she blurted out, peeping over Germain's arm at the scroll. The royal seal shone like a splash of blood at the bottom. *Louis XIV* was scrawled with a flourish.

"*Non*, mademoiselle."

"Why? There has to be a reason."

"I'm not at liberty to say." The officer proceeded to grip Germain's arms, holding a set of manacles in his hand.

Stiff with anger, Germain pulled away and drew his sword, but instantly the other guards surrounded him, pointing their weapons at his chest. He must either give up or forfeit his life. Choosing the first alternative, he let his sword clatter to the ground. A *lettre de cachet*. The King was giving him a *lettre de cachet*, the worst punishment of all! But why?

Germain's eyes were narrowed in wrath, and his face was deathly pale. A muscle worked in his jaw. "If this is some ghastly joke, you're all going to pay!" he snarled.

The guards refused to move.

"Are you paid by Fouquet to do this?" Madeleine challenged, her breath coming in shallow gasps of fear. Had yet another nightmare started?

"*Non*, madame. We are here on the King's orders."

"That is preposterous! I don't believe you! I spoke with him this morning," Germain spat, shaking his fist in a futile gesture. "It is a mistake."

The capitaine shrugged and climbed onto his horse. The guards led the struggling Germain to Apollo. It took three men to force him into the saddle. Two guards tied his hands to the pommel and handed the reins to the capitaine. Unable to move, Madeleine stared in disbelief. Like a parcel, Germain sat on Apollo and was led onto the road.

"*Non!* You can't do this!" She flew after them, clinging to Germain's leg. He looked down at her, his eyes slits of pain and bewilderment.

"You go on. I'll return as soon as this mad business is resolved. Please don't cry," he urged, but Madeleine could not stop the great sobs from tearing out of her. Apollo fidgeted, and she would have fallen under his hooves had not one of the guards dragged her away. Soon darkness swallowed the ominous group, and Madeleine fell to her knees in despair. A terrible foreboding spread in her heart.

As if in answer to that premonition of disaster, a bloodcurdling scream of rage rose to the sky.

"Germain!" she cried. "What are they doing to him!" In helpless terror and anger, she beat the ground. Kicking and screaming, she was lifted into the carriage. The horses strained, their harnesses creaking, rapidly widening the gap between the carriage and the prisoner.

In the coach, Madeleine lay sprawled across one seat, her face buried in her arms. Amul patted her shivering back, but he knew he could not comfort her.

The bewildering events had left him numb with fear. The act bore the stamp of Fouquet, and Amul suspected that the enemy was not far behind. To protect Madeleine from Fouquet, the King should have sent an army, Amul thought. Would it have helped? He suspected that most of the officers were in Fouquet's pay.

At last, Madeleine's sobs quieted and she lay very still.

"Please, Madeleine, collect yourself. I'm sure Germain will be back before long." Amul did not sound convincing. "Tomorrow at the latest."

Dejectedly Madeleine wiped away her tears. Her voice was thick as she spoke. "You know better than that. I thought we were safe with all the guards and the King's blessings—but more the fool I!" She heaved a deep sigh. "As for Germain, we'll be lucky if we ever see him alive again! I should have done more to help him."

She shuddered, envisioning a dark, empty road ahead without Germain. "It's my fault; I pulled him into my problems."

"Madeleine, you must focus on your mission."

"Bah! I'm *sick* of the mission! Let the King fetch the diary himself."

"You do not mean that. You have to carry on."

A new flood of tears burst forth, and Amul sensed the bottomless chasm of despair she was fighting.

Their adversary had been too powerful, making the mission impossible from the start.

"We will win," he whispered tensely into the darkness, but deep inside he was convinced they had already lost.

Chapter 23

The ancient convent was located on Rue des Boucheries-Saint-Quen in the town of Rouen. The air itself was steeped in history, crowded with ghosts from the beginning of time.

Madeleine felt numb, her tears spent. *Mon Dieu,* I need courage, she repeated silently over and over. For France, for France. As she heard the muted clang of the convent bells chiming for Angelus, she pinched her lips together in determination.

The kind eyes of a sister studied them through the grille in the door. Madeleine stood surrounded by the six guards and Amul.

"Sister, I need to speak with the mother superior."

Agnes, the mother superior, sat behind her desk, a stern expression on her face, her hands folded on top of the pristine blotter. Her old face was smooth and pink.

Madeleine had never seen her before, and she felt the older woman's assessing glance touch her like a cold prickle on her skin. She feared the mother superior would refuse her request. "I'm a former pupil of this convent, Madeleine Poquelin. My father was Jean Poquelin, the tax collector," she explained.

The well-known name in Rouen did not make the older woman's eyes light up in recognition. Madeleine sighed.

"In the convent wall I once hid a very important item, and I would like to retrieve it today." Feeling the suspicion and annoyance rise in her adversary, Madeleine held her hands extended in a pleading gesture. "I know it was singularly foolish to hide something in the wall, but you have to remember that I was in many ways a child then."

A weak excuse to be sure, but she could not afford to be stopped now. The mother superior pondered her words and carefully scrutinized each person of the group. The nun grumbled something like "Impertinent girl—sacred grounds." She rose reluctantly. "Highly improper, if you ask me! I've never heard such a story!"

Amul banged his elbow into Madeleine's ribs, making her want to giggle hysterically.

"Mother, I was distraught and frightened when my father died. He entrusted the item to me; it is very valuable. I assure you, I would not have used the convent as a hiding place, but I knew no better. I promise it will never happen again."

The nun eyed the guards, and Amul earned a withering stare when he snickered. "Do these men have to follow you onto the grounds?"

"*Non*, mother, if you please, only him." She pointed at Amul. "The guards can wait outside."

She motioned them to leave. Like a small shadow, Amul trotted after her. "Nothing saintly about *her*," he hissed in Madeleine's ear. "If you ask me."

"Shhh!"

"I've never heard of such reckless behavior in a pupil," the mother superior muttered with disapproval as she opened the door to the garden. "But then, my predecessor was too lax."

And so kind compared to you, Madeleine thought. In her chest leaped a flame of anger. What right did the nun have to judge her actions? She should be grateful that one pupil had thought so highly of the convent as to want to hide her valuable secret within its walls. Please God, give me patience. I cannot take another reprimand.

Diamond-sharp sunlight blinded her eyes as she stepped into the walled garden, and she had to squint. A peaceful silence reigned. The snow had melted, revealing bare garden plots. In the summer, it would be filled with sweet-smelling herbs and flowers.

With a disapproving nod, the mother superior left them. Madeleine concentrated on the search. A few minutes passed before she could remember at which end of the wall she had hidden the diary. Then she recognized the willow tree. One of the stones to the right of the tree concealed the diary.

With his sensitive fingertips, Amul helped her go over the surface of the large gray stones. Several were loose, and they began a backbreaking job of dislodging and replacing them.

"We should have brought the guards for this," Madeleine said with a moan as she broke a nail on one of the stones.

Luck finally came their way, and the fourth stone proved to be the right one. Mortar fell into the gaping hole, and Madeleine stuck her arm inside, immediately touching the oilcloth she had wrapped around the diary.

A fire of excitement consumed them, and after replacing the stone, Madeleine unwrapped the cloth.

The small book was in good repair; no damp stains marred the cover. Amul stared in avid interest as Madeleine flipped the pages.

"To think that such an insignificant thing has such powerful people jumping with nerves," he commented.

Madeleine smiled. "That is a slight exaggeration."

"People have *killed* for it!"

A sigh passed her lips. "It's true, alas." Clutching the diary decisively under her arm, she began walking back to the main building. "I can't wait to get rid of it. It has ruined my life." Bitterness tinged her voice. "My father was a fool to meddle in Fouquet's affairs." She drew a deep, shuddering breath. "Let the King take care of the rest."

"First we have to deliver it."

"Don't remind me! I'm so sick of this whole business; and I'm exhausted to boot," she complained, her brow dark with anger.

Amul knew better. Madeleine had been on the verge of hysteria ever since Germain had been hauled away. He wasn't sure how much longer she could last. The building strain of the last months was coming to the boiling point. Poor Madeleine. What a brave person she was—for a woman!

"I'm going to make the guards carry it to safety," she said, plunging into the dark interior of the convent.

The mother superior was in her office, and they thanked her profusely, showing her a corner of the diary.

Blessing them with a sniff of disapproval, she let them out onto the busy street.

Madeleine breathed painfully as if a heavy weight were crushing her chest. This was her hometown, but never would it be the same again. Nobody was waiting for her in her old home, only sad memories. The new tax collector and his large family lived in the house now.

Madeleine handed the wrapped diary to the capitaine of the guards, Monsieur Genet. Let them do some guarding, she thought coldly, and set off to the inn where they had taken rooms.

"We should get back to Paris at the highest possible speed," she threw over her shoulder. She wanted desperately to find out what had befallen Germain. She believed her heart was going to break with pain and worry. No tears remained, only a tight-lipped determination to find him.

The next evening, Madeleine dragged herself up the stairs to her room on the second floor of the small inn. Having barely touched her dinner, she wanted only to sleep. Her eyelids were drooping, and there was a constant pain in her chest. Having left Rouen early in the morning, they had traveled all day at a snail's pace, and she was sore all over and irritated with Capitaine Genet for leading them astray; they had lost half a day. Oh, when was she going to see Germain again?

The guards were making merry in the common room, including Amul in their jests. He strutted about, his thumbs inserted in his vest pockets, pleased at being treated like a grown man. The strong ale served at dinner had gone to everyone's heads.

Madeleine had counted six other guests who had already retired, worn-out travelers like herself.

Opening the window, she took several deep breaths of the fresh, nippy air. An owl hooted forlornly in the distance, and the moon hid behind a huge cloud, painting the edges with silver light. A bird or a bat flitted past the window, a tiny dark shadow.

The window faced a lane that wound like a light ribbon through a copse of oaks. A faint sound reached Madeleine's ears. She leaned further outside and strained to penetrate the shadows.

Apprehension rattled through her. You're being ridiculous, she silently chided herself. You see threats in every movement. A fox is out hunting, or perhaps the owl found a mouse.

Just as she was rationalizing her fears, another sound sliced through the still air. This time there was no mistake.

A rider, black and sinister against the night, emerged from the copse. Fear sat like a sick lump in Madeleine's stomach. She *knew*. This was disaster.

Transfixed, she watched the red glow of a torch flare in the copse. Behind the lone rider followed a group of seven men, one carrying the torch.

The slow *clip-clop* of the horses' hooves came closer, the men silent. It was a nightmare from which she struggled to wake up.

Whoever they were, the diary was their aim. She knew it.

Frantic thoughts rushed through her head. Where was the diary now? The guards—the guards! In despair, she watched the black knot of men turn into the empty yard of the inn.

Forgetting her exhaustion, she rushed out onto the landing and looked down into the common room. The guards were lolling over their tankards, their raucous laughter rolling toward the dirty ceiling beams. Amul was fast asleep, his head on the table.

Just as she opened her mouth to call the head guard, the stout door flew open with a loud crash, and three men stepped inside, their swords drawn. They were wearing dark, simple clothes and masks covering their faces. A silent menace hung in the air. More men crowded inside. The laughter died abruptly.

The first man, the obvious leader, pushed his way to the fore. Madeleine hid in the shadows, but still she had a good view of the room. Her legs shaking, she had to bite her teeth together hard to stop them from chattering. She swallowed a whimper.

The leader was dressed entirely in black, his hair concealed by a scarf under a wide-brimmed hat. Black gloves covered his hands, and the metal of his sword glinted evilly in the firelight.

Madeleine stared in horror at the scene enacted below. The leader grasped the guard closest to the door. "Where is it?"

"Huh? What?" Drunkenly he stared into the eyes of his attacker and feebly pulled out his sword. The attacker forcefully tore it from his hand and tossed it to the floor.

The other guards stood swaying, confused expressions on their faces. Drunken pigs! Madeleine thought. They had not listened to her warnings about the danger. All she had worked for was in jeopardy now.

The host sidled up to the group, wringing his hands in despair. "I don't want a brawl within these walls," he whined.

A brutal shove sent him sprawling to the earth floor. Madeleine bit her lip nervously.

"Well, where is it? Have you swallowed your tongues?" The leader's tone had turned impatient.

Monsieur Genet stepped forward hesitantly, his eyes clouded with fear. "The diary?"

An affirmative grunt came from the man in the mask, and he took a vicious hold on Genet's lapels, almost strangling the man.

The guard's words came in painful gasps. "The . . . young lady . . . has . . . it."

Madeleine could not believe her ears. The gall of the man! *He* was responsible for the safety of the diary.

The leader glanced around the room. "Where is she?"

Still in a stranglehold, the guard pointed up the stairs. "Number three."

Madeleine gasped. They would be after her now. The guards were all cowards. Soundlessly she sprinted into her room. Her eyes sought frantically for a hiding place. Under the bed or in the large wardrobe would be too obvious. She could already hear their thundering steps on the stairs.

The window. She leaned out. A narrow ledge ran along the wall. Seeming impossible as a hiding place, it was nevertheless her only chance. Hurriedly she clambered over the windowsill. She lowered herself, the ledge barely supporting her small feet. Holding on to a rusty hook fastened to the wall next to the window, she pushed the window shut at the same moment that the door swung wide.

Fervently she prayed that nobody had noticed the movement. She held her breath in terror.

The cool air seeped through her thin dress, and her feet turned stiff with cold. Trembling with fear, she decided to jump if they found her. She would rather die in a fall than be tortured to death by Fouquet's henchmen.

Screams and the thumps of furniture being overturned rang from below, terrifying sounds accompanied by the curses from the men searching her room. The brutes! Although they wouldn't find the diary, she knew they would tear her things apart as they went through them. She was of a mind to tell them the truth, to send them back downstairs to the feeble excuse for a man that was Capitaine Genet.

Her arms were beginning to ache with the strain of supporting her weight. Pressing hard against the wall, she was cloaked by the shadow of the eaves.

A loud crashing noise boomed. The wardrobe had been overturned. She realized her luck. What if she had hid inside? The thought made her teeth chatter uncontrollably.

Suddenly the casement window banged open, almost hitting her in the head. Compressing her teeth hard to stop them from chattering, she clung motionless in the shadows. Not seeing the man, she still heard the rasp of his beard against his collar as he turned his head back and forth, peering into the darkness below.

"She isn't down there," he yelled. "Too high a jump."

The window closed, and to her dismay, Madeleine heard him secure the latch on the inside. She was locked out. Why had she not thought of that earlier?

Helplessly her gaze wandered along the ledge. No hold for the hands, she concluded miserably.

She had a choice of breaking the window and releasing the latch or jumping. Looking down, she could barely make out the ground, but there was a drift of melting snow under the window. The choice was simple; she'd rather fall than face the villains inside. But if she started thinking about it, she would never dare to jump.

Closing her eyes, she released her hold and let herself fall, aiming for the snowdrift below. One desperate thought flashed through her head. Germain, help!

Before the thought was finished, she was on the ground. The snow saved her from injury, yet the fall jarred her bones and pushed the air out of her lungs.

Regaining her breath, she stood on shaky legs. Edging along the wall, she reached the grimy windows of the common room.

Peering inside, she was the witness to a horror scene that would give her nightmares for years to come.

Snarls and curses flew through the air. "You lied to me, you swine!" The leader attacked Genet, whose fearful whimpers pierced the air. "She's gone. Did she take the diary?" The air became so thick with menace that Madeleine flinched and started to cry soundlessly.

She pictured the other guests half dead with fear in their beds. One of the other guards threw himself on the back of the villain, who hurled him off savagely. As the guard tried to rise, the villain raised his sword.

A scream cut the stillness of the night. A petrifying gurgling sound followed, and a thud. Frantically Madeleine tried to see through the grime. The poor guard was lying on the floor, twisted awkwardly in death.

Before her eyes another one went down, his throat slit, and as if by a signal, the gang threw themselves like wolves over the rest of the guards.

A bloodcurdling melee broke out, the drunken guards easily overpowered. Slashing swords reflected the orange-red light of the fire, and Madeleine pressed her hands to her ears as more death screams rent the night. *Amul*.

Running around the corner of the inn, she crouched on the ground, her back against the wall. She could do nothing to help. To enter the inn would bring her death.

Tears trickled down her face, and she rocked back and forth to control her mounting hysteria. She did not feel the cold any longer. She was shaking uncontrollably.

Hearing the harsh voices and the heavy steps of the murderers, she pushed closer to the wall, placing her head between her knees.

As the men passed her only a few steps away, she heard every word they said.

"That milksop of a guard thought he could fool us. *Enfin*, he won't fool anybody ever again. The *bouffon* thought we wouldn't find the diary in his pocket. Too easy! A conceited fellow believing we would share our reward with him for giving us the traveling plans. But I have to hand it to the idiot, he made it easier for us with all those guards dead drunk."

One day and half a night, Genet had concealed the diary, and now his life was extinct because of it—and because of his own treachery. He had sold the lives of his fellow guards out of greed. Madeleine seethed with anger. Powerless, she watched the men mount their horses and gallop down the lane, the diary tucked safely within someone's clothing.

Following the murderers with her gaze, she hardened and got a hold on sanity once more. That diary had ruined her life over and over. She ought to be relieved to see it go.

Amul. Everything was so quiet. Her legs ached, but the only conscious thought in her head was to find Amul. She barely dared to glance through the open door of the inn, let alone enter, knowing full well that the sight would be forever etched in her memory.

Six guards and the host were bathed in a huge crimson pool of blood, their glazed eyes staring blindly at the ceiling. Their clothes were slashed to ribbons and their swords broken.

Mesmerized by the ghastly sight, Madeleine whimpered and looked for Amul. *Dieu*, let him be alive! She saw him sitting where he had been earlier, his head still resting on the table. His back was covered with blood where a single stroke of a sword had pierced through to his heart. Amul had never awakened from his sleep.

Screaming, Madeleine rushed to his side. In tears of utter despair, she seized his shoulders and tried to shake him back to life, but his eyes were never to light up again. Sobbing wildly, she stroked his curly head and his face, so young and so peaceful in death.

A wave of choking nausea welled up in her throat, and she fled outside. Leaning against the wall, she retched uncontrollably, perspiration covering her forehead, helpless to stop her trembling.

Afterward she felt empty and cleansed of all emotions, save grief. It started in her chest and spread its searing agony to the very tips of her fingers and to the soles of her feet. Grief sat like a blinding pain behind her eyes. The only way she could bear it was by moving. She staggered forward, one step at a time, not allowing herself to look back, to think. Amul, Amul—a terrible wail rose from her lips, and she tore at her hair.

Without her cloak, in thin, useless slippers, she began walking aimlessly along the lane. The brutal death of a child had caused an incurable wound on her conscience.

Chapter 24

Germain labored to pull his bloodied wrists from the manacles. He knew it was a futile struggle, but he could not stand to be chained to a wall like a dog. His muscles swelled and flexed as he pulled in fury at the unbending iron clamps.

Exhausted, he fell down on the pallet covered with filthy straw.

A rat was eating the leftover sops on the tin plate on the floor. Nausea and disgust gnawed at the pit of his stomach.

Incarcerated in the Bastille, he was totally isolated from the rest of the world. None of the usual favors due to his rank had been given him. For one thing, he was not kept in the tolerable part of the prison where the noblemen usually waited for the King's wrath to cool and the resulting pardon to come. In that part of the fortress a nobleman was allowed to keep his valet, and after passing out suitable bribes, to eat a good dinner every day. Germain was in the dungeons with the common thieves and murderers, the area filled with the stench of human filth and fear; the fear of knowing that at the end waited the gibbet, the ax, or the torture chambers in dungeons even deeper down than these.

For the thousandth time he asked himself, Why am I here?

Desperate wails and muffled groans pierced the air at regular intervals.

A thin slit in the stone wall let in wafts of cold air and told him of the passing days and nights. He had no idea how long he had been imprisoned. The perpetual damp cold of the stone gnawed into his bones, making him miserable.

RECKLESS SPLENDOR

How long would he be able to withstand the pain without going mad? He hated being locked up. A constant worry that he had failed Madeleine kept eating at him. He hated to sit helpless, chained to a wall, not knowing what had happened to her. With a snarl he punched his fist into the stone, only to regret it as a searing pain pulsed through his arm. *Merde!*

A thin mist of pink light spoke of a new day. Heavy footsteps sounded outside the massive spiked door. A grinding sound filled the cell as the key turned in the lock. Bolts and clanking chains were lifted from the door and, with a moan, it swung open.

Tense, Germain stared at the opening. A rough individual, a guard with a whip in his hand and a limp-brimmed hat on his greasy wig, stepped into the cell.

"What do you want?" Germain snapped suspiciously, his voice hoarse and his throat sore.

The jailed grunted and rattled his heavy key ring. "To the basement," was all he said, and pointed the whip toward the door. After unlocking Germain's manacles from the iron ring, he forced him to stand by digging the butt of the whip in his middle.

Snarling, Germain stood with considerable difficulty. Every joint pained him. His legs trembled, and his ankles burned with lacerations stemming from his attempts to free himself.

Their steps rang hollowly on the ancient stone steps winding in a spiral down, ever down, to what seemed to be the bowels of the earth.

In a cavelike room, four torches smoked on the walls, fouling the already dank air.

Germain saw the chilling contours of torture contraptions—the rack, the wheel, the many whips of various sizes. Behind a long rectangular table sat three dour men wearing wigs and gowns. He recognized Paul Falon in the middle, attorney of the King's Council and chief prosecutor.

"*Enfin!* Some justice will be done," Germain exclaimed, a flame of hope igniting in his chest. "First of all, why am I here, and when are you going to release me? I have a thing or two to say to the King—treating me like a common criminal."

Silence fell in the closed atmosphere.

"It will never happen. You will never see the King again—let alone speak with him. You have ceased to exist," Falon grated, his face a stern official mask.

Germain thought he was going insane. "Ceased to exist? Nonsense! Listen, this is not exactly the occasion for a jest."

"I'm not jesting. The King issued a *lettre de cachet*. You are nothing. Today you will be transferred to Pignerol where you will spend the rest of your days. You should be grateful that the King spared your miserable life."

"But—why?" Bewildered, Germain stared at the stern judge, whose pale lips curled into a sneer.

"Are you pretending that you don't know?"

"*Non, imbécile!* I have no idea what crime I'm accused of!" Germain snarled.

Falon bared his teeth in a cold smile. "That's rich. God only knows how long you've been a traitor to this country. You deserve to hang from the gibbet on Place de Grève like a common thief."

Germain went pale, anger welling in a hot wave through him. "I want an explanation, Falon. If you don't let me go, I will see to it that you'll regret it for the rest of your life." He straightened to his full height and glared down his nose at the judge.

The judge laughed, a cackling sound. "You should be more careful in choosing your mistresses, is all I say. Guards, take him from my sight! I have other more important business to attend to," he barked.

Germain could not believe his ears. The guards brutally dragged him from the chamber. This had been some parody of a trial! Struggling, he wanted to stay, to confront Falon. "I demand an explanation!"

Slamming an elbow in the midriff of one of the guards, Germain sent him squirming on the ground. He made a movement as if to lunge at the judges. Impotent fury was his fuel, but the fight was already lost. More guards burst through the door. The next thing he knew, a bright sun exploded into a myriad of burning shards in his head.

Madeleine!

RECKLESS SPLENDOR 223

* * *

Exhausted and deadened with sorrow, Madeleine crowded with the other petitioners at Saint-Germain. She did not care about her grimy, disheveled state. Proudly returning the furtive stares pointed in her direction, she waited in strained patience for the King to return from Mass. She would explain everything to him and try to forget that the diary ever existed. After that ghastly night at the inn, she did not care any longer what became of her.

A generous burgher family on their way to Paris had found her dejected and half frozen on the stone steps of a broken-down cottage along the road. They had offered her a seat in their coach, and she had silently accepted. After trying to feed her and pry some information out of her, they had given up when no response was forthcoming. Rocking back and forth, her knees tucked under her chin, Madeleine had cried all the way to the capital. Then, at the end, she had asked them to set her down on Rue Saint Antoine.

To see the heavy boards and the red official seals on the iron gates of *hôtel* Belleforière had come as a dreadful shock. She rattled the gates for twenty minutes, knowing in her heart it was futile. The *hôtel* had a closed, forbidding atmosphere. Hurrying around to the stables' wing, she came to the kitchen entrance.

Devastated, she saw the boards and the official wax and read: Property of the State.

A cold shiver coursed along her spine. Where was Germain? What had befallen him? She felt it in her bones that he needed her.

Stark desperation washed through her, draining away any hope. Fouquet had ruined Germain.

Once again she realized the immense power of her enemy. Once again she realized she had underestimated him.

The King's head appeared above the crowd in the corridor. He was flanked by his two Gardes de la Manche, their halberds pointing stiffly toward the ceiling. Wearing old-fashioned shirts of mail, they contrasted sharply against the satins and silks of the courtiers.

The King was dressed in a gold brocade vest and white and gold rhinegraves, his eyes sweeping over the assembled petitioners.

From her position of full curtsy, Madeleine boldly held her head up and fought to catch his gaze. She knew he would let her have an audience this time—*if* he recognized her in her ragged state. Embarrassment was far from her mind, numb as she was, but when the King halted in front of her, letting his eyes travel over her stained and rumpled dress and tousled hair, she flinched.

"Mademoiselle Poquelin!" The tone of his voice implied disappointment and resignation, like that of a father to a naughty child. "Come with me."

When the King entered the study, a man rose from a small desk. Madeleine instantly recognized Monsieur Colbert.

With a wave of his hand, the sovereign stayed the train of courtiers in his wake. The guards closed the gilded doors, and Madeleine found herself alone with the two men.

As a mark of her reverence, she remained standing by the door. The King sat down behind his desk, his face grim. Madeleine was flooded with misgivings. Surely he would understand . . .

"I take it you have the diary." The words came in a soft, expectant purr. She stared at him, and then at Colbert's sour face. *Mon Dieu!* He does not know!

"Sire, do you mean . . . ?" She swallowed the bile in her mouth. "I do not have the diary." Every word was painful to utter; she sensed the King's mounting displeasure.

His fingers tapped lightly on the mirrorlike surface of his desk. "I do not understand. Tell me everything."

Her body wracked with a nervous tremble, she told him about the horror-filled evening at the inn. "Fouquet is behind it. At this moment he's probably burning the most extensive records that ever existed of his crooked affairs."

She waited, her heart hammering dully. She could not bear it if he berated her. His voice was soft, but she heard the underlying edge as he spoke. "Perhaps the diary never existed."

Madeleine gasped. "Sire! Of course it does—or did! Why else do you think your guards were murdered?" she blurted out angrily, forgetting whom she was talking to. How dared he doubt her?

"All I have is your word, and . . . hmmm, if it is true, the dead guards. An investigation will be necessary. In the meantime, you're a prisoner. It will take time to untangle this web." He pondered in silence, and when he looked up, his expression was very grave. "Besides, I suspect you are an accomplice of Hautefort. There is no way of knowing how much information you have passed on to the Spaniards."

"The Spaniards?" Madeleine's mouth dropped open, and she stared at him.

A cloud of anger marred the monarch's handsome brow. Colbert explained. "His Majesty means that you have abetted Hautefort in treason against your country. An extremely delicate and distasteful matter."

"Treason?" The room spun slowly, and her legs began to buckle. The nightmare was starting all over. *Treason?* Feeling her knees touch the floor with a thud, she clasped her hands as if in prayer. "Sire, I beg of you to believe my innocence. After Germain was arrested, tell me—would I have stayed in the country if I were guilty? *Non*, sire. I had no idea why he was arrested. I dragged myself here without guards, without a horse, without any aid whatsoever to tell you what happened," she said, hearing her own voice as if from far away. Until today, I never knew why Germain was called back to Paris. I wish in my heart things were different, that I could deliver the diary today—and that Germain was free."

Her voice broke, and the seriousness of her situation seeped into her weary mind. "S-sire, I implore you. I have lost everything, including three persons I loved, my father, Hautefort, and the page Amul. And all because of the diary. We have to find and punish the brute who killed Amul," she sobbed and covered her face with her hands. Small black specks danced in front of her eyes.

Silence stretched endlessly.

She noticed that the King was deep in thought, a deep crease forming between his brows. It was a tiny consolation that he had heard her out.

"You are a fair and honest king," she began, but Colbert shook his head vigorously. "Hautefort is innocent," she finished. Colbert glared at her, and the King tapped his fingers impatiently on the desk top. Had she provoked the royal wrath by speaking out of turn?

He eyed her coldly, then turned to Colbert. "Send for Monsieur Molière."

Colbert walked briskly out of the room, his heels clicking on the polished parquet.

"As for Germain, he does no longer have that noble name of Hautefort. He sorrowed me greatly by betraying this country that I love more than anything. He is this day being transferred from the Bastille to spend the rest of his life in the fortress of Pignerol in the province of Piedmont."

"Without a trial?" Incredulous, Madeleine had to speak out of turn once more, but the King did not seem to notice. Truly he looked distraught. "No need for a trial. We found evidence in his *hôtel*, letters detailing all my military strategies for the Flanders campaign. The campaign was a state secret."

"Fouquet," she muttered. Nausea and fear flooded her, and she fought against swooning, her vision edged in black.

The King paced the floor, his hands clasped behind his back. Abruptly he turned to her. "What did you say?" He made no attempt to help her rise, and Madeleine could not do it unaided.

"I believe Fouquet planted those letters in *hôtel* Belleforière. Germain is your most loyal subject."

"Fouquet? Preposterous!" he snapped. "He knows nothing about my military strategies."

Madeleine gasped for air, and the stillness in the room pressed down on her. Why doesn't he believe me? I'm going stark raving mad. The numbness melting to despair inside, she wanted only to crumple to the floor and cry, but the presence of the King was enough to keep her spine stiff. She swallowed convulsively.

"Sire, please free Germain. We'll find the diary and bring it to you—if it isn't too late."

At that moment Colbert entered, followed closely by Molière, who had been doing his daily duty at court, making the King's bed. After bowing deeply, he hurried to Madeleine's side, and she swayed toward him. His expressive face was creased in worry. Colbert must have told him,

RECKLESS SPLENDOR

Madeleine thought, her head drooping. How she managed to live through the nightmarish interview was more than she could fathom. Only a desperate need to plead for Germain kept her from collapsing. From far away, she heard the King saying that he wasn't going to imprison her, after all. Each of his words etched into her.

"I have no evidence that Mademoiselle Poquelin is in fact guilty of treason. I will certainly order an investigation into the case. Molière, I expect you to look after her, keep her from mischief. I appoint you her custodian. She is not to leave your charge unless you see fit to send her to a convent."

"*Naturellement*, sire, it distresses me deeply—"

"Enough! Begone before I change my mind." Dismissing them, he turned his back.

Madeleine was utterly drained; Molière more or less had to carry her out. The only thought circulating in her head was that she had freedom, but the man she loved had not. He had lost everything because of her. Guilt lay like a heavy yoke on her shoulders. She would never be able to repay him.

Wide-eyed and pale, she stared at the towering nobleman barring her progress. The icy shock of recognition rushed through her. Lemont. Her eyes flickered to his face. He smiled, a sardonic curl of his upper lip. "You have lost. I warned you. Perhaps you should stay in your place from now on."

Anger welled hotly into her veins, giving her a spurt of strength. "I might have lost for now, but—listen!" She jabbed a finger into his chest. "My father's death will be avenged, and Amul's! If it is the last thing I do. Give Fouquet that message."

Her heart sick and aching, she leaned on her uncle's thin arm and passed the gloating courtiers with her head held high. Trembling inside, she thought she would never be able to survive the pain squeezing her heart like a giant, relentless vise.

Every jolt sent agony through his abused body. Raising his head from the hard surface, Germain experienced red-hot flashes of fire through his brain. Slowly he returned from the black oblivion that had mercifully let him forget his desperate situation for a few hours.

As his mind cleared, he noticed the rank smell of rotting straw, and rough timbers poking into his sore back. His hands, cold and lifeless, were bound behind him, and his shoulders ached relentlessly. Opening his eyes, he saw between the rough boards the dark blue sky studded with stars.

The wagon rattled over stones and holes, grinding and creaking as the wheels turned reluctantly.

A strong scent of horses wafted past him and, turning his head, he recognized the dark contour of a guard standing on the foothold at the back of the cart. Germain realized that he was in a cart normally used for transporting pigs.

Flexing his stiff fingers, he tried to untie the cord eating into his wrists. The effort forced perspiration to his forehead and as a gust of cool wind washed over him, he shivered. Straining his hands to the limits, he tried to break the cords. He bit his bottom lip until he tasted blood. Dizziness drained all energy from his limbs, and he slumped back onto the boards.

Pignerol. Nobody returned from there alive.

He had to get away, and there was no time to waste.

Grimacing, he forced himself up, propping his back against the side. His head hit the boards covering the cart. Like a pig to slaughter. He searched for a sharp object to cut the cords around his wrists. At least they had removed the manacles. His head pounded like fire; his eyes burned. Rolling over on his side, he fumbled along the sides of the cart for nails. He found none, and no other sharp objects protruded through the straw. His chances for escape were diminished.

Fortunately his legs were unfettered. Evidently the guards had not considered him a threat in any way. Good. The guards believed him to be more dead than alive. *Enfin*, that was how he felt—dead—but this was not the time to feel sorry for himself. He would get only one chance to escape, if any, and if he bungled it—well, then he would be chained hand and foot to the cart.

His tangled curls caught under his shoulders, and he shifted to release the pressure. If only he could get rid of the guard at the rear without drawing attention to himself.

RECKLESS SPLENDOR

An opportunity had to present itself first, he pondered gloomily.

His chance came from an unexpected source. Long before the gypsy camp came into sight, he heard them. Foreign-sounding violin tunes floated in the air, a wild sound. The rhythm of thumping feet and clapping hands echoed along the dry, hard ground. A group of gypsies had happened to camp in a clearing nearby, a common enough occurrence. In the spring the countryside teemed with the dark people in their gaily-painted caravans.

He prayed no outriders were riding behind the cart. As their equipage drew level with the camp, Germain set his teeth, concentrated all his force in his legs, and kicked out. The hard blow hit the guard in the groin, and he lost his hold on the cart and fell to the ground with a loud grunt. The loud music drowned every sound. Germain watched the man writhe in agony.

Tensely he waited for the rig to halt or outriders to bear down on him with swords, but none came. The cart ambled along. *It is now or never!* He wiggled through the opening and clumsily hit the ground, the sharp pebbles in the lane giving him a hard welcome.

He had to get away instantly, before the guard on the ground saw him. Like a shadow, the guard was already staggering after the cart. Soon his shouts would be heard over the music, and the other guards would be alerted.

Germain rolled into a ditch, wet slimy weeds twining around him. Too tense to worry about the foul surroundings, he waited, holding his breath. The guard, groaning and clutching his groin, passed his hiding place.

As soon as the man had melted into the darkness, Germain crawled out of the obnoxious ditch. Without the help of his bound hands, several precious seconds passed before he managed to gain an upright position.

Panting, he reeled across the clearing into the cover of the trees. A few moments later he heard the hue and cry of the guards. His escape had been detected. The sound of galloping horses from farther up the lane reached his ears.

At that moment he thanked his creator that the outriders had been ahead of the cart and not behind. What luck! Then he shook his head. He was not yet out of danger.

Weak-kneed, his head throbbing, he ran toward the sound of the music. His throat was as dry as parchment; he desperately needed something to drink. He paused in the shadow of the trees lining the camp, his eyes searching for cover.

One of the caravans was parked at the edge of the clearing. Still concealed in the shadows, he aimed his steps toward it. Having spied a low shelf beneath the caravan for carrying casks and boxes, he wished fervently that his tall body would fit there.

Crouching, he reached the wagon without being detected, and luckily the shelf was empty. How could he crawl onto it with bound hands? He had no time left; the voices and the music ceased abruptly, and the creaking wheels of the cart drew to a halt by the fire.

Using all his remaining energy and willpower, he inserted his upper body, face down onto the shelf. Lying flat, his wide shoulders barely fit on the shelf, but it was long enough to hold his long legs.

He listened to the guards' gruff voices as they argued with the gypsies. If they began searching, they might find him, but knowing that the gypsies were fiercely private, Germain doubted they would allow the guards to search through the camp. Savoring the knowledge, Germain smiled for the first time since he had been imprisoned.

After a long time the cart rumbled off, bearing the cursing guards. The gypsies' angry voices carried on the wind, and only when the music resumed did Germain relax.

He had done it! He was free.

Part II

Chapter 25

Madeleine stared out the window, her chin propped in one palm, the fingers of her other hand playing with the fringe of the velvet curtain.

A gust of hot air invaded the room, causing the curtains to billow and a small vase to topple over. Since she did not bother to keep the room shuttered, it soon grew as hot as an oven, and the stale scents of perfume and wax mingled with the stench of Paris. May was unusually hot this year.

Lost in thought, she worried about Germain. He was locked up at Pignerol, forever separated from her, and she was helpless to do anything about it. She had assumed that with time, the aching longing inside her would heal. But she was floundering in a bottomless pit of despair, her pain insufferable. What wouldn't she do to touch his lean face again, to feel his warm skin against her own, to taste his demanding lips? Never would she see the sunshine paint gilded streaks in his hair, or see his charming smile.

Madeleine jumped when a bird squeaked on the windowsill. The pain of her longing clung heavily to her mind. How would she go on without Germain? She *had* gone on, like a limping ship tossed to the raging winds, but what kind of life was that?

She was grateful to Uncle Jean-Baptiste, who had been very understanding and kind. He easily understood her desire for revenge, but it was impossible to confront Fouquet, who surrounded himself with guards everywhere he went. Her uncle insisted she should come back to the theater, but she had been too depressed to do anything but wander aimlessly through the rooms of La Béjart's apartment, where she was currently staying. She was sewing again, but now Molière was bringing the costumes to her.

He had berated her over and over. She recalled one of their conversations. "You'll have to return to work, to see other people. Holed up in a house, sewing by yourself, is harmful," Uncle Jean-Baptiste had claimed.

She had shrugged. "I will—someday." Without Germain, what did it matter what she did with her life?

Uncle Jean-Baptiste had shaken her shoulder, his bright brown eyes boring into her. "Go on living, Madi," he urged. And, yes, she was going to take up the threads of her life—soon.

"It hurts me to see you like this. Had you only come to me in the beginning—" Her uncle had gesticulated extravagantly as if on stage, his lean face vibrant with compassion.

"Oh, Uncle, we've been through this before. I was a fool for not believing that you could help me. But I didn't want to draw the family into my problems. I didn't want Fouquet to ruin your career."

Molière had looked at the floor, misery emanating from him.

"I have caused you nothing but trouble, Uncle Jean-Baptiste. Forgive me, but I still want to avenge Father's death."

His squirrel-quick eyes had rested on her. "Revenge is a disease. I want you to stop that wild idea! You have no business with revenge; you will only end up hurt."

She had let the words sink in. After a long pause she had said, "I feel so guilty. Somehow I should have been able to stop Father. He could have been alive today. Amul, too."

"Should—should!" he had mimicked. "Are you God? My brother was a fool, meddling in others' affairs."

"Nothing is going to be solved by talking about it now. The diary is lost, alas."

He had flung up his arms. "Thank God for that!"

Madeleine stared listlessly at the pile of costumes that needed altering. Later, she thought, feeling a twinge of guilt. The hot weather pulled her out of the house. Lately she had made a habit of taking walks along the Seine, on the lovely Cours-la-Reine.

Nature was at its most verdant. Flowers, an explosion of colors and shapes, bordered the shaded walks. The trees were cloaked in green; squirrels and birds bickered on the branches.

Wearing one of La Béjart's altered dresses, a pale blue muslin gown adorned with silver ribbons, and a white lacy apron, Madeleine admired the ducks on the river. Sunlight glittered on the water, and she had to shield her eyes from the glare with her hand. The only thing disturbing the peace were the horns of the barges and the vulgar voices of the lackeys at the back of elegant carriages.

A group of small children ran past her, playing with a cloth ball stuffed with rags. How carefree they looked! Madeleine sat down on a stone by the river, feeding the ducks bread crumbs from a bag that she had cajoled from La Béjart's cook.

Staring out over the water, she wished she could remain forever in the warm cocoon of sunlight enfolding her, but a cool breeze rippled over the blue-brown water and curled around her legs. The first herald of night. The nights were still cool. The sun, a burning orange globe, dipped beyond the jagged buildings of the city.

Madeleine shivered involuntarily. A piercing shriek cut through the air, and she jumped up, her first instinct to hide.

In the middle of the flower-edged lane stood a beautiful open carriage pulled by six magnificent grays.

Madeleine recognized the comtesse de Durenne, accompanied by a noblewoman with impressive jewels around her neck. Surrounding the carriage stood a gang of ruffians.

The lackeys and the coachman were held captive, swords pointing at their throats. The rest of the ruffians tore the diamonds from the ladies' throats, the bracelets from their arms, the pearls from their coiffures—this happening amid screams and curses.

The orange light glinted in long blond hair, painting it with fire. Had Madeleine been dealt a blow, she could not have been more stunned. She could have sworn the hair belonged to Germain. Even the tall body, all dressed in black, resembled that of her former lover, although it was leaner. *Non*, impossible!

Her mind was playing malicious tricks on her. Leaning against a tree, she shook with deep sobs, pressing her fingertips to her eyes to erase the image on her brain. Germain was in Pignerol, and there he would remain to the end of his days.

Hearing running footsteps and the enraged voices of the approaching policemen, Madeleine uncovered her eyes, catching a last glimpse of the thieves disappearing down the lane. The ladies in the carriage wailed, "Help! My diamonds! In broad daylight! Stop the thieves!"

The last thief to disappear around the bend in the road was the man with the golden hair, the man with Germain's hair. A black wide-brimmed hat was pressed deeply over his brows.

An urge to follow him came over Madeleine, but her legs were wooden, and she tottered behind a clump of trees before she would be called upon to give testimony. She heaved a deep, shuddering sob. The thinly healed wound in her heart had reopened. I'm seeing him everywhere. Am I going out of my mind? She massaged her temples and frowned.

That night, finding no peace at home, she fled to the theater at Palais-Royal, preferring to gossip with the actresses than sit alone with her tormented thoughts. In the dressing room she watched La Du Parc put a silver-backed brush into an elegant leather case. Noticing Madeleine's long look at the case, she opened it and displayed the luxurious things inside. The powder box had a jewel-encrusted silver lid and the same design ran along the edge of the comb.

"Lovely," Madeleine breathed. "The giver must be an admirer of some standing."

La Du Parc giggled. "Indeed, he is. Gros René is very jealous."

A smile flickered on Madeleine's lips. "I'm sure he is."

La Du Parc sent her a penetrating glance. "You're not yourself yet. Still brokenhearted, eh?"

"*Oui.* I don't think I'll ever get over this. There is a gaping hole where my heart used to be. The strangest thing happened today. I thought I saw Germain."

"*Mais non!* He's at Pignerol. You saw someone who reminded you of him."

"*Oui—oui,* I'm sure you're right. Germain was never a thief—well, perhaps a thief of hearts." She explained the incident of the robbery.

La Du Parc pouted her scarlet lips, and a tiny frown appeared between her eyebrows. "Hmmm. And the leader was blond?" When Madeleine nodded, she continued. "Have you heard about the terrible gang that has been pestering Paris lately? The police are desperate to catch them. The leader is a tall blond man, but that is the only clue. He is the Black Angel—always wears a mask and black clothes. Couldn't possibly be your comte."

"Don't call him comte! Germain was stripped of his title when the King gave him a *lettre de cachet. Oui,* you're right of course, couldn't be him."

"They are very daring, I've heard. The odd part is that they rob only aristocrats, and then preferably those connected to Monsieur. The robberies are always done in broad daylight in crowded places, as if they want all the world to know about it. Such a pack of rabble should hang!" She sighed and smiled, a slanted secret smile. "But one has to admit it is deliciously romantic! They are a cunning lot, eluding the police all this time. A sharp brain behind it, *vraiment?*"

Madeleine listened quietly. "That brain can't possibly belong to the man I *thought* I saw. Germain would never fall so low as to steal."

La Du Parc patted Madeleine's knee. "There, there, *ma petite.* Work and more work will take your mind off your grief. No better remedy for a broken heart."

Madeleine stood up so fast that her chair turned over. "*Oui,* you are right! It is time to go on living."

Chapter 26

When Madeleine returned to La Béjart's house, darkness shrouded Paris in a soft velvety cloak. Having no desire to sew, Madeleine decided to go to bed early. In her chamber, she lit a candle by the bed. She turned around, and her eyes widened in fear.

A man with a peculiar loose-limbed body and a pasty-white face with a huge black wart on the nose climbed over the windowsill. *"Mon Dieu,"* she gasped, and her hand flew to her throat.

"Don't be afraid, mam'selle, but the lackey would never have let me pass through the front door."

Baffled, her voice a harsh whisper, she demanded, "What do you want?"

"I mean you no harm." His small jet eyes regarded her with interest.

"I don't have any money or jewels." Petrified, she sank down on the edge of her bed.

"Don't worry about that. Just come with me." He pursed his lips in thought for a moment. "If the master didn't have claim to you already, I'd be very tempted to have you myself."

Amazed, Madeleine could not take her eyes off the odd man. His rough, mismatched clothing spoke of the underworld. Servants usually wore livery or some sort of uniform that established their status.

Fascinated against her will, she observed his long, slim hands. "I have no idea what you're talking about," she answered frostily. "The nerve! If you as much as touch me, I will scream. Who are you?"

"Weasel."

Madeleine wrinkled her brow. "That is no real name! Are you a thief? As I said, I have no gold."

He chuckled. "You're a fine enough treasure for me, but too large to actually steal. He peered at her narrowly. "I've never seen you this close before."

"Monsieur Weasel, stop talking in riddles! To my knowledge, I have never laid eyes on you before."

"Perhaps not; I'm a sly fellow, but I've seen you many times. I will take you to the master."

Madeleine gasped. "Who is the master? Get out of here before I call a lackey to throw you out."

"That would be a mistake. Just follow me to your lover. There is no time to lose."

Lover? Her heart made a somersault in her chest as if she already knew. "Germain?" She could barely speak.

"The same. The former comte de Hautefort, now an angel, *Ange Noir,* the Black Angel—the terror of Paris."

"It is impossible. He is at Pignerol, alas." Her whole world was hanging on his next words.

"*Non,* mam'selle, he is not."

"Where? Where is he?" She wanted to shake the man.

"Careful! Don't get overexcited. Seems like the master had a tussle with the authorities; he is wounded in his side, and he's in an awful temper."

"Did he send you here?"

"*Mais non*—took the liberty myself. Thought maybe the gentle hand of a loving woman could ease his pain." He paused. "He has more aches than one. Hasn't had a woman for a long time. Bound to sour his temper."

Madeleine went scarlet with mortification. "How dare you speak to me like that!"

Weasel looked surprised; he scratched his head. "What's wrong with that? Since you've eased his needs before, I thought—"

Madeleine's temper flared. "Of all the despicable—"

Raising his hands to ward her off, he begged, "Be careful—my ears are very sensitive. The master is badly wounded."

Madeleine relented immediately. "I will go to him. You have to come out the front door with me."

"*Non*, Mam'selle Madeleine. I will leave the way I came. I never go through doors."

Dumbfounded, she watched him slide over the windowsill and disappear into the darkness. She rushed to the window and looked down. He was climbing the brick with barely a hold for his slim fingers and toes.

"Don't fall!"

A snort of disgust wafted upward.

"What is your real name?" she shouted.

He had almost reached the ground. "I don't want to tell you," he replied.

After donning only a light cloak, Madeleine hurried downstairs and sneaked outside. Weasel appeared instantly at her side.

"Now, tell me your name," she prodded.

He muttered something unintelligible, but Madeleine persisted.

"Socrate Bouffon, mam'selle. And don't you dare laugh!"

A gurgle of laughter already poured from her lips. He looked displeased.

"Don't you ever call me that," he warned. "It's Weasel."

"I'm sorry, I didn't mean to embarrass you. But how can anyone have *fool* for a last name?"

"In the old times my ancestors had the post of fool at court. We were in high favor with the King, I assure you," he said with a sniff.

How odd. Here she was with a creature of dubious character, following him into the perilous streets. Had he only mentioned Germain's name to lure her out? The thought was frightening, but somehow she trusted the fellow. He had made her laugh. He led her along the narrow street around Les Halles, skirting the graveyard of Saint-Innocents. Bizarre chanting came from behind the wall, and Madeleine's skin prickled.

"Black Mass," Weasel muttered. "Did you know that they sacrifice infants? Their blood—"

"Stop it!" Madeleine pressed her hands to her ears. His words were too horrible to be true.

"It happens every night," he explained in a matter-of-fact voice.

She hastened to change the subject. "How badly is Germain hurt?"

"He has a slash down his side, not too deep but the wound is infected; he's running a fever. He's wild, I tell you. Thrashes about in bed something awful. He behaves as if the wound is nothing, but this morning he was too weak to get up."

A shiver of fear rippled through her. An infected wound could bring death.

"He refuses to see Big Hercule, the barber-surgeon on Pont-Neuf."

"Thank God. A doctor would without a doubt kill him off."

Weasel cackled. "Well said, mam'selle."

Although Weasel led her along foul-smelling backstreets and dark passages, she knew when they entered the law district on Ile de la Cité, not far from the Palace of Justice. The old gray stone houses huddled close together, the forbidding medieval façades accented with leering gargoyles. Madeleine noted the name of the street where Weasel turned, Rue de la Lanterne.

Swiftly he darted a glance behind him. They were alone. He rapped five succinct times on a door, then waited tensely. The door slowly opened, revealing a familiar moon face.

"Madame Barbette!"

"Shhh, you fool!" Weasel hissed.

Madeleine was crushed against an ample bosom and whisked into a musty-smelling hallway while Weasel carefully closed the door.

"It is good to see you, Madame Barbette. I wondered what had become of you," Madeleine said. "Quite different circumstances now."

Madame Barbette sniffed. "I would follow Master Germain anywhere. Except they wouldn't let me go to Pignerol."

"Where is he?" Madeleine asked breathlessly, barely able to contain herself. Weasel had disappeared without a sound.

Madeleine followed Madame Barbette, who panted and moaned as she climbed the steep dark stairs. She led the way along the upper corridor and opened a door at the very end.

Expecting to see Germain, Madeleine was disappointed when she found that the room was quite bare. Taken by surprise, she watched Madame Barbette practically walk through the wall. A hidden door, completely concealed in the wallpaper, opened before her. A dark passage bore them into another room similar to the one they had just left.

"This is the house next door," Madame Barbette explained. "The houses are wall to wall. From outside the place looks uninhabited, all the windows and doors boarded up. I'm a poor widow living alone with her son—in the other house."

"I see. This is Germain's secret hiding place."

Madame Barbette opened the third door off the corridor and stepped aside.

Nervously biting her lower lip, Madeleine entered. The room was shrouded in darkness, except for a candle's yellow globe of light by the bed. She discerned the black silhouette of a man lying against white pillows.

"Germain?" she breathed as the door closed behind her. A scent of lavender water clung to the air. She wanted to rush to him and throw herself into his arms, but he was so still. "Germain?" she repreated, and tiptoed to the bed.

A rapid movement on his part told her he was awake. With an enormous effort, he rose, floundering. Shivering next to the bed, his sword pointed at her, he barked hoarsely, "Who's there?"

"Germain, it's me, Madeleine." She noticed that the lower part of his face was covered with a curly blond beard. He glared at her for a moment. The sword wavered and finally clattered to the floor. He fell back onto the bed.

She rushed to his side. Had he fainted? He had. Around his bare chest a white bandage was stained with ominous red.

"My darling Germain," she sobbed happily. His forehead was burning with fever. His abundant curls, damp with perspiration, were plastered to his face and neck, and his face was flushed under the deep tan he had acquired since she'd last seen him.

She did not hear Weasel enter, and started when he spoke. "He lets no one touch his wound. That's why it is septic. Barbette is preparing a poultice."

"*Bien*. Help me put him back against the pillows. He stood and pointed a sword at me."

"I know. I was here the whole time."

Incredulous, Madeleine glared at Weasel as she tossed her cloak aside. "Don't you ever make any sounds?" she asked angrily.

He only shrugged and gripped Germain under the arms. "He is a big one. You have to help me."

Together they managed to make Germain comfortable. His bare torso gleamed wetly in the pale light. His black, tight-fitting culottes molded his body like a second skin. A powerful yearning to make love washed through her, but she grimly dismissed the unsuitable urge and unwound the bandage.

When Germain opened his eyes, they held a glazed look. "I must be dreaming," he mumbled. "*Diable*, Weasel, I'm seeing visions now."

"*Non*, you're not!" Madeleine retorted and placed a cool hand on his forehead. "You're burning up. What's this idiocy of refusing Madame Barbette's care? Do you want to kill yourself? Then I know any number of ways that are much less painful," she scoffed.

He muttered and licked his dry lips. "Water! I'm on fire. Life—oh, *diable*, water." His voice trailed off, and his eyes closed.

"He has lost consciousness. At least he won't fight when we clean his wound. You know, it's right on top of the one he received at The Greedy Cat last winter," she said pensively.

"I know. I was there." Weasel's face was gloomy. "He is in a bad way, isn't he? I'll fetch some boiling water; here is a pile of lint. If Black Angel dies, life will not be the same."

"Black Angel. Why that name?"

"My new name, Madeleine," came Germain's hoarse voice from the pillows.

RECKLESS SPLENDOR

She looked at him, joy leaping to her eyes. Falling to her knees by the bed, she clasped his dry, hot hand between hers and rained small kisses along the knuckles.

"You're awake. I cannot explain how much I have missed you. There simply aren't words great enough."

As if stung, he jerked away his hand. "Go! Leave me alone!" Moaning, he tried to twist away from her.

Believing the delirious dreams had returned, Madeleine shrugged and rose. Her proclamations of love would have to wait until he was better.

Nimbly she cut away the rest of the makeshift bandage. The wound did not look deep, but the edges were puffy and tainted an angry red. The surrounding flesh had a purplish cast, and Madeleine felt a wave of nausea rise in her throat. Closing her eyes momentarily, she fought her weakness. Why had he let it go this far, as if he didn't care? He would die if she couldn't stop the infection.

Chapter 27

Weasel returned with a bowl of steaming water, followed closely by Madame Barbette, carrying a tray with a cup of fragrant broth and the doughlike poultice.

Weasel pinned down Germain's flailing arms while Madeleine cleaned the wound.

"*Non!* I . . . will kill you . . . for this." Germain moaned, his head lolling back and forth.

"Now I believe he'll survive," Barbette said with an edge to her voice. "Foul-mouthed monster! He is as stubborn as a mule, not letting anyone near him. He has been taunting death ever since the imprisonment." With a disapproving snort, she rose from the foot of the bed where she had been sitting. The mattress bounced back when relieved of her weight.

"I will feed him the broth when he wakes up," Madeleine promised. She looked for Weasel, but he was no longer in the room. "That fellow's habits are very annoying. You never know when he has come or gone."

"You'll get used to it. Weasel is harmless and devoted to the master. You should see the other ruffians in the gang; they're fit to make your skin crawl."

When she noticed Madeleine's white face, she added, "Don't you worry, *petite*. Master Germain will explain it all when he wakes up." After patting Madeleine on the shoulder, she left the room.

Madeleine already knew. If what La Du Parc said was true, she knew he had become the most feared thief in Paris. Black Angel.

One wrong step and Black Angel would hang on Place de Grève. Why had he chosen to live a life of crime?

He stirred, his head jerking up from the pillows. He glowered at Madeleine, his eyes two sunken pools of piercing intensity. The unnatural brightness made him look half crazed.

"I'm going to kill him!" he barked, and Madeleine shivered.

"You'll be well soon," she said softly, pushing his rigid torso back down.

With the sound of a sob, he crumpled, his breathing coming in labored gasps.

Time slid silently toward dawn. When the first feeble light slipped between the boards across the windows, Madeleine's head slumped forward, and she dozed fitfully in a chair by the bed. Fragments of dreams flickered through her mind, giving her no peace.

"Madeleine? Is that you?"

She woke with a start. Her eyes focused painfully on Germain while her hand sought to rub the stiffness from her neck.

"*Oui.*" A rivulet of pleasure spiraled through her, and she flew to his side. "*Oui,* I'm here."

The coldness in his eyes halted her. Gone was the feverish light. His face looked gray and gaunt in the dim morning light. Beside the bed lay Ariel and Claudine.

"I see you still have your hounds," was all she could think of saying.

"What are you doing here?" he snapped, his voice full of disapproval.

"I . . ." The words snarled into a knot in her throat. Biting her lower lip, she did not know what to do or say. "Weasel brought me." She wanted to fling herself around his neck, but his icy anger denied her that pleasure.

"It was very foolish of him to do that."

"Why?" she breathed, her heart filling with dread. This was the last kind of reception she had expected.

"He acted without my orders."

His words sent her wrath soaring. Arms akimbo, mimicking Madame Barbette, she snapped, "If it weren't for the people who love you, you would be raving with fever this morning, possibly in the throes of lockjaw. One of your vile henchmen crawled into my bedroom through the window and lured me over here in the middle of the night to tend to you. High and mighty that you are, you wouldn't let anybody touch your lofty self." Fury oozed from her. "Weasel came to me because he was worried about you."

If he had smiled then, or at least softened the lethal glint in his eyes, she would have melted, but his eyes remained hard.

Her legs wobbly, she turned to the tray by the bed. "Before I leave, I'll redress your wound. The poultice will have pulled out the infection."

He did not resist as she began cutting the bandage from his chest; her cheeks burned in anger and humiliation. The scent of him, his virile warmth, made her sick with longing. His steely fingers encircled her wrists, and he forced her to meet his gaze. "You should not have come. I . . . we cannot go on as before. I want you to leave now, and don't return."

Her eyes were huge with pain. He shook her arm violently. "Do you hear me? I have nothing to offer you."

"Not even your love?" Her voice was barely audible. She searched for a hint of softness in his face.

"Not even my love. I'm dead inside," he grated and released his grip. "It was senseless of you to come here. Did it never occur to you that I could have easily found you, had I wanted to see you?"

His words hit her like hammer blows, and a wave of dread engulfed her. "*Enfin*, your words of love meant nothing then," she whispered to herself, crushed.

Had their love been more firmly anchored, had their previous days and nights together been less tumultuous, Madeleine believed she could have bridged the gap yawning between them. But she hesitated. Pride or fear were not her enemies this time; she didn't know if his love had really died or if he was lying. She stared for a long moment at his closed face, but it revealed nothing. Was it pure imagination to think that their love had been real? She was walking a tightrope and below her yawned an endless chasm.

She knew she loved him more than ever; she was at a loss, not knowing what to say to reach him. She said briskly, "I will dress your wound and then you have to rest. You should not be so careless with your health." She sensed his eyes on her, but she refused to return his gaze; she couldn't bear to see the coldness there. Noticing that he was leaner and harder than before, a sign of the hardships he had lived through, she dabbed lightly at his wound with a piece of lint soaked in water. Then she placed a new poultice on the wound and wrapped strips of clean linen around his broad chest. Obediently he lifted his arms. Several scars she had not seen earlier criss-crossed his wrists.

"Did they do this to you in prison?" she asked in a small voice, trailing a finger along one of the scars. She wanted to kiss him, to take the pain into herself.

Irritated, he pushed her hand away. "Enough! In prison the jailers take much pleasure in torturing the prisoners—but I did this to myself, straining against my leash you might call it."

She winced, could almost feel the intense misery he had experienced.

"Tell me about your escape—for escape you did, or you wouldn't be here."

He shrugged. "*Oui*, I escaped. I found some helpful gypsies on the road to Pignerol. They delivered me safely to the Porte de Saint Michel. My enemies will never find me now unless I want them to."

"I saw you on Cours-la-Reine yesterday. I thought I was seeing a vision." Her voice trailed off. He didn't know how her longing had tortured her for months, and now she could find no way to tell him. He didn't want to listen.

"*Oui*, you're right. I was there—the Black Angel, the terror of Paris."

Madeleine sensed the acute bitterness behind his words. She darted a quick glance at him and flinched when she saw the burning hatred in his eyes. How she yearned to smooth away that look! How she wanted to see his eyes turn warm and loving, teasing her as they used to. His wounds were much deeper than the slash in his side.

He was covered by a sheen of perspiration and collapsed on the bed. "I will not rest until I have punished my enemies for what they did to me." His words hung ominously in the air.

Madeleine hesitated for a moment, then spoke, wadding a piece of lint into a ball. "I lived for revenge. I lost everything—including you." She hung her head. "And the diary."

"*Non!*" He sat up, rigid, one hand gripping her arm so hard she thought it would break. "You didn't lose the diary!"

"*Oui*. The guards"—she took a steadying breath—"and Amul were murdered, and the diary stolen by masked men."

He tensed up like a coiled spring. "Amul? The little mite—dead? He can't be!" But when he read the stark grief in her eyes, he knew.

Several minutes of searing pain passed before he spoke again. "Do you know who the murderers are?"

"*Non,* but I thought there was something slightly familiar about the leader. His accents were those of a nobleman." She struggled to release his grip. "It hurts. It is no use, Germain. The diary is ashes now, and the King believes it never existed. I'm free only because no real evidence pointed at my involvement with your . . . treason. I barely convinced the King of my innocence."

Kneading her sore arm, she continued. "I am to blame for your present condition. *Non*—not the wound, but your ruin."

She wanted reassurance, but none came. Flashes of pain crossed his face, as if he was fighting with conflicting emotions. A sick feeling filled her when she sensed his withdrawal, his silent acknowledgment. She wanted to flee, but forced herself to speak. "Believe me, if I could ever change the past, I would do so. I caused the death of seven innocent men, including Amul. And your ruin." She chewed on her bottom lip to combat her tears. "I cannot bear the guilt."

He was tense, threatening. "Tell me, did you have anything to do with certain . . . letters incriminating me of treason? Did you hide them in my desk?" His voice was harsh. "And don't you dare lie!"

Madeleine's eyes flew wide, and she sank down on the edge of the bed. "Is that what they say?"

He nodded, his eyes narrow slits of suspicion. His forehead pearled with perspiration, and he was white around the mouth.

"*Non*, I swear to you, I didn't know about that letter until I returned to Paris. The King told me." She clasped his hand and squeezed it in agitation. "Please believe me, I implore you!"

He seemed to relax, his head resting now against the pillows. "*Oui*, I believe you."

Madeleine swallowed, able to breathe once more. "I'm sure Fouquet planted the letters in *hôtel* Belleforière. The deed reeks of his underhanded ways."

"*Oui*, he will receive his." Germain's voice was so hoarse, she could barely discern his last word.

Still holding his hand, she whispered, "It must be a fate worse than death to be a thief."

She was startled when he laughed. "Could be worse. Revenge holds a certain satisfaction. The comtesse de Durenne handed me a diamond necklace I once paid for. Last week Marquis D'Ambrose lost his carriage, his horses, and his diamond buckles." His voice shook. "They will pay—all of them!"

She drew a deep, shuddering breath. Germain drifted off to sleep, his skin feverish again. His face was haggard and sad, his eyelashes pale against the dark smudges under his eyes.

Even though she hadn't planted the letters in his desk, she was inadvertently the cause of his ruin, and she wanted to cry—cry until she died. Only because of her did he lie on a rickety pallet in a dilapidated house where paint flaked from the ceiling and mice scurried in the walls.

She had to wipe the bitterness from his eyes. Somehow.

As if sensing her distress, Ariel placed his wet nose in the palm of her hand. Somehow she felt comforted.

Chapter 28

Germain stirred, feeling a gnawing pain in his side. Moving his stiff limbs, he groaned in agony, then in a red haze of torment, opened his eyes. Twilight made the room appear ghostly, and the stillness held a waiting quality. The bells of Notre Dame echoed in his head. Was he in the world of the dead, the bells tolling for him? Was he in hell, where hot pokers probed his body incessantly?

Lifting his throbbing head with difficulty, he recognized his bedchamber, the Black Angel's lair. A sour smile spread across his lips. He tried to sit up, but the rapier-sharp twinge in his side made it impossible.

He was alone. Had they all left him to die?

The memory of Madeleine floated back to him. Had she been real? More and more he recalled their conversation, and another anguish amplified, this time in his heart. The pain swelled until he thought he was going to burst. Tears stood in his eyes, and he angrily dashed them away with the back of his hand. When she had touched him, he thought he would explode with despair. It had been so long since . . . He dared not finish the thought. Never would he be able to show her how much he loved her. What did he have to give her? Sooner or later he would hang—Black Angel would hang.

He expelled his breath, recalling her earnest plea of innocence. She had had nothing to do with the letters. A burden had fallen from his shoulders. He had never been able to convince himself of her guilt, yet a tiny nagging suspicion had poisoned his blood all this time.

Hatred and a lust for revenge had forced him back to Paris. He would not rest until he had found out who had placed the fatal letters in his desk. Fouquet. It could only be he.

Madeleine must be suffering deep pain after the loss of Amul, and he wanted nothing more than to console her. But the unlawful life he was leading—Germain didn't want to inflict it on any woman, however eagerly she offered herself.

Drifting in and out of sleep, he dreamed about Madeleine. He pictured her naked, her alabaster skin against cream satin, laces sliding over her alluring curves, her lips moist and inviting, her thighs parted . . .

With a start, he woke. A thin film of sweat covered him, and he ached from the tight, hot arousal in his loins. His blood coursing wildly through his body, he took a deep breath to ease the wave of desire attacking him. Each breath sent a stab of pain through his side.

Annoyed and aroused, he forced himself out of bed. On shaking legs, he stumbled to the boarded window. Through a narrow crack he discerned rose-edged clouds and part of the blue-greenish sky as the sun was sinking low in the west.

Wiping perspiration from his forehead, he noticed how hungry he was. When had he last eaten a full meal?

His legs barely bore him back to the bed. After downing a bowl of water on the nightstand, he lay back on the pillows with a groan, to wait.

Half an hour later Madame Barbette bustled through the door, carrying a tray. From the covered dishes wafted an appetizing smell.

"Ah, you're an angel, Barbette," he said with the ghost of a smile.

Madame Barbette eyed him disapprovingly, not easily mollified.

"I behaved like a bear, didn't I?" he asked when he noticed her scowl.

"Outright boorish, if you ask me," she retorted with a sniff. "Did you want to kill yourself? Would serve you right if you had died in the agonies of lockjaw!"

Germain grunted. "*Non*, not until I have had my revenge."

Barbette frowned in anger. "*Bouffon!* Forget vengeance and go into the country before they catch you."

"*Non!* No one can play me a bag of dirty tricks and believe I will say *merci* and meekly accept it." He pounded his fist into the pillows.

"*Enfin*, you would have been dead now had not Madeleine ministered to your wounds. How she could bear with you is more than I can understand." With her arms akimbo Barbette hovered by the bed, her fat face set in folds of displeasure. "At least you have the decency to look embarrassed. Haven't quite lost your gentleman codes. I will send her up so that you can thank her properly. A very sweet creature, Madeleine."

Disbelief clouded his face. "Is she still here?"

"*Oui*. Pale and tight-lipped, she sits staring out the window in the kitchen. I can't make her budge, and I can't get a word out of her, except for her mutterings of employment. Can't make head or tails of it."

Stirring the onion soup too rapidly, she slopped some over the edge of the bowl. She flung a napkin across Germain's bare chest and handed him the steaming bowl.

The door creaked open, and Madeleine stood on the threshold, her expression serious and closed, her hands clasped before her. "I'm here to make you a business proposition, Germain." She winced when looking into his cloudy eyes. He seemed so far away, even though a few steps could bring her to his arms. She had made a silent vow that she would not embarrass him with another emotional outburst.

"I would like to hire you to find out who killed Amul and stole the diary. Furthermore, I want to know if Fouquet received it and destroyed it. I cannot pay you much, but some. Molière pays me well for my sewing."

She sank down on the only chair in the room, her eyes riveted to his face and a stubborn tilt to her chin. She squarely met Germain's penetrating stare. He was eating his soup, but she could see the cautious calculation in his eyes. Did he suspect her of having ulterior motives?

"What makes you think I can do it?"

"Well, you are a—a—thief now." She spoke with a hint of sarcasm. "I'm sure you have connections. And don't worry, our association will be strictly businesslike."

His lips curled derisively. "I don't think you can afford my services. How did you plan to pay?" he challenged.

Madeleine bit her lip. She had very little money, but she wanted to be close to Germain at all costs. Only then could she win him back. And she wanted to know the fate of the diary. "When the diary is placed in the King's hands, he will reward us. You can name your price then."

Germain chortled. "*Alors*, I will only get paid *if* the diary still exists." He patted his lips with the napkin, hiding his mirth.

Madeleine stared at him stonily, her chin thrust higher. "You are right that the chances are small, but can we afford not to know?"

His lips parted in a smile that did not reach his eyes. "You're right, of course. As a thief, I do have valuable connections in every corner. But unless I can pay for the information, we might have to do some investigation on our own." With an elegant flourish, he drank from the goblet Madame Barbette handed him. Even in these sordid surroundings his noble origins could not be concealed. His arrogant bearing could not be hidden under an unkempt beard or rough clothing. But gone was the charming man she had grown to love. This was a man of wounded spirit and crushed pride. How she wanted to bring back the laughter to his eyes.

He finished his soup while Madame Barbette stood over him like a mother hen. She placed a plate of lamb cutlets and a hunk of bread in his lap, and he ate hungrily.

"Ah, delicious! Brings back my strength." He glanced casually at Madeleine. "Do you have any grand plans for this new adventure? I thought you had given up all thoughts of revenge."

She did not rise to his challenge.

"Who do you suspect the murderer is?" Germain's air had turned so forbidding that Madeleine could not keep her eyes on him. A sensation of futility shook her.

He continued relentlessly. "I suppose this is another one of your harebrained schemes."

Anger flared hotly within her. "I should have known better than to come to you—but then if I hadn't, you would have been dead by now."

"So I owe you now?" he asked ever so softly.

She met his blazing gaze. Silently they measured each other. Finally a smile tugged at the corners of Germain's lips. "You don't mince your words. Very much in control of yourself, *vraiment?*"

"*D'accord.* You know I owe you everything, but as it is, we have nothing to lose—except our necks."

Baffled, he stopped his knife halfway to his mouth, a piece of cutlet speared on its tip.

"Are you suggesting you want to . . . join my gang?" He studied her from under lowered eyelids.

"*Oui*, for now. I think that our problems stem from the same man, so it's no more than right that we should work together," she responded coolly. "Fouquet is at the root of our misfortune. For a while I forgot how much I wanted him to pay. Sorrow made me weak."

Germain fidgeted, struggling against a desire to sleep. "I don't know . . ." A wave of irritation flushed his face. "A woman . . ."

Madeleine stood, drawing herself up to her full height. "If you're insinuating that a woman isn't good enough for your gang, you're not being fair! You know what I've survived. If we don't solve this, it will haunt me for the rest of my days."

He had been staring at her during her outburst, and now he could not suppress a chuckle that jarred his injured side. Madame Barbette glared at him.

"You have, er, convinced me, although you might be a threat to my men's peace of mind," he said, wheezing.

"Stop right now!" Madeleine rushed to the bed and shoved him angrily against the pillows. His mirth gradually died with a few hiccups.

Touching his hot chest sent charged signals through her. Remembering their heated embraces, she blushed. She could not touch his skin and remain unmoved. This was the last time she would touch him, she vowed as she began changing his bandage.

Her fingers caused delicious torment on his skin. Her scent fanned his ardor to a boil, and he had to bite the inside of his mouth to restrain himself from pulling her into his arms and kissing her. He could not start all over with her. At his side, her life would be worthless. As soon as the diary business was over, he would force her to leave. At that thought, shivers of dread rushed through him, bringing back his dour mood. He couldn't bear the thought of losing her again.

He drank in the sight of her full, alluring breasts peeping over the edge of her bodice, the shadowed cleft in the middle enticing him. His gaze traced her narrow waist and rounded hips, another curve that drove him wild. He closed his eyes and pictured her naked buttocks, round and rosy.

"Argh!" he moaned.

"You're still feverish, but the wound seems to be healing nicely. Another poultice and you'll be as good as new," Madeleine said softly. Did he noticed how her heart raced, her hands trembled?

Neither of them saw Madame Barbette leave the room. Madeleine swallowed hard as she scooped the poultice made of mud, raw cabbage, red pepper, and garlic onto his wound.

"I'm fine," Germain said with a groan. He noticed the pulse beating rapidly at the base of her neck and stared hypnotically at her dewy lips, at the gold-tipped eyelashes framing her brilliant eyes. How he loved her! On the verge of succumbing to his longing, he turned away.

Sensing the mounting tension, Madeleine giggled nervously.

"What is it now?" he asked, his voice husky.

"I just remembered Grandfather's physician, Dr. Patel. His universal remedy is bloodletting, no matter how much blood the patient has lost already. In his care, you would have been dead by now."

"That is no laughing matter," he said gloomily.

"Tut, tut. There!" She patted the new bandage briskly and rose, turning away to hide the tears in her eyes. "Tomorrow you'll feel much better, and then we'll hatch the perfect plan to give our enemies some of their own foul medicine." Glancing around the barren room, she added,

"You don't know how sorry I am for this." With a wide sweep of her arm, she indicated the room, not daring to look at him, afraid of the silent accusation she might see. Breathless stillness pressed around them until, unable to bear it a moment longer, she fled from the room, slamming the door behind her.

Chapter 29

The next evening, Weasel escorted Madeleine down the stairs in the run-down house. "Do all the men live here?" she asked.

"Here and there," came the evasive response.

She persisted. "Don't the neighbors wonder about the comings and goings?"

"They never see us, so why should they wonder?"

"Oh." Weasel certainly didn't offer a wealth of explanations.

Madame Barbette had kindly made up a bed for Madeleine in the small room next to her own in the adjoining house. In addition to the bed, the room contained one decrepit chair and a tiny table.

Madeleine had sent a message to her uncle, explaining that she was well and had left Paris for a few days to think about her future. She hated to lie, but it would never do to tell him the truth; he would be furious if he had but an inkling of her real plans.

A single smoking candle lit a round table. Seated around it were a variety of individuals. Feeling ill-at-ease, Madeleine almost regretted her decision to pursue the elusive diary.

Her eyes grew as wide as saucers as she studied each character. Germain rose with difficulty and bowed, a mocking smile playing on his lips. He was very pale under the tan, and deep lines slashed from his nostrils to the corners of his mouth. His hair was matted and lifeless. Madeleine drew a long, aching breath.

"Let me introduce my men," Germain said. "Messieurs, this is our new member, Mademoiselle Madeleine."

Suspicious eyes observed her, and grunts and cackles greeted her.

"This is Le Souris—the Mouse."

"I met him once before," Madeleine said grimly, staring at the sturdy dwarf who was not much larger than a child. His hair, skin, and clothes were all gray. A sly grin lit his devious face, revealing stumps of yellow teeth. "He stole my purse once on Pont-Neuf."

The characters only shrugged their shoulders and chuckled evilly. Madeleine let her breath out slowly between her teeth, then pressed her lips tightly together.

"Capitaine Roland."

Madeleine gasped. "You." She turned to the man next to the capitaine, and knew who he was before seeing his long face and greasy hair—Spider.

The gang consisted of seven men, including Weasel and Germain, who introduced the remaining two.

"Father Jacques Legrand."

Madeleine stared at the huge man as he stood. The biggest man she had ever seen, he stood at least half a head taller than Germain. His huge hands resembled slabs of meat, and there was nothing saintly about his face. He looked outright mean with his toothless gap and sallow skin.

"He is meek as a lamb," Germain assured her with a cruel curl of his lip.

Madeleine crossed herself and coldly eyed the black robes and flat hat of the priest.

Germain chuckled. "He is not a *real* priest. It's just his latest disguise."

The last member of the gang did not look like a man, although Madeleine understood that under the gaudy harlot's disguise hid a man. She shuddered.

"Gaspard, our youngest and most innocent member of this assembly, is a man of many . . . talents."

"None of them honest, I bet," Madeleine murmured.

Germain glowered at her but did not return her barb.

Then she gasped. "Your valet! Gaspard Vincent."

"*Oui,* the same. As I said—a man of many talents," Germain explained with a quirk of his lips.

Madeleine nodded nervously to them all, feeling their silent assessment. Tense, she sat on the edge of the chair that Weasel had pulled out for her.

"I'm honored to meet you," she lied. How had Germain become involved with this loathsome group?

"Do you regret joining us? It's not too late to back out, you know." Germain's voice washed over her with deceptive softness.

"*Non*—I suppose we can work very well together," she answered with a conviction she did not feel. Had she been a fool to ask for his help? Without Germain's protection, she would fear for her life in this assembly.

"*Bien*. Now tell us everything about the murders," Germain ordered.

Madeleine told the story, her words faltering as she mentioned Amul. "I think we should start at Saint-Cloud. If anyone knows about the diary, or the murders, it would be Lemont."

Germain agreed and threw out a string of suggestions to the men. Madeleine listened with her mouth half open. These men had quick minds and florid imaginations. She could not believe the wild ideas each presented. From their combined efforts, a plan grew, so daring that Madeleine could not believe her ears.

Two weeks hence, a masked ball would take place at Saint-Cloud. Father Legrand suggested that Germain and Madeleine, disguised, should attend the ball and under cover of the night search Lemont's room.

Rubbing his bearded chin, Germain stared at Madeleine with hooded eyes. "Well?"

"It'll never work," she blurted out. "Everyone would recognize you."

The bogus father snorted, and sniggers cut the foul air.

"That is not the problem," Germain explained. "Are *you* ready for it? Will you hold up under the pressure?" His piercing gaze was once more riveted on her.

"*Oui . . . oui*, I'm ready." Her heart hammered in her chest. To act the part of a noblewoman might not be difficult, but what if they were identified? The gibbet of Place de Grève loomed. "People will notice your hair," she explained.

Germain chuckled. "When Legrand is through with me, nobody will recognize me. We will be guests invited to the ball. You see, it wouldn't do to go without an invitation."

"I see." Madeleine twitched nervously on her chair. In reality she did not see, but she was not about to reveal her innocence to them. These thieves were more resourceful than she would ever be. The nerve they possessed!

Germain led the way upstairs, pausing on every step.

"You should not be walking around. Your wound will start bleeding again," she scolded.

"I'll survive."

She was deeply aware of the tension forcing a wedge between them when they were alone. The surge was so intense that she could barely breathe. Climbing the stairs right behind him, she could smell his virile fragrance, that magical scent of moonlight and orris root. At that moment she would gladly have thrown herself into his arms, but as long as he resisted her, she had to wait. Would there ever be a time when he would give in to the attraction flowing thick as honey between them?

As Germain opened a door, she ceased to linger on such futile thoughts. Using the candle in his hand, he lit candles in a silver candelabra.

Madeleine gasped at the riches revealed inside the room. On all the walls hung rows and rows of sumptuous dresses and men's costumes. On the floor chests overflowed with jewelry, candlesticks, furs, gilt-edged frames, and other valuables. She stuttered, *"Mon D-Dieu!* Where—?"

"I have not been lazy." Germain eyed her coldly, expertly hiding his true feelings. He was sure by the dismay in her eyes that she abhorred him, or what he had become. He wanted to shout his frustration. It would have been much better had he never met her again. How long would he be able to withstand the battle inside?

"Here are the things we need to become aristocrats. As you know, all that matters is the outside of a person." His voice was harsh with sarcasm.

Madeleine's eyes flashed with indignation. "You know that is not true! You have to act like one, and that takes practice, or it is instilled from birth."

He chuckled and placed one long finger under her chin,

caressing her smooth skin. "Your hackles are always ready to rise." He traced her peach-soft cheek. "You can act the lady as well as anyone I know. You are one."

His touch sent hot waves of desire through her. With enormous effort, she restrained herself from throwing herself against his chest. She moved away, her face shut and distant, not allowing him to see the pain and tumult in her eyes.

"*Donc,* let me show you how we're going to hide my hair." He opened the lid of a small chest and pulled out something that looked like a lapdog. Placing it on his head, he pirouetted in front of her. A full-bottomed wig. Brown curls cascaded in perfumed and orderly abundance over his shoulders.

"*Voilà!* Do you like it? Legrand will curl it to perfection."

Madeleine crossed her arms on her chest and walked around him. "It will do."

"And now, let's choose our finery for the ball."

Madeleine sighed. "How will it ever work? It is the most preposterous plan I've ever heard."

"We will *make* it work. Have you so little faith in me then?" He pulled shirts from another chest and spread them over chairs and tables. His voice was as soft as satin. "Well?"

"I believe you can do anything you set your mind to, but you're a coward for concealing your true feelings for me," she censured him in a clipped voice.

His gaze sliced into her, and she held her breath. "We have been through this before, and those were my last words on the subject. There is no future for us, Madeleine." It appeared to strain him greatly to utter the words, and Madeleine shot him a glance as he bent over a chest to hide his flushed face.

"And you will never . . . change?"

The whispered words hovered. The silence quivered thickly.

"*Non,* I will not change."

"Then you are a greater fool than I thought!" She could not stand to be in the same room with him, and fled, tears streaming down her cheeks.

Chapter 30

Two weeks later, Madeleine leaned heavily on Germain's arm as they walked up the long, shallow steps of the palace of Saint-Cloud, Monsieur's residence. Her legs trembled. Her fingers tightly gripped Germain's sleeve, and her face was white and set behind the blue satin mask.

Germain's wound was almost entirely healed. The only sign of his recent ordeal was his unusually stiff bearing.

For one evening they were the marquis and marquise de Simonet.

After handing the invitations to the majordomo at the gilded double doors, Germain calmly led Madeleine into the crowded ballroom. Since it was a masked ball, the guests were not announced, though invitations were carefully scrutinized.

The majordomo could hardly know that at this very moment the real marquis and his spouse were bound in their beds with handkerchiefs muting their screams.

While Capitaine Roland and Spider had taken care of that detail, with the stern instruction not to steal anything except the invitations and the carriage, Legrand had been at work on Germain's disguise. Madeleine had not believed her eyes when she was admitted to his room an hour later.

In the middle of the room stood Germain, splendidly attired in a gold cloth coat. An exact replica of Simonet's well-known hawk nose and old-fashioned bushy mustache adorned his face. Legrand had brushed the brown wig into the style favored by the marquis. The Simonets had been chosen since the marquis resembled Germain in stature, as did Madeleine resemble his wife.

RECKLESS SPLENDOR

As Germain spoke, his voice held the affected lisp of Simonet. "It'll be a pleasure to escort you this evening, madame," he said and minced across the floor, waving a scented scrap of lace in the air with studied elegance.

Now, entering the hot ballroom, Madeleine thought her heavy makeup would melt, and her head itched abominably under the tight wig.

"Relax, my dear. I'll escort you to our host, and you only have to curtsy and remember to call him Your Royal Highness."

Terrified, Madeleine felt as if she was walking to her execution. Monsieur and Madame greeted the guests filing past them. Bright jewels flashed in the mellow light of the many candles, and their hosts' Roman togas shimmered with gold and silver threads. Madeleine noticed that most of the guests were dressed as gods and goddesses for the evening. She, on the other hand, wore the short ankle-length red skirt of a gypsy, the front covered with a black apron. A white blouse with a daring décolletage displayed her white shoulders.

Madame, the beautiful Princesse Henriette of England, smiled and held out two fingers for Germain to kiss. If she only knew that she was being kissed by the most infamous thief in Paris!

"Your Royal Highness looks lovelier than I can remember," he lisped.

Madame smiled. "Always a man of elegant words, eh, Simonet?"

Germain touched his bogus nose. "Ah! I'm betrayed! It's always the sad truth; I will have to cut off my nose."

"Nonsense, you look quite . . . distinguished. And your lovely wife."

Madeleine curtsied and smiled. The paste on her cheeks strained, and her smile stiffened into a polite mask. "You're too kind, Your Highness."

A rivulet of disgust coursed through Madeleine when Monsieur pressed his cherry-red lips to her fingertips, and she sensed Germain's revulsion when the prince toyed with his gloved fingers and pinched his cheek.

"Welcome," the prince chirped. "We have much to enjoy this evening," he added, his eyes suggestive behind the narrow slits of his black mask.

Madeleine admired Germain for not tearing his hand away and stalking off. Instead he bowed politely, completely in control of himself, haughtily eyeing the crowd and the sumptuous feast laid out on long tables. "*Oui*, I dare say." He spoke in the bored tones of a courtier.

Monsieur laughed throatily and with one last, hard squeeze, he let go of Germain's hand. "Always keeping me in suspense, marquis." He waved them away, ready to greet the couple behind them.

"I didn't know that Simonet shared Monsieur's taste in . . ."

"They're both pigs!" Germain wheezed between clenched teeth as they mingled with the other guests. "Disgusting!"

None of his interior turmoil showed on his face. With utmost ease, as if he truly were the marquis de Simonet, he greeted several other guests. Madeleine shrank beside him, not recognizing any of the faces behind the masks.

Lackeys scurried back and forth laden with trays, continuously replenishing the rapidly diminishing food on the buffet tables. Madeleine pulled away from Germain and disappeared into the crowd before someone asked her questions she could not answer.

Her nerves were raw as she edged her way to the buffet. What if somebody recognized her? Worried, she popped a tiny cake between her brightly painted lips. Her eyes darted from guest to guest, every moment expecting her charade to be exposed.

When a sudden hush fell over the crowd, she thought she would faint. She caught Germain's glance, and he joined her, having sensed her silent terror.

The King entered, a fanfare heralding his presence. The courtiers bowed and curtsied, having formed two lines between which he sauntered forth. He looked handsome in a red brocade coat with gold braid and exotic embroideries. Atop his brown curls he wore a hat of gold brocade adorned with a single red ostrich feather. With or without a mask, there was no mistaking his regal bearing.

Madeleine felt a stab of resentment. He had judged her too harshly at their last encounter. If only he knew . . .

She noticed Germain shaking with silent laughter beside her. After all, this was his small revenge on the sovereign.

The King ought to have known better than to believe that Germain was a traitor to his country, Madeleine mused. But then, Louis was known to be suspicious and jealous of the nobility.

Madeleine held her breath as he drew up alongside her and Germain. Staring at the floor, she was aware of his penetrating glance. To her relief, he moved forward and Germain underwent the same scrutiny.

"Ah! My dear marquis. Your nose has betrayed you. The most prominent nose at court, next to Condé's, of course."

What was Germain going to reply to that?

"Sire, at such an occasion as this, my nose gives me much grief, but I have to object when Your Majesty calls it the *most* prominent nose at court." Germain's drawl sounded exactly like that of Simonet.

"Oh? How is that?" the King asked, slightly amused.

"But, sire, *your* nose reaches into everything—and to every corner of the realm."

The blatant insult hit the assembly like a bolt of lightning. The tension grew explosive as the King's face turned a vivid red, and his eyes flashed with fury behind the golden mask. He was speechless.

Mademoiselle de la Vallière, who had been walking behind him, hurried to his side. "Sire, surely the marquis means that your power is unchallenged," she said breathlessly. Her blue eyes pleaded with the King, and she placed a coaxing hand on his sleeve.

"Hmmm. Simonet, I hope you realize that your wording was excessively clumsy." His angry glare bored into Germain, and everyone drew a sigh of relief as His Majesty continued his walk. Wrath still emanated from him, and the evening promised to be ruined by his displeasure.

"Why did you do that?" Madeleine hissed under her breath. She sensed Germain's amusement as he pulled her into the moving crowd. "A fitting revenge. He betrayed *me*—not the other way around. When I needed his help, he threw me in the Bastille with a *lettre de cachet*." Madeleine heard the bitterness behind his words. "I would have rotted in Pignerol for the rest of my life because of him."

"You were a hair's breadth from being recognized. I worried every moment that he would arrest you. You jeopardized our mission! After all, there is only one Germain de Belleforière."

Germain chuckled, pleased, and she felt the familiar stirrings of excitement. She would never love anyone as much as she loved this man.

"*Bien.* We have made sure that all the guests know that the marquis de Simonet is present. Perhaps we should fulfill the purpose of our jaunt here."

"*Oui.*" Madeleine eagerly assented. "Let's get it over with. Who knows what other wild idea you might take into your head?" She pulled him by the arm. "Amul told me once that Lemont's suite is on the second floor, in the east wing. What if we find Dubois lurking about?"

"He will most likely be there, but we'll find a way to lure him away for a few minutes."

The contrast between the brightly lit salons on the bottom floor and the silent darkness on the second floor was eerie. Madeleine's fertile mind imagined countless difficulties lying ahead of them. Germain's presence was comforting. Alone she would never have managed to play the game they were so daringly performing at this moment.

As they sped stealthily along the corridors, his long, warm fingers curled around hers. His touch ignited a bittersweet sensation. She wanted him to touch her, to hold her, and when she heard stifled giggles and laughter coming from curtained alcoves, she wanted to hide in one with him. But it was only a fleeting longing, as more pressing matters were at hand.

Someone came running from the opposite direction, and Germain pushed Madeleine behind some drapes. Having reached the corridor containing the apartments of Monsieur's permanent guests, they did not wish to be seen.

Madeleine's heart thundered with fear, and she was amazed at Germain's coolness.

"The coast is clear," he whispered, and taking her hand, he pulled her relentlessly toward the farthest door in the corridor. Putting his ear to the door, he listened for sounds.

The passage lay in silence, no noise penetrating from the festivities downstairs.

Tentatively Germain tried the handle. It yielded soundlessly, and the door swung open. A scent of stale powder and dirty linen assaulted their nostrils.

"Is this the suite?"

"I don't know."

"We need more specific directions."

"Did you recognize Lemont downstairs?" Germain whispered, stepping into the lofty room.

"*Non*. Unless he was the man in a rose costume with his hair powdered the same color," she responded.

Germain laughed softly. "You're right. The chevalier may be handsome, but he has no taste."

He continued to the next door and scratched. No response. "We need to find Dubois."

Madeleine drew a deep breath. "*Mon Dieu*, I'm not sure I'm ready to face that disgusting man."

"Too late to back out now." Germain knocked hard on another door at random. To their surprise it opened, revealing a sleepy servant.

"*Oui?*"

"Hmmm." Germain immediately became Simonet. "I have a message for Lemont's valet, from the chevalier. Where can I find him? I have lost my way." He eyed the servant with studied boredom.

"That will be two doors to your left, monsieur. The chevalier's suite."

"*Merci.*" Germain minced across the carpet after handing the servant some money. Madeleine could barely suppress a giggle as the man, like all suspicious underlings, bit into the coin.

Germain looked entirely the part of a bored aristocrat as he scratched on several doors in a row. "You'll do this one," he hissed and pointed to the door leading to Lemont's suite.

Madeleine shivered as she waited for a response to her knock. In the semidarkness Germain crouched behind a table in the corridor.

The door opened simultaneously with two others, and Madeleine stood face to face with Dubois. It came as a shock to see his evil face, and it took all her self-control to keep her voice steady as she yelled what they had planned earlier. "Hurry! An emergency! A man just fell down the stairs, breaking his leg—maybe dying. It might be your master!" Her voice rose to falsetto, and she moved as if to rush toward the stairs.

A wild scramble of steps echoed around her as the servants hurried past her, including a cursing Dubois. Pretending to be overcome with shock, she leaned against the wall, holding a hand to her forehead.

"Are you going to faint?" a maid inquired.

"*Non—non*, I will be fine. You must go and help the poor man," she muttered breathlessly, thinking that her faintness was not entirely false. Seeing Dubois again had brought back all the hideous memories. In her mind she could clearly see her father's dying face and Amul's lifeless body.

The corridor was empty and dark as she returned to Lemont's rooms. Peeping inside, she saw Germain rapidly searching the drawers and the wardrobes.

"Anything?"

"Not yet, alas. Keep watch outside. As soon as you hear Dubois, knock on the door."

Madeleine hid in the shadows behind a tall urn on a stand close to the door. Cold sweat covered her skin, and the tight bodice suffocated her. She breathed with shallow, nervous gasps. The strain of waiting for Dubois ate at her like a canker.

When the sound of shuffling feet reached her, she began to tremble. The servants were returning, talking loudly.

"I fancy he must have walked off one-legged."

"A prank to get decent people out of their beds. If I ever set eyes on that woman again, I'll wring her neck!"

A door slammed, but Dubois had not yet returned. She had to press her forehead to the cool wall to steady herself. Where was he? She could hear Germain pulling out one drawer after another.

Steps reverberated on the floor, and she heard more voices. In a frightened daze, she recognized Dubois's whine and lifted her leaden hand to knock softly on the door.

The sounds of Germain's search ceased abruptly, but he did not come out of the room as preplanned. What was keeping him? Fear coursed through her as she shrank against the wall.

The man conversing with Dubois was Lemont. She recognized his nasal tones. If Germain did not exit this instant, it would be too late.

No sounds came from within, and a few moments later, the two men opened the door and entered. Madeleine heard Dubois's words. "There was something about her that puzzled me. She had black hair like the marquise, but the voice was different. Too late did I realize that the voice belonged unmistakably to Madeleine Poquelin. Nobody has a voice like hers."

Mon Dieu! Madeleine thought. She had forgotten to distort her voice.

She flattened her ear to the door. Dubois's whine trailed distinctly through the wood. "Of course there was no man with a broken leg on the stairs," he responded to some murmured question.

"*You* would never bother to look for some poor wounded man, would you?" Lemont taunted.

"*Non*, I guess not, but I thought it important to find you and report that the Poquelin woman has not given up."

A curse burst from Lemont. "You're right! I thought we had finally cowed her. Too bad she wasn't snuffed with the others." Madeleine gasped, and terror struck her.

"If she was parading as Madame Simonet, what of the marquis?" Dubois mused aloud.

"He was the real marquis. No one else has that kind of nose. He even insulted the King." Lemont laughed harshly. "Wait! Simonet would not insult the King; he's too amiable, even when he's inebriated. Well, I suppose we can only speculate."

If only they knew how close they were to the truth, Madeleine thought. If they were to find Germain . . . She did not dare finish the thought.

"*Alors*, who was he then, the man with Simonet's nose?"

"I don't know, but I have a sneaking suspicion I've seen him before. I don't like it." Lemont's voice had become hard and calculating.

"Do you think someone suspects . . . ?" Dubois asked cautiously. "You know what."

"You know *I* was not . . ."

Madeleine held her breath, listening avidly, sensing they were on the verge of divulging some important information. So intent was she on eavesdropping that she did not hear footsteps behind her. A hand clasped over her mouth, and she froze in shock.

"Shhh, I'm here," Germain whispered in her ear.

Relaxing, she leaned against him, breathing deeply. A few moments passed before she could speak.

"I thought you were still inside," she hissed.

Not waiting for his answer, she once more pressed her ear to the door, and he copied her.

The sound of Lemont's voice came muffled through the door. "Monsieur says that the King is suspicious. Louis received an anonymous letter accusing me of the murders of the royal guards."

Madeleine felt Germain go tense next to her. Dubois's next words might hold the secret they eagerly sought. "*We* know you are innocent, but will the King? Well, there is no proof. The King will not let your reputation be sullied; you are Monsieur's very special friend, after all. He'll always protect the royal family from scandal. Yet it is a terrible accusation; you need to clear your name. Fouquet might—"

Lemont interrupted him with a snarl of impatience. Undaunted, Dubois continued, "But *who* sent the King the letter implicating you? It smells of conspiracy. I don't like it one bit."

Madeleine squeezed Germain's arm in excitement.

Rapid steps crossed the room. In the nick of time, Germain pulled Madeleine behind the urn, which barely concealed them. The door flew open.

"You can't be too careful here. Spies everywhere," Dubois whined and craned his neck to look down the dark corridor. Madeleine caught a glimpse of his white cravat and pale face. Germain held her tightly, and she closed her eyes, wishing she could sink through the floor.

"Nonsense! Your conscience is too sore." Lemont sounded bored. "I will don a clean vest and return to the ball. Damned clumsy of D'Ambrose to pour wine all over it. Perhaps I'll wear his favorite vest in retaliation.'' Lemont laughed coldly, evidently pleased with his joke.

The door closed with a slam, causing the walls to shudder.

Madeleine drew a breath of relief.

"Come, we must leave now before we are discovered," Germain whispered and pushed her toward the tall, narrow windows.

"But—"

"Shhh." Silently he opened the window and stepped outside onto a narrow balcony. Astride the railing sat Weasel, munching on a pastry. He smirked as they emerged. "Right on time. Roland is waiting with the carriage outside the wall. Testy as a bull he is. More than I could stand, so I climbed up here."

"What are you doing here? How did you know we were going to come out here?" Madeleine asked, baffled.

Weasel shrugged, silent.

Germain chuckled. "Weasel knew where to expect us, Madeleine. And he's not the only one here. You might not have noticed him, but Gaspard is a lackey tonight. He is doing a little snooping around."

Weasel sniggered. "*Oui*, I stole this from his tray; he didn't notice a thing. Do you want a taste?" He offered the half-eaten pastry to Madeleine, who shook her head. "No, thank you. I couldn't eat a bite."

Weasel shrugged. "Can you climb a rope ladder?"

Madeleine eyed him suspiciously. "Perhaps."

"I could carry you, but my wound would reopen, I'm afraid," Germain said.

"I did join the gang of my free will; I don't need any extra favors," she assured him angrily and swung her leg over the railing in an unladylike fashion.

Madeleine did not notice the tenderness stealing into Germain's eyes, nor was she aware of the rush of love moving through him as her hand touched his by mistake. She was only intent on finding a foothold on the swinging ladder. She hesitated.

"Go on, mam'selle."

Madeleine sent Germain a questioning glance.

"Weasel will unhook the ladder behind us. We don't want to leave any trace," he explained quietly.

"Oh." Madeleine frowned, thinking. "*Oui*, of course, I remember now. Weasel can climb a flat wall if he wants to." Strange creature! she thought as she descended the rickety ladder. She was glad she could not see the dark ground below; she liked to think it was only a few steps away.

Panting, she stood on the soft grass waiting for Germain, who arrived a few seconds after her. As the clouds separated, silvery moonlight bathed the earth. From the gardens at the back of the palace, she heard laughter and song.

Fearing they would be detected on this last leg of their adventure, she urged Germain to hurry. Obviously his wound was bothering him. One arm hung limply at his side, and he looked pale and drawn.

Running in the shadow of a hedge, they soon reached a small door in the stone wall. Waiting for Weasel, they leaned against the wall, panting. At last she could breathe freely. They had not been exposed, and she could hear the horses snorting on the other side of the wall. A seductive, sweet aroma of roses scented the night.

"How did you escape from Lemont's chambers?" she whispered.

Germain chuckled. "Easily enough. The rooms are connected to another suite, probably that of the Marquis D'Ambrose. I opened the door and stole through. As simple as that." He snapped his fingers to emphasize his words.

"Oh. I suspected they would catch you red-handed."

"You have little faith in me," he drawled. Lighting one of his black cheroots, he pulled further away from her.

"Perhaps it's difficult for me to picture you in this new role of thief," she replied acidly.

His laugh was brittle. "It wasn't exactly my choice."

"I know, all my fault. You don't have to remind me." She dragged a hand across her cheek, wiping away a tear of anger and frustration.

A deep sigh welled from his chest, but he did not speak until Weasel materialized soundlessly at their side. Madeleine was startled; she had not yet grown used to his sudden appearances.

Together they climbed into the waiting carriage, and Capitaine Roland let the restive horses spring.

Madeleine watched Germain on the opposite seat. Silver moonlight played over his stony features, and his eyes were two black, unfathomable pools. Lazily he met her probing gaze.

The gulf between them was wider than ever, and Madeleine sighed in despair.

Chapter 31

A shock awaited Madeleine as she descended from her bedroom the next morning.

Eating his breakfast, his shirt sleeves rolled up, the garment open to the waist, Germain leaned carelessly over his plate. His long hair was gone! Somebody had cut it at the nape of his neck in a coarse, jagged line.

"Your hair!"

Germain gave a crooked smile that never reached his eyes. "Good morning to you, too."

"What happened?" Sending an imploring glance at Weasel, she sat down at the table.

Weasel shrugged. "It didn't fit under the wig last night. We had to chop it off."

"Your handsome hair! How could you do it?"

"Pshaw, it's for fops—too conspicuous."

Madeleine's fingers plucked at the tablecloth. "Your hair was beautiful."

Madame Barbette snorted. "*Oui*, and he let that clod"—she pointed at Weasel—"butcher it off."

"Stop!" Germain snapped. "Sooner or later someone would have recognized me." He concentrated once more on his plate, his stance hostile. "You did," he reminded Madeleine.

Morning sunshine poured into the kitchen. The day was already sultry and oppressive. When she glanced at Germain's dear face, a dull ache pounded in her heart. His hostility made her feel sick.

"I think Lemont and Dubois know something about the slaying of the guards. If they have the diary, I don't know. I personally believe it doesn't exist any longer," Germain said to Weasel, who was sitting cross-legged on the stone ledge of the hearth.

"We will soon know something."

Madeleine ate a newly baked bun spread with homemade raspberry jam. The hot chocolate scalded her tongue as she listened intently to Germain's words. An especially pungent odor blew in from the streets. Nausea stole over her; her stomach revolted against the food, and she gasped for breath. Germain's and Weasel's faces blurred as she struggled against faintness.

Suddenly she had to bolt through the open kitchen door and relieve herself of her breakfast in one corner of the yard. Clammy all over, she leaned her forehead on the cool stone wall.

"Too lily-livered for our rough company, eh?" Germain drawled behind her.

Misery mixed with anger flooded her hotly, and she turned on him. "To see your sour face can turn anybody's stomach," she retorted as his body wavered in front of her eyes. It grew and loomed over her like a menacing black shadow; then she sank into soft oblivion.

When she came to, Germain was carrying her up the stairs to her bedroom. The sensation of his strong arms around her sent tendrils of pleasure through her languid body. She was protected, enveloped in his familiar scent. Here's where I belong, she thought. Shyly she glanced into his eyes. A ghost of worry flickered in their smoky depths, but as soon as he realized that she was awake, he looked away.

"You used to love me once, or was that in my imagination?" she muttered.

The only answer she received was the tightening of his arms, whether from tension or anger she didn't know.

He placed her on the bed and stood looking down at her, his eyes intent. "You'd better rest now," he said gruffly, unlacing her bodice so she could breathe more freely. Then he left her alone, and she could give free rein to her emotions.

She tossed and turned, crying softly into the pillow. Sick and exhausted, she drifted off to sleep and woke an hour later, refreshed. But her heart was still heavy in her chest.

Stretching like a cat, she lay staring at the stained ceiling. Germain's voice startled her.

"Better?"

She whipped her head around. He was sitting on a chair by the door, his long legs sprawled out before him and a brooding frown marring his forehead.

"*Oui*, much better, *merci*. This heat makes me sick. What wouldn't I give to breathe some fresh air again!"

"From now on you'll stay out of our expeditions. It will only hamper our work to have a fainting female on our hands."

"You . . . ! I've been through more than all of you put together. This is only a passing weakness." Anger flashed in her eyes and suffused her cheeks with red. "I thought we did well last night," she said, trying hard to swallow her wrath. She had to find out what had happened to the diary before she would get a moment's peace.

"The only thing we learned was about Lemont's possible involvement."

"I've known that the whole time," she parried impatiently. "He said the King suspected him." She wanted to hit Germain over the head with her pillow. How could he be so infuriatingly stubborn! Why didn't he make love to her? Now!

"We can easily find out more," she said, glaring at him, her eyes black with resentment.

"*I* will find out. You will stay here from now on."

Her anger converted to tears, but she choked them back. "You have no right to tell me what to do."

He laughed, a dry mirthless sound. "Is that so? I am the chief here. You came of your free will, and now *I* decide if you may leave this house or not."

"You're an insufferable oaf, stuffier than when you were the comte de Hautefort," she retorted scathingly. She averted her head so he could not see her tears. "Go to hell!" she spat.

"You have been listening too closely to Capitaine Roland. His vocabulary stems from the gutter."

She threw her pillow at him. "Leave me alone! If you came here to aggravate me, you have succeeded splendidly."

"I came here out of concern for your well-being."
"Absurd!"

She heard him rise. "I will return when your mood has improved," he drawled and exited, leaving her fuming.

Her communication with Germain deteriorated even further during the following days. The mounting tension made her snap at everyone.

One morning, she was sitting at the kitchen table, the tight laces of her bodice loosened, revealing a generous portion of her firm bosom. A cloud of irritation surrounded her, and tears stood in her eyes as she chopped yellow onions for Madame Barbette. The summer heat lay like a foul blanket over the city, and a sheen of perspiration covered her skin. Her hair hung heavy down her back, and Weasel, chewing on a straw, thought that she presented a most alluring picture.

He had noticed there was something seriously wrong between the master and this lovely little morsel. The master had certainly not eased his manly needs, and he was becoming more insufferable as the days went by. They all chafed against each other. It was the heat. *She* was dissatisfied as well. It stood written all over her.

He would not mind taking her in his arms and satisfying her, letting his fingers caress those enticing globes swelling over the edge of her bodice. Weasel had never been in love, but this young woman stirred him like no other had. Still, she belonged to the master, who was an idiot not to take what she so blatantly offered him. There he was now, scowling at her from the doorway. As Germain's eyes rested hungrily on her, Weasel thought it was perfectly clear what the man wanted.

Since they would not help themselves, Weasel realized he had to push them together for everybody's peace of mind.

"Master, why don't you take the mam'selle for a walk along Cours-la-Reine, or in the Bois de Vincennes? It's cool under the trees, the air is fresh, and I've heard the cabaret girls at La Pissotte are exceptionally good this season. You cannot stay confined here indefinitely."

"She's not going anywhere. I will not let her ruin everything for us," Germain snapped.

Weasel glanced briefly at Madeleine, who looked ready to stab Germain with the knife she was using to chop the onions.

"Now, listen here," Weasel insisted. "I think she has as much courage as any of the men. She didn't even bat an eyelash when Legrand spoke to her sharply the other night, and he's no less terrifying than he looks."

"So you're *both* in league against me now. See? She has corrupted us all." Germain sat down on a chair at the table, his disapproving gaze directed at her.

Weasel exchanged a speaking glance with Madame Barbette, who rolled her eyes heavenward in silent disgust.

As long as the master and Madeleine were at loggerheads, life in the house on Rue de la Lanterne would remain intolerable. And the master's being so crotchety spelled danger. In such an emotional state he was liable to make some grave error. Weasel had no wish to dangle from the gibbet on Place de Grève. Their profession was a dangerous one, and it was important to stay alert at all times.

"You clearly need a rest," he said bluntly. Germain turned to him wrathfully, but nothing could move Weasel. "Take Mam'selle Madeleine into the country for a spell," Weasel persisted.

"*Oui*, I agree," Madame Barbette added fiercely. "And—"

Germain shot her an angry glance, and the older woman snorted in disapproval, opening and closing her mouth like a fish.

No more was said at that point because just then the Mouse came running into the kitchen. "We have it now," he blurted out between gasps, rivulets of sweat coursing down his grubby, gray face.

Germain stood immediately. "Let's go!"

The dwarf led the way, followed closely by Germain, but Weasel did not move.

"What's going on?" Madeleine cried, forgetting the onions.

"Today we'll know if the diary still exists."

"And nobody told me?" She was on her feet in an instant. "What are you waiting for?"

"I'm not needed," Weasel answered with a yawn.

Overcome with fury, Madeleine stomped her foot on the floor, her eyes twin daggers directed at him. "Tell me about it this instant!"

"Gaspard is a temporary lackey in Fouquet's household. He was going to inform us the minute he could ferret out the truth, which he obviously did today."

"Well, don't sit around here like a hay sack. Let's go!" Madeleine shook him impatiently.

Weasel rose grudgingly. "The master will slit my throat for this."

"Non, non! Don't be a coward!"

Weasel stared at her darkly. "Don't you ever call me that word!" At a leisurely pace he accompanied Madeleine out of the house. She could have screamed in frustration.

"Where are we going?" Madeleine asked as she lay hidden in the hay of a lumbering wagon.

"Shhh, do you want to be thrown off the wagon?" Weasel muttered. "The meeting point with Gaspard is in the woods at Vaux-de-Vicomte."

"Fouquet's country estate?" That explained why they had changed conveyances twice. They had left the city far behind.

"Oui, and you'd better calm down. We won't get there any faster if you fret."

"You intolerable—"

"Don't say it! Spare your invectives for the master."

She glared at him. "What do you mean?"

"If you were the sweet girl you *look,* you would have the master wrapped around your little finger by now."

Madeleine snorted. "He's the one to blame. He wants nothing from me—thinks I'm only a nuisance."

Weasel broke into muffled laughter, wheezing terribly.

"It's not funny!" Madeleine exclaimed.

"You only have to wear him down. The man is not made of rock."

"Oui, he is." But already she felt a flare of fierce hope inside. Could the odious Weasel be right?

The dust from the sweet-smelling hay made her nose itch, and the subject was pushed to the background as she had to stifle a series of sneezes.

Unnoticed, they slipped off the wagon as it rolled past the gates at Vaux-de-Vicomte. How Weasel knew all the lanes and paths, Madeleine could not guess, but before long, they approached a clearing and he halted her with a hand on her arm.

"The master does not want to see us here," he whispered.

On a small slope he forced her to lie down on her stomach, her face pressed against the damp, musty-smelling earth. She prayed she wouldn't come eye to eye with a spider or some other disgusting insect.

From the clearing she heard Germain's cautious voice and the chinking of the horses' harnesses. "Gaspard?"

Tense silence fell, but almost immediately, Madeleine heard footsteps and the snapping of twigs. The trill of a swallow pierced the air nearby.

"That birdcall. It's so loud," she whispered.

"A sign that the coast is clear. Spider is probably posted on the path."

The sound of hissing voices reached them—Germain's and Gaspard's. Madeleine strained to hear what they were saying.

"This is extremely dangerous! I hope you have come up with something important," came Germain's voice.

"I've been keeping an eye on the mail and the messengers. They come day and night. Not an easy task to—"

"Get on with it!" Germain sounded impatient.

Madeleine waited tensely for Gaspard's next words, sensing that they were of utmost importance to her.

"It's true that the diary still exists, but Fouquet doesn't have it. He's a raw bundle of nerves! Somebody is squeezing him."

Germain's excitement was palpable in the air. "Who?"

"I don't know."

"Merde!" came Germain's lethal whisper.

Calm down, Madeleine thought, but she empathized with the hope building in Germain because she felt the same sensation.

"No names have been mentioned, master. Someone high up has it."

RECKLESS SPLENDOR 281

Madeleine heard the crackling of paper and assumed Gaspard was handing Germain a note.

"Now, go, and keep your eyes and ears open."

"*Oui*, master."

The stillness was broken by the hoot of an owl.

"An owl? In the middle of the day?" Madeleine commented, filled with surprise.

"It's a warning signal. Someone is approaching. Remember, no sounds!"

Madeleine held her breath in fear. Would Germain get caught now that they were on the brink of finding out the truth?

Peeping between two tufts of grass, she saw Gaspard slide into the shadows of the trees. Germain sneaked behind a tree, but was pounced upon from behind by a large, burly man. She gasped, and Weasel clapped a hand over her mouth.

"Shhh—don't move!"

At that moment another man arrived on the scene, pushing Spider in front of him. Spider's arms were bound at his back, and he walked with difficulty.

Madeleine watched breathlessly as Germain struggled with his attacker, flinching every time a fist rammed into him, feeling the pain herself. Stop, Stop! her mind kept screaming, but Weasel firmly held his hand over her mouth.

Yet another man, dressed in the green costume of a bailiff, attacked Germain and, while one man pinned him to the ground, the other firmly bound his hands.

"Fat catch today," the man in green growled. "Poachers, filthy thieves!"

Gaspard had slipped away unnoticed. Madeleine heard Weasel draw a breath of relief. Something moved at her feet, and she whipped her gaze sideways. Crawling soundlessly to their sides was the Mouse. Where he had come from Madeleine had no idea.

"Shall we take them?" he wheezed.

Weasel nodded. Putting his lips to her ear, he whispered, "When we surprise the men, hurry to cut the master loose with this." A sharp knife glinted coldly in the sunlight.

Madeleine bit her bottom lip, and her hand trembled slightly as her fingers curled around the metal handle, her heart thundering in fear.

With a hideous cry, Weasel and the Mouse catapulted from the ground and threw themselves on the astonished men. The Mouse looked like the small animal he was named after as he clung to the huge man whose knees were pressing Germain to the ground.

Keeping her eyes on Germain, Madeleine darted forward, her legs weak and jellylike.

A snarl erupted from the man in green as the Mouse's teeth found a good hold in his neck. Throwing himself backward to crush the dwarf, he let go of Germain.

The anger in Germain's eyes changed to disbelief when he saw Madeleine kneeling beside him.

"What the hell are you doing here?"

"We're helping you out of your predicament," she snapped and began tugging on the tight leather thong around his wrists. Her hands were shaking so badly, an eternity passed before she managed to insert the knife beneath the leather. She was afraid the sharp edge would cut into his already mangled flesh.

The moment the bailiff managed to shake off the dwarf, Germain was freed. With catlike grace, he jumped to his feet and threw himself at the bailiff, sending the man crashing to the ground with a well-aimed fist, his nose bleeding profusely. Germain grasped a thong and swiftly bound the man, who roared savage curses at him.

Madeleine tried to free Spider, but his wrists were bound so tightly that she could not insert the knife.

Weasel had overpowered his opponent and was sitting on the man's chest.

"Spider . . . I can't do it . . . I'll cut you," Madeleine squeaked, the tension taking its toll.

"Here, give me the knife," Germain snapped as he kneeled beside her. Anger poured from him in waves.

The Mouse and Weasel tied up the other man.

With a sigh of relief, Madeleine sank to the ground. Germain's eyes raked over her darkly, making her heart begin to thud hard once again.

Within seconds, Spider had been released and stood massaging his sore wrists.

"Phew, that was a close call. They hang poachers in these parts—without questions asked."

Germain was not listening. He kept glancing at Madeleine, an inscrutable expression in his eyes.

"Now, tell me, *what* are you two doing here?" he demanded, his eyes shifting to Weasel, who wore his usual calm mien.

"Don't blame him, Germain. It's all my fault. I *made* Weasel bring me here." Madeleine's voice quivered, and Germain's hard gaze was like a blow in her middle.

"*Made* him? Nobody makes Weasel do anything he doesn't want to do."

"Well, the mystery of the diary is more my business than anybody else's." Her voice rang more firmly as her anger started to boil to the surface. "You have no right raking us over hot coals. If it weren't for us, you'd be dangling from that tree over there." She pointed at an ancient oak. "I think you should thank us. You should be grateful that you have such faithful men!"

She saw a muscle working in his jaw, and his bronzed face turned pale with wrath, but he did not speak further. She swallowed, her distress a sharp pain in her chest. Everything she did turned out wrong. She was a millstone around Germain's neck. Never would he have helped her if it weren't for his own interest in revenge. She had to get it into her head—her romance with Germain was over, and it had been over ever since he had lost everything.

Chapter 32

Madeleine found herself struggling against Germain as he lifted her up on his horse.

"Stop, or you'll be walking back to Paris," he threatened. When he saw her flashing eyes, he added, "The other men refused to take you, mumbling some nonsense about you belonging to me." His voice dripped with sarcasm. "On the other hand—if I make you walk, I'll have the men turning against me. I've no idea what you've done to capture their hearts."

Stiffly Madeleine sat on the horse, nothing of the surprise she felt registering on her face. Did the men really accept her?

Her thoughts were brutally interrupted as Germain swung into the saddle behind her. Her senses reeled at his closeness—the heady virile scent of him, of sweat, horses, and desire, assaulted her nostrils. The hard, lean touch of his body against hers made her weak with longing. As his muscular arm snaked around her waist, securing her against him, she wanted to swoon. A torrent of desire, so strong that she feared he could sense it, engulfed her.

The horse trotted off at a leisurely pace. In the hot midday sun perspiration broke out over her body. Her blood pounded with mounting need. Every jolt that brought their bodies closer was sheer, agonizing pleasure.

To ward off the clamor of her dissatisfied senses, she said, "I'm glad to hear that the diary has not been destroyed after all. Gaspard did not find out who has it, then?"

"*Non,*" Germain muttered. He shifted in the saddle and fished out a note hidden in his shirt. "Read this."

RECKLESS SPLENDOR

Madeleine received the stiff folded note. The paper was of the finest quality and the handwriting bold and elegant.

This is my last answer. Either you do as I advised or you will never see the diary again. It certainly has some very interesting information concerning your affairs. When you have exonerated my name, the diary will be in your hands forever.

The note had no signature.

"Exonerate whom?" she mused.

"I don't know. It could mean anybody," Germain said. "Perhaps Lemont. Fouquet is the only one who can acquit him if he's guilty of the murders."

Germain was growing more and more frustrated as he tried to prevent the hard, aching bulge in his culottes from coming into contact with her body. It would not do to let her feel it. She would laugh at him! He had immediately smelled the sweet scent of her arousal, and her body was soft, her skin glistening like a dewy rosebud in the golden sunlight. He wanted desperately to place a kiss in the hollow of her neck, to undo the untidy knot on the top of her head and watch her tresses cascade like a waterfall down her back. He wanted to lay her down on a meadow full of flowers, spread her legs wide, and plunge into her, teasing her to ecstasy, tasting her arousal, caressing her softness, strewing kisses over her heated skin.

That was why he had been caught today. His mind had been filled with her, her breasts, the curve of her hips. He had become careless and had risked his men's lives.

And now she was so close, so unbearably exciting. When her head jolted to his shoulder, he could glimpse her alluring cleavage. To him she grew more beautiful every day, her mysterious appeal more pronounced. She was a deadly poison in his blood. If he pulled her bodice down a bit, he would be able to feast his eyes on the rosy crests.

The horse stumbled with fatigue, and Germain was painfully jerked back to reality as Madeleine's elbow jabbed him in the newly healed wound on his chest.

"Oh-ahhh," he groaned, all his ache and longing pouring forth with the sound.

Madeleine swiveled around, staring into his eyes, dark and smoky. For the first time she felt a small chink in the invisible armor he had donned. His sexual desire almost oozed from his pores, and he could not hide the hunger in his eyes. She wiggled her hips provocatively.

Irritation winning over all other emotions, he abruptly pulled the horse to a halt.

"We'd better stop at this inn to rest the animals."

Madeleine wanted to reach out and smooth the frown from his forehead, run her hands through his crude hairdo, and ruffle his curls. His lips formed a sneer behind the thick beard.

"What are you staring at? Your spine will be permanently deformed if you keep turning like that."

He slid off the horse, at the same time pulling his shirt from the waistband of his tight culottes to conceal the telltale bulge in the front.

Without helping Madeleine down, he stalked through the low door of the inn.

Spider lifted her from the mount, and she studied her surroundings. The inn was an old gray stone building with blue painted shutters and a thatched roof. Huge trees shaded it, and old rosebushes hugged the walls. Bumblebees buzzed sleepily through air that was heavy with the delicious scent of full-blown roses.

"Such an idyllic place!" she exclaimed, but nobody heard her; the men had disappeared through the dark mouth of the doorway.

An ostler watered the horses, and Madeleine wiped perspiration from her brow. The contrast between the bright day outside and the dark room inside blinded her for a few moments. When her eyes had adjusted, she saw Germain leaning on the counter, a large tankard of ale in front of him. He looked far from the aristocrat he was; he was harder, sharper, with an attractive strength exuding from him. The barmaid, her cheeks flushed, was making sheep's eyes at his brooding face.

Madeleine felt a stab of jealousy. He was hers! But there was that anger in him, keeping them apart. She refused to believe that their love was over; his desire for her was too blatant to ignore. But as things stood between them, she would be foolish to read anything more serious in their relationship. The diary was the only reason they were together now. The thought depressed her.

Swallowing her misery, she stalked over to the table where Weasel and the others sat drinking ale.

Weasel pushed his tankard toward her. "Good for parched throats," he said, wiping his mouth with his sleeve.

Madeleine cautiously took a sip. "I'm sorry, but I don't have any money to pay for one." Turning to the Mouse, she blurted out, "You owe me something. You stole my purse, so you might as well pay for my ale—even if my purse was empty."

The Mouse showed his yellow teeth in an embarrassed grin. "I should not have done that to a friend, but—"

A tankard crashed down on the table. "Here," Germain barked. "And stop that bickering."

Madeleine's eyes glowed mutinously. "I don't need *your* charity."

"*Oui*, you do. Drink up and be quiet!"

Madeleine was dizzy from anger and thirst. Germain's hard words finally made her emotions boil over, and she rushed outside.

Weakly she leaned over the fence behind the stables and cried until she thought her chest would burst. How silly!

A cool, wet cloth was placed on her forehead.

"I'm sorry," came Germain's husky voice behind her. With a steadying arm around her waist, he wiped her face with the cloth. The fresh scent of lavender water eased her. With closed eyes, gulping for air, she let him pat her face. She hiccupped, and a tremor ran through her as he softly slid the cool wet cloth across the visible expanse of her bosom.

She felt sore everywhere. His arms lay protectively around her, and she leaned feebly against his chest. The hair in the vee of his open shirt tickled her face.

"I don't like to see you suffer," he said gruffly against her hair. Anguish held him in its cold grip. He could not stand to see her so upset.

"I'm fine now. I'm being foolish, that's all."

"Weasel was an idiot to bring you out here."

"*Non*, he's a good friend—if somewhat odd, of course." She could barely speak. "Let me rest for a while, and I'll be as good as new."

Without comment, he lifted her into his arms and carried her to the shadow of an apple tree out of sight of the inn. After tenderly lowering her onto the grass, he sat down, leaning against the trunk. She did not protest when he placed her head in his lap and slowly began stroking her forehead and hair.

With that divine touch on her skin, she drowsed, dreaming of Germain's lips on hers and the air filled with the warm scent of ripening strawberries.

Hot desire pulled her slowly back to reality. She was drowning in a sea of pleasure. Blinking in the filtered light, she looked into Germain's eyes, two fountains of silver fire. Gradually she realized that the feeling came from a featherlight teasing of her nipple, the one closer to him.

Unable to move, she sighed deeply and felt the crest of her breast tighten with unbearable sweetness. Expectation as thick as honey settled in her womb. A swelling need in her loins begged for his touch. But as soon as he realized that she was awake, he abruptly withdrew his teasing finger from her breast and pulled up the tight bodice.

"It's time to leave," he rasped, pulling her into a sitting position. Hurt and despair washed over her.

"How dare you touch me when I'm defenseless!" she scolded.

"It was too tempting a moment to waste." His voice was hoarse with desire.

Her face went red, but he held up a hand to ward off the angry words gathering on her tongue. "Let me help you with your hair. You look like you've been pulled backward through a hedge."

Confused, she weakly put a hand to her head. The chignon was askew, and a mass of curls fell in a wild tangle over her shoulders.

She wanted to pound him with her fists as he began taking the pins out of her hair, but she sat in quiet defeat.

Expertly he untangled her hair and, with a proprietary air, rearranged every sunlit strand into a gleaming curtain down her back. Finally he secured it at the nape of her neck with a leather thong he cut from his wrist.

"There, now you look much better. If you can get some color into those pale cheeks, you'll look like a goddess."

Under his tender grooming her vicious anger evaporated, and she felt strangely deflated. *"Merci."*

"Do you feel better now?"

"Oui." She was then on the verge of throwing herself around his neck, but memories of old disagreements still created a barrier that she did not dare to step over.

Weasel's voice echoed in the yard. "Master?"

The intensity in Germain's gaze relaxed, and the moment of intimacy vanished.

The ride to Paris with Germain's body pressed so close to hers was pure agony, when all she wanted was to be gathered into his warm embrace, not cloaked in a mantle of rejection.

Chapter 33

In his elegant library at Vaux-de-Vicomte, Nicolas Fouquet fumed. His majordomo trembled in his silver-buckled shoes.

"Where is that confounded note?" Fouquet yelled for the fourth time.

"I—I truly don't know, monsieur. I saw you reading it yesterday, and I haven't seen it since."

Fouquet's forehead furrowed. He paced back and forth, thoughtfully rubbing his chin. "I would bet anything that there is a connection between the disappearance of the note and the poachers. Send for the bailiff immediately and then get to work on finding out who is a traitor in my household."

Ten minutes later, the bailiff stood nervously in front of Fouquet.

"I want you to describe the man to me again." Fouquet sat behind his desk, his glittering black eyes fastened on the minion.

"At first I saw two men, one of them large with hacked-off hair and a beard. The other was a mean-looking, dirty ruffian with long, greasy hair. We had them trussed up like hares when out of nowhere a young woman, a midget, and a skinny fellow fell upon us. The midget bit me in the neck, and it's still aching. The woman freed the other man, and that was the end of it for us." He rubbed his bandaged neck.

"What color hair did the large man have?" Fouquet stared intently at the twitching bailiff.

"Blond, monsieur, like ripe wheat. A dangerous rascal, full of hatred."

"Had they stolen any fowl or rabbits?"

The bailiff scratched his head. "*Non*, I don't remember seeing any. But they could have hid it for all I know."

Fouquet leaned back, a sly look creeping into his eyes. "Do you recall the woman?"

"Oh, yes! She was beautiful; ripe and lovely with very light-colored hair."

Fouquet's breath was a barely audible hiss. "That will be all."

When he sat alone in his sumptuous study, a great fury slowly ignited within him. In the dark recesses of his mind, he already knew the answer to the query he was dashing onto paper. When the answer from Pignerol came, he would know for certain.

The comte de Hautefort was still alive, and the girl knew it. He slammed his fist onto the hard surface of the desk. *Nobody* was going to make a fool out of him, the most powerful man in the country.

At the palace of Fontainebleau sat another powerful man, the king God had chosen, according to the Frenchmen, to rule France. His fingertips in a steeple, elbows leaning on the gilt desk, the King was deeply immersed in thought.

Colbert, in his usual brown velvet, eyed the sovereign with bright eyes.

Without looking at Fouquet's assistant, the King spoke. "Are these figures accurate? You could have made a mistake."

"*Non*, sire, they are correct. Fouquet is showing you falsified accounts every day. It has taken me many months to uncover the deception. He has been extremely clever."

In his thoughts, the King went over his conversation with Fouquet, who had lied straight to his face. It enraged him that a member of the inner council was cheating him—and with such daring schemes as lending funds at staggering interest rates and concealing the fraud by registering the capital larger than it was. In the treasury registers Fouquet had made up a multitude of false expenses to rectify the balance between receipts and expenses.

What gall of the man!

"Do we have enough proof to arrest him?"

"*Non*, sire, we'll have to be extremely careful. He holds the post of attorney-general in the Paris parlement, and if you start attacking him, you risk another civil war. Sire, you know that your finances are not strong enough to bear that strain. Fouquet has powerful allies."

Irritated, Louis flung the accounts to the floor. "The man has more power than I have."

"Not for long, sire. We'll let him put a noose around his own neck. If we only could have laid our hands on that Poquelin diary, that proof would have been enough."

The King paced the floor. "It's too late. We'll have to find another strategy, a plan more cunning than Fouquet himself would have thought of. You can be sure that the diary has been burned by now, *if* it ever existed."

Colbert sighed. "That diary has been the root of much evil."

The King frowned. *"Oui.* By the way, are there any more clues as to the identity of the men who killed my guards?"

"*Non*, sire, except that anonymous letter."

"I refuse to believe for one moment that Lemont is involved in that sordid affair."

"He was paying a hasty visit to Rouen at the same time Mademoiselle Poquelin was there. That is all we know, except that the leader of the murderers had the air of a nobleman and that he spoke with a lisp."

"Bah! Everyone at court speaks with a lisp. But if any more evidence pointing to his guilt turns up, I want it hushed up. It won't do to have Monsieur's name dragged through the mud along with Lemont's."

"I understand, sire." Colbert rubbed his chin. "If I may speak, sire, I have an idea how we might trap Fouquet." When the sovereign nodded, he continued. "We have to make him resign from the parlement; the only way we can accomplish that is if you offer him a higher post. Once he has left the parlement, we can arrest him."

"*Dieu*, that is a brilliant stroke!" The King rubbed his hands together. "I will bait him with Mazarin's post. Then he'll have to give up the attorney-general status. That man has too many titles as it is!"

Madame Barbette prepared a stew of mutton and beans. The whole house was filled with the aroma, and Madeleine complained that mutton smelled woolly. Despair had made her lose her appetite; all she wanted was to make peace with Germain.

She had been in the house on Rue de la Lanterne for several weeks, and she worried that she should return to La Béjart's home before Uncle Jean-Baptiste began searching for her. The mystery of the diary had not yet been solved, and she grew increasingly impatient. As strange comings and goings occurred during the dark hours of the night, she also sensed that Germain was keeping her out of his operation. Time was rapidly approaching when she would have to leave. She had no wish to have to explain to her uncle that Germain was hiding in Paris.

Legrand had a fondness for the theater, and he went to the play at Palais-Royal every Saturday, respectably clad in a snuff-brown velvet suit and a wig concealing his own oily strands. This particular Saturday, he came rushing in, wig awry and a smile softening his usually sinister face.

"Your uncle is getting married!" he blurted to Madeleine, who was sitting at the kitchen table embroidering a rose on a piece of white batiste.

"Married? He's almost forty years old! To whom?"

"Armande Béjart, La Béjart's daughter."

"Armande? Impossible!" But instinctively she knew that Legrand was speaking the truth. Her uncle had behaved like an infatuated schoolboy in the company of Armande. How La Béjart must be raving!

"Oh dear, that means I can't return to the Béjart residence."

"You're not going anywhere," came Germain's voice from the doorway. Madeleine turned her head, her haste betraying her eagerness. "I—"

"No use arguing, Madeleine. I'll not have you running about Paris with your madcap schemes. You know Fouquet must be desperate by now, and he might get it into his head to assault you again."

"I'm no child! And Fouquet knows that I don't have the diary," she parried hotly.

"He's vicious enough to blame you for everything," Germain grated, at the end of his patience. "He might choose to punish you for his failure." Carelessly he sloshed wine into a chipped glass and drank deeply.

Madeleine stared at him in surprise. "I hadn't thought of that," she muttered.

Germain's eyes bored into her. "You have no choice. You'll have to stay in this nest of thieves." His voice dripped with irony.

On the verge of launching herself into another verbal battle with him, she took a deep breath, but somehow she couldn't find the words. Sending him one dark glance, she turned, skirts swishing, and fled from the room.

Madeleine was sitting in the window of her room, racking her brain for a clue as to the whereabouts of the diary. Since Germain would not let her participate in his activities, she would find out for herself. If Lemont was innocent of the murders, he did not have the diary, but then, who did? And why was that person trying to blackmail Fouquet? The issue had gotten completely out of hand; it was too confusing to unravel with the scanty information she had to go on.

Germain waited patiently for the coach to come around the bend. For two days, his men had been lying in wait for Fouquet's gold-encrusted coach to leave Vaux-de-Vicomte, and at last they were in luck.

He felt no fear at the prospect of attacking the coach in broad daylight. His men were ready, perched on the thick branches that formed an arch across the road. The guards following the coach would not have a chance of warding off the attack of his seasoned men.

As the well-sprung carriage reached the arch, he shouted, "Now!"

The coachman stared in disbelief as a dwarf jumped onto the back of the leader horse and forced it to a halt. The animals neighed in distress. Spider assaulted the coachman, and the guards found themselves surrounded by a motley crew armed with swords, cudgels, and lethal daggers.

Fouquet craned his head through the window and inquired peevishly about the delay.

As Germain left the shadows and rode up to the coach, Fouquet stared with dawning understanding at the masked man.

"Highwaymen," he croaked. "Guards!"

"No use, minister. We have to apologize for this untimely interruption of your journey, as you must be on important business of the state, Monsieur Fouquet," Germain said ironically. "But a certain issue has to be cleared before you may continue."

Fouquet stared hard at the bearded man whose head was concealed under a large hat. There was something familiar about his voice and bearing.

Germain alighted from his horse and climbed into the coach, sitting down on the seat facing Fouquet.

The minister felt the eyes behind the mask searing into him, and a shiver of fear rippled through him.

"Do I know you?"

"No, I'm dead and forgotten." Germain's voice was a menacing hiss. His gaze strayed to Fouquet's manicured hands clutching the knob of a silver cane. On his little finger glistened the diamond that had been the comtesse de Hautefort's wedding ring.

A powerful urge to break Fouquet's hand gripped Germain, but he only whispered, "Hand me the ring."

As Fouquet began to pull off the ruby on his index finger, Germain snapped, "The diamond!"

Fouquet's hands were clammy with fear as he handed Germain the ring. "Is that—all you want?"

Germain pocketed the jewel and very slowly reached for Fouquet's jabot. With a twisting motion, Germain cut off the whimper rising to the man's lips and watched him struggle for air.

"I could kill you now and nobody would know. Would you like to be buried like a common thief in unsacred ground? We could easily dig a grave under any of those trees outside." He jerked Fouquet's terrified face inches closer to his own. Choking, Fouquet managed to shake his head. Crimson flooded his features as he gasped for breath.

Germain shoved him back against the squabs. "This is only the beginning of your sufferings, Fouquet. If you want to keep your life, tell me one thing. Where is the diary?"

Fouquet went rigid, and the crimson turned to purple.

With a disgusted grunt, Germain let go of his stranglehold. For a few moments Fouquet gasped desperately for breath. Holding a hand to his throat in protection, he wheezed, "I don't know what you're talking about."

Germain threatened to grip his jabot again.

"Non! Don't . . . Lemont has it."

Germain's gaze bored into the face of his hated foe. He sensed that Fouquet was telling the truth—or what he believed to be the truth. "Who killed the guards?"

"Lemont did. He's begging me to exonerate his name. If I don't, he'll deliver the diary to the King."

Germain jerked his fist up, and Fouquet squealed in terror.

"How did you get involved with Lemont in the first place?" He pressed Fouquet's chin higher. "Answer me!"

Fouquet wheezed, pushing ineffectually at Germain's arm. "He owes me a hundred thousand livres. Please, let me go," he begged. "I'll pay you anything you want. I am very rich. This matter has to stay between us."

Germain let his hand fall. Against his own inclination to take his revenge then and there, he stepped down. "I don't want your money. My revenge has just begun. The King will deal with your punishment in due course. It'll be so much more humiliating for you than to die here—away from the eyes of the world. Oh, yes, I'll enjoy watching you grovel in the dirt. And I want everyone to see you for what you really are, worse than the slimiest cutthroats living in the sewers of Paris. Remember, this is only the beginning."

Germain jabbed a hard forefinger into Fouquet's heaving chest, making the slighter man cringe.

The Mouse whipped the horses, and they leaped forward at a frantic pace. The guards were relieved to follow the coach at the highest possible speed, their throats still intact.

Germain stared after the carriage with a small measure of satisfaction. After the conversation he had overheard between Lemont and Dubois, he knew that Lemont had not murdered the guards. Lemont was playing some game with Fouquet to get his name cleared, but more likely he was trying to force Fouquet to wipe out his debt by withholding the diary. Germain whistled between his teeth. One hundred thousand livres! Now it only remained to find out who really had the diary.

As morning light filtered through the threadbare curtains in Madeleine's room, her thoughts drifted to the stunning news Legrand had delivered. She found it hard to picture her independent uncle married to the flighty Armande. Would Armande understand how lucky she was to win a man like Uncle Jean-Baptiste?

"Mam'selle Madeleine."

As usual, Weasel had slipped into the room without her noticing him.

Irritated, she turned on him. "Don't you ever scratch on doors?"

Weasel shrugged. "Madame Barbette has packed a picnic basket. We're going to the Bois de Vincennes. Do you want to join us?"

Excited at the prospect of leaving the seething, foul-smelling city, Madeleine jumped at the invitation. "*Oui*, I'd love to." Then she hesitated. "Is, er, Germain coming?"

"*Non*. When he's in one of his black moods, nothing and nobody tempts him."

"He has changed a lot. He used to smile, to always tease me."

"*Oui*." Weasel scratched his head. "Perhaps you can help him."

Madeleine knew what he was implying, and a scarlet blush tinted her cheeks. "Weasel, if you don't stop harassing me, I will empty the chamber pot over your head!" She wanted to shock him, but nothing could ruffle the thief's composure.

"I don't know why I even listen to you!" she continued huffily.

A smile lit up his pasty face. "You don't have any choice. You'd better be nice to your friends in this den of iniquity. We are no cutthroats—the master won't allow it— but it can be unpleasant to have us as enemies."

If she had not seen the twinkle in his eyes, she might have suspected he was threatening her. "You're incorrigible."

With his usual shrug and soundless gait he left the room, followed by Madeleine.

Setting off on foot, the ruffians separated so as not to draw attention to themselves. In a group, they looked sinister enough. Serving wenches and matrons made the sign against the evil eye as they passed them in the street.

Madeleine enjoyed the warmth and the golden light of summer. She was dressed as a servant in a short blue cotton skirt and a white blouse, the drawstring loosened to reveal her creamy shoulders. Around her hair she had wound a colorful kerchief.

"Just like a gypsy," was Madame Barbette's comment when Madeleine had entered the kitchen.

"This is so much more comfortable than suffocating corsets and triple petticoats."

Of Germain there was no sign. Madeleine furtively looked for his tall frame among the other ruffians. Although she already knew he wasn't going to be present, a sharp pain of disappointment twisted in her stomach. He had become more and more reclusive, spurning every cheerful suggestion. Madeleine yearned to know what dark secrets churned in his mind.

Between them, Madame Barbette and Madeleine carried the food basket. An urchin tried to run off with a loaf of bread sticking out of the top, but Madame Barbette, amazingly agile, grasped him by the scruff of his neck and shook him. "A shame on you, stealing honest people's food like that!" she bellowed, and Madeleine could not help but smile. Honest people, indeed!

Madame Barbette bristled. "By the time we reach Bois de Vincennes, all the food will be stolen."

"Not with you guarding it." Madeleine waved to the driver of a passing wagon full of hay. "*Maître*, may we travel with you as far as the Bois de Vincennes?" she cried with a beguiling smile.

"*Mon Dieu*, who can withstand that smile?" Madame Barbette muttered sarcastically.

He stopped, and Madeleine helped Madame Barbette to hoist her fat bottom onto the hay.

The oppressive heat and smells of Paris slowly subsided, giving way to a soft, playful wind filled with the exquisite fragrance of newly scythed grass. The forest was at its most lush, deep emerald green interspersed with warm, golden shadows.

Madeleine drew a breath of profound delight as she watched the downy clouds glide across the sky and the sun create diamonds in the gray ribbon that was the river Marne.

"I needed this. How beautiful is France!" she exclaimed, riding on a wave of euphoria.

On the paths along the river, couples strolled and children played. Madeleine found herself wishing she was walking arm in arm with Germain, listening to his whispered endearments. She imagined the feel of his arm pressing into her breast, and it sent a warm flow of excitement through her. She had waited patiently for him to come out of the icy fortress of contempt that he had built around himself, but he had not, except for the one brief occasion under the apple tree when he had almost succumbed to his desire.

A delicate blush crept into her cheeks at the memory. She would never love another man the way she loved Germain. Would their love ever have the chance to deepen, to expand? Not if Germain kept being so pigheaded, she thought.

"Lost in dreams again, eh? Your eyes are wistful, as only they are when you're thinking of Master Germain." Madame Barbette's voice had grown uncharacteristically soft.

"I'm a fool to think about him. He hates me."

"Pshaw. If he hates you, I'll eat my slipper," Madame Barbette snorted.

"He blames me for his misfortune."

"That is understandable. Had he not been involved with you, he'd still be the comte de Hautefort, prisoner at court. He *hated* that life. No, dear, you'll have to remind him with all your charm that he loves you. I believe that things can be set right again. He has to stop being the terror of Paris first, of course, and that before he gets caught. It's the only thing that has me worried."

"*Oui.*" Madeleine shivered as if a cold draft had brushed over her skin.

The cart halted with squeaky wheels. "Here we are, mesdames. I wish you a pleasant outing."

Madame Barbette puffed and heaved to extricate herself from the hay. Straw stuck to her ample form, and Madeleine giggled.

"You don't look so ladylike yourself," the older woman muttered.

Madeleine pirouetted in the lane. "This is a heavenly spot. Can you feel it?"

Madame Barbette mumbled and wheezed as she walked across the meadow, and planted herself in the shade of an ancient oak. "Youth," she sniffed.

It was no real surprise to see Weasel's head sticking out of the hay. Madeleine had not spied his presence before, but she had become used to his appearing in the most unlikely places. The driver had not.

"Cursed skunk! Sneaking into my wagon—get out of there!" The thongs of a whip whined in the air.

Quick as the animal he was nicknamed after, Weasel slid to the ground, at the exact moment the sharp lash bit into the hay. With an apologetic lift of his grimy wide-brimmed hat, he darted across the meadow, followed closely by Madeleine, who had no wish to taste the driver's wrath.

One by one the other men arrived and sat down under the tree, forming a ring around Madame Barbette. During the months she had followed Germain to the other side of the law—and to squalor—Madame Barbette had become a pillar of strength and a haven for the ruffians flocking to Germain. She held an unflinching belief that this was a transition period in her life, and she gave freely to all and sundry passing through her orbit.

Madeleine felt a surge of tenderness at the older woman's staunch support of Germain. Had she possessed only a morsel of that strength, nothing could have stopped her from reaching Germain across the gulf of estrangement.

With a grunt of contentment, Legrand stretched his gaunt body on the ground and munched on a leg of mutton that Weasel had stolen from a stall on Pont-Neuf. The Mouse, Paris's most audacious cutpurse, was sharpening his tool of trade, his most cherished possession, a small pair of scissors hanging from a golden cord.

Capitaine Roland, a black scowl on his face, foraged through the hamper for a bottle of ale. Madeleine was still cautious in his company, for she often recalled her first terrifying encounter with the huge man and his thin shadow, Spider, who was picking his nose with a clawlike fingernail.

These men were her family now. She wanted to laugh at the absurdity of the situation.

The proper townspeople looked askance at the assembly under the oak, but the ruffians were completely oblivious to their reaction. Grunts and snores spoke their own language of contentment.

Having downed three strawberry tarts and two glasses of wine, Madeleine was affected by the drone of Weasel's snores and yawned hugely. The temptation to stretch out in the soft, sweet grass was overpowering, but she was jerked out of her drowsiness when she saw Germain leaning against a tree trunk nearby, staring at her.

"Master Germain! Come and join us. There is still some food left," Madame Barbette called upon noticing him. Madeleine's heart began to pound hard. She could barely breathe. To her delight, he sauntered toward the group and sat down next to her. A shuttered look was on his face, but she sensed a softer note in his movements.

The sun gilded his hair as he discarded his wide hat, and Madeleine remembered how his curls used to ripple across his shoulders. As if reflecting his severe mood, the short golden curls were brushed back severely, away from his face. She felt a sudden longing to ruffle them into a wild cloud. A nervous giggle escaped her lips, and Germain's gray gaze raked her with disapproval.

"You look at me as if I'm some distasteful insect you found under a stone," she snapped, tired of his sulks. "I was here first, and one of us has to leave."

"You're exaggerating," he drawled.

"Whatever I am—to see your dour face is enough to send me elsewhere." She stood and brushed pieces of grass from her skirt. Sending him a dark venomous glance, she stalked off down the path.

"Childish games!" Madame Barbette burst out. "You should be ashamed of yourself, Master Germain! Don't you see she's madly in love with you?"

The ruffians began to fidget and mutter. The ground had suddenly grown lumps and holes, and they rose, one after the other to walk away, while giving Germain furtive, apologetic glances.

"See what you've done; ruined our outing, alas," Madame Barbette scolded. "Go and speak to the poor girl."

Germain grimaced and threw a piece of pie on the ground, where sparrows busily attacked it.

"She's nothing but a large problem," he snarled.

Madame Barbette's formidable temper flared. "I've had enough of your tantrums! Where are your manners? Where is the gallant gentleman I used to serve?" She waved away his attempts to speak and, standing with difficulty, stood over him, arms akimbo and a belligerent scowl on her face.

"You will not disgrace yourself further! Although your fortune has changed, it's written nowhere that it cannot change again." Hastily she packed the leftover food back into the hamper. "And don't come back to the house until you have made peace with Madeleine. If the old comte knew, he'd be turning in his grave, the poor soul," she added fiercely, wagging a fat finger under his nose.

Germain's face darkened, but not with anger. Pain registered in the depths of his eyes, and his powerful shoulders sagged.

He watched Madame Barbette waddle through a patch of poppies. She was more of a mother to him than the woman who had given him birth.

Struggling against the gloom that had haunted him for so long, he felt weak, as if he had no fighting spirit left. He knew he had to make some kind of truce with Madeleine. Tension sat like a coiled spring in his stomach. God knew, he loved her, perhaps more than ever, but her constant presence in the house on Rue de la Lanterne created a violent conflict with the ban he had laid on his feelings.

He both cursed and praised the moment she had come back into his life. Then he had been too feeble to send her away. His body had failed him then, and it was betraying him now in a clawing hunger for her. Love pounded in his veins. In his loins, a constant ache reminded him of when he had bedded her for the first time. It grated on his nerves that she was the only woman who could assuage his needs, and he almost hated her for spoiling him for all other women.

As if by a will of their own, his legs bore him down the path she had chosen. His nostrils filled with the heady scent of wild honeysuckle, and bees droned past his head. He walked in a dream, searching for his lost love.

Pain and fear grew in his chest like a canker. What if she coldly refused him? The ache rapidly flooded every inch of his body, like poison under his skin.

In a haze, he did not notice the play of golden sunlight and mysterious shadows under the trees or birds bickering over his head. To him it was the path of uncertainty, the path of fear of being rejected by the most important person in his life.

The suffering became unbearable as he stumbled forward. Then he saw her.

Chapter 34

Sitting on a boulder at the river's edge, Madeleine was throwing pebbles, one by one, into the glittering water, watching the rings swell wider and finally disappear. Just like life. Young and full of energy, she made big waves, but with the passing of time the swell would weaken until there was no more proof of her ever having existed. What a depressing thought! She wanted to make waves that would go on forever. Was she wasting her life waiting for Germain to return her love?

A rustle of leaves alerted her, and she turned quickly.

Germain stood in the shadows, his face white under his tan, his eyes unnaturally bright. With fear? No, that could not be possible. She had never seen Germain afraid of anything.

The sunlight caught the whiteness of his shirt, blinding her as he stepped forward, as hesitantly as a sleepwalker.

The only sounds in this secluded spot were the gentle gurgle of the water against the shore and the swishing of birds' wings through the air.

"If you've come to humiliate me further, you may leave immediately," she said sullenly. "I've had enough of your foul temper, and I'll never return to Rue de la Lanterne with you."

Immediately she sensed his changed mood. Despair oozed from him. Instinct made her rise, sensing that he was on the verge of saying something very important. She wanted to run to him, but a flare of pride stopped her.

Warily they eyed each other, the silver flames of his gaze boring into the dark blue pools of her eyes, drowning in the unfathomable depths.

Germain's voice broke, dangerously close to tears. "I've tried so hard to shut you out of my life, but I know now that I can't do it; I have no power over my heart. Will you please forgive me? I will always . . . love you."

As if to hide his pain from her, he raised a shaking hand to his eyes.

Joy, a flame, sprang to life in her chest. It flared and shone brightly, flooding her whole being. Her feet, on wings of love, bore her toward him. "I've waited and waited . . ."

Sensing the floodgate bursting in her, Germain spread his arms wide, wonder creeping into his eyes.

Body embracing body, love touching love, made them both brim over with soaring happiness. The bridge crossed, the tension soothed, Germain's legs shook like jelly, and he gently eased Madeleine's clinging form to the ground, sliding down next to her. "I've been such a fool," he murmured, touching her face reverently.

Their bed was a thick carpet of grass interspersed with daisies and bloodred poppies waving lazily in the wind. The breezes bore away the sound of their blissful sighs as their lips touched after the long, agony-filled separation.

Germain could barely contain the explosive pressure of his long-suppressed desire. The rage of his emotions made his body tremble like a leaf, and Madeleine placed a hand to his forehead, gently caressing his face. Her hands riffled through his hair with exquisite tenderness, and his flattened curls became an unruly mass, mirroring his emotions to perfection.

His tongue played slowly across her generous lips, savoring each inch of the inviting curves. As the rosy tip of her tongue met his, he could not stop himself from crushing her pliant mouth hard under his, from tasting deeply of the honeyed recesses whose intoxicating quality he had almost forgotten. Ravenous, he softly drank her love, so freely given. Their mating tongues satisfied a profound need for affection, slowly softening the desperation inside. At the same time it heightened the urge of their bodies to become one, to once more seal the bond that no words could.

Germain's hand slid down the silken column of her throat and wandered across the satiny span of her shoulders. Madeleine ached for the moment when he would claim her breast with his lips. Her nipples hardened in anticipation, and her heart pounded wildly. Only Germain's moist tongue and demanding fingers could transform that pounding into a glow of contentment.

"Germain . . ." she whispered ecstatically as his warm hand closed around one of the swollen globes.

"I need you so much. You're the only one who can free me from this agony." His voice was ragged.

Madeleine wanted to open herself up, to fold him into her heart that was flooding, filling her whole being with love.

"I'm yours . . . have always been," she whispered against his mouth. She clung to him, drawing his head down to her breasts. A shock of pleasure coursed through her as the tip of his tongue touched her nipple, his hot breath caressing her skin.

She loved the feel of his taut muscles as her hands slid beneath his loose shirt. His skin was smooth and warm, exuding a virile, musky scent of arousal mixed with the lavender scent of his clean shirt. That, combined with the rich smell of earth, river, and sunlight, blended into a kaleidoscope of delight.

His starved fingers moved across her flesh, bringing glorious sensations to her every pore.

Germain drowned in her sweet, feminine scents and the feel of her soft hair on his bare skin. Although desire drove him wild, he wanted to keep the moment forever. This was more than he had ever dreamed possible. She lifted him beyond heights of rapture just by lying pliant and warm in his arms, eager for his embrace.

He savored the moment when his fingers reached the inviting, moist core of her womanhood. As she quivered in his arms, he mirrored her sensations. Every pleasure that filled her was echoed in him.

He watched a delicate flush of desire rise in her alabaster cheeks, her lips half open, begging to be kissed.

He answered her need and tasted again the well of sweetness she offered him.

As she drowned in his kiss, Madeleine's fingers worked on the fastenings of his culottes. She felt no hesitation or shyness as she freed the hard proof of his desire.

RECKLESS SPLENDOR

With a knowledge as old as time, she set forth to enthrall him, her fingers closing around his velvety flesh. As his agonized gasps intensified against her neck, she knew she was succeeding beyond her dreams. In her caressing hand he grew larger, throbbing with need. She felt his rapid heartbeats reverberating in his loins, and a frenzy overtook her, a fire erupting in her. He slid his fingers into her, bringing her to the edge of intolerable pleasure.

The soft grass supported her naked body as Germain pulled off all her garments, letting her skirt lie like a brilliant splash of blue over a bush. She relieved him of his shirt and culottes. Naked skin brushed naked skin, bringing moans of delight to their lips.

Placing himself between her widespread legs, he clasped her face between the palms of his hands, looking fully into her eyes.

"You're mine," he whispered, and thrust into her with savage gusto. "And I'm yours."

For a moment the world stood still and then turned to a divine blur as he began moving thickly, deeply within her. His fierce possession brought her into a sea where his thrusts were the waves, the waves of rapture washing over her, washing in her.

Faster and faster, the waves pounded into and over her until a cry burst from her, mingling with his, and she dissolved into ecstasy as he hotly filled her with his seed, his body transported into blinding rapture.

Chapter 35

Dulcet contentment cradled Madeleine all the way to her toes, and happy laughter trilled from her lips. She opened her eyes and saw Germain watching her, his eyes bright with love. One of his hands slid up and down her body as if he could not get enough of touching her.

"Germain . . . *merci*. These were the happiest moments of my life," she whispered tenderly, threading her fingers through his mass of sun-kissed curls. "And you're smiling again."

It was true. Gone was the shuttered cold mask, leaving room for a peaceful and open face with a warm grin spread across it.

"I love you, sweet woman. I never thought I could love anybody as much as I love you." A fierce fire blazed for a second in the smoky depths of his eyes as he gently slid the pad of his thumb over her peach-soft cheek.

Her breath caught in her throat. Mere words could not describe the emotion in her heart, and she swallowed convulsively. Germain chuckled and let his index finger glide across her mouth. "You don't need to speak," he muttered and placed a feather-light kiss on her reddened lips. With infinite care, he wiped away the tears that had gathered at the corners of her eyes. "I've been such a thickheaded idiot."

"I—I never lost hope that you would come out of your bitterness, but I was on the brink of giving up today."

"Had it been me, I would have given up a long time ago."

"I hate giving up!"

RECKLESS SPLENDOR 309

Germain laughed, a happy sound. "I know, but sometimes it is preferable." He stared out over the shimmering water, the guarded look clouding his face for a second.

"Don't let anything ruin this day, please," she urged and saw the shadow pass instantly.

The leafy canopy rustled above them. "What if someone should happen to pass by?" Madeleine suddenly became aware of her nudity. Not far from their secluded haven people surely continued to meander on the paths.

She squinted toward the sun, noticing how the light had shifted, slanting down on them, a rose-orange sheen.

"We must have been here all afternoon! The sun . . ."

Time had melted the afternoon into one long golden hour of ecstasy.

"Shhh, yes, and my stomach is protesting loudly."

"Well, you didn't deserve any food the way you ruined the outing—scaring off the men like that!"

"You saw that?"

"*Oui*. I hid among the trees for a few minutes. You were a veritable ogre."

Germain's lips curved into a rueful smile. "*Oui*, Madame Barbette gave me a piece of her mind."

He rose with one lithe movement and gathered Madeleine's garments. From the pocket of her skirt tumbled a few copper coins and a leather thong. As he bent to retrieve the thong, he glanced quizzically at her. She snatched it from his fingers, pink tinting her cheeks. "*Oui*, it's the one you used to bind my hair. Sometimes I touch it and remember those wonderful moments."

"Come." He cradled her in his arms, and a low chuckle rumbled in his chest. "That was an awful day. I don't believe I've ever been as aroused as I was then. I brought the agony upon myself, of course. Pride always makes one suffer."

They dressed quickly as the sun delivered its last light. The sky shone eggshell blue, painted boldly with lavender and red streaks. In the dying light, their hair was aflame with red, and their skins were tinted amber.

For one breathtaking minute, the world seemed unreal as the daylight fought a dramatic battle to survive. But the shadows lengthened and night had already reached under the trees, cloaking them in black velvet.

"Let's have supper at a tavern here, since I don't have any particular longing to return to Paris just yet," Germain suggested. "Let's celebrate our newfound love."

"*Bien.*"

Arms twined around each other, they walked to a tavern called Coq d'Or next to La Pissotte, the cabaret. The low-ceilinged common room was filled with smoke and drunk patrons, their harsh voices slicing the air. The aroma of roasting pig permeated everything.

As Germain and Madeleine squeezed their legs under a table in a dark corner, they did not notice the avid attention of a guest, a man leaning against the ale-soaked counter.

A young boy with a too-large apron around his slim middle came to their table. Germain ordered wine, roast pig, and rolls. Madeleine felt her mouth water in anticipation.

Germain could not take his eyes off her glowing face, so soft in the flickering candlelight.

The man at the counter glanced furtively over the edge of his tankard as Germain took both her hands and kissed them lightly. The blond-bearded man dressed in rough clothing did not look like the comte de Hautefort he had once served, but he knew his former master well enough to recognize his haughty bearing, which no misfortune could erase. Maurice felt an overpowering satisfaction to see the aristocrat reduced to such humble circumstances. The triumph was so fierce that he almost choked on the ale. A malicious smirk bared his yellow teeth.

Passing on this tidbit of information to Fouquet would earn him a fat reward.

He slunk out of the crowded tavern.

Oblivious of their surroundings, Madeleine and Germain were aware only of each other. The pork could have been a piece of wood, and they would not have noticed the difference. The wine warmed Madeleine inside, amplifying her soaring euphoria. Nothing could perforate the protective bubble of love surrounding them.

Germain's warm voice washed over her. "You're not turning up your nose at this meal as has been your custom lately."

RECKLESS SPLENDOR

"It's just that I've been too miserable to eat well. This evening has changed everything."

A surge of protective tenderness welled up in him. All he wanted was to shield her from every unpleasantness. "*Oui*, the strain has been hard on us both. Let us make up for lost time."

They savored the food, the wine, and grew closer as every minute passed. After the meal, they left the tavern. Once outside, Germain held her in the circle of his arms. "It's so beautiful here, so peaceful in the forest."

"I don't mind sleeping outside. The night is balmy. The heat in Paris is unbearable, and we would not be able to sleep anyway."

Retracing their steps, they stood again on the edge of the river Marne, the mellifluous fragrance of flowers weaving around them. Silver moonlight played over the quietly moving water, casting an enchanted spell over the sleeping landscape.

"This is paradise," Madeleine whispered, caught once more in the magic of Germain's touch and the wonder of the night. "I will always remember this place."

Birds chattering in the trees disturbed their peaceful sleep. Germain opened his eyes first, glancing at Madeleine, whose head rested on his arm, her cloud of blond curls spread across his chest. Gently he kissed her rosy lips and was rewarded by a smile. Sleepily she opened her eyes.

Dawn lay like a mauve shimmer over everything. A warm wind rustled through the leaves, but the world was quiet.

Together they savored the beauty of the hour, watching gilded streaks pierce the mauve veil. Before long, the light would chase away the hesitant shadows of the night.

"Come, let us take a dip in the river," Germain said and rose, stretching his powerful body. The long scar along his side glared a vivid red in the morning light.

With a playful smile on his lips, he lifted her into his arms and waded into the water. As he lowered her, she squealed.

"It's not cold," he parried, easing her relentlessly into the water.

Gasping, she clung to his neck, but as the water embraced her, she enjoyed its coolness on her skin. Laughing, she splashed a cascade of silver droplets in his face.

"You little vixen!" he growled and pushed her under water.

Spluttering, she resurfaced, her hair like a wet mantle around her.

"Beast!" Her eyes flaring with mischief, she hurled herself at him, causing him to lose his balance. With a mighty splash, he went down and she laughed, a high merry sound. But she soon regretted her mirth as a wave of water drenched her.

As the first hot rays of the sun glistened on their wet bodies, they joined in a long, breathtaking kiss, a peace offering.

"Wonderful! Nothing like a bath to heighten your appetite. What we need now is a hearty breakfast," Germain said, his lips nuzzling her neck and making her giggle.

"I cannot bear to leave this spot. This paradise is made for lovers, and we found it," she said.

"We have to take it with us, in our hearts. I will never forget this time. I will enter the world a converted man. Let everyone envy me!"

Madeleine's knees went weak as his breath flowed into her ear. "*Oui*, neither will I forget," she whispered, emotion choking her.

Germain banged on the locked door on Rue de la Lanterne. Long minutes passed before it opened a thin crack.

Madame Barbette put a belligerent eye to the opening, and her look did not soften when she recognized them.

"Open up, Barbette," Germain commanded, peering at her from under the wide brim of his hat.

Madame Barbette did not mince her words. "Not if you're still behaving like an idiot."

Germain laughed. "Ask Madeleine."

"She's with you?" Madame Barbette's eyes widened in disbelief.

Shyly Madeleine stepped forward from her hiding place behind Germain.

A slow smile creased the wrinkled face of the old cook. "*Mon Dieu*, you have made peace with each other!"

The door flew open with a crash, and they found themselves crushed in the woman's fleshy arms. She smelled of flour and cocoa. Madeleine sniffed the air. "What are you baking?"

Madame Barbette beamed at her and winked slyly. "Come and see. The men are in the kitchen filling their bellies. We will celebrate your reunion."

The aroma of freshly baked bread filled the house. Grunts and harsh laughs met them in the hallway. As they entered the kitchen, a deafening roar rose to the ceiling, making the windowpanes vibrate in their frames.

Madeleine had rarely seen all the men gathered together in the kitchen. Mostly they sneaked in and out during the dark hours of the night.

"Welcome home!" everyone bellowed, and Madeleine had to clap her hands over her ears for a moment.

The gang surrounded Germain, each of them eager to show his approval with slaps and handshakes. Madeleine found herself lifted onto a chair, looking down on Capitaine Roland's evil face. In the depths of his eyes, she discovered the beginnings of shy respect, and she felt an urge to cry.

"To the happy couple!" Legrand growled as cups of cocoa and tankards of ale were slammed against each other in celebration.

Chapter 36

Night lay like diamond-studded black satin over Paris. Madeleine rested peacefully in the arms of Germain, who was playing with one of her curls, running it up and down her nose until she giggled.

"Stop it! You're tickling me."

"You should pretend you like it, or you will pay." He nuzzled her peachy cheek.

"You big brute!" she chided, but without conviction. Her forehead creased in thought. "Tell me, where did you meet the thieves? I thought you and Capitaine Roland were deadly enemies, after what happened at The Greedy Cat."

Germain chuckled. "In the days before I fell in love with you, I was a deeply unhappy man. To dispel my boredom, I frequently haunted low taverns and gaming hells. At those places you hobnob with everybody. The patrons are mostly crooks." Thoughtful, he paused for a moment.

"The two most valued assets in a villain are strength and stealth," he continued. If you have both, you can become a powerful man in the underworld. I defeated Capitaine Roland once by rescuing you. In his eyes, you became my property because I beat him in a fair fight. He holds no grudge. Since then, he has lost his ship and has been happy with me. You see, I could not be too choosy either. My men have been more faithful and honest than the best men at court. These are my real friends; at court I had none—well, I thought the King was one, but you know how ready he was to believe my guilt." He sighed sadly.

"The only threat we have now is other gangs. Paris is teeming with them, all claiming their territories. I would be dead in a moment if I stepped outside my boundaries."

"Oh." Madeleine had to digest the information he had given her. "Do you not fear them?"

Germain laughed. "I have nothing to lose—except you. Furthermore, I have the best men. I have forbidden them to kill, and they obey. The Mouse and the Weasel can steal anything, and the large men act as guards. Capitaine Roland loves a good fight. So there you have both strength and stealth."

"It sounds simple, almost too simple."

"The most important thing is to keep watch at all times. If we are caught unawares, we will die."

Madeleine shivered and curled closer to Germain's warm body, to draw on his strength. "Do you think we'll ever find the diary?"

He was quiet for a few moments. "I'm sure we will."

Madeleine's intuition told her he was not telling her everything. "If Lemont stole the diary, why has he waited so long to hand it over to Fouquet?"

"He's the only one who knows the exact reasons. Perhaps Fouquet has met his match in Lemont. Two cunning foxes. Lemont owes Fouquet a hundred thousand livres. It's about time Fouquet was brought down," Germain lashed out. "And if Lemont's game helps our cause, so much the better."

Madeleine stared at him in the downy darkness. "I believe Fouquet has every advantage over us, even over the King."

"As with all greedy men, he will ruin himself in the end."

"*Mon Dieu*, you sound sure of yourself."

Germain laughed, a loud happy sound, and Madeleine tingled all over in delight. He was no longer the arrogant comte de Hautefort or the bitter crook. He was a real man, a free man, secure in his love. Yet he was also a wanted criminal. There were posters all over Paris with a crude picture of his face and the words *Black Angel* in large letters. One thousand livres was the reward on his head. Madeleine could not stop a sense of unease from flooding through her, and she burrowed closer to Germain. "Tell me about your childhood," she begged.

He smiled and tweaked her nose. "I thought Barbette told you every sordid detail. She loves to gossip."

"*Non,* she hasn't, just that you and Gaspard were two naughty boys, indeed."

"*Oui,* we were spanked many times for our pranks. I guess I was lonely sometimes, but there was always Gaspard. Father spent most of his time in Paris with the old King, and my mother was always at Les Étoiles with me. She was not a very happy woman. I think she loved Father very much, but he was indifferent to her. It was an arranged marriage. When he was at home, he taught me to fence and to shoot. We hunted together every day." Germain chuckled. "I think he worried that under the authority of women I would turn into a weakling. Mother was a hard woman, but she was not unkind—except when she caned me, of course."

"Perhaps you deserved it," Madeleine teased.

"I certainly did."

"Well, I know how it feels to be an only child, but that is probably the singular thing we have in common. My childhood was very different from yours."

"You never did any mischief, *non?*" he teased.

"*Oui,* some, but my mother was strict. She always complained that I was too wild." Madeleine laughed. "She was of proud burgher stock, very conventional, always dressed me in demure dresses of good quality and starched petticoats. She was as severe as my father was gentle."

Madeleine stared dreamily up at the ceiling. "I can still remember the all-pervading scent of furniture polish and the tilt of Mother's head as she sat in her favorite chair working at her embroidery frame. Father spoiled me every moment he had a chance. I know they both loved me, even though Mother seldom showed her feelings." She sighed. "I truly miss them—always will."

He smoothed the curls on her forehead. "They are right here with you now. You're as sharp as a needle—that's your mother—and as gentle and kind as an angel—that's your father."

Madeleine giggled. "You always have an answer for everything."

"I wish I did! Things certainly would be easier." He heaved a sigh. "If it hadn't been for the *lettre de cachet,* I doubt I would have been able to tear myself away from court. My disgrace was a blessing in disguise, even though I don't have the funds now to do what I want the most—experimental farming at Les Étoiles. That is the place I want to be—not sailing around the world, not being King Louis's mindless appendage." He blew tenderly at one of Madeleine's curls lying on his chest. "It has taken me a long time to realize what I want out of life. What do you want?"

You, a life with you, Madeleine thought, but she only shrugged. "I suppose I was groomed at the convent to become a dutiful wife and mother to some hapless burgher in Rouen. That was the road my mother had firmly in mind. But she died before she could see me securely wed, and Father never forced me to do anything I didn't want to. I stayed at the convent longer than most girls, yet I had more freedom. I suppose I'll always remain a seamstress now . . ."

She could feel Germain's searching eyes on her. "At this point we can only live one day at a time," he said. "I don't like it that you're in this lawless den with me, but nor do I relish the thought of a life without you." His voice grew husky. "But this will soon be over, I promise you that."

"This is paradise to me," Madeleine whispered. "I am fulfilled."

He squeezed her shoulders tightly, and she heard him swallow hard. "You have made me a happy man. Yet we cannot be entirely happy until Fouquet's threat is removed."

She nodded and silently cursed the day she had first heard the word *diary*.

"Right now I'd like to know who put the treasonous letters in my desk," he continued.

Madeleine snorted. "Your old friend Fouquet, of course. Who else? More important, we will prove it."

"I envy your optimism, *ma petite*."

At Vaux-de-Vicomte Fouquet was eating his breakfast in a dining room full of treasures rivaling in beauty those of the royal palaces.

His majordomo entered and bowed reverently. "Monsieur, Maurice is here to see you. He is most insistent."

"Maurice? I told him to leave Paris," Fouquet said peevishly. Glaring at the motionless servant, he ordered, "Send him away!"

But before the majordomo had reached the door, Maurice stormed in. Fouquet rose, angry at having his peace disturbed so early in the day. "What can be so important you have to blunder in here at this hour?" he said sarcastically, wiping his lips on his sleeve. "You have been paid."

Maurice twisted his hat between his hands. "I have information that will interest you greatly." He could barely suppress his excitement.

Fouquet glanced at him slyly. "Already squandered your large reward, eh?"

Maurice fidgeted. "I assure you, you will be pleased to find out about . . . about the comte de Hautefort—*former* comte, that is."

Fouquet's breath caught in his throat. That name made his bile rise and his hatred gnaw like a rat in his stomach. He suspected he already knew what Maurice was going to say. "I will give you whatever you ask for the information," he said softly, a speculative glint in his eyes.

Maurice licked his lips, consumed with greed. "I need a thousand livres."

Fouquet cursed silently. Not to show his dislike, he turned his back on Maurice. "Done!"

"I saw Hautefort in the Bois de Vincennes. He was having a rendezvous with Molière's niece, Madeleine Poquelin. He had eyes for no one but her." He snickered. "They stayed in the forest all night. I spied them—from a safe distance, of course. It wouldn't do to have Hautefort noticing me. He's dangerous when he's angry."

"Get on with it! Or is that all?" Fouquet demanded, a cynical twist on his lips.

"I followed them the next morning to a house on Rue de la Lanterne. I'm sure it's Hautefort's hideout because I saw the cook, Madame Barbette." He rubbed the coarse stubble on his chin. "I must say the comte has changed. I hardly recognized him."

"He's nothing. You should stop calling him by his old title."

"You don't seem surprised."

"Let's say your story corroborated my suspicions. I now know the answer to the inquiry I sent to Pignerol." He motioned to the majordomo waiting quietly just inside the door. "Show Monsieur Maurice out."

"But—my reward?" Maurice fought the servant who had grabbed him.

Fouquet looked merely bored. He pulled the bell rope, and two guards entered. "Get rid of this man, and make sure he never sets foot on my grounds again."

Before he left the room, he saw hatred flare in Maurice's eyes.

Living day to day without knowing what would happen next gave Madeleine and Germain's relationship a vibrant immediacy. They strove to give each other their all—while they still could. Every day Germain brought her armfuls of sweet-smelling flowers, stolen at the market. She prepared delicacies in the kitchen for him, driving Madame Barbette out of her mind.

Their intense love was contagious. More often Madeleine saw smiles creasing the men's faces, and many a wistful glance was cast in her direction. Sometimes they passed on small trinkets they had stolen for her.

Considering the abundance of loot, Madeleine was surprised that the thieves were always short of funds, but no one was complaining.

One evening after sunset Weasel sneaked into the kitchen where the gang members were bent over their bowls of pork and beans. For once his face did not hold its usual placid look; he was shaken and pale. Germain rose immediately and pulled out a chair for the smaller man.

"Gaspard sent word that Fouquet knows you're here in Paris. He knows about this house. Not only that but Fouquet found out that Gaspard was your man and had him . . . killed." Weasel's voice was dry with tension.

Madeleine gasped and bit into her napkin with fear. The ever-loyal Gaspard, Germain's childhood friend! Was there no end to Fouquet's evil? She watched Germain, whose face was creased into a thunderous scowl. She knew how he felt. He was blaming himself for his valet's death, just as she still blamed herself for Amul's death.

The air in the room took on a quality of alert tension.

"Who gave you this message?"

"Maurice, your ex-steward."

"His word is worth nothing! He betrayed me."

"He appeared to be telling the truth, said that Fouquet had cheated him. He wanted to pay him back."

Germain turned to the men. "There is no time to lose. At any moment we could be trapped here like mice in a cage. Leave! You know where we will meet, but whatever happens, don't return here."

Without protest, the men rose and hurried from the room. Germain turned to Madame Barbette. "Go to Les Étoiles."

When she began to argue, he pressed a well-filled purse into her hand and pushed her out the door. "My things!" she wailed.

"I will bring them to you later."

Madeleine stood rigid with fear, waiting for his command.

"Come, I'll have to fetch another purse upstairs. We will have to stay at an inn for a few days until we can find another place."

They raced up the stairs, Madeleine panting with the effort. "We have no indication that they will be here tonight."

"They will. Fouquet doesn't let grass grow under his feet. It was sheer luck that we weren't caught before." He gripped her hand and squeezed it reassuringly. "It won't be long before Fouquet pays for all the evil he has done."

Madeleine wondered what he meant by that, but she would have to ask him another time since all her concentration lay in staying on her feet on the dark stairs.

They passed through the secret door and into the uninhabited house. The treasure room was still full of various costumes, but the chests were empty.

Germain pulled a sack from the floor. "Put a dress or two and shoes in this."

Madeleine complied, her lips set in determination. Germain added some clothes of his own and slung the sack over his shoulder.

After returning to the other house, they hastened toward the stairs.

Suddenly Germain halted and placed a finger to his lips. Wide-eyed, she stared at him, her heart pounding. Then she heard the sounds. Men's voices drifted up the stairs, and heavy steps echoed on the floor below.

"They are no friends of ours," Germain muttered.

"Did they hear our steps?"

"Perhaps."

The voices sounded closer now as the men neared the bottom of the stairwell.

Madeleine gasped. "We'll be captured."

Germain shook his head and took her hand. Walking quietly, he led her to another room.

"A proctor once owned this house. To escape the wrath of his clients, he built a secret stairway," Germain explained in a tight voice. "That's why this was a perfect hiding place—until now."

Next to the fireplace he pressed the center of a carved daisy on the wooden paneling, and a door swung open with a groan.

Hot, fetid air met them as they stepped through. Germain lit a candle and closed the door behind them. The yellow globe of light hardly penetrated the dense darkness.

"Careful now. Steps ahead."

As Madeleine advanced cautiously, something soft and sticky clung to her face. She swallowed the scream rising in her throat and clutched convulsively at Germain's arm.

He chuckled softly. "Cobwebs." He swept his arm through the air. "There, the passage is clear." Leading the way, he crept forward until he almost fell face first down a set of steep stairs. *"Par bleu!* Here they are. Now take my hand."

Madeleine's toes touched something soft and woolly on the floor. It moved! She shivered and swallowed a whimper. As Germain's steps stirred up clouds of dust, she suppressed a need to sneeze. When she heard voices from behind the wall, she pressed her nostrils together to quell the urge. Panic rose in her. What if their enemies found the entrance? They sounded so close. Germain sensed her distress and wound his arm around her waist, practically carrying her down the steps. He drew a deep breath of relief as the door at the other end opened to the dilapidated stables in the back. No horses had inhabited the building for the last ten years, and it smelled of decaying wood and mold.

"We are free!" Madeleine exclaimed, heaving a sigh of relief.

"Not yet; we have to pass through that door in the wall to be free. Guards could be posted outside." Germain's face looked grim in the pale light of the moon. "We have to keep very quiet; one sound, and we'll have a horde of men after us."

Madeleine followed him hesitantly as he glided like a shadow under the trees. She was so eager not to make a noise that she lagged behind; he waited for her patiently.

"You will make a good thief yet," he joked.

Madeleine could not fathom how he could be so composed at a moment like this.

Upon reaching the door, Germain put his ear against it. The street outside was quiet, and he motioned to Madeleine to stand right behind him. Her muscles were knotted in fear.

With a creak that she thought could have wakened a dead man, the door swung on its hinges. Furtively Germain slunk outside, glancing this way and that way. A shadow moved, and Germain was hit from behind. The blow aimed for his head caught him on the shoulder. Madeleine stifled a scream. The man was standing over Germain, wide-legged. Madeleine remained as if rooted to the ground, waiting for a blow to fall on her, but the attack did not come. Only one man had been standing guard, and he was now trying to tie Germain's hands. She searched frantically for a weapon, anything. *Mon Dieu*, help! Her fingers closed around a stone. Holding her breath, she hoisted it over her head and threw it with all her force at the guard. It hit him in the back, and he grunted, losing his foothold. Germain folded his legs and kicked out, striking the man in his solar plexus. The guard fell with a hoarse grunt.

"Run, Madeleine." Panting from the exertion and the pain in his shoulder, Germain stumbled to his feet. He gripped the lost sack and beckoned to her. "Come! We are detected."

She heard more voices calling and steps pounding. Her feet seemed to grow wings; she ran down the dark street, followed closely by Germain. An owl hooted from a roof.

"Weasel—a warning," Germain whispered. None too gently he pushed Madeleine into the blackness of a portal and placed his hand over her lips. Only moments later, running footsteps reverberated on the cobblestones, and more men bounded up the street carrying clubs.

"Policemen! They are excited tonight, thinking they will catch me," Germain whispered with a chuckle. "The police have long sought to bring me to justice. Fouquet must have alerted them."

Madeleine hugged him fiercely, her legs still shaking. Imagining the noose closing around Germain's neck, she stifled a sob. She could not bear the thought of ever being separated from him again—least of all by death.

"There, there," he soothed. "Nobody is going to catch me as long as I have you to care for."

As stealthily as cats, they sneaked along the walls until they reached Rue de la Colombe. There, leaning against a tree trunk and chewing on a straw, was Weasel.

Chapter 37

The thieves often slept under bridges or in thieving dens, or whiled away the night in lowly taverns, but, having all his life been accustomed to comfort, Germain liked a bed under his body and a roof over his head. The inn he took Madeleine to, The Golden Horn, was a dark, dilapidated building in Faubourg Saint Michel—enemy territory. The bed was lumpy, the floor and windows dirty, and the air permeated by the scent of rancid fat.

The grime on one window was being partially rubbed off by Weasel, who was sitting on the windowsill. True to his habits, he had not entered the room by its only door. Many times Madeleine had itched to ask him why he had such aversion to doors, but the opportunity had not arisen.

It was clear that the strange man was deeply attached to Germain. Why, she had no idea, but she was grateful to him. Without his cry of warning, she would have been sitting in a cell at the Châtelet by now.

Germain had thanked him several times, hinting that he should leave, but Weasel showed no inclination of doing so.

"You need some rest, Weasel. It has been a harrowing day," Germain tried. The thief did not move, only kept chewing on his perpetual straw.

"*Bien*, spill it out, whatever it is," Germain said impatiently.

"Fouquet has invited the King to a celebration at Vaux-de-Vicomte, on the sixteenth."

Germain tensed. "Where did you get your information?"

"Maurice. He had just returned from the estate, where the preparations were in full swing. According to him, the

RECKLESS SPLENDOR

feast will be grander than anything ever seen before. Also, Maurice begged me to deliver his apologies to you. Heaven knows I'm loath to do it. That rat deserves to be boiled in oil!'' He wrinkled his nose in disgust, his wart bobbing.

Germain chuckled. "Maurice discovered too late that he was working for the wrong side. *Alors*, our enemy is already celebrating. He must see himself as the future prime minister."

"*Oui*, Maurice said the servants at the estate were all abuzz with the news that the King had dropped hints that Fouquet could not hold the posts of prime minister and attorney-general at the same time. It's what Fouquet has hoped for all along—to follow that old fox Mazarin as prime minister of France."

"There is no end to his ambitions; he will stop at nothing to reach his goal now." Then Germain added cryptically, "If all goes well, he will be digging his own grave."

As if Weasel had suddenly had enough of their company, he disappeared out the window. His eyes level with the windowsill, he said, "See you tomorrow," and merged with the shadows of the night.

"Do you have a plan you haven't told me about?" Madeleine asked, planting herself in Germain's lap, the most comfortable "chair" in the room.

"How would you like to go to a lavish banquet at Vaux-de-Vicomte?" His lips caressed her throat lazily.

Madeleine gasped. "I suppose it would be, er, entertaining. But I have the sneaking suspicion that we won't be attending the ball for entertainment." She moaned as the tip of his tongue laved the erect nipple of the breast he had freed from the confines of her bodice.

"You're too suspicious, *chérie*." His attentions made her too weak with delight to pursue the issue, and she gave herself up to his ardent lovemaking.

Much later, sated and full of peace, she lay pressed against him, one leg thrown across his thigh. She was drifting in and out of sleep, but noticed that Germain was fully awake, deeply concentrated in thought. Very gently he eased away from her and climbed out of the bed. Standing in front of the open window, he lighted a cheroot, the smoke of which wafted to Madeleine's nostrils.

Her eyes heavy, she pulled herself into a sitting position. The air was sultry and airless, and the rough sheets were soaked with perspiration.

"What is wrong, *mon cher?*" she asked sleepily. He did not answer, but sadness emanated from him.

"Gaspard?"

"*Oui*. If I had not told him to take a position in Fouquet's household, he would be alive today."

"You don't know that. Besides, he knew the risks he was taking, and still he wanted to do it. The way he lived, it would be only a matter of time before he was hanged. He was very reckless."

Immediately she regretted her words. They all ran the same risk, Germain most of all; not only were the police looking for him, but Fouquet as well, and Fouquet was a much more formidable opponent than the law.

"*Oui*, my hours are limited. I was a fool to pull you into my life again. I fought so hard to hold back my feelings for you, but in the end, the heart won out."

"I don't regret a single moment," she said passionately.

"You know it has to end. I have *nothing* to offer you, least of all security, and, as you said, it's only a matter of time before I get caught. But first I will have my revenge on Fouquet."

Madeleine's heart bled. Every word stabbed her with merciless truth. "I'd go to the end of the world with you," she whispered. "No! I'd crawl to the end."

He laughed, a dry, harsh sound that was more like a sob. "*Oui*, and we'll be married and live happily ever after."

Madeleine remained silent. It was the first time he had ever mentioned marriage.

"I can't give you anything but my body," he continued savagely. "And you loathe the fact that I am a thief." He shook her roughly by the shoulders. "Don't you?"

"You could find some honest work." Her words were almost inaudible.

"*Oui?*" He shook her again. "Only to be betrayed to the police by someone wanting the reward for Black Angel; to lie in a dungeon trussed up like a pig, waiting for the trial that will send me to the gibbet. I would not even be allowed an aristocrat's death on the block." His voice dripped with bitterness. "*Non, ma petite,* we have lived on borrowed time. After the sixteenth it will be time to say goodbye."

She could not bear the thought of losing him. How could he coldly determine the date when they would separate?

Wild sobs racked her body. "You cannot calculate love," she cried. Finally Germain took her into his arms and cradled her until her despair subsided. She fell asleep, her face pressed against his chest. Tenderly he wiped the tears from her cheeks. When the first light of dawn filtered into the room, he was still wide awake, his eyes dry and aching, his thoughts far away.

Having tucked the sheet around Madeleine, he washed himself with a cloth dipped in the tepid water of the cracked basin on a stand. When Germain was dressed in his culottes and a clean but wrinkled shirt, Weasel showed his face in the window. Germain eyed his friend in the spotted mirror and brushed his hair straight back with severe precision.

He put a finger to his lips and motioned toward Madeleine's peacefully sleeping form. Weasel disappeared. Germain slipped out of the room and walked down the dark stairs.

The host greeted him and showed him to a stained table in the common room. "A bit of trouble, eh? Or else you wouldn't be showing your snout in the Faubourg de Saint Michel. Not your area," the host said jovially.

"One moment, Jacques." Germain went to the door and looked outside. In the dewy light of dawn, he saw Weasel leaning against the wall. "You can come in now."

Hesitantly, Weasel followed him through the door, glancing suspiciously around the room.

"Jacques, I knew I could count on you!" Germain slapped the proprietor on the back. "Now, let us have a sturdy breakfast and some ale. But first"—he rolled a gold louis under the host's blue-veined nose—"could you see to it that the lady in my room gets breakfast served in bed, preferably cocoa and rolls with strawberry preserves, and a hot bath. Your wife . . . ?"

The host rubbed his hands, his eyes gleaming to rival the brightness of the coin. "Right away, Black Angel, right away."

The aroma of frying eggs and ham drifted in from the kitchen, covering up the odor of sour ale and grime.

Weasel looked uncomfortable. Germain laughed mercilessly at him. "Are you expecting someone to rush in here and slit your throat? Relax. The cutthroats of Saint Michel went to bed an hour ago. Our habits are diametrically opposed to those of our fellow ruffians. None is as daring as we are," he bragged to put Weasel in a better mood. "Now, my dear friend and most trusted man, this is what I want you to do . . ."

When Germain returned to the bedchamber, he was met by a radiant Madeleine. She was rosy and clean, her hair still damp from being washed. Rose fragrance clung to her, and Germain breathed deeply in appreciation. "Lovely. You're the sweetest lady who ever walked on this earth," he said in a fit of inspiration. He embraced her, burying his face in the bosom barely covered by her low-cut blouse. "When you're ready, we're going to pay a visit to your Uncle Molière."

"Uncle Jean-Baptiste? Why?" she asked, wide-eyed.

"He is going to help us with a difficult detail."

"If you don't tell me about it this instant, I will . . . I will scream!"

Germain laughed and ducked as her fist came flying, but he remained as secretive as ever. "Trust me. I want it to be an amusing surprise. We're going to the most lavish celebration of our lives."

Her eyes filled with suspicion. "Whatever it is, I don't like the sound of it. And Molière will kill me. He thinks I am in Normandy visiting friends."

"Do you take him for a fool?" Germain lit a cheroot and leaned lazily against the door.

She whirled on him. "What do you mean?"

"Has he not always known about us?" he challenged.

She gave him a measuring look. "Perhaps."

"Don't deceive yourself. He knows you're with me, although he pretends to all and sundry that you're in Normandy—to protect you. He has never berated you for your love for me, has he?"

"*Non*, he's a fair man."

"Now, let's go and pay him a visit."

Puzzled, but catching the excitement emanating from Germain, she wound her hair into a chignon and followed him. Gone was his brooding bitterness of the night before.

Molière was alone in the theater of Palais-Royal when Germain and Madeleine entered, their steps echoing in the cavernous room as they walked to the closet that was called Molière's study.

"Greetings, Uncle Jean-Baptiste," Madeleine said softly to the man scribbling furiously on a script. He was surrounded by papers strewn all over the floor and on the chairs. With a distracted air, he glanced up from his work. His face split into a wide smile. "Dearest Madi! You're back at last." His gaze went from her to Germain. "How was your stay in Normandy?"

"Oh, Uncle, we don't have to pretend any longer. You know Germain Belleforière, of course."

"I believe we have met," he said cautiously. "I've seen you at court many times." He gestured to the littered chairs. "Oh, let me clear off this mess."

"It's not necessary. Uncle, Germain has a favor to ask of you." She nudged Germain in the ribs. Strangely enough, he was behaving shyly. He cleared his throat.

"Monsieur, first of all, I'd like to tell you how much I like your plays."

"*Merci.*" Molière's eyes lit up with mischief and pride. "What can I do for you?"

Germain came right to the point. "Help us to crush Fouquet."

A tense silence fell.

"I will help you if I can," Molière responded at last. Madeleine felt a rush of gratitude toward her uncle. He was the most generous person she knew, and so quick to understand.

"You are very sure of Fouquet's guilt?" Molière asked warily, sticking the goose quill behind his ear, making a blue ink mark on his cheek.

"We need to get inside the gilded gates of Vaux-de-Vicomte. You do have an invitation to Vaux, don't you?" Germain asked.

"*Oui*. As a matter of fact, I've been asked to provide part of the entertainment."

"Perfect," Germain breathed.

"I have written a new play, a short farce called *Les Fâcheux*, that will be performed there for the first time. You can come as part of the ensemble. I've hired many extras for the evening. Excuse my curiosity, but are you sure you can catch Fouquet this time?"

"Absolutely certain," Germain responded firmly.

Madeleine wondered what information he had that made him so sure of himself, but she knew he would give nothing away.

"Be here at noon on the sixteenth. I have certain costumes I want you to wear." A smile played over Molière's bold lips, and Madeleine could only guess at what mischief her uncle was planning.

"Are we invited to your nuptials, Uncle Jean-Baptiste?"

She watched his cheeks suffuse with red. "So you've heard, then."

"*Oui*, it is the most astounding piece of news I've received in a long time. I wish you all the happiness."

He rubbed his nose in a gesture of embarrassment. "Armande is very young, alas, but I love her."

"I hope she realizes how lucky she is."

Molière rose, his movements mercurial. "What are you going to do, Madeleine? Are you coming back to us?" He patted her kindly on the shoulder.

Madeleine glanced at Germain, whose face had turned into an inscrutable mask. "I don't know. I cannot see my path clear yet," she said softly, her eyes directed to the floor.

"You will always have a place with Armande and me."

"Thank you, Uncle." She kissed him on the cheek and walked away, tears filling her eyes.

Chapter 38

The King was staying at Fontainebleau outside Paris during the hottest months of the summer. On the sixteenth of August, he and the court set out for Vaux-de-Vicomte to attend the festivities. Three hours later the royal carriage entered the imposing gates at Vaux. Lawns like thick emerald carpets reached all the way up to the moat. Standing in the courtyard, Fouquet and his wife welcomed their august guests.

Louis had difficulty concealing his suspicions from Fouquet's quick eye. As he was shown around the luxurious *château*, he could not but think that the sumptuous interior had been paid for by the impoverished people of France, and by him personally. If only he had real proof! If Fouquet stepped into the trap he had set for him by resigning the post as attorney-general in the firm belief that he would be appointed the next prime minister, then he could be arrested without Louis's fearing vengeance from Fouquet's powerful friends in the Paris parlement. Fouquet would stand alone, at his most vulnerable.

This day was a day of triumph for Fouquet. He shone as brightly as the King in power and in riches. He gloated over the fact that, in reality, he was richer than the King.

Fouquet delighted in showing his treasures to the sovereign. For fifteen years he had been saving funds for the building of Vaux. The splendid creation was finished at last, a rare gem of classical symmetry created by the leading French architect, Le Vau. Two wings flanked at right angles the imposing main block with its heavy central dome. Inside the ceilings and wall panels were painted with light pastoral scenes, and the house was packed with treasures—cloth of gold, Persian carpets in jewel tones, silver vases and chandeliers, rose marble and translucent porphyry tables. The sumptuous supper in the King's honor would be served on gold plates.

The ladies of the court gaped and clucked like hens. Anne, the King's mother, made polite noises while the King glowered at her.

One guest who held an invitation handwritten by Fouquet himself had not yet arrived—the chevalier de Lemont. He was still at Saint-Cloud worrying about the upcoming ordeal. Contrary to what he had let Fouquet believe, he did not have the diary, and he did not dare think what the minister of finance would do when he found out. Nervously he tied the lace jabot at his neck. Sooner or later Fouquet *would* find out. It was no use trying to escape. Fouquet had spies everywhere, and before the month was out Lemont would probably find himself in some river with a slit throat. No, best to make a clean breast of the whole mess.

Lemont's fingers trembled. How would he face Fouquet and tell him that he never had touched the diary?

Madeleine was sweating in the confines of her costume. She was dressed like a faun, her upper body concealed in a tight skin-colored blouse with bogus hair glued to her chest. On her head she wore a tawny wig complete with horns. The thick culottes fashioned out of wolf's fur chafed against her tender skin, and her feet were ensconced in sabots resembling hooves that were very difficult to walk in.

On top of that, Germain was laughing at her. She could not see any humor in being forced to sit in a wooden cart dressed as a faun, crowded together with perspiring nymphs, deities, satyrs, and trees.

She made a face at him.

"You have the temper to match a wicked faun," he chided.

"You should talk!"

He was dressed as a satyr, his torso gleaming golden in the sunlight and his behorned head magnificent with its evilly painted face. He was unrecognizable, which was a

RECKLESS SPLENDOR

blessing when it came to passing the close scrutiny of the guards at the gate.

They were on the grounds at last, where, according to Germain's cryptic words, Fouquet would write the last chapter of his career. In response to Madeleine's questions about the diary, Germain only shook his head. Madeline nudged Weasel with her hoof, teasing him. He was the back part of the satyr's costume, and he was suffocating under the heavy fur. In the cart behind them rode Legrand and Capitaine Roland, dressed as trees, while the Mouse, due to his small stature, had become a nymph in pink tulle with pearls wound in his blond wig. Madeleine had never seen him in a worse temper. His lethal glances bored into anyone who dared to snigger.

Molière's word was law here. When he told them to be quiet, they were quiet. When he told them to move, they moved.

As the carts entered the main *allée*, Madeleine was enchanted with the beauty of the gardens. Sprays of hundreds of water jets created shimmering walls of water. She had never seen anything so grand in her life.

Molière hurriedly shepherded his troop to the outdoor theater at the end of an *allée* of firs, before they started blabbering uncontrollably about the surrounding splendor. Relieved to alight from the uncomfortable cart, Madeleine stretched and tottered on her hooves to a carved stone bench under a rose arbor. She felt nauseated with nervousness and prayed that she would not disgrace herself by being sick in this garden of Eden.

"Not feeling well, eh? That head contraption could give you a sunstroke with all the heat it traps," Germain said.

"The sun is setting. It will soon be cooler." She drank in the sight of the lovely flowers and the hundreds of trees, painted orange by the sunset. "Look at those water cascades; like millions of tiny diamonds showering the earth."

Germain placed an arm around her. "I wish I could give you all this." He swept his other arm in a wide gesture. "You deserve to be walking in these gardens every day, dressed in silks and satins in summer and furs in winter. All for your courage alone."

Love flowed through her veins, and tears pressed against her eyes. How she loved him!

As darkness fell, servants lit hundreds of torches in the gardens, and the grounds took on a magical atmosphere, much of it due to the gaiety of the guests.

"Do you miss this—the court? You should be among them, laughing and flirting," Madeleine said softly.

Germain seemed to ponder her words before he answered. "My only regret is that I can't give you any luxuries. And being a satyr is much more entertaining than wearing uncomfortable court dress. As for flirting, those so-called ladies have acid tongues. It is very easy to get singed if you get too close. *Non*, I count it a blessing to sit here under the trees with you tonight. We *are* at the festivities, after all." He tickled the nape of her neck, and she sighed with pleasure.

"My only regret was losing my family's estate in Brittany, Les Étoiles. By now the walls must be crumbling; Fouquet made certain to lay his hands on it. I'm sure he has done nothing for its upkeep."

Although Germain tried to keep his voice light, Madeleine heard his underlying bitterness. She wanted to comfort him, but knew it was futile. The personal hell he had gone through was more than she could fathom. He had had to fight alone for so long. But now she was at his side, however much that was worth.

The aristocrats gathered at the theater. Madeleine stared avidly at the soft, floating, brightly hued gowns of the ladies adorned with pearls, diamonds, and emeralds against the luster of precious fabrics. They were clothes for frivolous dragonflies who lived only for a day, or for birds who sought to attract each other with dazzling feathers. As the courtiers laughed and flirted, no one suspected that under the painted face of the satyr standing motionless under a tree was an aristocrat as highborn as any of them.

The odor of cloying perfume blended with the more subtle scent of sun-warmed roses. A hush fell over the assembly as the King arrived, flanked by Fouquet and Queen Anne.

Madeleine felt a rivulet of excitement roll along her spine. Concealed behind a bush next to the stage, waiting for Molière's cue, she watched as the King sat down in an armchair covered with Chinese plush. He was magnificent in a heavy midnight-blue velvet vest richly adorned with silver embroidery and crusted with pearls. In contrast, a gossamer-thin white shirt billowed around his arms, and knots of ribbons flowed from his right shoulder as he lifted his hand to make the sign for the show to begin.

Molière appeared alone on stage in his town clothes. With an apologetic smile he announced that he had lost his troupe somewhere. Had not unexpected help arrived, there would have been no performance. With a deep bow, he swept his arm wide. Suppressed excitement embraced the audience.

An enormous pink seashell opened slowly to reveal a naiad dressed in filmy multicolored chiffon that clung to her exquisite body. Madeleine recognized Madame Du Parc, but the actress was cleverly disguised. In a clear voice she ordered the statues to walk and the trees to sing for the King. That was their cue. Madeleine sent a reassuring glance to Germain and stepped onto the stage with the other satyrs and deities, who danced a pastoral to the delight of the court.

The satyrs, part man, part stag, brought laughter to the assembly as the men in charge of the back legs had difficulty matching their steps with the men in front, producing comical results. Madeleine saw a pained expression on Germain's face as he tried frantically to keep his balance with Weasel staggering aimlessly in the back.

"He's no good at this kind of work," Germain hissed between clenched teeth to Madeleine as they passed each other on the stage. "Molière sure knows how to set the mood. He has the whole audience roaring with laughter."

He was right. When the play *Les Facheux* began, it was already a success. Nobody noticed as the fauns and satyrs faded into the shadows of the night.

"That was the last time I'll ever walk on stage," Weasel vowed as he joined Germain and Madeleine. The rest of their group assembled in a ring around them, swearing and muttering.

"I will not tolerate anything like this again," Legrand spat, and the other men echoed his words.

Germain could not suppress a low chuckle. "I thought your faces were greatly improved with a bit of paint and powder," he teased, and they answered with grunts and growls.

"Now, back to our *real* reason for being at this estate. You all know what you have to do, and I won't tolerate any mistakes. Is that clear?"

The men hissed *oui* in unison. Germain pulled off his sabots and then proceeded to help Madeleine with hers. "You can run better without these. Let's go."

Madeleine curled her bare toes into the soft, spongy grass. She sensed a sudden change in the men. From being angry and rebellious, they became quiet and efficient.

Tension mounted, reminding her of the times when they had gathered around the table at Rue de la Lanterne before leaving on various shady missions.

Laughter rolled from the audience, weaving through the trees as the thieves sneaked along the *allée,* keeping away from the lighted areas of the gardens.

Feeling Germain's warm grip on her fingers, Madeleine felt reassured. Nevertheless, she wasn't sure she liked this latest adventure. Germain was acting more reckless than usual, as if he could already taste victory, but many questions swirled in her head. He had been very secretive about this mission, and now there was no time to ask questions.

Panting, they arrived at the back of the east wing. Pressing against the wall, they were shrouded by deep shadows. The Mouse, droll in his pink nymph costume, began picking the lock of a door in a corner. There was no sign of the guards, who patrolled the estate at even intervals.

"Hurry! We don't want to get caught before we have accomplished our task," Germain whispered.

The Mouse grunted that he couldn't crack the lock.

Suddenly the door swung open from the inside, and in the weak moonlight Madeleine recognized Weasel's pasty face and long nose.

"What are you doing here?" Germain sounded angry.

"I slunk in the window. The coast is clear, no guards in this part of the building—only bedrooms with a lot of beautiful jewels. If we pick a few things here, we will never have to work again."

"That is not why we came." Germain shook Weasel furiously. "If you lay your hands on as much as a pearl, I will personally wring your neck. Is that clear?"

Madeleine wondered at his fury. He was a thief; why did he refuse such obvious pickings?

But she abandoned the thought as she was pushed into the silent, dark corridor.

Chapter 39

As Fouquet paced the floor of his study, laughter floated to his ears from the theater in the distance.

It had been difficult to creep from his seat in front of the stage, but this was more important than the temporary displeasure of the King. At last he would hold the diary in his hands again. Eight people had lost their lives over that document, but he felt no regret, and he could almost taste victory now. The only threat standing between him and the title of prime minister was one stupid mistake—the diary in which his illegal transactions were recorded. How idiotic he had been to record anything in the first place!

Although the weather was balmy, he had built a small fire in the fireplace. The damned diary would burn the moment he laid his hands on it. He could afford no more mistakes.

He glanced at the clock. Where was Lemont? He should have been here by now. A fireball of nerves turned in his stomach. He went to the open window and breathed deeply. The sweet scent of roses permeated the air . . . and another scent that reminded him of—what? Greasepaint? *Non*, that was impossible. The theater was too far away for that scent to reach his nostrils. He shook his head. You're imagining things, he told himself sternly.

Just because you have a new mistress in the Italian theater doesn't mean you smell her everywhere. He felt a rush of desire when thinking of her lush body. This evening he would visit her and celebrate his success, seeking to forget that the diary ever existed.

A faint scratch on the door alerted him. Lemont, at last! Forgetting his usual poise, he rushed to the door and opened it.

RECKLESS SPLENDOR 339

Lemont looked ghastly, his face void of any color, his hand shaking as he patted one of his perfect curls. Behind him cowered Dubois, who was as pale as his master.

Immediately Fouquet sensed that something was very wrong. He motioned for both men to enter and carefully closed the door after making sure that the guards outside were at their positions.

"What happened?" he asked abruptly, anger slowly filling his dark eyes.

"N-nothing," Lemont stuttered, watching fury flare in Fouquet's face.

"Where is it? I want to burn it. You have been exonerated, as I promised."

"I, er, lost it."

Silence roared in the room. Fouquet's face was transformed into an evil mask and fire spewed from his eyes. "You—*what?!*"

"I lost it." Without being invited, Lemont sank into an armchair because his legs could no longer hold him up. He fanned himself with a handkerchief. He had confessed, and he knew that Fouquet would be merciless in his anger. Disdainfully he glanced at his servant, who was no support in his hour of need. Dubois looked as if he would faint at any minute.

Fouquet stalked up to Lemont and gripped him by the embroidered lapels of his vest, ruining the exquisite cascade of lace at his throat. He wanted to squeeze the neck below the lace until the pulse stopped beating under the skin. "*Enfin,* who has the diary?"

Lemont's life was spared as a wild tumult broke out in the corridor. Dazed, Fouquet released his hold on Lemont and stumbled to the door. He rushed out, almost losing his balance over a guard who was sprawled on the floor, groaning loudly.

As he eyed the wild fight under way, Fouquet thought he must be dreaming. Satyrs, fauns, and trees were rolling on the floor with guards or parrying back and forth with swords drawn, steel glinting in the light of the torches.

"What's going on here?" Fouquet bellowed. Instantly his breath was pushed painfully out of his lungs as one of the guards was hurled against his chest. His eyes clouded over, and he slumped to the floor. But before he fell into oblivion, a strong hand jerked him back to a standing position, and he felt the cold prick of a sword on his throat. He shifted his eyes so that he could see the man with the painful grip on his arm—and stared into a pair of gray eyes blazing silver fire.

He knew those eyes, but it must be a bad dream. The man was a satyr, his face full of deep grooves and a thatch of wolfskin on his head, goat's horns sticking up on the forehead.

Germain de Belleforière.

The name bored into Fouquet's brain like a lance. The cry ringing out came from his own lips. The mêlée in front of his eyes was like a picture straight out of hell. Priceless Chinese urns lay crushed on the floor, water from broken crystal vases had soaked into the carpets, and mangled flowers lay strewn everywhere. Shattered swords and ripped clothing littered the floor, and the walls were splattered with blood.

A small faun cowered against the opposite wall, flinching every time someone wailed in pain. Swords glittered, and the air was thick with the smell of fear and perspiration.

The faun was Madeleine. She cringed every time a blow touched flesh, and she fervently prayed that the fighting would end without death. Holding her hands to her ears, she tried to shut out the sounds, but it was fruitless. Once again she relived the horrors at the inn outside Rouen. Then, just as she thought she was going to faint, Germain let out a piercing whistle.

The fight slowly died down. The thieves were surrounded by twenty guards, and more were coming, their running footsteps pounding in the corridor.

Twisting Fouquet's arm, Germain pushed him into the study, the point of his sword still thrust against the finance minister's jugular, a drop of blood shining red from a nick in the skin. Germain motioned with his head for Madeleine to follow him, but she could barely walk, her legs rubbery. Yet with effort she obeyed, keeping close to his side.

Germain shouted, "If anyone dares cause any harm to my men, I will slit your master's throat."

The thieves and guards in the corridor stood completely still, their heaving breathing the only sound.

Germain pushed Fouquet into a chair and ordered Weasel to tie him down. Germain was not surprised to see Lemont and Dubois in the room, their frightened eyes darting back and forth, their faces deathly white.

"Truss them up, too." With a cynical twist to his lips, he added, "The King will know what to do with them after we hand him the diary." He took enormous pleasure in seeing their faces turn gray with shock.

"No!" Lemont whimpered.

Everyone's eyes were directed at the imposing and fearful satyr. Germain tore off the wolfskin wig, and Fouquet gasped as the light of the fire caught Germain's golden curls.

"You! I knew it," Fouquet croaked.

"*Oui*. I'm still alive and well, though you tried your best to get rid of me. How you must have gloated over the thought of me wasting away in some filthy dungeon, the rats finishing off the remains of the last Hautefort." He uttered the last words leaning over Fouquet, his face mere inches from that of the perspiring minister.

"*Enfin*, you succeeded," Germain added. "I am nothing now, only the most feared leader of thieves in Paris, the Black Angel. You have all met me at one time or another. The proceeds from the jewels I stole from you have gone to finance an orphanage outside Nantes, and you will never lay eyes on them again." He swept out his arm. "*You* made me a thief! I had to live in the twilight, hiding like a mouse in his hole because you would have killed me had you known that I was back in Paris."

The bitterness that had nourished him for so long in anticipation of this moment, and the triumph of victory, came pouring out with furious power.

"When you thought I was broken"—he slashed through the air with his sword—"I learned how to be a thief to survive. I've lived for this moment." He pointed to Weasel. "My teacher—the best burglar in France." He leaped across the room to the door and bellowed, "Legrand, bring him in."

Legrand entered, pushing a sullen Marquis D'Ambrose before him, holding him by the collar. "He tried to sneak away, but I caught him by his scrawny neck," Legrand said with a leer.

Germain took a deep breath, his chest expanding. Finally he addressed D'Ambrose. "You thought you were very clever, *non?* Weasel helped me to steal this back from you." Germain pulled the diary from the wolf's hide covering his legs and turned slowly, holding it high in the air. Gasps filled the room. "This is my revenge, and how sweet it is! Watching you squirm before the King's wrath will give me no end of pleasure. You deserve death, but I'm not in the habit of killing people—not like some of you. You will lose everything! You will rot in some dungeon, the exact fate you planned for me. Death is too light a punishment for you." He laughed harshly and loomed once more over Fouquet.

"*Oui*, Monsieur Minister, your brow is perspiring. Do you want to know how the diary ended up in my hands? Would you like to know how your victims paid you back?"

Fouquet swallowed audibly and croaked, "I'll pay you a fortune for it. I'll have your titles reinstated, I—"

Germain laughed. "You cannot buy me, Fouquet. It is over, don't you see? Let me explain."

All of a sudden D'Ambrose tried to make a dash for the door, but Legrand's hand twisted around his neck.

"Ah, D'Ambrose, you don't like the truth?" Germain spat. "Well, you'll have to listen anyway." He addressed the entire room. "D'Ambrose isn't as weak-kneed as Lemont here. He saw an opportunity to pad his slim purse— and you would have paid to the end of your days, Fouquet, because you didn't know who was blackmailing you. You *thought* it was Lemont." He swept out his arm, indicating D'Ambrose. "He did it! He got to the diary before Lemont did. He killed the royal guards . . . and a child. Not alone, *naturellement*. Who told him about Lemont's whereabouts so that he could beat him to the inn where the massacre took place?" Germain whipped around and grabbed Dubois by the collar. "This little rat, who does anything for a gold louis. He is your valet, Lemont, but also Fouquet's slave and D'Ambrose's informant. And, worst of all, a murderer."

RECKLESS SPLENDOR 343

He paused. "By now, Lemont, you must have figured out that D'Ambrose is no friend of yours—however often he hangs on your arm. I wager he'd rather hang on Monsieur's arm, therefore he sent a letter to the King naming you the murderer of the guards. He wanted you out of the way. Very clever, eh? It could have worked, but we were more clever. And this little book has brought defeat to all of you. Justice has won."

Madeleine squealed in delight. Her feeling of relief was so great that she threw herself around Germain's neck, tears streaming down her face.

For one moment he was distracted, and a nimble guard flung himself at Germain's legs, toppling him. The diary flew out of Germain's hand. Madeleine was knocked to the floor right next to the diary. Instinctively she reached to take it, but Lemont kicked it viciously across the room, and it slid beneath the heavy draperies, coming to a stop just in front of the fire.

Fighting broke loose. Vases flew like missiles through the air, flowerpots connected with heads, and a full inkstand smashed against the wall.

The thieves were experts at extricating themselves from tricky situations. One by one they slipped from firm grasps and melted away from the scene, leaving puzzled guards holding empty coats and limp wolf pelts. In the ensuing chaos, guards fought guards until Fouquet ordered a halt, his voice breaking.

Released at last, he rushed to the fire. *There was still a chance.* But the diary was gone. Furious, he turned on the guards. "How many did you catch?" he roared. "They will hang before morning."

The guards scratched their heads. "None, monsieur."

Fouquet's face took on a purple hue of unspeakable rage. He opened his mouth to scream, but instead fell into a chair, clutching a hand to his heart.

"He's dying! Do something, you nincompoops!" Lemont shouted.

Silence fell suddenly as the guards stood dumbly staring at their suffering employer. Curtains billowed from the open window through which some of the gang had escaped— among them Germain and Madeleine.

* * *

Germain heaved a sigh of relief. They had made it outside in the nick of time. One moment longer and they would have been irrevocably captured by the guards. Thank God they had stood right by the window the minute the fight broke out! He had fallen hard when throwing himself outside with Madeleine in his arms. But no bones were broken, and Madeleine was safe with him.

"Phew, how close!"

"I am so sorry! I should not have thrown myself at you like that," Madeleine said in a small voice, holding Germain around the waist, half afraid he might leave her. "Did you catch the diary?" She held her breath nervously.

"Non." He sounded deflated, resigned. "And you didn't either, *vraiment?* Let's leave before they find us."

Weasel was waiting for them at the end of the hedge. Madeleine would not have noticed him if Germain had not halted abruptly.

"We're all safe," Weasel whispered. "The best way to escape is over the wall. We'll have to swim the moat. But first, I have something to tell you, something that will make you very pleased. We found Gaspard in the dungeons below. He is still alive and well, if a bit weak. Roland and Spider have released him and helped him escape."

Germain laughed in delight and rubbed his hands. "Thank God! At least we won something tonight, even if we lost the diary."

Weasel stared at them, a smile breaking slowly over his face. It was the first time Madeleine had ever seen him smile. Triumphant, he lifted his wig and handed Germain the diary. Germain drew his breath in sharply, then he spontaneously embraced Weasel, thumping him in the back. Since they could not shout their triumph, suppressed tears stood in three pairs of eyes as they silently shared the blissful moment.

"You'd better leave with the others. Madeleine and I have some business to take care of here."

Weasel nodded and slid into the shadows.

Germain seized Madeleine and cradled her within the warm circle of his embrace. His lips fastened hungrily on hers as if to reforge the bond between them. The kiss was full of sweetness and peace.

"Let us find the King."

By now the play had ended. Colored lanterns had been lit along the enormous terrace at the back of the palace, and lackeys were setting up tables filled with sweetmeats and refreshments. Germain was grateful that the gang had managed to escape. To avoid the zealous guards who were scurrying around the grounds like ants, Germain pulled Madeleine through the darkest part of the gardens. As the nobility, led by the King, walked slowly back toward the *château*, splendid fireworks were shot into the air from the amphitheater at the end of the main *allée*, cascading like thousands of falling stars. The ohhhs and ahhhs of the guests filled the air. The next spurt of fireworks spelled the names Louis and Marie-Thérèse, and showered them with *fleurs de lys*. On the canal glided a boat in the shape of a whale that sent off more fireworks to the music of trumpets and drums.

As the King slowly climbed the long, shallow stairs leading to the terrace, thousands of rockets went off, creating an arch of fire above him.

From the shadows of a tree next to the stairs, Germain and Madeleine watched, awed by the magnificence of the entertainment.

"You'll have to reach him before he enters the house," Germain whispered, his voice urgent.

"I? What about you?"

"I can't show myself to him—I might forget that he is the King and do something foolish. But I will be watching you, knowing that the King will reward you greatly and that Fouquet will get his just punishment."

Knowing it was no use arguing with him, Madeleine hugged him fiercely. Clutching the diary in her hand, she ran to the landing and waited; the King was slowly approaching. Her heart thudded in her chest.

"Sire!" she cried out over the noise of the rockets, forgetting to curtsy in her eagerness to speak to him.

His dark gaze swept over her, and she remembered her place and fell to her knees. She looked up, boldly meeting his scrutiny.

"A faun! Have we business?" the King asked disdainfully, tapping his beribboned cane on the stone step.

"*Oui*, sire. Don't you recognize me?"

"I can't say I do."

"Oh." Realizing she had forgotten to take off her wig, she hurried to rectify that error, letting her blond hair flow like a soft cloud down her back.

"Mademoiselle Poquelin—a faun?"

A group of aristocrats gathered around the sovereign, but with an impatient wave of his hand, he dismissed them. Many curious glances were directed at the strange little creature at the King's feet.

"Here, sire. I'm extremely pleased to hand you this diary, and I trust you will punish Fouquet appropriately." Breathlessly she eyed the King, willing him to take the small book she was holding out to him.

An egg-shaped ruby glittered on his finger as he gingerly grasped the bound volume. A wisp of lace from the cuff of his shirt caressed her hand, and Madeleine remembered the times when Germain had been dressed in satins and laces, his hands adorned with jewels.

"Mademoiselle! Is this the Poquelin diary? How . . . ?"

"Sire, the story is very long, alas. The blood of eight people has been shed for that journal."

The King smiled. "You have pleased me. Just the proof I needed. Steps will be taken—I promise you." He eyed her for a long time and slowly reached out to take her hand. The aristocrats, keeping at a respectable distance, avidly stared at the scene. The gossips would be very busy relating the strange events at Vaux-de-Vicomte to the unfortunate members of the court who had not received an invitation to the festivities.

"A faun looks singularly ridiculous curtsying—it's the pelt on your legs that does it," the King said, smiling.

Self-conscious at last, Madeleine blushed and lowered her gaze. He pulled her up, and she dared to respond to his warm smile.

"I will call you to Fontainebleau as soon as this business is cleared up." With a bow, he walked off, leaving Madeleine staring after him.

Surprised, she saw Fouquet emerge from the *château,* leaning heavily on his majordomo. When the King reached the terrace, Fouquet fell to his knees and stretched out his arms in an imploring gesture. The King eyed Fouquet speculatively, his cane tapping the floor. Silence stretched from one side of the enormous gardens to the other as everyone held his breath.

"Arrest him!" the King ordered in his most official voice.

Madeleine's feet had wings as she ran back to Germain and threw herself into his arms. He laughed and lifted her high into the air.

"You were perfect."

"The King said I look foolish with pelt on my legs."

Germain laughed happily. "I tend to agree with him. And Fouquet will get his just reward, don't you worry."

Tears sprang to her eyes. "For Amul. I can never undo the wrong I did to him," she said thickly. "And for Father."

Germain's expression grew serious. He hugged her fiercely, sharing her pain. Her tears wet his bare shoulder. Tenderly he caressed her hair until she quieted and the sadness faded to the background. How he wished he could make her forget the sorrow. Eventually time would heal her wounds, as it would his.

"Let's catch up with the others," he said.

Dawn was coloring the sky over Paris light pink as carts carrying the exhausted players pulled through Porte Saint Antoine. Germain had wrapped one arm around Madeleine and the other around his old friend Gaspard, who had escaped certain death by starvation in the dungeons of Vaux-de-Vicomte.

Madeleine was at peace at last.

Chapter 40

As the bells of the city tolled, Germain stirred. He counted each chime—"three, four, five, six."

Six o'clock! They had slept all day. Wide awake now, he turned to Madeleine, who was sleeping innocently next to him.

"Wake up, you sleepyhead!" He growled in contentment and planted a kiss on her soft lips, watching her stretch, her deep blue eyes clouded with sleep. Some greasepaint still stuck to her eyebrows and cheeks.

"You are adorable," he whispered into her ear, his hands eagerly seeking her warm, rounded contours concealed by only a thin sheet. His hands were like waves of water caressing her skin, and slowly the urge to make love stirred in her, building to a honeyed fire in her loins.

Cradling his aroused manhood within the depths of her being kindled such need, such torment, and such joy that she wanted to cry with happiness. Each time was a gift, one more beautiful than the other. He held nothing back from her, waited patiently until she quivered with unbearable desire, then brought her glorious release, over and over. He was like rain on her desert, warmth on her cold, always bringing her more when she believed no higher enchantment could be reached.

She clasped him deeply within her, her eyes fixed on his laughing eyes. As she clung to him in abandon, he began throbbing and growing within her until his breath came in hard gasps. Together they plunged into a sea of bliss.

Two hours passed before they were ready to leave the bed, and then it was with much reluctance.

RECKLESS SPLENDOR 349

"Well, would you rather starve?" Germain asked as Madeleine complained. Filled with energy, he washed himself thoroughly, erasing every trace of his satyr disguise. "You have changed so much, *chérie*. At first you'd jump out of bed bright and early, and now all you want to do is to stay in bed."

Madeleine giggled. "Before, I did not have you to wear me out."

Germain's gaze narrowed in mock anger. "*Oui*, blame it all on me, vixen! You are making me into an old man before my time."

"Oh, *zut!*" Madeleine flung her legs over the edge of the bed. "What are we going to do now?" She patted the mattress. "Please come and sit here and tell me."

He stiffened slightly but obeyed. "We have been over this before, *ma belle*. I love you, you know that, more than anything. But think, Madeleine, think! I can give you nothing."

"Your love is enough."

"Madeleine, I . . ." He rose, shoving a hand through his hair. "I don't even have a name to give you!"

She sat up, her hair falling like a golden waterfall down her back. "I don't care as long as we can be together."

Germain paced the floor, feeling that a solution to the problem was beyond his reach. "*Chérie*, I will not allow you to continue to live a life on the wrong side of the law. I have decided to leave Paris and start a new life, an honest life. I've had my revenge. I'm satisfied."

"I want to go with you!"

He shook his head, his face pale.

"How could you plan a life without me?" Madeleine felt hot tears fill her eyes, and fear gripped her heart.

"*Ma petite*, you knew that our time together was limited. It hurts to say this, but you will be better off without me. I am a wanted man and will always be hunted. You will be rich, and you will have the King's protection. I know him; no one will dare to scorn you. You will make a good marriage at court."

"Excuses, excuses! Just say it! You don't want me anymore," Madeleine stormed, then pinched her lips together. This was worse than she had dreamed.

With a groan Germain folded her into his arms, crooning softly into her hair. She was not aware of his sudden tears soaking into her curls, and she could not feel the pincers of grief in his chest.

As their tears dried and their misery was shared, the subject became too tender to bring up again. Madeleine could not bear more rejection, and she could not understand why he did not throw caution to the wind and share the rest of his life with her, marry her, with or without the blessing of the church. She had thought their love was greater than anything in the world. How foolish! But she wasn't going to beg, refused to be a millstone around his neck.

They dressed in silence, the lightness of the evening gone. Trying to penetrate the gloom, Madeleine spoke at last. "You never told me how you managed to get your hands on the diary."

Germain sighed and explained. "When I didn't find the diary among Lemont's possessions, I suspected that he didn't have it. We didn't know if it still existed, but after overhearing Dubois and Lemont that night at Saint-Cloud, we knew that Lemont was innocent of the murders."

He massaged his neck. "Then Gaspard found that blackmail note among Fouquet's papers, and we knew for sure that the diary existed. We ambushed Fouquet and discovered that he thought Lemont had the diary. He admitted he had forced Lemont to run his errands since Lemont was deeply indebted to him. Lemont pretended that he had the diary so that Fouquet would have to exonerate him from the murders. When I heard of the massacre, I suspected that Fouquet was responsible somehow. Who had he hired to do the deed of stealing the diary? Lemont. But, as we know, Lemont never reached the inn. He didn't kill anybody; D'Ambrose and Dubois did, and they took the diary."

Germain chuckled suddenly. "Used to the constant intrigues at court, I put two and two together and figured out that D'Ambrose wanted the diary to thwart Lemont.

"D'Ambrose had hidden the diary under his cravats in a chest. Weasel nabbed it in thirty seconds, after scaling up the wall and going through the window. D'Ambrose's goal was to oust Lemont from Monsieur's affection. He sent the anonymous note to the King, hoping that Lemont would be convicted of the murders. Perhaps he thought he had won when Lemont failed to confess to Fouquet that he didn't have the diary. Perhaps he even thought that Fouquet might kill Lemont when he found out the truth. I can't read every twist of their crooked minds. Furthermore, Lemont was afraid of the King—deathly afraid that Louis would behead him for the murders."

Taking a deep breath, he added, "I think Lemont was appalled to hear that Dubois was involved in the massacre. Dubois served many masters, he was a very dangerous man. In fact, I think he is unhinged. I'm certain Louis will go to the bottom of this and mete out suitable punishment for all of them. At least the sordid business is out of our hands."

Germain threw his head back and laughed. "Such conspirators!"

Madeleine frowned, not inclined to join in his mirth. "You knew for some time, yet you didn't tell me!"

"If I had, you would have ordered me to hand the diary over to the King immediately. I wanted revenge. I wanted to see them sweat and squirm. Lemont feared for his life, while Fouquet had trouble finding a trustworthy alibi to prove to the King that Lemont had been nowhere near the inn at the time of the massacre. Several people knew that Lemont had, in fact, gone to Rouen at the same time we did."

"Germain! You *must* make Fouquet admit that he planted the treasonous letters at *hôtel* Belleforière."

Germain snorted. "He'd rather die than admit that. He was very clever; ruining me was a much more devious punishment than telling Jules Delchamps of Brigitte's and my little *faux pas*. Fouquet has won in the end, he's achieved his lifelong revenge on me for helping you. Listen, *chérie*, I would never have kept the diary from you had I known some other way to make him pay."

She smoothed an errant curl from his brow and sighed. "However much I hate to admit it, I might have done the same thing."

She turned away from him, her tears threatening to overflow. Stillness filled the room. How could she convince him that he could not live without her? She could find no immediate answer, and misery flowed through her.

"I will go back to bed. I'm still exhausted," she said, and listlessly pulled off her dress. The bed was lumpy and uncomfortable, but she would rather suffer its discomfort than deal with Germain's oddities. How could he be so blind! They belonged together! Feeling his eyes on her, she pulled the sheet over her face. He quietly walked to the door.

"I will ask Maître Jacques to send up a tray of food," he said and left the room, closing the door soundlessly behind him.

Madeleine did not respond.

Loud banging on the door pulled her out of the nightmare that had haunted her sleep. Dazed, she fought to extricate herself from the tangled sheets.

"Open up, Madi."

Recognizing Molière's voice, she stumbled out of bed. Germain was not in the room.

After flinging a wrap around herself, she opened the door. "What time is it?" she asked sleepily as her uncle entered.

"Seven o'clock."

"In the evening?"

"No, silly, in the morning. You look awful. Have you slept too little?"

"*Non*, rather too much. I must have slept eighteen hours." She yawned widely. "Is Germain downstairs?"

"I didn't see him. You'd better hurry up dressing. A royal coach is waiting downstairs. The King has ordered you to Fontainebleau."

"Oh." Disappointment tinged her voice. "I don't want to leave before I've spoken with Germain. We have some important things to settle."

Molière snorted. "More important than the King's command?"

It occurred to her then that Molière was serious, and her nerves began to flutter.

"I have nothing to wear!" she wailed.

"I know. I've taken care of it." He walked to the door and called down the stairs. A servant entered carrying a dress of peacock-blue silk embroidered with silver threads. Madeleine drew a sharp breath of surprise. "Beautiful!" she whispered as spiderweb-thin petticoats and a bodice covered with lace were spread out on the bed. She noticed that the blue matched the color of her eyes. "You thought of everything, Uncle."

He cleared his throat noisily. "I can't send my niece to court in rags."

She smiled hesitantly. "I'm not sure I look forward to my meeting with the King."

"The red carpet is going to be rolled out for you."

Perhaps, but I'm going alone.

"You'd better make haste. The King doesn't like to be kept waiting."

Madeleine's elegant dress was a far cry from the faun outfit she had worn during her last meeting with the King. She followed the stiff Swiss Guard down the long corridor to the King's salon. The new shoes pinched her toes, and the corset ground into her ribs.

How she wished Germain was accompanying her! He had not returned to the inn, and it nagged on her mind. Where was he? What was he doing?

The gilded double doors opened on well-oiled hinges, revealing priceless Persian carpets and gleaming gold and silver furniture, polished crystal reflecting the bright sunlight.

The King looked more elegant than she could remember. He seemed to have grown; more power exuded from his person. She sank into a deep curtsy, her eyes fastened on his diamond shoe buckles.

His beringed hand reached out for her, and she trembled as she placed her hand in his, feeling as if she was offering herself to him.

"Lovely. You will be a great asset to the court, Mademoiselle Poquelin. Or should I say Marquise D'Aubry?"

"Sire?"

"I'm bequeathing the title of marquise on you. With the title goes the *châteaux* of D'Aubry and Dampierre. I am also giving you an annual pension of a hundred thousand livres. I expect you to stay at court from now on to illuminate it with your fair presence."

Madeleine stared at him in disbelief. Her breath came in shallow gasps, and she felt on the verge of swooning. "Is it true?" The air seemed to close in on her, thick and heavy.

He laughed, amused by her reaction.

She swallowed convulsively. "I—I don't know what to say. My deed was but a small thing."

"The diary was beyond my expectations. I value it more than I can express. You have pleased me greatly. My gift is a small token for my appreciation."

Madeleine opened her mouth to protest, but he stopped her with a gesture. "The subject is closed."

Was the interview at an end? She decided to be bold; this might be the only chance to speak to the King in private.

"Sire, I would like to beg of you one more favor." She regarded him seriously.

"Favor?" He sounded incredulous.

"Oui. Certainly not for myself, but for a friend. He helped me to recover the journal. Without his assistance, the deed could not have been accomplished."

"Oh? And who is this paragon?"

Madeleine took a deep, shaky breath. "The former comte de Hautefort. Please, sire, can you find it in your heart to pardon him? He is innocent. He was falsely accused of treason, another one of Fouquet's tricks."

The King regarded her thoughtfully, then clasped his hands behind his back and stepped forward until he was looming over her slight form. His dark eyes penetrated to the depths of her conscience.

"He has done much harm to my courtiers. Not a day has passed without one or two of them losing some valuable trinket. Black Angel—deplorable behavior!"

"So you know already. What was left to Germain? You took everything from him except his dignity. With the stolen jewelry he founded an orphanage in Brittany. He has lived in squalor." She defended Germain heatedly, for a moment forgetting whom she was addressing. "He has always been loyal to you."

A shadow of amusement flitted across his eyes. "You do have spirit. Black Angel should consider himself fortunate to have your esteem. When I heard that he had escaped from prison, I knew I had not heard the last of him. If Fouquet admits his guilt, I will give Germain his title back. But for riches, alas! They are all gone. Fouquet saw to that. All the estates were sold except Les Étoiles. I believe Fouquet kept that one himself. Since he is now arrested, his estates belong to the crown."

"Sire, Germain is innocent."

"It must be proved. You can tell him that, if he continues with his unlawful activities, he will be hunted like a rat and hanged on Place de Grève, like the common criminal that he is."

Madeleine swallowed convulsively and could only nod in response.

The King sat down at his desk, thus indicating that the audience was over. As she backed to the door, he spoke once more. "Your *appartements* have been prepared in the palace. You can take immediate occupancy. With your new status I advise you to keep your friend at a discreet distance."

Dismay washed through her; she was relieved when the doors closed behind her. Sinking onto a chair by the open windows leading to a long terrace, she fanned her face vigorously while staring at the immaculate lawns and the courtiers strolling down the paths. The weather was sultry, and her face was flushed. Where would she find the strength to live without Germain, and why did she have to stay at Fontainebleau when all she wanted was to return to Paris and Germain? Where was he? Before leaving Paris, she had scribbled a hasty note to him. He would grow suspicious if she did not return. As they had separated on a bad note, he might think that she wanted to leave him.

"You fool!" she whispered. "He loves me. He will come for me; then I will go with him—to the end of the world if need be."

Now she realized what he had meant by comparing the court with a prison. Had her right of choice been taken away when the King created her a noblewoman? She felt a hysterical need to laugh, but bit her bottom lip and glanced furtively at the stone-faced guards outside the King's salon. Drained of all strength, she rose, her legs still trembling.

A black page stepped forward and bowed deeply. Madeleine had to swallow hard. He reminded her of Amul.

"Madame la marquise, allow me to escort you to your *appartement.*"

New living quarters. Another ordeal to live through in one day. Her heart was heavy as she stepped through the door to her lavish apartment located on the same floor as those of the most important courtiers, an additional show of the King's favor. Her silken prison.

Chapter 41

The King sent a message that she should prepare herself for an indefinite stay at court, meaning she should go back to Paris and purchase gowns and cloaks befitting a marquise.

Madeleine had never felt less excited at the prospect of squandering funds on frivolous clothes. Her heart was not in it, and she was bothered by a nagging worry about her future, which looked bleak to say the least. How could she enjoy her new life of luxury without Germain? It was unthinkable.

She shivered, although the sun shone hotly on her head as she walked to the coach waiting to take her back to Paris. She ordered the coachman to drive her to The Golden Horn in Faubourg Saint Michel, where she had stayed with Germain. Telling him to wait, she ran up the stairs and into the room. It was empty. Her clothes were neatly packed into a portmanteau by the door, but she could see no sign of Germain's sack. An envelope leaned against her pillow. Fumbling, she tore it open, pulling out a dirty piece of folded paper.

Beloved Madeleine, I know that the King called you to Fontainebleau. He will have rewarded you greatly by now for the favor you did to France. You deserve it all. Seldom have I seen man or woman with your determination and courage. I cannot put into words how much I love you, but it ends here, as you must understand.

The gulf in our stations is wider than it ever was; ironic, *non?* I am certain that you spoke to the King about me, but should I, against all odds, be pardoned, I have decided that I do not want to live my life at court. I am sure the King knew all about me; he always did. He will be a powerful and magnificent king, but I do not care to live in his shadow for the rest of my life. I have tasted freedom. Tears come to my eyes when I think of you and the great love we shared. Grim is fate that I could not marry you. We have lived for the moment, and I do not regret a single minute. You have showed me the meaning of true love. I deeply wish you will find a way to live happily at court.

I am leaving Paris today.

You are always in my thoughts, and life is gray without you. I love you, always. Germain.

Tears streamed down her face, and her legs could not support her. Sinking down on the bed, she buried her face in her hands. Sobs shook her body until she thought she was going to break apart. How could he leave? Not even to kiss her good-bye. Coward! Sneaking away!

Then she realized she could not have borne to see him go; he had shielded her from that heartrending moment by simply leaving a note. Had she been here, she would never have let him go. He knew that. Still, she bled as if a dagger had been thrust into her heart.

A soft knock sounded on the door, and Maître Jacques entered. Clearing his throat, he said, "I heard your sorrow all the way downstairs. Black Angel was greatly distressed when he left, and I had to promise him several times to help you, if the need arises." Hesitantly he stepped forward. "He left this."

Madeleine regarded him through swollen eyelids. In the palm of his hand lay a ring with a large diamond. She immediately recognized it; Germain had worn it that first night at Versailles. Grasping it eagerly, she pressed the cold stone to her lips in longing. She thought of his hands, so tender in her hair, on her body. A new bout of crying racked her.

"*Merci*," she mumbled and blew her nose. "I . . . will leave in a moment."

Rubbing his greasy hair, not knowing what to say, the kind host left Madeleine to cry in peace. "You may stay here as long as you like," he muttered before he closed the door behind him.

She had to leave. To be reminded of Germain in the room where they had been so happy together was too painful. He was not coming back. On the rickety stand by the bed, she left several gold coins to cover the expenses and give the host ample reward for sheltering her. She was sure Germain had already settled their debts, but she felt a need to leave something more behind.

With her head bent, she climbed into the coach and gave the coachman the address of La Béjart. She needed help. Alone she could not manage to get through another day.

The King waved at Madeleine as she entered the crowded ballroom. It was her first official appearance as the Marquise D'Aubry, and she felt extremely awkward under the arrogant glances of the courtiers. Dressed in a pale blue gown lavishly adorned with silver flowers, she was as elegant as any of the other ladies. Curls spilled in artful spirals over one shoulder, and a strand of pearls was woven into the gathered tresses on top of her head. At her throat glittered sapphires and diamonds, and on her finger flashed a perfect diamond—the one Germain had given her.

"Step forward, marquise. You will be given a taboret," the King called.

A gasp of surprise swept through the crowd. Only royal princesses and duchesses sat in the King's presence, and then only as a favor. Madeleine had been shown the highest favor, and speculation was rampant. Was she to be his new mistress? But the King was still infatuated with La Vallière. Whispers flew around the room.

Blushing, Madeleine sat on the gold-tasseled taboret placed at the feet of the King. She smiled shyly, carefully hiding her desolation, and he gave her a benevolent nod.

With a wave of his hand he ordered the music to begin. Frail violin tunes floated through the room, and all eyes were fastened on the sovereign, who rose and bowed to La Vallière.

Madeleine watched as they opened the ball, a handsome couple at the heart of splendor. She felt stifled, like a bird in a cage; to make matters worse, the envious glances of the other courtiers felt like sharp pinpricks on her skin.

No one asked her to dance, and she grew increasingly uncomfortable. Restlessly she walked to the tables laid with delicacies and placed random pieces on a plate without noticing what they were.

"Th-there—*hic!*—you are—*hic!*—my love—*hic!*" came a voice from behind. She turned sharply, and Lemont's wine-laden breath washed over her. "A marvelous ball, eh, Mademoi—*hic!*" he slurred, and Madeleine was nauseated. So he was not under arrest.

A group of men snickered as Lemont almost lost his balance. She edged away from him before he could fall on her. Steadying himself against the table, he clumsily swept a silver plate filled with artichokes to the floor. Two lackeys hurried forward and led him to a chair.

Madeleine was mortified. With tears burning in her eyes, she hurried out of the ballroom to the terrace.

Pacing up and down, she slowly relaxed. She did not belong here; she never would. She began fanning herself vigorously. How could she extricate herself from this situation without displeasing the King?

Returning to the ballroom, she almost collided with the chevalier de Lemont. She glared at him, but in place of his usual arrogance was a pitiful air of shame. Holding himself upright with difficulty, he mumbled an apology and staggered away, a hunted look on his face. She heard him topple over behind a pillar, and then came the sounds of retching. Placing a hand to her throat, she choked back her own nausea.

She knew a beaten man when she saw one. Although Lemont was in attendance at court, she knew the King had doled out a fitting punishment—the entire court's rejection.

"*Oui*, your disgust is quite understandable," said the King. "Tomorrow he is going to the Bastille to spend an uncomfortable month, and then to his estates in the country until I see fit to recall him. Perhaps never!" the King exclaimed angrily. "He made a fool of me."

"Sire, he mostly made a fool of himself," Madeleine replied softly. "He dared not defy Fouquet."

"Ah, that snake in the grass! He is at present in the Bastille awaiting his trial. I would like to see him hang, but he has many powerful friends in parlement. I must be careful. I have decided to send him into exile."

Madeleine whirled around, the silk of her gown whispering against the parquet. "Sire, may I protest?"

The King looked puzzled. "Protest?"

"*Oui*. If he is free—abroad—he could raise an army against you, one so large that you would be destroyed. Fouquet is capable of anything. He's a fanatic. He would never rest, not until he had done everything to ruin you. Sire, you must incarcerate him. It's the only way you can control him. I know him." Her eyes pleaded with him. How dared she tell the King what to do? But the fear of seeing Fouquet free again made her bold.

Suddenly the King chortled. "*Mon Dieu*, you're right! I've underestimated him. Your advice is very sound. Now, mademoiselle, let us dance."

He captured her hand and led her regally to the middle of the floor. A smile lurking in the depths of his eyes, he bent over her fingers and pressed a light kiss to their tips. She should have been moved by his attention, but she felt nothing. Something had died inside when she was forced to separate from the only man she loved.

"So young and lovely, and so wise," he muttered. Brushing his fingers across the large ring on her forefinger, a curious smile lingered on his lips. "The Hautefort diamond. Always passed on to the oldest son to give to his bride." He shrugged out of his sudden trance and smiled at her. "It's a trifle large for you."

His words had the effect of shaking loose the coldness in her heart. The Hautefort diamond, she thought in a daze. A flood of tears threatened to drown her, but she forced them back. Germain had never told her about the significance of the ring! It was his way of saying that he considered her his wife. Oh, Germain!

Biting her lip hard, she concentrated on following the intricate dance steps. Only once she was alone would she allow her tears free rein. It was all she did these days—cry. Her lips trembled, and her eyelashes grew wet.

"You love him very much, don't you?" the King whispered as the steps brought him to her once more. When she did not answer, he added, "He's so much a man, isn't he?" He studied her closely, and she blushed. Was the evening never going to end?

"If you love him that much, you have my permission to go to him. But remember, he's a hunted man. Think very carefully before you give everything up for him," the King advised kindly.

Standing at the open window of her bedroom, Madeleine let the cool night breeze play over her body, which was covered by only a thin shift. Gently she massaged her ribs, which had been so abused by the corset and the tight laces of her ballgown. She could stand this no more! She drew deep breaths of the fragrant night air, laden with the sweet scents of honeysuckle and roses.

"Germain, are you suffering a sleepless night also?" she whispered into the night.

"Psst!"

She jumped with fear. What was that?

"Psssst!"

Peering outside, she saw a pasty face and a long nose with the telltale wart at the tip.

"Weasel! What are you doing here? The guards might catch you," she breathed as the thin man scaled the wall to her window and crawled inside. She threw a wrap around herself and frowned at him.

He chuckled. "There doesn't exist a guard who can catch me," he scoffed.

"You're too careless. Sooner than you think, the noose will close around your scrawny neck!" she admonished.

Silence hung between them.

"Did . . . Germain send you here?" She held her breath, realizing how much she wanted him to say yes.

"*Non*, he has left. I want to follow him. Paris no longer holds an interest to me."

Madeleine saw that he was disturbed and sad. "*Oui*, I agree. I'd gladly exchange my riches for one more day with

Germain. He abandoned us all." She heaved a tremulous sigh. "He doesn't want me."

"I think he does, but he wants to do the honorable thing by you." Weasel hesitated. "He wanted to marry you—to protect you always—but he is a wanted man. He cried when we left the inn. I have *never* seen him cry. Of course, he would never admit to such a weakness." Weasel's rounded shoulders sagged. "I have no desire to hang on Place de Grève. As you said, sooner or later—"

"I know! Weasel, from now on you will be working for me. You'll be my majordomo." She paused. "To be that, you'll have to learn to walk through doors, of course." She scrutinized his face, seeing it light up.

"I will learn."

"*Bien.* You will have a livery, the most elegant clothes you've ever seen." Delighted, she clapped her hands. "Where are the other men?"

"At The Greedy Cat, drinking themselves into oblivion. Black Angel provided for all of us, but the men have squandered their lot already."

Madeleine had an idea. "You will go back to Paris and hire all of them for me—that is, if they are willing. I need coachmen, lackeys, and grooms. They may choose what they want to do, under one condition; there will be no thieving! Or drinking. You'll have to make that clear to them."

Weasel twirled his hat between his hands, a smile wreathing his face. "*Merci!*" he said thickly. "You are an angel." He slid onto the windowsill, eager to fulfill his assignment.

"Wait!" She tossed him a filled leather purse. "Make sure they are clean and shaved, with their curls brushed, before they present themselves here. I don't want the guards to become suspicious; the ruffians' faces are terrifying enough."

Thus Madeleine acquired a group of odd servants. She had difficulty adjusting to giving orders, since she considered them all her friends. It was strange, but she trusted them more than any of the courtiers who always made a point of showing her that she was an outsider, an upstart who had managed to charm the King with much cunning.

For days she lived in a twilight world of dreams and longings, trying to summon the courage to join Germain. What if he rejected her? But already she knew the answer; she had to leave.

Then one morning she was sitting in bed eating breakfast from a tray when from the open window the first brisk herald of autumn pierced the ripe summer air. Time was passing, time too valuable to waste on a life she found stifling and unsatisfactory.

She called Weasel to her room. He had changed tremendously; he was now clean-shaved and well groomed, his muslin jabot impeccable and his dark velvet suit pressed and well fitting. The only signs of his former life were his reluctance to go through doors, his darting eyes, and his refusal to accept any name but Weasel. His life now had direction; he filled his post admirably.

"I want you to find out who owns Les Étoiles," she said, excitement tinting her voice. "And I want to purchase the estate if possible."

The request baffled him, and she laughed. "How would you like to live at Les Étoiles, Weasel?"

"Well enough, I believe," he answered, concealing his excitement with a shrug. "Especially if Black Angel is there. I will do your bidding immediately, mam'selle."

He was the only one who called her "mam'selle," and no matter how many times she told him to stop, he never did. As he approached the door with utmost caution, she halted him. "Tell me, why do you dislike doors so much?" It was the first really personal question she had ever asked him.

He rubbed his wart, clearly embarrassed. Looking at the floor and shuffling his feet, he said, "My father hanged himself in front of a door." Before she could speak, he slunk out.

She shivered, but her dismay was followed by growing hope. Her life was not the only one strewn with tragedies. Others had survived deep losses and gone on living—with scars, but still living.

A sensation of euphoria filled her. She would take fate into her own hands and live, no matter what.

Colbert, dressed as usual in his favorite snuff-brown velvet, was studying the fashionable young woman in front of him. She had come a long way since the first time he had laid eyes on her in this same office. He had come a long way, too, had gained an increase in power. But unlike Fouquet, he was an honest man. He worked toward improving life in France, not to fill his own coffers with gold.

"Mademoiselle Poquelin, I do not understand why you want to purchase another country estate when you already own two."

"Monsieur Colbert, you don't need to understand. Just sell me the estate. The crown needs the funds."

A slow smile spread over his face. "You are not willing to discuss it further?" he teased.

"*Non,* please don't hold me in suspense. I will sign the papers before I leave. This time you will not be able to fob me off so easily," she parried, a small smile of triumph on her lips.

He lifted his hands in a gesture of mock defeat. "I'm glad to sell you the crumbling heap. It'll cost you a pretty fortune to restore it."

"That will be my problem, Monsieur Colbert."

The sun seemed to shine brighter as she stepped outside Colbert's narrow house. The birds sang louder and more beautifully. Everyone appeared to be smiling, even the beggars on Pont-Neuf. As her carriage passed, she flung out a handful of gold louis at their feet and shouted, "*Vive la France! Vive l'amour!*"

Chapter 42

Germain was working hard to mend the hole in the roof before nightfall. Perspiration covered his torso, and he swore when he hit his thumb with the hammer. Defeated, he sat down and suckled the offended member. From the roof he had a splendid view of the surrounding buildings and the forest. His heart ached with love at the sight. The gray stone of the turreted main building blended perfectly with the lush verdure of the forest and the stony hills.

The landscape was wild in these parts of Brittany, far from the sophistication of the large towns of Nantes and Rennes. He knew no other place he would rather be. He had no pride left, and when he had heard that a bailiff was needed at the estate, he had applied for the job under an assumed name. The state official in Rennes had barely glanced at him, having no interest in the estate himself. As an official, he had only to hire bailiffs. He didn't care if the estate went to seed. There had been a constant stream of bailiffs over the last year, and this rough customer from Paris was just another one who would leave in a few weeks, he thought.

Germain had been hired, and now he lived in the gatehouse with Madame Barbette, who cooked simple meals and mended his clothes, and with Gaspard, who shared his simple work. A bailiff's salary was meager, and any sous they could spare went into materials for necessary repairs.

Now the estate had been sold, never again to belong to the proud name of Hautefort. It hurt.

He glanced at the drive where it met the piercing blue of the September sky. Weeks had passed since he'd last seen Madeleine. Often his gaze drifted to the road, as if he unconsciously expected to see a carriage there. The thought of Madeleine was always in his mind, and he yearned unbearably for her. Had he been a fool to let her go?

At the time, there had seemed to be no other choice. He had no right to her. But now he had decent work. Should he send for her? Would she be content to be married to a bailiff?

Aching despair pierced his chest. What would he not give to hold her in his arms once more.

Night was falling, and a stiff, salty breeze from the sea beyond the forest blew in, bearing a fresh pine fragrance. He climbed down off the roof, greeting the dogs waiting for him on the ground.

"Ariel, Claudine, you lazy beasts! You only sleep or chase rabbits these days. Why did you not help me on the roof, eh?" He rubbed them fondly behind the ears.

"On the scent of another rabbit?" he cried as they rushed away, their deep barks slashing the air. Then he heard the sound of wheels crunching over gravel. From the roof he had seen no carriage, but it might have just entered through the gates. Who could it be, visiting so late in the day? All the neighbors knew the house was closed.

Suddenly, as if by instinct, he knew who it was. Madeleine! Running as fast as his legs could carry him, he met the coach halfway down the path.

He saw blond hair shining in the twilight.

"Madeleine, *chérie!*" he cried, oblivious of the gleeful laughter greeting him. Had he looked closer, he might have recognized Weasel sitting next to Capitaine Roland on the driver's seat, or Legrand, Spider, and the Mouse perched on the back of the coach. But he had eyes only for Madeleine. As the horses came to an abrupt halt, he flung the door wide and lifted her into his arms.

"Germain . . ." she whispered, her voice overflowing with emotion, telling him of her endless love and longing.

Laughing, he swung her around. Without a thought to the spectators, he kissed her deeply, desperately, like a starving man.

"How could you leave me! I've pined for you, cried for you, and cursed you," she admonished softly as he reluctantly released her lips.

"I was a total, utter fool, that's what!"

Their arms entwined, they strolled toward the gatehouse. Madame Barbette waited on the steps and folded Madeleine to her ample bosom. "Positively emaciated! Some stout country food will put that to rights," she puffed, staring fiercely at Madeleine. "Aren't you dressed prettily!" she exclaimed, eyeing the pale green velvet traveling dress.

"*Oui*, the King tried to make me an aristocrat, but I was no success—thank God!"

"Bah! I'm sure you were."

"*Non*, real aristocrats don't like upstarts like me. I was considered an adventuress." Madeleine turned to Germain with love in her eyes. "I have come to stay, if you still want me." She regarded him closely, afraid he would turn her down.

He shoved a hand through his rumpled hair. "What about the King?"

"He gave me permission to leave. I'm not going back to Paris." It hurt to see Germain's hesitation, and she followed Madame Barbette into the warm kitchen.

"How did you find out that we were here?" Barbette asked as she put the water kettle on the hob to boil.

"Weasel knew. He is with me, as are all the other men. They are working for me now, having left the unlawful life behind in Paris."

Madame Barbette chortled. "We'll be like a big, happy family. The men are strangely attached to Master Germain."

"They certainly respect him like no one else."

"The estate is lost now, so I don't know what the master is going to do with all of you."

"Lost? Les Étoiles?"

"*Oui*, it was sold two weeks ago to some rich noblewoman in Paris. Master Germain could never stand waiting on some demanding madame, so he's leaving."

Madeleine laughed. "*I'm* the new owner. A real surprise, eh?"

Germain's voice came from behind her. "*You?*" He stared at her incredulously. Behind him crowded the men, their ugly faces wreathed in smiles.

"*Oui*, she is as good as gold," Legrand said. "Is planning to give it to you."

"Legrand! You were not to tell him! I wanted to tell him myself."

"And keep us in suspense? It's not fair. What do you say, Black Angel?" Legrand asked expectantly. "Well?"

Germain's face had turned white. Unexpectedly he stalked out of the room, leaving the men scratching their heads in consternation.

"See what you've done now," Madeleine scolded.

"Don't worry," Madame Barbette soothed. "Master Germain needs time to think this over. After all, it was a real shock. Come in boys, and have a cup of wine. I predict the master will be the happiest man in the world when he has gotten over the fact that a woman owns Les Étoiles." She rolled her eyes at Madeleine, who giggled nervously.

As the men entered, Madeleine went to find Germain. A single light shone in a window in the main house, and she ran all the way, knowing that he would be there.

A musty scent assaulted her nose as she pushed open the massive door. The house had been closed up far too long. Her steps echoed in the empty rooms. A few pieces of furniture were covered with sheets, resembling ghosts. The atmosphere was ancient, but friendly and warm. She knew she could learn to love living at Les Étoiles.

She pushed open the door to what had once been a library. Smoking a cheroot, Germain was seated in an armchair of old worn leather. He glanced at her as she stepped inside, his eyes burning with love and admiration.

"I never dreamed I would see you stepping through that door."

"But I did, and I will stay." Unceremoniously she plunked herself onto his lap, where he held her tenderly.

"You have grown more beautiful since I last saw you, and so sure of yourself," he murmured.

"It's the time to live. We have only one chance, you know." She let her fingertips travel down one lean, cleanshaven cheek. "I'm glad the beard is gone."

He chuckled. "Too rough, eh?"

"Germain . . ." She held his face between the palms of her hands. "I need you," she whispered. "Without you, life is worthless."

"Oh, *ma petite*," he whispered and buried his face against her bosom. "Can you spend the rest of your life with a former thief?"

He looked very humble, and Madeleine's heart contracted. "That is all I want," she whispered. They savored the moment, then Madeleine continued. "I had the deed to Les Étoiles made up in your name, Germain, and I have the funds to put the place back in order. It's my gift to you, to thank you for all you did for me. It's but a fraction of what you lost, but I implore you, accept it. It's all I have to give." Her heart fluttered. Was he not going to accept her offer?

She left his lap and went to stand by the window. Without noticing, she began wringing her hands in despair.

His warm fingers closed on her shoulders. "I accept. You have made me the happiest man in the world, and I will be happier still if you promise to marry me."

With a whimper, she turned and threw herself into his arms. "Oh, yes!" she breathed with starlight in her eyes.

As their lips met, he lifted her easily into his arms. "Welcome to Les Étoiles. I must show you the master suite. The bed is very comfortable," he growled into her ear.

Epilogue

Les Étoiles, June 1662

Leaning against lace-covered pillows, Madeleine nursed her infant daughter.

"She has lusty lungs, the little devil," Germain commented softly as he touched the downy cheek. "All pink and white," he added.

"And blond like her father."

"*And* her mother."

"A stubborn streak like that of her father—and mother," Madeleine said with a giggle.

Madame Barbette burst through the door after the merest scratch.

"This came by royal messenger," she exclaimed, her eyes almost popping with curiosity.

Germain lazily opened the stiff parchment and read aloud—to Madame Barbette's delight.

His Majesty King Louis XIV is pleased to congratulate you on the birth of your child, the firstborn of the new generation of Hauteforts. Loyal Germain, we see fit to return your title and the remains of your estate. Fouquet had his trial, a complicated affair that took almost a year. He made a full confession. He will spend the rest of his life at the fortress of Pignerol. Lemont is away in disgrace, although we may have to call him back to court since Monsieur misses him. After confessing that he planted the treasonous letters in your *hôtel,* Dubois was hanged this morning at Place de Grève for the murders of my guards and the little page Amul. D'Ambrose was found hanging from the ceiling of his *hôtel* in Paris. He couldn't face the mob on Place de Grève. We have arrested the rest of the men who assisted in the massacre; they will follow Dubois's fate. Can you find it in your heart to forgive me, Germain?

The last line was scrawled in the King's bold hand.
Germain and Madeleine exchanged incredulous glances.
"There is still justice in the world," Germain said.
"I will call our daughter Louise after the King."
The infant wailed in protest.

Author's Note

Dear reader, please forgive me for taking some historical license in writing this story. Nicolas Fouquet in reality embezzled large sums of state funds; it was the discovery of falsified ledgers, not a diary, that led to his downfall. Also, he was not arrested until a month after the fête at Vaux-de-Vicomte, as he was trying to escape.

Madeleine's father, Jean Poquelin, was the playwright Molière's older brother, but in reality he died from natural causes, not from a murderer's dagger. I took the liberty to create his character since very little was mentioned about him in the history books.

MARIA GREENE

A native of Sweden, MARIA GREENE is a blonde, blue-eyed echo of her long-ago ancestors the Vikings. Like them, she roamed the world looking for adventure until she settled down with her American husband, Ray, in New York State's beautiful Finger Lakes region.

Maria likes to read books by Susan Howatch, Jennifer Wilde, Patricia Veryan, James Herriot, Sidney Sheldon, Barbara Pym, and Charlotte Vale Allen. When she is not writing, she does needlepoint, gardens, plays with her cat, Max, and sometimes goes fishing for lake trout and salmon with Ray, an avid fisherman.

Maria loves to hear from her readers!

KARLEEN KOEN
THROUGH A GLASS DARKLY

The Beloved Bestseller— in paperback!

70416-1/$4.95 US; $6.50 Can

As opulent and passionate as the 18th century it celebrates, THROUGH A GLASS DARKLY will sweep you away into a lost era, an era of aristocrats and scoundrels, of grand style and great wealth. Here is the story of a family ruled by a dowager of extraordinary power; of a young woman seeking love in a world of English luxury and French intrigue; of a man haunted by a secret that could turn all their dreams to ashes...

"IT SPARKLES!" *Chicago Sun-Times*

Buy these books at your local bookstore or use this coupon for ordering:

Avon Books, Dept BP, Box 767, Rte 2, Dresden, TN 38225

Please send me the book(s) I have checked above. I am enclosing $_____
(please add $1.00 to cover postage and handling for each book ordered to a maximum of three dollars). Send check or money order—no cash or C.O.D.'s please. Prices and numbers are subject to change without notice. Please allow six to eight weeks for delivery.

Name _____
Address _____
City _____ State/Zip _____

Finally!

The beloved, bestselling saga of Steve and Ginny Morgan continues, as their legacy of passion shapes the destiny of a new generation...

ROSEMARY ROGERS

BOUND BY DESIRE

On Sale: February 14, 1988!

The passionate tale you've been wating for, by the only woman who could tell it...

Begun in *Sweet Savage Love*, *Dark Fires* and *Lost Love, Last Love*, the bestselling story of Steve and Ginny Morgan has thrilled readers as only Rosemary Rogers' novels can.

Now, their beautiful, headstrong daughter, Laura, and an untameable rogue, Trent Challenger, find themselves swept from Paris, to London, to Spain's dark castles, drawn together by love, and
BOUND BY DESIRE....

ASK FOR OUR SPECIAL 16-PAGE PREVIEW SAMPLER IN YOUR BOOKSTORE BEGINNING JANUARY 1st 1988!
It's an exciting taste of the delicious new tale to come!